THE HUNGER

The night whispers continued to beckon Emma on her evening runs. She wasn't sure what was happening to her, but she was still changing. What had once seemed monstrous to her — the drinking of human blood — didn't seem so any longer. She was so . . . *hungry*. All the time.

She grew lean, her eyes haunted and glittering with the hunger. She found herself tormented by the thought of sinking her fangs — just once . . . just a little — deep into Matthew's luscious throat. And the very idea of that repulsed her. Petrified her.

If she didn't find prey soon, she'd have to leave Matthew . . . or she'd end up preying on him.

That she couldn't do. She'd promised herself. But it had been a human promise . . . *and she no longer felt human . . .*

HAUTALA'S HORROR—HOLD ON TO YOUR HEAD!

MOONDEATH   (1844-4, $3.95/$4.95)
Cooper Falls is a small, quiet New Hampshire town, the kind you'd miss if you blinked an eye. But when darkness falls and the full moon rises, an uneasy feeling filters through the air; an unnerving foreboding that causes the skin to prickle and the body to tense.

NIGHT STONE   (3030-4, $4.50/$5.50)
Their new house was a place of darkness and shadows, but with her secret doll, Beth was no longer afraid. For as she stared into the eyes of the wooden doll, she heard it call to her and felt the force of its evil power. And she knew it would tell her what she had to do.

MOON WALKER   (2598-X, $4.50/$5.50)
No one in Dyer, Maine ever questioned the strange disappearances that plagued their town. And they never discussed the eerie figures seen harvesting the potato fields by day . . . the slow, lumbering hulks with expressionless features and a blood-chilling deadness behind their eyes.

LITTLE BROTHERS   (2276-X, $3.95/$4.95)
It has been five years since Kip saw his mother horribly murdered by a blur of "little brown things." But the "little brothers" are about to emerge once again from their underground lair. Only this time there will be no escape for the young boy who witnessed their last feast!

THE LAST VAMPIRE

KATHRYN MEYER GRIFFITH

ZEBRA BOOKS
KENSINGTON PUBLISHING CORP.

*And again . . . a special
thank you to my husband, Russell,
for all his special knowledge on
survival in the wilds and Indian lore.*

ZEBRA BOOKS

are published by

Kensington Publishing Corp.
475 Park Avenue South
New York, NY 10016

First printing: June, 1992

Printed in the United States of America

Prologue

The end of the world had come, but it was like nothing anyone had ever imagined. Its virulent earthquakes had rippled under the skin of the globe, tearing open the fragile earth; spreading destruction as they devoured towns and cities like a monstrous hungry beast; exploding lethal missiles in their silos; creating chaos and fear that eventually released the doomsday cries of every religious fanatic on the planet . . . but worst of all, they unleashed a vicious plague that could not be stopped. A plague that would finish what the earthquakes and wars could not.

Soon there were few places left to run to — to escape from the devastation and the dying.

Not even in America.

And so the world ended . . .

One

"I can't believe I'll never see this place again, Larry."

"Me neither," Larry replied somberly. But he was too busy packing to look up, so she couldn't see the expression on his face.

Emma sighed as she moved away from the windows on the ninth floor, her packing done. As far as she could see through the dirty glass, the sick and the homeless camps stretched, crawling along the fringes of the roads and across the dead grass and concrete of St. Louis, like a huge undulating blanket of ants; even through the windows she could sometimes hear muffled wisps of their squabbles, their sobbing, their misery, as if from faraway. It was chilly for April—it was always chilly lately—and tiny campfires sparkled among the drab tents.

People everywhere. They'd stripped the city of everything edible or useful, like an ocean of voracious locusts.

The city—once beautiful and strong—was dying, and she felt sorry for it. But it was the humanity suffering below her that tore her soul apart.

She wanted to weep for them, but she had no tears left.

The people had nowhere to go; no way to live since their homes and cities had been destroyed by the contin-

7

uing earthquakes. Their lives had been shattered by homelessness, hunger, and . . . plague.

Plague, the evil the scientists believed had been released by that first mammoth earthquake six months ago, as it had ripped a new fault across Nevada and Arizona. Nine point three on the Richter scale. It'd been the worst one in human history — until the next one in California. A nine point nine. That one had leveled every large city in two states; killed nearly two million people; reactivated a chain of long dead volcanoes that spewed forth miles and miles of molten lava and atmospheric debris; and then sent shock waves across five other states for months. It had sent temperatures plunging nationwide, while clouds from the erupting volcanoes and the flash fires darkened the whole nation and turned the days into long twilight.

But the worst thing the earthquakes had accomplished, was the destruction of a secret underground military chemical and biological weapons laboratory somewhere in Nevada that — the government finally admitted — might have caused the mysterious plague that then swept across the country. A sickness that was a thousand times more lethal than the feared AIDS virus of the nineties, because it could lie dormant for hours, weeks, or months, and then strike, its victims then dying in agony in *days* . . . and it sickled through the people left after the earthquake, killing everyone . . . everywhere, especially the children. Nothing could stop it. Like the earthquakes, the scientists had no explanations or solutions for it. Millions more died.

In six months' time, it had spread like wildfire.

The scientists christened it the Red Plague, because it — like the AIDS virus before it — attacked the blood. It heralded the beginning of the end. So started the great migration east.

The people had begun to panic.

Emma and her two children had all grown sick with it, but miraculously had recovered, while their friends and neighbors had died in droves. Her husband, Danny, escaped it completely. It was extremely rare that someone survived it once they'd caught it. Emma wondered why God had spared them. But she had no answers.

Welfare and all the other social services collapsed, toppled over by the sheer weight of the number of people unemployed, sick, and homeless. The survivors had to fend for themselves, and with every month humanity was becoming more savage. These days many people lived out in the open in patched tents, makeshift abodes, or in burned-out buildings, without electricity or running water. They survived however they could: stealing, begging, maiming, and killing.

You were a fool if you walked the streets unarmed.

The problem had swiftly escalated into one of catastrophic proportions that the government hadn't been able to solve, even with all their new laws and their police state.

Glancing back outside one last time, Emma knew it was only going to get worse.

The hordes had been migrating into St. Louis for months now. Blank-eyed with shock or fear. Hungry, sick, and angry. Misplaced, soft city-dwellers who had long ago forgotten how to survive without their air-conditioned homes and microwaves.

They must have believed that things would be better here. They wouldn't be, Emma mused sadly. They'd all eventually die in one horrendous manner or another. If the plague didn't get them — or some third-world religious fanatic leader who'd illegally obtained a nuclear weapon didn't drop another bomb on them — starvation or murder would. Despair. Many, in the end, every resource and avenue of hope exhausted, would opt for dying at their own hand.

Mass suicides.

It was happening all over the world, they said.

And looking at the bewildered crowds terrified Emma. Soon she, her husband, and two children would be sharing their fate.

She gazed slowly around at the familiar room, with the bright cubicles and the rows of shining Macintosh 10's. It had been her second home for so long. In the old days she'd rarely have come into work on a Saturday morning, but she hadn't wanted to face the others while she packed up her belongings.

Larry, her coworker and friend, had had the same idea.

She turned to him and said, "There was a time I would have said I'm not all that sorry to be going . . . I haven't been happy here for a long time . . . but now . . ."

"I know," he answered. He met her worried eyes this time and shrugged. There'd been too much office politics involved since the new art director had been hired three years ago. Emma had never been one of his favored people. Years of snubs and tons of uncreative busywork, for a longtime graphic designer of her status, had taken their toll and left scars.

Emma's face still reddened, remembering. It'd been a bitter pill to swallow. After all those years of being one of the top artists, she'd been humiliated to find herself teamed with a much younger woman, who suddenly had had the right to tell Emma *how* to do her job, *and* make the final decisions on everything Emma did do. Emma had been threatening herself with quitting for years, but with the world situation steadily worsening, she'd held on, and was glad she had.

But now Corporate Graphics, the ad company she'd worked for for over twelve years, had finally folded.

Her eyes turned haunted. "I really needed this job since Danny lost his.

"I don't know what we're going to do now." She was biting her upper lip again and her eyes misted over as if she were ready to cry.

Until three months ago, Danny had been a manager at one of the city's top restaurants. But expensive restau-

10

rants were one of the first luxuries to go. People could hardly afford to keep a roof over their heads and feed their families these days, much less spend a hundred dollars for a fancy supper out.

Now she was out of a job, as well.

Larry didn't respond to her remark about needing the job. He had needed his, too. Millions of people did these days. Being unemployed had become commonplace, as the nation's economy had plummeted.

Three months ago, a 747 loaded with nuclear weapons had come from one of the Middle Eastern countries—some of which had been in open warfare with us for years—and had dived into the heart of New York. It had wiped half of the city's population off the map. There was speculation that the stock market wouldn't reopen. Ever.

"Well, think of it this way, Emma." Her fellow artist was giving her a halfhearted grin. "You won't have to get up early anymore . . . and you won't have to be humiliated anymore, either."

"Yea," Emma muttered, thinking that her humiliations would probably come in some other form from now on. "You know he told me last year in my yearly review—before things got so bad, I mean," she gestured symbolically at the world outside, "that when he first came on board, he'd wanted to fire all the older artists. But the big boss wouldn't let him. He said that he didn't think too much of any of us. He insinuated that I was deadwood, because I'd been here so long. That I should have moved on a long time ago, and that, no matter what I did, I would never be a senior artist under him. Never."

It seemed like a lifetime ago, but Emma still winced at the old hurt. Though her job had never been her whole life—like some people she knew—she'd wanted to be an artist since she'd been nine years old and in pigtails, and his words had been a cruel shock to her. Until then she'd been proud of her time at the company and her abilities.

11

She'd always worked so hard; loved her job. According to him, though, all that meant nothing.

"The man had a lot of gall. If someone'd said that to me, I would have punched him out."

"That's you, Larry. I was so flabbergasted at what he was saying to me — with a smile on his face, mind you — that I clammed up and just nodded like a dummy, instead of fighting back. I thought that if I worked even harder, proved myself to him, if I was as nice to him as I could be, I'd win him over in time. I guess I was naive. He never did accept me."

"Yep, you sure were." Larry nodded as he scooped up more of his belongings and stuffed them into brown paper bags. He'd heard this all before, but like the good friend he was, he let her go on talking.

He knew how hard leaving was for her.

"The worst thing was," she confessed, glancing out the window again nervously at the sudden rise in noise, "I feared for my job after that. And I was consumed with hate at the way he was treating me. I used to lie awake at night, planning revenge. It was horrible."

He snorted, "I still can't believe that he *told* you all that to your face. Not very diplomatic for someone who was supposed to inspire confidence in his workers. I never did think much of the man," he admitted, but his voice was strangely subdued.

"He didn't want me to feel confident. He just wanted me to give up and quit. But I showed him, didn't I?"

"Yes, you sure did."

Larry had been hired by the new art director. But he'd turned out to be a little too headstrong, and, like Emma, had never enjoyed the privileges of the inner circle, though everyone had liked him, including Emma. They'd become friends.

He stood up, his arms full of books and drawing pads. "Don't know if I'll ever need these again, but I'd better take them home." He was a tall man, heavyset with a chubby, bearded face and compassionate eyes; because

12

of his size he reminded Emma of a grizzly bear. Gentle Ben.

Emma found herself back at the window, her thoughts darkening. Below, the people were scurrying around pointing and shouting soundlessly. Emma noticed that some of the tents pitched in the park near the fountain had fallen. Someone was crying somewhere.

She paused, the commotion out in the streets forgotten for a moment, as she tilted her head and said softly, "And now, what difference does any of it make?" Her feud with the art director seemed so trivial now.

He had died of the plague two months ago.

"None," she answered her own question, as if Larry weren't even there, and then fell silent. Outside she could hear the crowd screaming.

Larry must have misunderstood her silence, for he offered kindly: "You never should have doubted yourself so much, Emma. You're a damn good artist. He just never gave you a chance. You should have fought for your place."

"No," she replied tersely, a frown on her face as she glanced back over her shoulder at him. "I'm just not like that. I'm not the kind of person to jump through hoops, just to get a pat on the back. If my work doesn't speak for me, then there's nothing to say."

She took a deep breath and let it out painfully, looking around. "Let's face it, there's not going to be much of a future anymore for artists. Scientists, doctors, soldiers, and survivalists, yes.

"Not artists. Not right now." He knew she was right. "Maybe, someday . . ." her voice trailed off weakly.

She went back to intently observing the crowds.

Larry cleared his throat self-consciously, ready to go. He walked up to her and gave her a quick hug, embarrassed, then stepped back to look at her. "Well, it's been great working with you, Emma. I wish things were different." Fear tinged his voice and Emma caught it.

"Don't we all?" she answered sarcastically.

"Someday . . ." he echoed her own words, his eyes ignoring the crowds below and instead scanning the honeycomb of artists' cubicles, light tables, and drawing boards. He reached over and gingerly touched one of the shelves that held the paper cutter and wax machine. "We'll say that these were our golden days. The best."

Emma walked over to her desk, her eyes evading his; filling with tears, even after she'd promised herself she wouldn't cry.

I'm going to miss all this. "I'm going to miss you, Larry," she told him, letting her fingers play idly over the keyboard of her own Macintosh, her mind mulling over the memory of how she had once fought learning it and how she'd ended up loving it. In the last eight years, she'd done nearly all her designing on it. When would she ever use another one?

Their eyes met over the edge of her cubicle. She was tall for a woman: five-eight in her stocking feet. Her hair was shoulder-length and pale blond, her eyes so dark a blue, they were almost black; her face long and narrow, and right at that moment very weary-looking.

"You *were* the best damn graphic designer I've ever known, Emma," he said sincerely as they headed toward the elevators, as if it could make up for all the rest. "No matter what the art director said."

"Thanks. You weren't so bad yourself," she laughed back, but her eyes remained unhappy.

"Maybe I'll see you at the next place?"

"Sure," she responded tiredly, but instead thought: *This awful new world. If things get any worse, I might never work again.*

It'll never be the same.

Emma reflected on her drive in that morning. All those *people* everywhere; crammed in together like dying blades of grass under a shadowed sun; cooking heaven-knows-what over little cookfires and trying to stay warm. The police had long ago stopped chasing them off. There were just too damn many. Too many dying of

14

hunger and plague right there on the streets, huddled in the doorways and living in the alleys. The hospitals could no longer handle the overload. The plague wagons rang through the city all hours of the day and night.

Emma saw their lost, pinched faces again, watching her as she maneuvered past them carefully in her car. She could imagine what they were thinking: *She still has a car, a home to go to, and decent food to eat.* Unlike them.

But for how long?

"I finished that underground shelter," Larry told her proudly.

"You mean the one you were building along the Missouri bluffs outside the city?"

"Yeah. It wasn't easy. You know how hard getting certain materials and supplies have become. But I did it. Now . . . we're ready. It's even stocked with food and bottled water. Enough for the both of us for a whole *year.* Medical supplies, too. Joanie pilfered them from work. All I have to do now is transfer my guns from the house to the shelter, or some of them anyway."

"Smart you," Emma commented, genuinely happy for him. Larry was one of those survivalists who believed in being prepared for the worst. He'd been saying for years that when the big one came—bomb or earthquake—he wanted a safe place to go to. Now he had it.

Her husband Danny wasn't a survivalist, he was a pacifist. He'd say, *If it comes, it comes, baby, and if we live, we live.* He didn't believe in being prepared, though he had taught her a little about how to live out in the woods. He'd been a boy scout; an eagle scout.

"Joanie still working for the hospital then, huh?"

"Yeah. It depresses the hell out of her sometimes, but she won't leave. Says it makes her feel like she's doing something worthwhile, you know?"

"Yes, I know." Emma flashed him a smile. "She's got more guts than me. I can't stand the sight of blood. Faint dead away. Can't stand to see people suffer.

"She's a special woman. Do you know how lucky you

15

are to have her?" she teased him.

"Oh, I know," and there was love in his deep voice.

"How are Danny and the kids doing?"

"Under the circumstances, they're holding up pretty well. Danny's busy with the garden. We've gotten a lot of food from it already, but it's about played out now that the weather's become so unpredictable."

"Fresh vegetables are worth their weight in gold these days."

"Tell me. We had to put fences all around to keep out the poachers. Danny keeps joking that he'd electrify it, if the electricity wasn't already rationed. He has to keep a constant watch over the garden, or thieves would devour every leaf."

"Times have changed, all right. When we have to guard our food like it was gold."

Emma couldn't have agreed more with him. But saying so wouldn't change a damn thing. Nothing would change what the world was evolving into. She could only hold on tight for the wild ride, and pray.

The first tremors came when they were almost at the door, arms loaded down with their belongings.

Earthquake.

Now she knew why Midnight, her cat, had acted so weird this morning, when Emma was doing that load of blue jeans. She'd found him crouched, shivering, behind the dryer, and when she'd tried to pick him up, he'd scratched her and ran off. He'd never acted like that.

They said that animals sensed earthquakes before they happened.

"Larry, did you feel that?" Emma whispered, her heart faltering. She lowered the stuff in her arms slowly to the floor; then the next jolt came.

"My God!" she moaned, shoving herself away from the wall she'd fallen against, pulling herself up on her feet, and then running back toward the windows.

"Emma, get away from the glass. It's dangerous!"

Her wide eyes frantically scanned the city. Union Station was still there. Untouched. The Arch was still standing. Nothing looked wrong, and yet . . . there was a shimmering, a shifting of things. She shook her head wildly. She wasn't wrong. The world outside was *moving*. People were running around on Market Street like frenzied sheep. The roar grew swiftly into a screeching chorus, as people began to realize what was happening and panicked.

As she looked on in horror, unable to tear her gaze away, a pencil-thin line crackled down the middle of Market Street, and began to yawn open like a hungry black mouth. People, cars . . . buildings . . . slid into the chasm and disappeared.

"Get away from those windows!" Larry was suddenly behind her, grabbing and drawing her away as the building began to sway. "We've got to get the hell out of here," he hissed. "Half the place is glass, and I don't know if it's even built to code —"

Another jolt hit, almost knocking them down. Hairline cracks shot down the solid wall to their right with violent whiplike sounds.

Emma screamed. Frozen.

Just in time, Larry grabbed her, spun her around, and started dragging her toward the hallway. The wall of windows behind them shattered and rained glass. In shock, Emma gazed down at her arms as tiny rivulets of crimson appeared. There was no pain, but she had to fight from passing out at the sight of her own blood.

Her thoughts were with her family across the river in Cahokia.

Danny is probably working in the garden, salvaging the last of the harvest. Peter and Jenny are watching cartoons in the living room, trying to stay warm. They hadn't been allowed to turn their furnace on yet. Soon, they're predicting, they'll be rationing electricity.

Oh, God.

Then the first explosion came, and there wasn't time to think of anything but escaping.

"The stairs!" Larry yelled. "We don't dare take the elevators."

Larry herded her through the door to the stairs, but not before she'd caught a glimpse of the mushroom cloud billowing across the river, framed in the Arch. About where Cahokia and East St. Louis were. The ugly blood-red smoke permeated the sky.

Emma cried out, yanking Larry to a complete stop. The land across the river in Illinois was a wall of fire leaping toward them.

Cahokia. Home.

The whole east side was an inferno. No one could live through that.

"Oh God . . . some bastard's dropped a nuclear bomb on us!" Larry wailed disbelievingly, his face ashen. The hand on her arm tightened until she gasped out in pain.

"Don't look at it, Emma. Oh God in heaven," he muttered, "we've got to get to the shelter . . . *now.*"

Larry hauled her along behind him, slamming open the large door that let out onto the corridor, just as the rest of the glass windows imploded. A roiling wave of heated air and wreckage hurtled them through the opening. The next thing she knew they were sprawled on the floor, the door lying on top of them.

Emma must have lost consciousness, and when she came to, she could hear fire crackling hungrily somewhere close. Very close. The city shrieked as the ground rocked beneath her. Faraway there were more blasts. The air had turned heavy, hard to breathe.

Groaning and shaken, she crawled out from under the door. Her eyes were burning, her vision blurry. She brought her hand up to her numb face and trembling fingers came away sticky with blood.

"Larry?" she whimpered, her fingers reaching out for him. He wasn't there. "Where are you?"

She spied him, propped in the corner, grinning up at her through a dirty, pain-grimaced face; his legs were trapped under the door and other rubble.

18

"You all right, Emma?"

It touched her that he thought about her first, especially since he was the one obviously hurt. "I think so. It's you I'm worried about."

"I'll be okay . . . but we've got to get out of the building, Emma. Out of the city." A bewildered look settled on his bruised face. Emma noticed that his eyes were fever-bright, but vacant.

"Larry?"

"I can't get my legs out."

It took her three tries to get the door and the chunks of concrete off him, tearing her hands in the process. She didn't care. Her face wasn't the only part of her body that was numb. When she looked at his shredded legs, she tried not to let the fear show on her face, tried to keep her stomach from emptying right there.

His wounds were bad.

How in the world was he going to get out of the building—much less the city—if he couldn't *walk?*

"It hurts terribly, doesn't it?" It sounded lame the minute it slipped out.

"I'll make it somehow, Emma, I swear I will. And if I can't . . . I won't hold you back." But the plea in his eyes was clear enough: *Don't leave me.*

She reached down and helped him to his feet. He moaned in pain, teeth gritted tightly, as the weight resettled. Even with all her support, he could barely stand, and he was a heavy, big man. Blood was everywhere. Swallowing hard, she fought to keep her stomach as another explosion rattled the building.

"Gas lines going sky high," he told her, his eyes studying her face. "There'll be more. Looting, killing. Flooding from the river. Real soon. If it hasn't started already. If it *was* a nuclear bomb, radiation cloud should be coming across the water about now—" Her apprehension flashed like neon across her countenance.

Frustrated, he shoved her away and toppled back to the littered floor. "Get out of here, Emma. Get away while you can. I'm not going anywhere." He slapped his hands angrily against his useless legs. There were tears trickling down his filthy face. "I'd only hold you back. Get you killed."

"No . . ."

"GO!"

Emma stared down at him with steely eyes, canted her head stubbornly, and held her hand out to him again. "I'm not leaving here without you. You're the only friend I've got left. You're *all* I've got left.

"Come on, let's get out of here," she said sternly.

His eyes shone, glittering with gratitude. "Oh, Emma."

Between them they made it down all nine flights of stairs and into the lower garage where he had parked his Land Rover; only stumbling once when the steps behind them crumpled away. They were safer taking his new Land Rover than her old beat-up Buick Skyhawk.

The Rover was meant for rough terrain.

"What we're heading into might be pretty rough. The shelter's on the Missouri side, thank God, hidden up in the bluffs. Not too far from here. *If* we can get there.

"But you'll have to drive," he confessed, leaning against the side of the big black vehicle for a moment to catch his breath. He fumbled the keys from one of his pockets. "Don't think I can."

"We have to get you some help—" she started to protest, seeing the blood dripping into puddles where he was standing.

"There's *no time,* Emma." His eyes were desperate. "I have an extensive first-aid kit in the shelter and medical books, too. I'll deal with it when we're there . . . safe."

Emma collected the keys from his battered hands, and nodded.

She knew that since the first shock wave only a few minutes had elapsed, but it felt like an eternity. She was drained already.

The garage was crumbling around them. "Let's go,"

he announced anxiously, after she'd helped him into the front seat on the passenger's side. She revved up the engine and screeched out of the garage, just as the section they'd been parked under disintegrated with a shuddering crash.

As she floored the accelerator pedal, Larry tore a strip of cloth from his shirt and tied a tourniquet tightly around his left leg, the one that was still bleeding.

"You gonna make it?" she asked, peering over at his pain-filled face.

"I have to make it. You'll need me — and I'm the only one who knows where the shelter is."

Then, "Hurry, Emma."

The streets were a nightmare. The smoke so thick, Emma couldn't see two feet in front of her. Market Street had been ripped into a ragged scar, full of smashed cars and dead or wounded people, so she maneuvered onto one of the smaller side streets. But bricks, glass, and dirt soon forced them to a rolling crawl, while crippled or stalled cars and trucks blocked most of the roads. Water was rushing down the streets from somewhere, getting higher every second.

"The river's flooding the city. If we don't get out soon, we'll be floating."

Larry didn't have to tell her to get off the street, she sharply spun the wheel and the Rover jumped the curb and headed for land that was clear enough to drive through. Parking lots. Grass. Sidewalks.

But there were people running everywhere, or lying injured, and as hard as Emma tried, she couldn't miss all of them all the time. Some of them; when they saw the Rover was still moving, ran alongside screaming and begging for a ride out of the city, or for help. Emma wanted to stop.

"Keep going." Larry glared out the window with a cold gleam in his eyes, as his hands fumbled under the seat and came out clutching a gun. "It's a Beretta M-10. I got it off an old Army friend of mine. They used it a lot in

21

the nineties. He swore it could drop an elephant."

"I don't see any elephants," she commented feebly, but he didn't laugh.

"I mean it, we're not going to stop for *anything*, or *anyone*," he warned her heartlessly. "There's no more room at the shelter. No more supplies. Just enough for two people. I'm sorry." Guilt washed over his face, and he covered it — still clutching the Beretta — with his trembling hands in shame.

The crowd turned violent, ugly, when Emma refused to stop. They pounded out their rage against the side of the car with their fists or pieces of metal, as they splashed through the swiftly rising water. They cursed them; threw bricks at them.

Larry leveled the gun's long barrel against the window; and threateningly pointed it at a woman's outraged, fire-scarred face.

Get back. *Get back.*

All of them did, except one man. He was in a tattered pin-striped suit, his hair still smoking. Emma glanced at him and thought: *Maybe I drove by you this morning on my way to work, you in your pin-striped suit and matching briefcase. Maybe you even worked in one of the other offices in my building.*

He spat at Larry through the window; shook his fist. The whole left side of his face seemed to be gone. But he fell back, and Emma watched his slumped figure dwindle into a smudge on the side of the road as they drove away, the water knee-deep already.

Emma accepted it all without a whimper, hardening her heart.

There was just too many of them.

"You're learning. From now on, Emma, all that matters is survival. Nothing else." His voice didn't even sound like the Larry she'd known.

He gave her directions to where they were going.

They raced across Bell Telephone's smoldering lawn, cut through the edge of a large parking lot, and up onto a sidewalk with benches. At times, they were driving through swirling water mid-tire high, and Emma wasn't sure what she was driving over. She winced every time something crunched under the Rover's tires. Building rubble or bodies. Maybe a child . . . like Jenny . . . like Peter.

"Oh, Lord. *They're all dead,*" she whispered, narrowly missing a screaming black man who had suddenly jumped out in front of them, a human torch.

The tears rolled down her cheeks and she drove faster, as if she could escape all the pain.

Larry knew she was speaking about her family. "Yes, they are," he whispered back, desperately trying to keep from passing out. "Joanie, too." One of his hands found hers on the wheel and gently squeezed. When she glanced over at him, he was crying silently.

"I . . . wish . . . we had moved to the Missouri side. Joanie and me." He took his hand away, gripped the safety strap above him, and leaned his head back against the seat, holding on tightly, as they bumped across sections of a shattered building. The car's tires splashed through racing water. "I was going to have us move as soon as the shelter was done. Was gonna build a tiny house next to the shelter . . ."

Larry's home had been across the Poplar Bridge, too . . . in Dupo, Illinois. Now it was hell.

". . . but time ran out," his voice was anguished.

Tears slid through the gore of his face. He'd loved Joanie more than himself. Loved his wife as much as Emma had loved her husband and children.

I have to get home! Something broke inside of her. Maybe they escaped . . . maybe they're still *alive.* And here she was running away with another man to a hole in the hills.

"I should go home, Larry," she exclaimed, as if it had just all dawned on her. "They could still be alive. Might need me. I've got to find them . . ." Emma was suddenly overwhelmed with the urge to turn around right there and then and drive toward the east side. She put on the

23

brakes with all her might and brought the Rover to a breathtaking stop; muddy water gushed over the front.

Larry pulled himself together. He knew shock when he saw it. He didn't have much time, a crowd had already spotted them and was closing in. He had to make her understand. Now. "No, Emma. No one made it through that. Whatever it was, nuclear bomb or earthquake, they're all *dead*. The east side is gone. The bridges are gone. Believe me. I'll show you. I know it's hard to take . . . for me, too."

Her eyes as she turned to him were like a dying animal's. Glazed and suffering.

"You know it's true." His voice was gentle, as if he were talking to a distraught child. "I'm sorry, Emma."

Her heart finally cracked into a thousand pieces. She knew he was right. She froze at the wheel, her mind trying to destroy itself. How could she be so damn selfish . . . so many people had died; who was she to think that only her people mattered? That she mattered? She laid her head on the wheel as the world spun. The water was lapping at the bottom of the door.

"Start it up now, Emma. Or we haven't got a chance." She looked up. The rabble was just feet away.

Larry, his face scalded and slashed with slivers of glass, looked frightened and sick.

"We've got to get to the shelter while there's still time. Please."

"Yes," a mouse voice. Then self-preservation kicked in with a vengeance. She turned the engine on, and the wheels spun furiously, then caught.

The foundation of the building towering behind them rumbled like an angry beast as they drove away. The ground started to shake again; things began to fall on the car. The front window smashed in around them.

Emma brushed off what she could, and kept driving.

As they raced through the city, buildings rocked and tumbled to the streets, landsliding over cars and screaming people, and narrowly missing the Rover at times.

She didn't stop.

But she really didn't give a damn if she made it or not. It was Larry she was fighting for.

All she wanted was to die; be with her husband, her two children, her parents, and her two brothers and their families.

Everyone she loved was dead, except for one older sister who had moved up to Maine years ago.

They made it out of St. Louis and headed for the woods, paralleling the river. Larry had been right. Illinois was just a glut of flames. The Jefferson Barracks Bridge was burning. She could see it down the horizon. The Mississippi River had split into two separate rivers, flooding its old banks, and water was everywhere. Half the highways were already under water.

The Martin Luther King Bridge was gone.

The Poplar Bridge was gone.

Both had slid into the river with all their human travelers. The river was stained red with blood, and tips of colored metal bobbed along wildly in the filthy water.

Even though she tried to block it all out, Emma could still hear their shouts and cries down below her.

She'd hear their cries forever.

Her last sight of St. Louis was seeing the Arch topple into the growing river. The towering Metropolitan Life Building went down next, and the Adam's Mark Hotel, Union Station followed . . . like crazy dominoes, as the earth continued to quiver violently. A pulsating fireball was skimming across the water and gulping up everything they'd left behind just seconds before. If the city and land around it wasn't drowning, it was burning.

She couldn't bear to look again.

They were driving the last leg of their journey down a winding narrow dirt road, and had left the rushing water behind them, when she brought the Rover to a hasty stop. "We can't go any further, Larry. The road's got fallen trees all over it." And the fire was roaring close behind them.

"Yeah, I see," he growled. "Looks like we haven't got any choice but to get out and hoof it. It's not that far now."

"Can you make it?" she asked. He was obviously in great pain. He'd already passed out once or twice since they'd left the city.

"I have to." He shoved open the door and waited for her to get over to him. "We have about five minutes' jump on that fire, and then we'll be crispy critters."

Then they were on foot stumbling through the woods, fleeing before the voracious fire, rapidly opening fissures, dodging flying limbs and other debris.

They kept being knocked to the ground every time it shook. "Don't know what the hell's happening, Emma," Larry sighed once. "But whatever it is, it's bad. Maybe the end of the world finally . . ."

Emma had nothing to say to that, except that maybe he was right, and that maybe she didn't care.

But Larry urged her on, when she wanted to just sink to the ground, sick and exhausted, and give up. He wouldn't let her.

The rest of their flight she could barely remember, except Larry pleading that they were almost there and *keep going!*

Then a tree came falling out of nowhere. Larry had just enough time to scream and throw her out of the way before it crashed, pinning him to the ground. He went into convulsions, blood welling from his mouth, nose, his eyes.

Sobbing aloud and wiping the sweat and tears from her face with the back of her grimy hand, she tried, but she couldn't budge the tree.

Emma knew he was dying.

So she cradled what she could of him in her arms as the rest of his life slipped away; with his last ounce of strength he took a key from his pocket, whispering hoarsely, "Go straight . . . Emma, only a mile or so further down the dirt path. Three huge rocks mark it . . . a

26

cave . . . door recessed . . . you can make it.

"Get inside and stay . . . for at . . . least . . . six months. . . . if nuclear strike . . . *have* to stay below *six months*. Emma. Don't come out for *nothing*." His mouth grimaced, and more blood spilt down his chin.

When she was sure he was dead, she hauled herself up on weak legs and started trudging in the direction he had pointed.

She found the large rocks and the cave, the door, just as Larry had said; just as another blast singed the whole of her right side and back. Her clothes caught fire, and she was slapped to the ground like a weightless rag doll. In spite of the pain, she tore her burning blouse off, crawled the last few feet, poked in the key with unsteady hands, and somehow yanked the door open — then shut it behind her.

It was the last conscious thing she would remember doing, because she rolled across the dirt floor and passed out. The next few days were spent in fever and delirium, as the world outside destroyed itself.

Two

Matthew Whitefeather was gutting a deer when the earth began to tremble. As the ground shifted, he calmly wiped his bloody knife blade off on the side of his worn blue jeans, and slipped it back into the leather sheath at his waist. His tall, lanky frame stiffened as the ground rocked again.

"Earthquake," he muttered, regarding the trees around him with narrowed eyes the color of bitter chocolate, eyes almost as dark as his long ponytailed hair. The trees were shaking off their limbs, like dogs shaking off their fleas. The scientists didn't have any explanations for the severity and continuation of the earthquakes, just that the world's crust was shifting; they didn't know why. But Matt did. Since he'd been a child on the reservation, the old medicine men had predicted the end of the world.

This was it.

In the far distance he heard a series of huge explosions. Out toward St. Louis. He scooped up his old shotgun, his sharp-boned face grim. He had to get back to his truck. After the loss of his welding job last fall, there wasn't any money to buy another one. Even one as decrepit as his old Chevy. Without it, how would he be able to go where he had to go? The deer were frightened and had been foraging farther and farther away from the cities, as if they had sensed the coming cataclysm. He'd had to drive deeper and deeper into the wilderness to find game. He hated leaving the venison — his family needed the meat — but if he hurried, it would still be there when he returned.

He jogged back through the woods, surefooted, to where he had left the truck, dodging bombarding tree branches and jumping splits in the ground that grew under his feet. A hurtling rock from out of nowhere hit him on the side of the head, brought him to his knees, and knocked him senseless. When he awoke, there was fresh blood seeping down the side of his left cheek . . . and the woods were burning.

He stumbled around, dazed, until he came to the place he'd left his truck. It wasn't there. And since his father, a full Cherokee, had taught him how to hunt and track when he was a child, and had always sworn that Matt could track a squirrel through a snowstorm, Matt knew it was the same place. It just didn't look the same. The earth had sifted itself like a loose deck of cards. Instead of grass and trees, it was a sea of moist, churning, black-colored earth and burning tree roots.

His red Chevy was nowhere to be seen.

There were columns of heavy smoke curling over the horizon when he looked toward his home, and its implications terrified him. His wife, Maggie, and daughter, Sara, were at home alone in Fenton, Missouri. He ran until his exhausted body screamed, then kept on running.

It took him most of the day to get back to the tiny house on the edge of town. The quake had demolished it.

Looters were already fighting over the remains. Two bloodied men in ragged clothes, and one filthy, bedraggled woman, were filling large sacks with his food and his family's belongings.

"Where is my family?" he demanded fiercely, when they turned to peer insolently at him.

"This your place?" one of the men growled, a burly

guy with bad skin and tattered clothes.

"It was," Matt replied scathingly. He raised his shotgun and leveled it even with the man's eyes. "What are you doing here? Where's my wife and daughter?"

Perhaps the looter saw the cold fury lurking in the Indian's slitted eyes, because he backed up and gestured to his friends to leave. "We haven't seen them, man," he groveled. "We're just passing through. Thought everybody was dead here. We were hungry." He spread his hands, nodding, as he continued to inch away. "Just came from Fenton. The town's burning . . . the factory exploded or the gas lines. We didn't see anyone left alive—"

"Nothing worse than looters after a disaster," Matt interrupted coldly, "my daddy always told me. Likened them to vermin. He also told me to shoot 'em."

The man's mouth had dropped open in indignation, then he caught the hatred in Matt's eyes. He looked down the barrel of the shotgun and his face went white.

"I swear, I haven't seen nobody. Haven't seen that wife and kid of yours," the man blubbered. "Don't shoot me! Here . . . take your stuff back. I'll find food somewhere else." He had dumped the bulging sack at Matt's boots, and raised his empty hands. "Please?" he begged. His friends had already run back into the woods.

"Just get the hell away from here and don't come back—" Matt cocked back the gun's hammer. "—or I'll blow your fucking head off."

The man turned and rushed off into the woods after his friends.

When the man's footsteps had crunched away into the mist, Matt stood staring at what was left of the house. Faintly, in the distance, came more explosions. Then, abruptly, silence, and the loss settled on him like a heavy blanket.

It began to rain, a soft intermittent drizzle, and that's when he heard it: Muffled sounds coming from somewhere in the wreckage before him.

He set his shotgun down under a ledge of plaster to keep it from getting wet; listened carefully.

He heard it again.

"Maggie! Sara!" he howled at the top of his lungs, and started tearing through the debris like a madman, yanking off bricks and shattered pieces of lumber in the area where the bedroom had once been.

He'd left Maggie in bed this morning with some kind of flu; Sara, a precocious six year old, would have run to her mother's bed when the trouble started.

As he clawed at the remnants of his home, he prayed that the noises he heard were them.

Maggie.

He'd found her late in his life, she'd been twenty-three and he thirty-two when they'd met. In a grocery store, of all places. She'd been in front of him in the checkout line and had looked over her shoulder at him, smiling shyly, and asked him if he always wore his hair in braids. He'd replied, straight-faced, "Only when I'm not wearing it in a ponytail." Maggie had laughed, and that's when he'd noticed how pretty she was, with her wide green eyes and short red hair; no taller than his chest. She'd been an English teacher, so smart sometimes it had scared him. What had she ever seen in an outcast like him?

He hadn't loved Maggie in the beginning, but had grown to love her in the seven years of their marriage. She'd changed him, made him grow from the drunken, crazy unskilled half-breed he'd been — a real loser — into a good man. She'd helped him leave the reservation, kick the bottle, and eventually encouraged him to go to welding school.

She'd changed his whole life, and he owed her. And he loved their daughter, Sara, more than anything in the world. *Little feather* he called her, and her innocent Indian brown eyes haunted him as he continued to dig.

Someone was calling, "Daddy, daddy." He dug faster.

It didn't take him long to find them. Maggie was dead and already going cold on the bed where he'd left her. A

31

piece of the ceiling had smashed her skull. Sara, he found hiding under the bed, weeping, and in shock. He gathered her into his strong arms, and wept with joy that she was still alive, then wept in grief over his dead wife. He covered her in a blanket, lifted her body from the bed, and carried it to the back of the house.

After he'd calmed his little girl and tended to her cuts and bruises, he cleared a space on the bed and laid her down to rest. She was asleep within seconds, now that she knew her father had her safe. As she slept, he buried his wife out behind their home, as the last of the day trickled away into dusk.

The house was a mess. It would take a lot of work to rebuild. For the night, Matt dug out his old tent and the sleeping bags, set the tent up next to the ruined house, and they moved into that.

He didn't get much sleep that first night, but sat, legs crossed, on guard through most of it. Worried about Sara, worried that other looters or worse would find their way to his home again.

He had no doubt whatsoever in his mind that he would kill to protect his daughter. Before Maggie had tamed him, he'd been a fighter, a warrior. A survivalist. He knew how to live off the land. Maggie had teased him about it, saying that he had more than half Indian in him.

He stared into the rainy night and reminisced about Maggie: their first night together . . . the exact moment he'd suspected that he loved her. A dull ache took hold of his heart and begun to squeeze mercilessly. Gods, he'd do anything — *anything* — to have her in his arms at that moment. His head lay on his knees, his hands clenched into tight balls, as he fought back tears. He couldn't afford to let the grief touch him, or he would soon be howling out his misery to the moon, like a wolf who'd lost his mate. He had to be strong for Sara.

Behind him in the tent, his daughter woke in the night, crying in terror. He went to comfort her.

Three

Emma gazed out over the city, or what was left of it, her eyes flat. It still made her want to cry over the waste of it all, but she'd shed all her tears long ago. There were none left. Five months alone in a bomb shelter with all her ghosts had wrung all the grief from her. She'd stayed down there as long as she could bear it without going stark raving mad, and five months had been her limit. In the end, what had kept her down in the shelter even the five months had been her final promise to Larry.

She'd never completely accepted Larry's premise anyway, that a nuclear bomb had been dropped in the area. Because of the type of devastation on the Metro East Side that she could see from the bluffs, she now believed that what had really occurred was that the New Madrid Fault had ripped open, and when it did, the Phillips Petroleum Plant across the Mississippi River must have exploded. That's what had created the mushroom cloud.

Below her sprawled an alien land. What hadn't been demolished by the explosions, the earthquake, and the fire, was now underwater, because the Mississippi had *changed course*. She'd once read somewhere that that could happen, but she'd never have believed it if she hadn't seen the beginning of it with her own eyes the day of the earthquake. And now before her was the final result.

Her home was truly gone.

"What am I going to do now, Danny?" she mourned under her breath. "Why couldn't I have just died with you and our children?" But Danny's ghost didn't appear this time when she spoke to him. Sometimes *they* didn't answer. Ever since she'd left the shelter, they had visited less and less.

Oh, her being alive was a miracle, she knew that.

All those awful weeks when she'd been in agony, sick with her burns, some tenacious sense of survival had refused to let her die. Larry had had extensive medical supplies, and books on how to self-treat wounds. Somehow in her pain, she'd doctored herself and had made it. Danny had helped. He'd sat right beside her and had talked to her for hours at a time, showed her what to do, encouraged her.

Sometimes, Larry had come to see her. Sometimes, even her children.

She'd never realized just how strong her will to survive was.

Emma sniffled, and wiped her nose off with her cold fingers, careful not to touch the burnt skin that trailed down the right side of her face and body. The burns were still healing. She could bear the pain now, but she'd carry the horrendous scars for the rest of her natural life—however short that might be. Then there was her leg. She must have damaged it, too, in their flight, because it hurt to walk on it.

Emma limped over to the tree and retrieved the knife. She'd practiced throwing it every day since she'd emerged, and was becoming an expert at it. Larry had had knives in the shelter, but no guns. There were gun racks, but they had been empty. She vaguely recalled him saying that last day, that he hadn't had the time to bring the guns up to the shelter yet. Well, she was lucky to have the knives. She'd probably need them.

Larry had had a gun in the Rover, but she couldn't remember now what had happened to it. Perhaps she should locate the Rover and search for the gun. She could do that.

Well, and if she found Larry's body? Emma shuddered. She could give it a decent burial. She owed him that.

Emma closed her eyes for a second, the chilly breeze playing wistfully with her loose hair. Larry appeared and gave her the thumbs up, grinning broadly, then his image just as swiftly dissipated. Emma smiled. She'd studied Larry's survival magazines: *Soldier of Fortune* and *American Survival Guide*. She knew if she wanted to stay alive, she'd have to learn how to take care of herself, defend herself. She'd also have to learn how to hunt, and eventually how to grow her own food.

Emma peered into the cool, heavy mist that hung over everything day and night. Daytime was a perpetual twilight of gloom. It had been like this since she'd come out. Emma guessed it had something to do with all the atmospheric debris that the world had been spewing out. Thick clouds hid the sun from the earth. And besides the constant dusk, she was afraid the planet's climate was changing. It was *cold,* and it was only September. Heaven knows what the winter would be like.

She threw the knife a couple more times, and studied the clouds above her, shivering. Thank God there had been blue jeans and sweaters; a jacket almost her size had been stored in the shelter. They had probably been Joanie's. Joanie had been thinner, so at first the clothes hadn't fit. But Emma had lost a great deal of weight, now the clothes were almost too big.

Yanking the knife out of the charred and blackened tree, she felt pity for the poor earth. Nothing but destruction everywhere she looked, except there were already little touches of green sprouting here and there. Nature was so resilient . . . and savage. Without people to compete with and be killed by, the insects were crawling, scurrying and swarming aggressively everywhere.

Emma sidestepped silently away from a cloud of droning bees, fully aware that if they came after her, their combined stings could kill her. She'd only been foraging for a week or so outside, but she'd learned not to panic. The bees hovered a few feet away for a while, and then shot off into the gray sky.

"This world's not going to be easy to live in, is it, Danny?" she asked aloud. Again, he didn't answer. It was beginning to worry her. Where had he gone?

She looked down at St. Louis again, or what was left of it. Once it had been a great city. The tall proud buildings that had once glittered in the sun were burnt-out ruins, husks that poked like blackened pieces of decayed teeth above the water. She could see the jagged stumps of the Arch a few feet under the waterline, the rest of it gone.

All the evenings she'd driven home from work threading through the busy city streets, heading toward the Poplar Bridge and Illinois, when the sun would splash the Arch in soft shades of apricot or pearly pink. The clouds swirling behind. A metal rainbow.

Now there was no Arch, no bustling avenues and sidewalks, no bridge, no puttering cars . . . *no people.* Just a silent watery graveyard of twisted metal and dying memories, a lingering putrescent smell, wafting up even as far as these bluffs.

Where were all the people? Were they all dead?

Was the whole world like this now?

There must be *some* other survivors, she rationalized, but where the hell were they now? The city looked deserted.

Emma muttered under her breath, sliding the knife back into the homemade sheath that hung from her thin waist, and moved away from the cliff that overlooked the remains of the city. She had made a decision.

Home. I want to go there. Across the water. See for myself what's left. If anything. Stink or no stink. Treacherous or not.

Somewhere in the distant recesses of her mind, she

still had this crazy hope that perhaps one of them was still alive. That someone else had made it. Even if it was just the damn cat. She knew it was impossible . . . yet, it was a hope she'd held close to her heart, and protected like a fragile flower since that first night in the shelter.

Anything was possible, wasn't it? *She* had made it.

She wove her way carefully through the dead leaves and crunched across the dried grass.

If none of her family had made it, then all she had left in the world was her older sister, Margaret, and her husband, Ken. They'd moved up to Maine a couple of years ago. They had no children. Emma prayed they were still alive.

And if none of her family here were left, more than anything, at that moment, Emma knew what she wanted to do. Go up to Maine and find her sister. She had to believe that someone she loved was alive somewhere. But Bar Harbor was so faraway. It might as well be on another planet.

Emma walked faster toward the shelter, suddenly longing for its safety. If the truth were known, it was the thought of leaving the shelter now that terrified her. The shelter was safety. Like a womb. It had enough prepackaged dry food and bottled water to last her another year and a half. *Thank you, Larry.* How could she leave it? For what?

This awful new world scared the hell out of her.

She produced the key back at the shelter, first peeking around nervously, unlocked the steel door, and slipped in.

Emma squinted her eyes in the semidarkness. It was cool inside the shelter. Almost as cold as outside. But it was well built. A shame, she reflected sadly, that the ones who had built it had never gotten to use it.

"Don't feel so sad, Emma," Danny was smiling his misty smile at her from one of the two cots. "Larry's glad someone put it to good use."

"Oh, Danny." Emma ran to him, her face breaking

37

into happiness, leaning in close, but not touching. "I was afraid you'd left me."

"I'll never *really* leave you, Em, you know that. I love you."

"You just haven't been around much lately," she sulked.

"You don't need me as before . . ."

She started to shake her head, but his melancholy eyes stopped her. He looked just like the last time she'd seen him: plaid shirt and his old tattered blue jeans, his long blond hair combed back away from his square jaw, his brown eyes troubled in a deeply lined face. He had aged so much that last year.

"You know, Em," the ghost's voice grew gentle, "I'm going to have to go away soon. You know that, don't you?"

"Why?" Emma protested, the fear creeping in again.

"I was only here to help you through the worst. I don't belong here anymore."

"I still need you," she said softly.

"No, you don't. You're getting stronger every day, Em. You're a survivor. I always told you that. I have to go."

Emma saw that he wouldn't be swayed, so she answered, "I'll *miss* you." Tears collected in her eyes.

"You'll see me again someday. None of us really die, you know. Not as long as you remember us."

"Please, don't go." Emma's arms longed to hold him, though she knew she couldn't. When she tried to touch any of them, they evaporated like smoke.

But he was already gone. Fading away into the shelter's dim interior. One blink there, one blink gone. Only his love lingering and making her even more lonely.

"I know you aren't real," she murmured defiantly, lying down on the cot, closing her tired eyes, her head swimming. But for a long time, she had needed to believe he was, that the others were. It had saved her sanity.

She turned over on the hard cot and moaned, snuggling her head into her arms. She was so afraid. So alone. Sleep stole over her anyway.

He'd been aware of the human woman for days. Her thoughts were clear, strong on the air currents around him, unlike most humans. It was the first sign of any healthy life he'd come across in weeks. Intrigued—and lonely for the first time in centuries—he found himself drawn to a human. At first, listening to her mind and watching her in the evenings as she forayed from her hole in the ground, he'd been wary that she was insane. She was talking to people that weren't there. Then he realized it was only her way of staying sane. Clever.

There was something about her. She had the glow for one thing . . . and she was learning swiftly to survive. She was magnificent with that knife of hers, the way she stood, proud and straight, even with her hideously burned face and crippled leg.

Low to the ground, in beast form, his glittering red eyes devouring her slim figure as she moved through the woods, he tailed her cautiously. So many of the humans had that terrible sickness. He had to be careful. Sometimes he didn't smell it until it was almost too late. Unbelievably, it killed his kind, too.

Soon he had to accept that he wasn't following her as he would have his usual victims, for sustenance or entertainment, but for something else . . . perhaps she would be the one. Perhaps. There wasn't much to choose from these days, to be truthful. And he hadn't seen or heard from his own kind in ages. It was beginning to worry him.

The shaggy shadow drifted behind the woman as she stood pensively studying the swollen river from the cliff, and disappeared without a sound back into the woods as she turned around and headed back toward her lair.

It was too soon to decide, too soon to make his move.

He had to think about it for a while, see if she made it. It'd been so long since he'd done such a thing. His ancient mind clicked back over the centuries, as he galloped with the setting sun. Europe near the end of the fifteenth century, he thought it had been . . . somewhere in the south of France. That lovely human female with the flowing auburn hair they'd been trying to burn for a witch . . . just because she had possessed psychic powers. Barbarians. Still barbarians. Vanessa something or other. There'd been so many back then, he soon forgot their names. But she had been unique, even for a human changeling. And she'd been even more striking with silver hair. Those eyes. He'd forgotten everything else about her, but he could still remember her eyes. But, in the end, the change had warped her like it did so many of them, made her careless, and after he'd tired of her and turned her out, years and years later, he'd heard from another of his kind in passing that she'd been caught and destroyed. Pity. She'd been so . . . pleasing under the covers.

Oh, well, his sharp teeth flashed in the dark as he left the human woman and went in search of prey. There was a town not faraway, and there were a few humans left among its ruins. Hungry, weak. He could hear their minds babbling in fear. He hurried. He was ravenous.

He'd decide about *her* later.

The next day Emma went searching for the Rover, to see if there was anything in it she could use — and if she was ever going to leave this place, a gun would be better protection than just a knife.

Leaving bits of cloth tied in tree branches (a clear return trail, so she wouldn't get lost) she went out and eventually located the Rover. The fire had changed it into a black skeletal frame on four melted mounds of rubber. Completely useless. There was no sign of the gun.

Or Larry's body. The fire had taken care of that, too.

Disappointed, Emma spent the rest of the day exploring the territory around her, stretching her weak muscles. She saw no signs of people anywhere, but kept having the unpleasant feeling that someone or something was following her. She never caught sight of them, though. Only a huge lone wolf at the edge of a clearing, who loped back into the shadows when her eyes discovered him. The animal terrified her. What was a wolf that big doing in these parts? The earthquakes, she reasoned, trying not to show her fear before the animal disappeared, the earthquakes must have driven the beast down from the mountains. She prayed it would leave her alone.

Toward evening, tired, as the sun begun to settle closer to the horizon, she headed home.

She was nearing the shelter when she heard the commotion and slid behind a clump of shrubs. Her hand hovering over her knife, she froze.

People.

They'd discovered her home.

For one heartbeat, Emma desperately wanted to just run out and greet them. She hadn't seen a real person for such a long time. But something in the way they were acting, alerted her sharpened senses and warned her in time.

This wasn't the world she had grown up in.

These weren't friends.

From her hiding place, Emma counted three or four of them. Sickly, emaciated, dirty. And armed to the teeth. Their bodies bristled with knives and guns. In the lengthening shadows, they seemed sinister, not of her world.

Stay away from them. They're trouble.

"Hey, someone's living here," one of them declared. "Looks like one of them underground homes or something." He turned, and in the fading light, Emma could see that he was a hulking man with scars on his face, a

41

scraggly beard, and only one ear. He had an old shotgun pulled up close to his chest. His clothes, fatigues and a dark jacket, were torn and filthy.

"I'll be damned, Wildman, you're right. I think it's one of those bomb shelters, though," another, deeper voice. "I bet there's food and guns in there."

"Fuck . . . maybe, women," one of the others snickered greedily.

Emma's skin prickled, and her heart pounded so loudly in her ears she was fearful they would hear it.

"Goddamn it, Wade, all you think about is getting pussy," another voice snarled back, angrily. His back was to Emma, all she could see of him was a massive blur.

"Well, shithead, if you would've let that last one live a little longer—"

"I told you there was something wrong with her."

Emma thought he twirled his finger in a lazy circle near his ear, but it was hard to tell. It was getting darker every second.

"And she was another mouth to feed. Would've brought us more trouble than she was worth, especially after you roughed her up, she didn't walk too good . . . looked disgusting, too. *Had* to carve her face up, didn't ya?"

Emma's blood went cold, colder than the coming night.

"Couldn't help it, Foster, she pissed me off, that's all," the one named Wade snorted.

"Couldn't help it, huh? You make me sick. Her screaming could have brought any one of the other gangs down on us—or worse yet, Plagues. Could have all been dead, 'cause of you."

Gangs? Emma reflected, puzzled. She was beginning to get a picture of what this new world was like, and she didn't care for it at all. She shifted her position so she could see the men better. Her food, medicines, everything she had was in that little hole in the ground. Could she just walk away and let them have it?

42

Did she really have any choice? A knife was no match against guns.

Maybe they wouldn't be able to get in . . . she had the key.

"Shut up, all of you." One of them swiveled more toward her, and she caught a glimpse of him, a small stocky man with a hard face. "Right now, I'd say we have more important fish to fry. We gotta get in there." He gestured toward the door they were all staring at.

"I know it's full of goodies."

Emma held her breath as they tried first one way after another to get in. They had tools. She wanted to rush out at them, kick and hit them . . . make them go away.

But she was smarter than that.

"Got it!" the cheer went up, as they all scuttled into her home like advancing parasites.

No. That's my home.

As she watched in disgust, silent tears coursing down her cheeks, they ransacked it and carted everything of value away into the forest, amidst shouts of glee.

She waited until it was totally dark. She huddled behind a tree, her teeth chattering. The nights were getting terribly cold. They waited around for most of the night. Would they never leave?

Finally, half-frozen and discouraged, she heard one of them say, "Damn, let's get the loot and get the hell out of here. It's freezing. Go back to camp. Ain't nobody living here anymore, Wade."

She made sure they were long gone before she dared to come out of hiding and scurried back into the shelter. She lit a match from a booklet she had in one of her pockets, and looked around.

There wasn't much left. They'd taken the oil lamps, most of the blankets, the cots, medicine, and all of the food. They'd even taken the portable potty. It was a mess. Most of what they'd left behind was paper and trash . . . like the vestiges of her life.

43

She had felt safe here. It had been her home. No more.

"Now what am I going to do?" she groaned in the darkness when the match went out.

She slumped down to the floor. What would she do if they came back? Unlikely. They had everything of value already.

"Danny?" she sobbed achingly. If she had ever needed him, she needed him now. No answer. Emptiness.

She was truly alone.

She curled up on the floor, pulled bits of paper around her, and drifted off into a shivering, fitful sleep.

When she awoke the next morning, her body was sore, and her belly was rumbling, demanding sustenance. No longer could she just reach up to the shelf and find bags to rip apart or cans to knife open. It wasn't going to be that easy anymore.

All she had were the clothes on her back, her knife, a pack of matches, and whatever she could glean from the trash the men had left behind.

It stole over her then that she'd already made the decision to leave, even before the men had ransacked her refuge. She'd known almost from the beginning that she couldn't stay locked away in the shelter forever. So her hand had been forced a little sooner than she'd anticipated: she was going to try to make it to Maine. Her sister Margaret. It was an impossible idea. An impossible trek across the whole country. But if there was the slightest chance that Margaret and Ken were still alive . . . God, she would do anything to find them.

And then for the first time in a long time, Emma smiled. Hope. A purpose to keep living. Maybe she wasn't alone after all.

But first she wanted to see her old home one last time. Useless, sentimental journey that it would be.

She hobbled outside and answered nature's call, glancing around nervously, still afraid that those men were lurking around somewhere.

I'll have to defend myself . . . learn to make a camp . . . travel across miles and miles of perhaps hostile territory . . . hunt for my own food—real soon.

The prospect of her coming journey both excited and dismayed her. She wasn't exactly sure where Bar Harbor, Maine was. Much less how to get there. On foot. She didn't know, either, how bad it really was out there.

She trudged back to the shelter to see what she could salvage.

A short while later she stood outside the door, a meager pack fashioned out of an old shirt strapped on her back. The thieves had left behind a metal box where Larry had had maps of the whole country, a compass, a coil of rope, and more matches. Thank goodness for tiny favors, she thought, as she studied the map against a tree trunk.

This is the right way, she told herself, looking through the trees. East. If the landmarks were still where they should be, the roads and the towns. With a great sigh, she hefted the pack higher on her back, turned, and without another look, limped away.

Got to find food. Hungry.

Again she thanked fate, or whatever watched out for her, that she'd had all that time in the shelter . . . and for Larry's survivalist magazines.

Now she'd really put what she'd learned to the test.

Her eyes scanned the ground as she moved through the woods, searching for edible foods, berries, roots, seeds . . . furry squirrel or rabbit parts bouncing through the foliage. She'd always loved animals, so she worried if she could actually kill them. With a knife? Skin them?

Damn right, her stomach growled painfully.

But I won't eat grubs, yeck, she promised herself as she pushed a low hanging branch out of the way and forged through a tight crack between two boulders. *Or insects!*

The sun climbed the sky, but it was just a shadowy circle behind the clouds. And Emma walked.

The world had changed. Emma felt, once she had come out of the woods, she might as well be on another planet. Devastation lingered everywhere from the earthquakes, the fires, and the water. Aftershocks were still jarring the earth, some of them pretty sizable. Yawning cracks lacerated the ground. Some of the chasms were so deep Emma couldn't see their bottom, and some bubbled with something that resembled molten lava, which baffled Emma. What was it? She didn't know. There weren't any volcanoes around that she knew of. Perhaps the crimson flow came from deep in the earth. Perhaps it had something to do with the severity of the earthquakes. The steam that rose from these, drifted up to join the heavy clouds above her. If there were as many elsewhere as here, she brooded — as she gave wide berth to the fissures — then the land must be truly scarred.

Twice that morning she saw paw prints in crusted-over puddles of icy water. Big cats of some kind. In the distance, wolves howled. Deer, rabbit, and squirrels bounced across her path all the time, but they moved so damn fast. Well, she wouldn't go hungry — if she could catch them.

Fighting the sharp-edged brush, she shoved through and crouched in a weary heap at the edge of a cliff overlooking the Mississippi. Staring down, a whimper escaped from deep in her throat, and her heart nearly stopped.

So here's where all the people went, she thought bitterly.

The earthquake had changed the river's course, but where the remnants of the Poplar Street Bridge, trees, cars, and decaying bodies had choked its flow, it had thinned almost to nothing and dammed up. Parts of the bridge rose out of the water, creating a sort of link most of the way across. It looked very unstable. She carefully studied the ragged hunks of concrete and steel that spiked above the water like steppingstones.

A person could crawl or climb most of the way across the river . . . and only have to swim short distances. It was relatively dry on the other side.

But the stench was so overpowering, she had to cover her nose with her hand. The river always did have a powerful aroma all its own, but now with all the decaying bodies floating in it, it was putrid. And the water would be freezing.

Would all the towns and cities be like this? St. Louis was. But the other towns and cities? Some must have people left in them. Somewhere. But what mystified Emma was: Where were the police, the rescue and clean-up crews . . . where was everyone?

Then a horrifying truth presented itself. Maybe there *wasn't* any place to go. No people left alive anywhere, except a few demented stragglers like the ones that had plundered the shelter.

What if she made it to Maine, and it was like this? *Dead.*

Yet, she glanced over her shoulder, there was nothing behind her, either.

Scared and uncertain of what she should do, she only knew that she ached desperately for the family she'd lost. Her grief had become a soul sickness. And her sister's face from the last time she'd visited her up in Maine haunted her memory, as she started working her way tediously down the crumbling hillside toward the water.

Well, one impossible task at a time.

Pacing along the edge of the river, flapping her arms like a crazy bird to stay warm, she judged that she could get across where the water was its narrowest. Doubt nagged her. It was in the opposite direction of where she was eventually heading, but she had to see one last time the place she'd known as home. She had to keep a promise to herself.

While mulling over the situation, she found some of the last of the season's wild blackberries on bushes along the bank, dried and shriveled, but delicious anyway. She gobbled every one she found, even the rotten ones. She was so hungry. Lose any more weight, she fretted, and

47

you'll be nothing but a walking skeleton.

Well, the bridge it would have to be. She couldn't walk on water. And there were no boats left anywhere. People had probably fled in them after the earthquake.

But not until morning.

She shaded her eyes, peeking up at the dim sun. It had to be around five or so, and in the new world that was almost dark. She wanted plenty of sunlight to make that crossing. Strength, too. Her atrophied muscles were screaming from the day's workout.

Now to find a safe, warm place for the night. Maybe a cave. There were lots of them along the bluffs. Since the earthquakes, there had also been horrible storms. The weather had become unpredictable, like everything else.

It was when she was searching for a place to sleep, the evening shadows closing in on her, that she first suspected someone was still following her. Watching her.

Had those men pursued her . . . were they ogling her from somewhere along the cliffs at this very moment?

She ran, stumbling with weariness and fear, skulking along the cliff and hiding behind anything she could find, using some of the evasive tactics she'd read about in Larry's magazines, until she found a tiny cave. She squirreled into it.

Until the feeling of being watched was gone. She'd scraped her leg down the calf in her flight, and she whimpered with the pain as outside it grew dark. The storms came, fierce and vicious. Then, exhausted, she curled up and fell asleep on the cave's floor, ravenous and frozen as she was, thankful to be safe and have shelter.

She dreamed of Danny and her children; dreamed of the world before the cataclysms . . . and cried softly in her uneasy sleep.

The next morning, Emma faced the bridge.

She wanted to run away. Back to the shelter. Hide her head in the sand. Die. It was insane, trying to go *home* . . . and this whole scheme of trekking out to Maine like some brave person. When she wasn't.

No. She could do it. She had to do it.

She looked at the bridge, the water shimmering before her. It had become a sort of a test. Cross that bridge, go home, and bury her past . . . and she could do anything. Even make it to Maine.

Her stomach growled in protest.

She promised herself she'd find food. Afterwards.

"Here goes nothing," she grumbled, and waded into the frigid water. She regretted that she didn't have a change of clothing. There was no help for it, she'd just have to build a fire afterwards and dry her clothes out. Taking the rope out of her pack, she held it close. She'd use it as a safety line.

The sun filtered down on her in the quiet early morning, as she swam toward the first stretch of half-submerged bridge. She was a strong swimmer, but she knew her limits, so she took it slow and easy. She braced herself mentally against what floated in the water around her, or what she would find sandwiched in the sections of the bridge. And the smell. God.

She was shivering so badly from the cold water when she got there, that she could barely claw her way up on the first section. Her hands cramped up. Tears of anguish stained her haggard face. She tossed the rope, snagged a broken girder, then torturously pulled herself from the river. After she'd rested a few minutes, she started working her way across the bridge, carefully. She had sturdy tennis shoes on and was glad of it. Waterlogged, they squeaked and left round, wet spots behind her. At the places the bridge dipped or plummeted into the water, or was blocked with debris, she had to find alternative ways.

Once everything under her fell into the water, and the only thing that saved her from being sucked down with it and crushed was her lifeline. As she was hanging out over thin air, twirling at the end of the rope like a dead fish on a hook, she wondered again why she was doing this. Maybe she was touched.

But she gritted her teeth, wiped her tears away with numb fingers, and kept crawling along the perilous bridge.

Not all the cars had toppled into the water. Most of the vehicles on the bridge were empty, some weren't. Emma tried not to look at the rotting bodies, but it was difficult. They were everywhere.

"This is really stupid, Emma . . . this is really, really . . . dumb," she moaned under her breath, as her weight accidently dislodged a loose piece of the structure, and, with bated breath, she watched it plunge into the misty depths below her.

"Really *s-t-u-p-i-d* . . ."

Her bad leg gave her more trouble than she expected, soon she was dragging it behind her like a useless dead thing.

It took agonizing hours to cross the bridge, and when she finally made it back onto safe land, her body was shaking with the exertion, and her hands were scraped bloody. Her clothes were frozen to her like an icy shell. The first thing she did was gather wood and build a huge fire, then huddled over it until her clothes were almost dry. It was too chilly to take them off.

As the fire crackled and her body thawed, she surveyed the miles of scorched barren ground that lay before her. Whatever had happened here, it had melted the steel bridge trestles, buildings, and industrial plants into a glob of something that might have resembled the carnage left on a futuristic battlefield after the aliens had won. Or after a nuclear strike. The ground was as gray as the sky, but rippled through with blood-red veins of boiling lava, like one of those rocks streaked through with fool's gold that she remembered from her childhood. As she picked her way through the gullies and the ruins, silhouetted against the dirty sky and devastation like scarecrows with their scrawny arms outstretched, were the burned telephone poles and lines . . . marching into the distance as far as she could see, like wooden soldiers along the side of the empty highway.

There'd be no food on this path, she realized. There was nothing left, no trees or shrubs or game. How long could a person last without food or water? She didn't know, but she would find out eventually, she had little doubt.

The ground started to rumble and shift under her feet. Thank God she was off that bridge. She froze, her heart racing in fear, until the quaking subsided. It hadn't been a bad one. This time.

For a moment, she almost turned and went back the way she had come, but something wouldn't let her: the incredible microscopic hope that Danny or one of her children might still be alive. Suddenly it hit her that she'd never really given up hope.

She mentally shrugged. If another major earthquake came, it wouldn't matter where she was anyway. It could kill her anywhere.

Tilting her chin up and wiping her tears away with a grimy hand, she trudged toward the direction she believed she should go, her feet crunching over the black ash and dead earth. She'd driven down this highway to home so many times, she could have walked it blindfolded. It was about six miles to her house. The trees' burnt limbs, like emaciated fingers, waved at her as she passed.

Twice during the day, she was sure she was still being followed — spied on — and it made her skin crawl. There was no place to run to, to hide. But no one bothered her, and hard as she tried, she saw *no one*. Not once. *Where the hell were they? Who were they?*

By nightfall, she was so hungry and weary she could barely set one foot in front of the other. The roadway not only had deep crevices slicing through it at different places, but deep ravines and pits. It had been hard going with her bad leg and exhausted body. And another storm was roaring in.

But she found her home, or what was left of it. She stood and looked at it with misery in her eyes. Once it had been a beautiful old two-story frame and brick house. Danny had done a lot of work on it, though, and it had always been kept up. Now it was just a burnt-out ruin.

There was no one there, and no sign that anyone had been there in the recent past.

As the raindrops began to fall, she stalked around the grounds, calling for them hysterically: "Danny? Peter? Jenny! Anyone . . . is anyone here?" she sobbed over and over as the rain fell harder. No one answered.

"Here kitty . . . kitty, here kitty —" she yelled into the rising wind, remembering Midnight, her cat; stopped as her foot brushed up against a tiny, feline skeleton half-buried in the rubble at the front of the house. "Oh, no," she moaned, kneeling down to stare at it in shock, water and tears mingling to trickle down her face. "Midnight!" She reached out and touched its paw. "Poor little thing . . ."

She saw the fingers of a human skeleton peeking out from under a section of fallen plaster . . . and Emma knew without a doubt that it was her husband's hand. She tediously dug until she partially uncovered the other two pathetically small bodies — revealed them just enough to prove to herself that all three were there. Buried. Then she recovered them. Let them rest in peace. This was where they belonged after all.

They must have been caught when the house collapsed. Emma prayed they hadn't suffered. Now all that was left were the bones . . . and Emma wept her final grief, as the skies emptied their tears along with hers.

Later, she huddled forlorn inside the blackened shell of her old house for an endless time, as the wind slapped at her, drenched her to the bone under night clouds. She mourned in the dark for the family she would never see again, the children she would never smile at again, the husband she would never hold in her arms again.

Now *she* felt like the ghost. Which was what she was, wasn't she? An apparition. Something that no longer belonged where it was. And she accepted, maybe for the first time, that Danny and the others had just been her hallucinations. They had been dead all along. All dead. Like Larry. Like most of the world.

Letting the water gather in her cupped hands, uncaring if the liquid was polluted or not, she drank greedily to quench her thirst.

As the night settled in, it grew frigid, and she knew she had to get out of the rain. She collected wet rubble, bricks, and charred boards with her bare hands, to build a crude shelter in one corner of the gutted house.

It felt strange to be home again. Even though the house was just wreckage, she could still see in her mind the way it had once been. She didn't care that her family's remains were just feet away. At least she wasn't alone. But she would have done anything for some of the old civilized comforts: a furnace, electric lights . . . a microwave and a couple of those delicious TV dinners. A dry bed.

Keep dreaming, she told herself wistfully. Wet, shivering, and hungry, she settled uneasily down for the night.

Because *it* was back. Whoever or whatever was stalking her. She could *feel* it. She was still under scrutiny, even though the rain and the night were a dark curtain surrounding her. She unsheathed and clutched her knife tight to her shivering body, and after a long time, when nothing happened, she dozed off.

As he scrutinized the scene, the beast's eyes glowered like amber beacons in the blackness and rain. She was huddled now in those human ruins, her thoughts full of sadness. He could almost hear her weeping, even from where he was. Never could understand why humans cried the way they did. His kind had no use for it. The woman had made it across the treacherous bridge, she was still alive . . . what was she so damn upset about? Something about family from what he could glean from her troubled mind. Humans were such sentimental fools. The creature shook its huge head, water cascading off its rippling fur. It had been crouched down in the wet weeds watching her, had been surprised when it had awoke and picked up her trail earlier in the evening, that she'd crossed the river. How on earth had she accomplished that feat? He'd had no trouble swimming it. Nothing could stop *him*. But a puny human? Amazing woman. What was she searching for? They were all dead. Most everything was dead now.

The beast glared around him. The trees were silent sentinels alongside of him, their branches and dying leaves swaying with the rising wind. His stomach growled in deadly protest. He hadn't fed in two days. Soon he'd have to move on, widen his search. Kill and feed on the woman, or take her with him. One or the other. There wasn't much time.

He sniffed the wet night with flared nostrils, his long ears twitching. Another earthquake coming. Weeks, maybe less. A big one. Devastating. He'd be wise to be faraway from this area when it did.

He'd almost decided what he was going to do. Almost. He was still sending out calls for his own kind. If they didn't answer soon . . . he could do what he wanted with her. There'd be no one to be horrified at it. No one to stop him. With a muffled grunt, he rose from his haunches, his monstrous paws nervous on the soaked ground, and skittered back into the night in search of food. He'd catch up with the knife-woman in a few nights or so, and take her for his own. If she was still alive, and he was still alone. He had time.

The rain came down harder and the world closed in like a black curtain. Faraway a lone wolf howled into the wind.

When the sun rose, Emma wiggled out of her cubby-hole, feeling emotionally and physically beaten from her exposure to the raw elements and the lack of food and water.

The sun was a hazy ball low in the sky, and the temperature was even lower. Miserable, she sniffled and tried moving around to warm herself. As badly as she needed warmth to dry out, everything was too wet to build a fire.

But that wasn't her most pressing concern, food was.

She rummaged through the ruins and found a cache of can goods buried below the surface, where the kitchen pantry had once been located. The labels had dissolved, and the cans were dented, crusted with dirt. Yet, she felt as though she'd discovered diamonds. With her knife, she worried a slit into the tops, peeled back the metal, scooped out, and devoured every bit of what she found inside. Pears, stewed tomatoes, and Spaghettios.

Digging further into the earth, she discovered another six cans and stashed them in her pack. For later.

Then she strode away from her old home headed toward the bridge, not looking back once, anxious to be away from the ghosts of the past. She'd grieved enough.

At least, going back home had served a purpose . . . she'd finally succeeded in burying that past. And she had found food.

She retraveled her route to the bridge, recrossed it, and before dusk, scrambled tiredly down on the other side.

That night she found shelter in a huge cave, carried in armfuls of dry leaves, and prepared herself a bed. Leaves underneath and then leaves scooped on top of her, just like Larry's magazines had taught her. Amazingly enough, it worked, and they kept her warm.

For once rain didn't come with the night, and there was no water for her. One can of soup was all she allowed herself. She knew that finding food like she had that day in the wreckage of her house wouldn't always be so easy.

It had been *her* house, she'd known where the food had been kept, where to dig. In other peoples' houses she wouldn't be so lucky.

As the days dragged by, where she was headed and where she was, became secondary to her basic survival. Her food ran out after the first few days, and hard as she tried, she couldn't catch any game. She didn't find anymore berries. Nothing edible. Three times she went into abandoned houses and tried to find food. No success. Two places had already been ransacked, and the third house . . . she dug everywhere with her knife, searching, until the ground looked like a giant mole had gone crazy, but found no food.

Starving wasn't going to be pleasant.

Slowly, the parched days and chilly nights, the constant moving, the hunger, drained her of her energy.

And someone or something was still following her. She could just never catch them at it.

Every town she came to had been destroyed by the earthquakes or fires. She walked, dazed, through a nightmare of empty streets and past leveled houses, sleeping in caves at night in beds of leaves.

There were dead bodies, or their decomposing remains, everywhere. The plague had been real busy in the last six months, she thought glumly. No matter how many times she came across the bodies, in the roads or in the buildings, she could never get used to them or their stench. She knew she never would.

But she saw no one in all that time. There were no live people anywhere.

Though fear would have kept her away from strangers, even if she did see any. She couldn't get those men who had looted her shelter out of her mind. Day by day, she hated them with an evergrowing passion for what they'd done. Leaving someone without supplies, food, and water was worse than killing them. She lost weight. She lost hope. Her feverish mind began to play tricks on her. Sometimes she was sure what followed her was that same huge gray wolf she had seen weeks before. Of course, that was impossible. A wolf as large as a man stalking her this long, this far, without attacking? Ridiculous.

Unless it was waiting for her to drop. Waiting for her strength to fail, so she'd be easier to bring down.

So she never stopped moving. Always tracking the small game, praying to get close enough to use her knife. As good as she believed she was with a knife, she wasn't good enough yet to bring down a swiftly running hare or a squirrel.

When she became hungry enough, she fell to eating leaves and pieces of tree bark . . . and with her eyes squeezed shut in revulsion . . . insects, like she'd read in the magazines. Anything to stop the pain in her stomach.

In the end she raided any house she found, regardless of the risks, in search of sustenance. Sneaking in, sneaking out, terrified that the thing stalking her would catch up to her, or that the rickety building would cave in under her weight. Sometimes she even found food.

And with the help of her compass and her maps, she kept heading east.

She was hiking parallel to a main highway late one afternoon, somewhere outside of Effingham (or where the maps said Effingham was supposed to be and no longer was), when she first heard their voices. As weary and weak as she was, she still panicked and ran until her weak leg gave out. Miles later, panting and trembling at the knees, she'd thought she'd lost them, when suddenly they were standing right in front of her.

The men who'd cleaned out her shelter weeks before.

"Well, we finally ran the little fox down." The one with the long stringy hair was breathing heavily. "You were right, Wade, there was a woman, after all." When he grinned, he showed a mouth full of rotten teeth. "Not much to look at, but better than nothing. Since we haven't had a woman in weeks now."

"Nope, not much to look at, but mighty sweet anyway." The man without the ear leered at her.

"You've . . . been . . . following me . . . all this time?" Emma gasped, her hand stealing to her knife hilt. She backed up against a tree into the lengthening shadows as they cornered her.

"We've been tracking you, yessiree . . ." his voice was as ugly as his face as he sneered at her. "And looks like we caught you. You sure can travel, honey. Was your mama a cross-country jogger or what?" He laughed at his own joke. "We almost didn't catch you at all."

"What a pity," Emma spat sarcastically. "Just leave me alone! Do you hear me. I don't want any trouble . . . I just want to be left alone."

"Well, what a pity," one of them mimicked her. "We don't want to leave you alone, baby.

"We just want to have a little fun. Now don't you want that, too? I mean, there aren't many of us left, you know. You ought to be happy to see us. You ought to be more friendly to us, if you know what I mean?"

Her eyes narrowed. "Oh, I know what you mean. But I don't want to play. And I'll knife the first one who comes near me. I mean it," she said fiercely, waving the knife at them and trying to look brave. She mustn't let them see how afraid she was of them. She had to catch them off guard, get away.

They all looked at each other and laughed, as if they had this juicy secret between them.

Emma remembered what they'd said they'd done to the last woman.

Wordlessly, they moved in closer to her. She slid around the tree, eluding their grasping hands, and took off at a hobbled run, her gimpy leg handicapping her. She didn't get very far, before they had her backed up against another tree. They stunk. She wondered when they'd last had a bath, or—worse yet—if any of

58

them had the plague.

"Leave me alone!" she screamed it louder this time. The words bounced away into the silence.

"Goddamn, the woman must be part rabbit!" the one with the scarred face swore, breathing heavily, as if he hadn't heard her. Before she could stop him, he strolled up to her and ran his rough hand tauntingly down her cheek, her neck, and under the top of her shirt. Emma slapped him. With a nasty grin, he took his hand away and covered the spot on his face with it. His eyes going into mean slits.

"Well, friends," the one she believed was the ringleader whispered. "Who goes first?" He rubbed his hands and stared at Emma like she was less than a bug.

"I get first dibs on her."

"After me, Wildman . . . then you can have her."

"Then me next, Wade."

How could she hope to fight all four of them? Running for it was still her best chance. Soon it would be totally dark, and she could hide in the woods behind her.

The leader was unbuckling his pants when she made another dash for it.

She hurtled into the woods but was knocked to the ground before she got very far. One of them straddled her and slapped her hard across the face, while another one tried to pry the knife from her fingers. Like a leech, she held on.

She didn't waste any of her energy yelling. She fought to plunge the knife into one of them. But her body wasn't responding like it once might have. The last months and weeks, the lack of food had taken their toll. She was a weakling.

But as the fist descended again and again, somehow the strength came from deep inside her. She freed her hand for a second; the knife flashed; one of her attackers screamed a string of curses and fell away from her, sprawling on the ground.

The knife rose again, but it was knocked from her

hand and flew away like a metal bird. One man was holding her down as another tried to tear off her jeans. Emma got in a kick shot to his groin, tore free, and scuttled along on the ground trying to find the knife.

Her hands closed frantically over it. She had it!

Someone kicked her viciously in the ribs. This time she screamed, curling up on the ground in agony, before she rolled and jumped to her feet to face her tormentors. The rocks cast deeper shadows across her tear-streaked face, as she held the knife in front of her.

"You might get me in the end, but, by God, I'll hurt some of you first!" she said in a cold voice through the pain. She was badly hurt, she knew it. If she passed out now, she was as good as dead. Worse than dead. After what she'd done to two of them, they'd make sure she suffered . . .

"Give us the knife, bitch, or it'll go worse for ya." A threat. A promise.

"You can't get away."

They reminded her of a pack of ravenous dogs, and she their intended dinner. The one she'd wounded with the knife was still whimpering in the dirt. The other three had circled her, closing in for the kill, unconcerned over their partner's pain.

"Hell, she's a little spitfire, I'll give her that. Even if she looks like a burnt marshmallow."

Emma hadn't thought about her appearance in a long time. But the words still stung, and scattered her concentration just long enough that one of them kicked out with his foot faster than she could move, and the knife went spinning from her hand again — and the three of them were on her that fast.

Emma tried to fight them. It did no good. They were stronger than her. More of them. She bit and kicked gallantly, even as they brought her down.

They beat her mercilessly, and later she would recall little of it except that when the leader — old stringy hair — was naked and ready to mount her . . . in her twilight nightmare of horror and pain . . . somehow . . . there was suddenly this . . . man.

Yet, not a man.

Her vision was playing tricks on her again. They'd kicked her in the head too many times. But she thought he was tall and dressed in dark clothes, and he was *so strong*. He seemed to be everywhere at once.

He flew into her attackers and lifted them high above his head, tossing them around like shadows as they cried out. She heard bones breaking and men dying. She'd heard the sounds before, so she should know them well enough. There were other sounds. So horrible, she blanked them out.

After the night grew silent, he knelt over her with a grim smile, not touching her, and consoled her, "You're safe now, little one. No one will ever hurt you again."

His eyes were ferocious and hungry and *old*. Feral. They reminded her of a wolf's eyes. Even though he'd saved her life, she was unsure of him.

"Didn't need to help me," she gasped, grabbing at his arms. "I would have beat them in the end. Somehow. Those bastards!" Anger made her voice quaver.

The man laughed. "You are a fighter, aren't you? Just as I had thought."

She looked into his face, and almost smiled. The night was finally pitch-black, but his eyes were like tiny moons above her. She turned her head away. "Why did you save me?" she then asked weakly.

"Because you have such . . . spunk, my girl. Spirit. I admire that. I've been following you." He hesitated, then went on in a deeper voice. "For quite a while."

"Ah, it was you," she murmured, amazed, but not relieved. What did *he* want from her?

"I wasn't the only one," his tone chilling.

All Emma could do was nod, fighting to keep from going under completely. She had hurt so badly before, but now her body was going numb part by part. The beating had left her broken, bleeding on the ground, half-naked and some . . . stranger was hovering over her like death. She couldn't pass out now.

A great inner sadness began to invade her whole being. *I'm dying,* she thought, astonished. *After all I've survived . . . I'm dying.*

"No, I won't let you die," her protector hissed. "I promise.

"But you must sleep," he told her. He touched her forehead with fingers so cold they made her head hurt.

"What's your name?" he asked, his strange voice already faraway, but still commanding.

She didn't want to answer him, her lips were bloody, torn — but she did. She couldn't stop herself.

"Emma . . . Emma Bloodworth," barely audible.

And the world was spinning, going away, the pain and the humiliation dragging her down into oblivion.

She couldn't be sure, but she believed the last thing she heard was his soft laughter as obscurity claimed her.

Four

The following weeks and months were like a bad dream that Matt woke up to each morning and had to conquer. It never ended.

At least they had food. Game was plentiful and close, and Maggie had been caching away bottled water and canned goods for months. She'd had this premonition that the next earthquake to hit would be for them — and she had been right. Matt missed her more than he could have imagined.

Sara never fully recovered, never spoke another word. She was like a ghost of herself, trailing along behind her father like a tiny deaf and dumb creature, her frail hand in his. She wouldn't let him out of her sight for a moment. And since he wouldn't leave her alone to go see, he had no idea what was happening in the cities and towns.

From the remains of their old home, he slowly rebuilt a modest two-room building: a common room and a small bedroom for Sara. They needed the shelter, and it gave him something to do. When he'd just begun the new house, a particularly nasty aftershock knocked it back to the ground, and he had to start all over again. The next time he made sure it was sturdy and very low to the ground.

There were weeks and weeks of storms. If they hadn't been up on such high ground, the place would have flooded like half the state already had. One day as Sara slept, he'd ascended the nearby bluff, climbed a tree, and looked out over the area. Water was everywhere. In the distance he could just make out St. Louis rising out of the muddy river. He'd seen enough to not want to see anymore.

The air was full of steam and soot from the continual earthquakes, and layers of clouds hovered low to the earth day and night, keeping the world in constant twilight. It was bearable at first, but Matt suspected that the longer the sun was obscured behind the veil, the cooler the temperatures would become. He was right.

Soon Matt had to go hunting not just for meat, but for the fur. Though he'd caught the looters in the act that first day, they'd still gotten away with some of their possessions and most of their clothes, so he caught foxes, skinned them, and painstakingly sewed long coats together for himself and Sara, just like his tribe had done every winter on the reservation when he was a child.

The old ways came back easily.

When he wasn't hunting or gathering, Matt huddled in their small abode, comforting his daughter, telling her stories, talking to her, trying to get some response. She seemed to drift further away from him every day, as the rain drummed relentlessly on their roof.

She'd loved her mother so much, and the trauma of watching her die had done something to Sara.

He considered trying to find a doctor . . . but where would he look? If there were any doctors left alive, they were far too busy with the other survivors. If there were any.

Sometime during the third month after the earthquake, Sara fell deathly sick. The fever hit her and then the rash, and Matthew knew what she had. The plague. He remembered someone saying once that it could stay insidiously dormant for weeks or even months, but he still couldn't believe Sara had it. It'd been so long since they'd had any contact with anyone.

As dawn's weak rays touched the earth on the fourth morning of her illness, Sara died in her father's arms, quietly, and seemingly toward the end, without too much pain. Matthew was grateful for that, because he'd seen people die of it often as not in excruciating agony. Sara was spared that at least.

He buried her next to her mother.

Then he stoically packed up an old pup tent left over from his camping days, any supplies he could carry, slung his old shotgun across his arms, and headed east.

He had no idea where he was going, and he didn't really care. Any place was better than near those graves.

He spent the next few months in the hills. Isolated. Reliving his seven years with Maggie and Sara. Being miserable. Growing to hate himself.

When the loneliness had eaten deep into him like acid, he'd gone into a few towns searching for survivors. He had never seen anything as horrible as what he saw in those places. One town was almost all underwater, and there were dead bodies drifting along, stinking and bloated. There were people. Poor things. A lot of them were starving or dying with the plague, and even though Matt had cared lovingly for his own sick daughter, he was apprehensive about getting close to any of them for long. Right after Sara died, he had waited for the plague to take him as well. It never did. He figured that God must have some further use for him, and wondered at times what it was. He didn't have a clue.

Then there were the scavengers.

In the second town he was caught off guard and attacked, and had to savagely defend himself or die. He ended up shooting two men that day, knifing one, and then retreating back to the hills and his tent, sick at heart. He wasn't a killer, but the new order of things had turned him into one.

From then on he stayed away from the cities and towns. From people. He hunted alone in the hills for food, and spent hours, days, reminiscing about the way it had been before the world had become a hell.

And slowly closed up inside himself.

Five

"You've been out for a long time," the voice coaxed her from the murkiness.

She wasn't sure if it were that dark, or if she just couldn't see. By a touch of her fevered fingers, she could tell she was bundled into a thick pile of something like fur, and yet she still shook.

"I'm so cold," she sighed on a shiver, and someone tucked the fur up closer around her chin. When she moved just the slightest bit, her body pulsed with pain, a moan escaped, and the world blurred.

"How long have I been out?"

"Five days."

Terror nibbled at the edge of her consciousness; alarmed, she shoved it away.

Something terrible had happened. Something . . . She had been beaten, almost raped, almost died. *She had died.*

Emma's mind retreated, unable yet to cope with what had happened to her out there at the edge of the woods . . . and since. She had these images, misty and unreal, yet still there, of being enfolded into someone's arms, smothered under someone's gentle weight; of someone making love to her, their mouth at her neck . . . and then, nothing.

She could never remember anything else.

But it frightened her even more than what those men had done to her.

Minutes might have elapsed, perhaps hours, until she was aware again.

"Where am I?" she asked. It was still pitch-black.

"My home." By his voice, she could tell he was the same man who had saved her.

His face floated in a velvet circle of light. His eyes seemed to glitter in the dimness like chips of diamonds. He had a comely, but hard face, with high cheekbones, an aquiline, hookish nose, and brilliant eyes as black as a moonless night. He leaned toward her, his body moving like some carnivore's, fluidly silky and silent. His shaggy long silver hair added a wolfish touch.

He had *butchered* those men who had attacked her . . . with his bare hands. She hadn't seen a weapon. His glittering gaze studied her. There was something in it that wasn't human.

She tried, in vain, to sit up; fell back to the pillow. "You killed *all* of them —"

"Did you prefer that I had not? They were trying to kill you . . . after they had finished with you, that is. Four against one, not my idea of very fair odds. I've always been a great defender of the underdog."

"And I was the underdog?"

"Yes. You were badly hurt: broken ribs — one pierced your lung and collapsed it — there was a massive loss of blood internally . . . and you stopped breathing. Those men are better off dead." His voice showed true emotion — intense hatred — for the first time. "I was afraid for a while that you wouldn't make it, even with the blood. I can only do so much." He shrugged gracefully.

What was he talking about? *Stopped breathing?*

"Are you a doctor or something?"

He chuckled, denying it by the expression on his face. Emma stared at him, uncertainty seizing her will. Those awful sounds as those men had died.

She was shaking her head. "But how did you defeat all of them? Who are you?" she demanded, her voice trembling from the strain. *"What* are you?" blurted out before she could stop it.

"My name's Byron Shelly, this century anyway. I'm what you Others would never truly accept existed. I'm a myth." That enigmatic laughter she remembered so well echoed after the words, and then he became serious just as swiftly.

His face was above her, so near she could feel the taintedness of his breath. As his fingers brushed her eyelids, they gently closed. There was something very *wrong* about him . . . *but he had saved her life and* . . . *and* . . .

"Rest," his voice was stern, hypnotic. Emma found herself slipping back into sleep, and whatever she had been about to remember went with her.

The next time she rose to consciousness, her mind was more in focus and the pain was bearable, but she found herself alone.

Her mysterious benefactor was nowhere to be found.

Emma tried to sit up, but her body wouldn't obey.

Looking through the darkness, she could see objects surrounded in a faded glow, the way you can just as dawn creeps into the night. No windows. No . . .

In the muted light she spied a candle, and a box of matches on the floor next to her. She opened the box and struck a match; lit the candle. The light, soft as it was, hurt her eyes, and she shielded away. Her vision wouldn't completely focus.

She was in a cave, a comfortable one to be sure, but a cave nonetheless. But it was the strangest cave she'd ever been in. There were curtainlike coverings over the walls, perhaps to keep drafts out; plush throw rugs were scattered all over the cave floor. An empty chair sat low to the ground, as the candle's flame lapped at the cold air. Emma's breath made gauzy white clouds.

And she *was* lying in a pile of furs.

"So you're awake?" The voice startled her, for her savior was watching her from the chair, as if he had been there the whole time.

"You weren't there a moment ago! I would have sworn it." Emma slid back under the covers and clasped them closer to her chest. She'd just discovered she was completely naked.

"Sorry if I frightened you. I forget sometimes." He got up and walked over, lowering himself sinuously to sit near where she was lying; he smiled thoughtfully at her.

"Forget what?" she asked.

"How it upsets you Others."

"Others? That's the second time you've used that term."

He nodded his head, an amused look on his face. "Not of my kind."

"Your kind?" The word *vampire* just popped into her mind, and she watched in horror as his face lit up.

"Yes." He made a gesture of resignation. He was serious.

Emma snuggled back into her furry bed, closed her eyes. She felt funny. She'd never felt exactly like this before. He'd read her thoughts. It was ridiculous, and yet . . .

"Nothing else to say?"

"What is there to say?" she replied carefully. Of course, he was insane. She imagined many of those left alive were. Off their rocker, that is. "You believe you are a vampire."

He laughed again. "Oh, you are priceless. Yet if I were you, I would be just as doubtful. I, too, would believe I was insane."

Emma's mouth tightened; only her fever-bright eyes showed her confusion.

"But you will accept all that, vampires, reading minds — in time. Believe me," he finished in a more compassionate tone, a knowing glint in his eyes. Was he playing with her?

She glared at him.

"And concerning your clothes . . . they were in despicable shape, so I took the liberty of disposing of them. I've brought you some clean apparel. In the wardrobe over there. I think they'll fit.

"And there's a robe at your feet."

Emma began to deny it, "No." Her eyes slid downwards.

There was a robe.

"How did you do that?"

For a moment she thought he was going to truly answer her, but then he seemed to stop himself. *Too soon, too soon,* he thought. "Do what?"

Emma's face drained. Too much had happened too fast. The earthquake, the death of those she loved, five months in solitary, and then those beasts attacking her. Those queer dreams. This bizarre situation she found herself in.

I must be sicker than I thought.

"Thank you for the robe." She reached out and clutched the robe to herself, and going under the cover, she wriggled her body into it. She was surprised that he was still there when she came out. She'd hoped he wouldn't be. She needed time to think.

"How did you get those burns?" he asked, not unkindly.

She told him about Larry and fleeing St. Louis that last day. He didn't interrupt her, even when she broke down and hid her face in her hands. He waited until she collected herself.

She finally looked up. "And if I haven't said it before, thank you for saving my life. I would be dead if not for you. I don't know how you did it or why, really, but I thank you . . . Byron."

He smiled because she hadn't forgotten his name.

"I've never done this before. Saved a human." His look was unreadable. "But I've been lonely, Emma," a sigh. "There aren't many of us left, you see. And we feel loneliness, just like you. We are capable of love.

Deep love, because it can span centuries."

He stood up and began to pace in front of her, his head hung. "I haven't heard from any of my people in months. I've looked for them. No luck. I fear they may be all destroyed. I'm alone." He paused, seeing Emma's eyes fill with pity. She knew what it was to be lonely. To love and lose. She knew.

"The plague kills us also, Emma. If we drink your blood and you have it . . . it makes us sick and then kills us. The first human ailment in history that has ever been able to do that." He seemed disturbed. "It takes us longer to die, but, in the end, we do die from it as well."

Emma said nothing. Her fingers clutched at the fur.

He stopped in his path and turned to look at her sadly in the candlelight. "Of those four men who attacked you . . . three had it. I could tell by their . . . smell." His delicate nostrils flared, as if he could smell the sickness still. "They would have been dead within a few days, at the most. I couldn't get nourishment from them. Just the one.

"That's why we're dying," he whispered. "There aren't enough of you left alive to — well, to feed us any longer." For the first time Emma sensed fear in him.

His black eyes held hers with an intensity that made her quiver down to her soul. She couldn't look away; she didn't want to. It had been so long since she'd been able to talk to someone, and her need scared her. Even if he was insane. If he'd wanted to hurt her, he would have done it before now.

She wanted to weep for him, herself, the world, but she found, for some reason, she couldn't cry.

"Where have you been since the earthquake, Emma?"

She sighed tiredly, "It's a long story."

"Time is the one thing I have plenty of. Tell me."

And she told him about herself, her life before the quake, her family, and how she'd hid in the shelter for five months, and why. And he listened patiently.

"Those men — and you — are the only people I've seen

71

alive since I've come out," she finished. "Is it that way everywhere?"

"Yes," he answered. "Far worse than your worst nightmare. That is the world now. I've traveled long distances. After the last series of worldwide earthquakes, the plague ravaged the rest of the population. There aren't many people left. Anywhere."

"Worldwide?" Emma repeated incredulously.

He sat back down in his chair, and his gaze searched into someplace she couldn't follow. "Yes, everywhere, Emma. The earth's crust has somehow . . . shifted . . . like an angry snake shedding its skin. Rivers that were there before, sometimes are gone now. Whole towns — cities — in some cases have disappeared off the face of the planet. Oceans moved and took back some of the land."

How does he know this? she thought.

"I know it, Emma." His eyes shone at her. "I told you — "

He had read her mind! How did he do that?

Vampire.

Emma gasped, flinging her arm over her face. "Stop, please," she begged. She thought she was weeping, but was astounded to discover there were no tears on her cheeks.

Then, in a whisper, "Maine. Is it still there?"

"Some of it is. Some of it has been reclaimed by the sea. I'm sorry. I know your sister lived there."

"How do you know these things?" she demanded angrily.

"I know many things, Emma . . . and I'm *very* old." His voice was like rustling leaves.

Emma stared at him. His handsome head reclined in his pale hands. He was dressed in dark clothes. Old-fashioned. A long coat and tailored slacks, dusty and worn now. That's all she'd ever seen on him. His long silverish hair hung to his shoulders in wild waves. He looked perhaps thirty-five or so. No older. Not a large man, or exceedingly tall, and yet he projected the image

72

of pure raw strength. A sharp, rare intelligence. His charisma was undeniable.

He swiveled in the chair to meet her gaze, and there was something about the way he looked at her. So hungrily. Possessively.

Emma felt nauseous. The room was spinning. Perhaps she was really still out in the woods, broken and dying, and he and this whole vampire thing were all part of her death delusion.

"Could I sleep now, please? I'm very tired," she said between clenched teeth, sweat breaking out all over her body. She turned her face into the soft fur, clutching her screaming stomach. Her blood was boiling in her veins.

She was dreaming and yet she was awake.

What was wrong with her? Why did she feel so . . . wretched? Then the pain hit her. It wasn't the first time.

"Oh, God, Byron . . . what's happening to me?" she moaned.

He enclosed her in his strong arms as she cried.

"Hush, Emma. Hush . . . soon it will be over. Soon." And this time as he began to caress her, make love to her, she didn't fight him. She knew and gave in to it. His strength was unbelievable, his lovemaking savage; yet strangely, she trusted him. She didn't even care when later he set his mouth to her neck and began to feed.

The pain dissolved into numbness. Reality faded into a swirling river that carried her away. Though something elusive — a warning — fluttered frantically inside her breast, she couldn't capture it, and it scurried away to a dark corner of her tortured mind. She could hear it crying, and then realized it was herself. She was weeping deep inside.

"You will not be afraid, little one. Not of me. Never of me. You will sleep now," he told her as they lay together later. "Forget. Like the other times before."

For a dark moment she captured the truth, and she *knew.* "You should have let me die," she groaned bitterly, hopelessly, before sleep claimed her. Her eyes fought to open—he was no longer there—and she plunged back into oblivion.

What would become of her?

Time was no longer a concept she could grasp. How many hours, days, had she been here in this cave? She had no idea.

She tried desperately at times to make sense of the dreams that kept eluding her. Nothing.

She was still sick. Weak. *Why?*

"Byron," she called out, somehow knowing he would come as soon as she spoke.

He was there.

"What's wrong with me?" The panic made her voice shrill.

"You'll be all right. In time." He took her cold hands in his, yet his eyes were worried. Hiding secrets, as always. "I promise you that."

How, she thought, *when I don't eat? He doesn't feed me. Why aren't I hungry? Oh, God. I feel so . . . strange.*

"I must go out for a while," he told her, standing in the shadows.

Who was he? she fretted for the millionth time. *What am I doing here?*

There were never any answers.

"Am I a prisoner?" she asked him.

But he was already gone.

He didn't come back. Emma wasn't sure exactly how long he'd been gone, because, alone, drifting in and out of delirium, she couldn't be sure.

Time passed.

She began to slowly grow better. The chills and the fever passed.

In the end the loneliness, the fear of how long she had truly not eaten or drank, forced her from her bed of furs, forced her to get out of bed. She found and put on the clothes Byron had left her: a simple dark top and dark loose pants. Silk.

Outside it was twilight. She greedily gulped the lovely evening air and leaned back against the rocks of the cave's entrance. She was high up on a cliff. A thickening mist clung to the land below her. She could see that it was very cold out. Her breath froze before her. But she didn't feel cold. In fact, she didn't feel any way at all. Warm or cold. She scratched where her skin itched, around her burns, and was amazed as great hunks of scarred flesh sloughed off. Underneath, the skin was healed. Smooth and pliant. No scars.

Astounded, she stared at her new skin. It was so . . . white.

She sat down on the ground and watched the sun set, feeling better than she had in a long time. Whatever illness she had had, was leaving her.

She wondered where Byron was. Or if he truly existed at all.

She dragged herself back into the cave and slept some more. Waiting for Byron. Waiting.

The next time she awoke, more of her burns had flaked off. When she ran her hands over her arms, her body, the skin was normal. Almost. It was cold, like stone.

It was black in the cave, but she could see as if it were day.

She wasn't hungry, either. Not for food, that is. Something else . . . but what?

Then she heard the howling of a lone wolf. She sat up, alert, listening; remembering the huge gray wolf that had trailed her all those weeks ago.

The wolf cry came again, closer, but much weaker, and her heart speeded up. Closer. Closer.

It was coming into the cave.

She scooted far back into her bed of furs. But as the

large wolf stumbled into the mouth of the cave and limped heavily, painfully, toward her, she realized she wasn't afraid of it.

She somehow knew it was dying, and that it wouldn't hurt her.

When it was inches away from her, she met its black glowing eyes and recoiled in shock. "Byron?" she cried.

The wolf fell to the ground, panting. Its tongue lolling and its eyes pleading with her to help.

Emma jumped from her bed and knelt on the hard cave floor above the wolf, her arms reaching out to wrap around it.

And before her eyes, it began to change . . . into a naked man. Into Byron.

"So it was you following me all those weeks? You!" Emma gasped. "You're the wolf! It wasn't my imagination."

"Yes," he wheezed, a death rattle. "I followed you for a long time. Protected you. I sensed you were . . . acceptable."

She ignored that, more concerned about his deteriorating condition. "Where have you been so long, and what's wrong with you?" Her tone was anxious.

"I'm dying, Emma . . . drank contaminated blood. Plague." His hands clutched her as his agony raged. "So . . . hungry. Couldn't take any more from you, or I'd kill you. I made a costly mistake—" He began to convulse.

He was truly dying. "No! You can't die. You can't leave me alone now. There's something wrong with me—"

He smiled ghoulishly, nodding. *"There was so much yet to teach you, Emma . . . I'm sorry . . ."* His voice faded, even as he desperately tried to finish what he was trying to say to her. Warn her. The spark extinguished from his piercing eyes.

"NO! DON'T DIE!" she begged. But she already knew that he had.

She touched him softly. No matter what he was—or

76

what he had done to her — he had saved her life. She owed him. She had even begun to understand him in a strange way.

The body began to smoke. Transform. Melt in her hands.

Then it was gone. Puff. Like it had never been there at all.

Stunned, Emma got slowly to her feet and walked to the entrance of the cave; she peered out into the morning twilight.

She no longer limped. She no longer felt the cold. Her burns were all healing. She'd held a strand of her long hair in her fingers a moment before, and saw that her hair had turned silver white. She wondered if her eyes were black now.

And she was alone again.

Six

The days passed and Emma grew stronger. In ways
that astounded her. Soon there wasn't a trace of the
burns that had once marred her face and body. Her
skin was smooth, like milk glass. She no longer
limped, felt pain . . . or the cold. Which was good, because outside the cave it had begun to snow, drifting
through the misty cloud-covered world. Days on end.
Snow. Ice. It covered everything she could see for
miles. And she could see for miles, or what she believed was miles, her eyesight as keen as a hawk's; she
could see in the dark like a bat.

There were times when the physical changes terrified her. Because it meant that, perhaps, whatever she
was becoming, wasn't human.

Vampire.

That's what he'd said he was. *Vampire.* And she'd
laughed at first. But now . . .

All the horrific images from childhood crowded in
on her, making her head reel. *Blood-sucking fiends with
hypnotic glowing eyes . . . the walking undead . . . death-
bringers . . . monsters with fangs dripping in innocent victims'
blood . . .* all the myths and stuff of a child's worst
nightmares.

*Not reality. Surely, not real? This is just another of my bi-
zarre hallucinations, isn't it?* she kept asking herself.

Sometimes being an imaginative artist was definitely a drawback.

But since Byron's death — if that was what she could call it — she'd fallen deeper and deeper into a mysterious depression. She didn't know what was happening to her. Or she did know, but wouldn't — couldn't — accept it.

The only other option was that she was insane. Had been insane since that first day of the earthquake, when she'd had to watch the world die in front of her eyes; had had to watch Larry die in her arms. Or perhaps the agony of her burns in those first few weeks, and the months of loneliness afterwards, had done it? She shook her head despondently. It was too easy. All this felt *too real* to be imagined. *Too real* to not be happening.

She'd never felt like this in her whole life. So full of raw energy. Power. So restless. So unlike herself.

Emma sighed aloud, rose from the bed of furs, and walked, straight and strong, toward the mouth of the cave. It was still snowing, and the glaring white hurt her sensitive eyes, though even the snow couldn't brighten the grayness too much. She stood just within the circle of the cave's shadow, and glared over the brink into the amazing wintry wonderland. By her crude calculations, it could only be October. She thought of the poor people that might have made it through all that had come before . . . but she didn't see how they could ever hope to survive *this*.

Miles away she could see a volcano erupting, a huge pillar of smoke rising up from the crater, mushrooming higher and higher into the leadened sky; down the side a mixture of hot gas, mud, rocks, and other material flowed like a slow oozing wound, instead of the usual boiling lava. Tons of black ash and vapor feathered into the skies and mingled with the snow, tainting it, further polluting the air, and tons more covered miles and miles of the ground around the volcano itself like a dark blanket, desiccating all the land under it.

This area, and probably the very volcano she was observing, was part of the Ring of Fire, a circular zone stretching from Alaska to Japan and south to New Zealand. Mount St. Helens in Washington, which had erupted devastatingly back in the 70's, was part of that Ring of Fire.

Emma vaguely remembered Danny (he was the scientist of the family; he had the mind for it) talking about it all, when the earthquakes and volcanoes first began to erupt last year. About vast tectonic plates in the earth's crust pushing against each other, of ocean plates subducted beneath continental plates, causing the solid material brought down from the surface to melt or boil in intense heat beneath the earth's crust. When it became light enough, it would force its way upwards, erupting into the atmosphere in the form of ash, vapor, and molten rock, called lava.

Emma suspected that the destruction she was witnessing was playing itself out across the whole planet. How many volcano chains were there in the world? She didn't know. Danny would have known, though.

She might be the last person alive in the world, and that terrified her more than anything. The last days with Byron had taught her how she desperately needed other people.

For, heaven help her, she missed Byron. Missed their strange conversations and his company. Missed expecting him. Even missed his sardonic humor. Missed him making his savage love to her.

Something fragile and elusive fluttered deep inside her, when her memory brushed against the erotic dreams of their lovemaking. But the passionate memories, the guilt, no longer jarred her. If they had just been the wild imaginings of a love-starved woman, then they had been damn vivid. *Damn good,* she frowned into the wind.

She lifted up her hand and stared at it. So stone-

80

white. So perfect. Like every part of her body that she could see. So strong. She'd crushed a piece of solid wood yesterday. Broke it into splinters. My God, how could she do such a thing?

She spun around and stalked back into the cave. Her home now with its plush wall hangings, carpets, and fur bed.

There were books, too, she'd discovered with delight. All the classics. Even a large box of romance and horror paperbacks. She'd devoured the romances, but couldn't bear to even read a page of the others. Her life had turned into a horror novel, so why would she want to read one?

Byron had had strange tastes in books, as in other things.

Byron.

Her abductor. Savior. Her enigma. Byron was gone. Emma's eyes blurred . . . the wolf had died at her feet. The *wolf. Byron.*

What did you do to me?

All the strange changes in her body. She could read without a candle. She'd snuffed them all out days ago, she had no need of them.

Emma paced back and forth, just as Byron had done so many times before. She felt like a caged animal.

Hungry.

But not for meat, nor vegetables, milk, or water. Even the thought of a TV dinner or a juicy roast turned her stomach. Now.

But the thought of blood made her mouth water. She craved *blood!*

Emma slammed her hands against the cave's granite wall in frustration. Then letting her body sink down to the floor in a despairing heap, she screamed one long piercing wail after another into the darkness. Screamed until her voice was only a raspy echo of itself.

81

She wasn't one of them. She wasn't . . .
She'd never be. Never.

All she needed was food. So after a while, she roused herself. It was a darker shade of gray outside. Night was coming. Snow or no snow, she was going out there to hunt. Since she could see in the dark, what difference did it make what time of day she went out?

If she could *catch* something to eat, perhaps her hunger for food would return. Maybe it'd just been too long since her last good meal. Continued malnutrition might create a feeling of not being hungry, she soothed herself.

Now that she'd decided, she was anxious to get out. Sheathing her knife, which she had found among her things in the cabinet against the far wall, she left the cave. Almost out of habit, she wished she had a coat and gloves, but she didn't. She had to go out just as she was, in the black shirt and pants Byron had given her.

She didn't dwell on the fact that all she needed was what she had on; that from the moment she stepped outside, she didn't feel the cold.

Night was coming. She crouched at the edge of the cliff outside the cave, turning her face upwards to catch the falling snow. The sun was a ghost of itself, as it slipped down below the dim horizon. A tawny colored ball hiding behind the sheer curtain of flakes and mist. She could see her breath freezing before her mouth.

Emma felt nothing. Not cold, not warm. Just nothing.

She reached her fingers down and buried them in the white stuff, brought her covered fingers to her mouth and tasted. Her mouth puckered, and she wiped her fingers off on her thigh. She wasn't thirsty — for water that is — either.

The cave was niched high up on the side of a hill.

Had to be a mountain goat to even get up here, she mused. It was a long way down. How had Byron carried her all the way up here? Or had he flown? she chuckled softly to herself.

Another mystery.

Emma could barely discern the bottom, where the steep hill stopped and the level ground began. It was that faraway. With the deep snow, it looked almost as if she could just jump, as if her fall would be cushioned by the white feather bed below her. But it was just an illusion. Yet some voice whispered impishly in her brain that she *could* jump . . . and not be hurt. She brushed the annoying pest away and concentrated on how she could get down.

Carefully placing her hands and feet, crawling backwards, she began her descent, continually amazed at her strength as her journey progressed.

Halfway down, her fingers slipped, and the next thing she knew she was clawing for a handhold, sliding and tumbling as she fell. She didn't even have time to scream before she was out in thin air.

She landed in the snow with a loud grunt, moaning, afraid to move. Surely such a fall should have killed her? Or at least broken bones. A few moments later, she sat up. She seemed all right. Moved her arms, got to her knees, and then cautiously to her feet. Except for her clothes being dirtied and soaked through, she was unhurt.

Her lips slid into a long wondrous smile. She couldn't believe it, but it was true. She was all right.

Somewhere an owl hooted, high up among a tree's branches. The wind sloughed through the woods, singing its eerie, night songs.

The dark forest called to her like a lover, and she went to it. Strode deep into the tall trees, the icy whiteness. Surefooted across the rocks and frozen creeks. The night animals were out searching for their prey. Every living thing was hungry.

Emma was hungry.

Her eyes adjusted quickly, and though she realized that it was now dead night, she could see everything clearly. The owl huddled up in the far tree stared down at her, unconcerned, knowing it was safe so high up. She saw a tiny rabbit burrowed snug in the entrance of its hole before it disappeared. She even saw a larger predator, a big cat of some kind, a female, slinking along hidden in a thicket, probably tracking a meal for its ravenous young.

Emma saw them all.

As if something was awakening deep inside her, she began to move through the woods quietly, her feet light on the soft snow. Then she ran. It felt so good to be free.

So good not to hurt any longer. Not to limp.

All the restrictions and curses laid upon humans.

And then she caught herself. Thinking like one of them already, huh?

God, was she dreaming all this? Was it really happening at all?

The snow was knee-high, but she had no trouble getting through it. She didn't seem to get tired. She walked and searched the woods for hours. Loving the night and its inhabitants. Learning about her new world.

Don't overdo it, though. You still don't know your true limitations. Yet.

A short while later, she caught a movement out of the corner of her eye, pivoted slowly toward it on the balls of her feet. A rabbit, maybe, lurking there in the penumbra of the underbrush behind that tree. Furry ears twitched against its background. Holding very still, Emma watched it as it hopped past her, thinking it was safe. Unnoticed. Then it cocked its head, hearing something. Sensing that its life was in danger. It ran.

Pulling her knife in one fluid motion, she aimed,

84

and the knife flew swiftly to bury itself deep within the head of the rabbit.

She'd done it!

What she had tried vainly to do for so many weeks and couldn't accomplish—catch food with just her blade—she'd done. In the snow. In the blackness of night. So easily it scared her. Apparently all of her senses were now enhanced.

As she stooped down and lifted the small carcass in her hands, she experienced a pang of guilt. She'd never killed a *living* creature before. *Sorry, little creature . . . sorry I had to kill you. But I have to survive, and I threw as hard and fast as I could, so you wouldn't suffer. Forgive me.*

You should take it back to the cave now, skin it, gut it, and cook it. Eat. But the warm furry body lay still in her fingers, something sticky and warm dripping down her hands. She hadn't moved. Her fingers touched the blood and brought it to her lips.

Sweet. So sweet.

God, she was so hungry.

She brought her mouth down on the wound, and before she grasped what she was doing, she had voraciously sucked off half of the animal's blood. The flesh didn't interest her.

She stopped, and held the mangled bundle of fur away from her. Even in the dark she could see its tiny staring eyes, its still form.

"Emma, what are you doing?" she groaned, as she angrily tossed the dead thing away in disgust. She could feel the blood trickling down her chin. Nausea churned her stomach, but she ignored it.

She couldn't do this.

But she was terrified that she was losing the battle. The smell of the fresh blood taunted her, lured her back to the tiny corpse in the underbrush, like a child spying the first colored egg on Easter morning. Leaning over it, her very fingers itched, wanting to pick it up and plunge her teeth back into it and drink . . .

But when she did, she gagged, her stomach fighting what she'd just sent down. One more taste . . . then she fell to her knees and retched it all up violently into the snow, her body heaving.

Was it only human blood she could keep down, or was this just another part of the fantastic initiation?

"What will it be next time, huh, Emma . . . a person?" And with revulsion she knew that part of her—a small part, but still a part—wanted that. To drink human blood . . . how delicious it would be, how . . . NO!

Tears wanted to form in her eyes. But she couldn't cry.

Instead, she raged at the night, the damn world for tearing itself apart, God for ignoring them in their time of direst need, Danny for abandoning her, and . . . at Byron for making her what she was becoming. A monster.

I'll hate you forever, you demon. Forever.

And I'll never be like Byron, she swore to herself fiercely, to the heavens above, and the stars. Wherever in the hell they were these days.

Emma dropped the bloody carcass from her fingers, her fear of what she was becoming driving her to scramble and tear off into the woods, as if her very life depended on it. To the cave. Home.

Her keen eyesight led her safely back. Even the climb up the cliff was easily achieved. Where was all this surefootedness when she'd had to cross the destroyed Poplar Street Bridge a couple of weeks ago? She could do almost anything now. Superhuman, that was what she was. No . . . *un*human.

She torpedoed into the cave like a wounded animal and hid there for hours . . . days . . . she wasn't sure.

She wanted *not to have to survive by draining other people's blood.* She wanted to die. She wanted . . . all this to just go away, and she be back at work on a normal sunny day, clicking at her Macintosh and nitpicking

86

with the art director over some job or other; Danny and the kids waiting contentedly at home for her. The world she had had before the earthquakes, losing her family, and meeting Byron. That's what she wanted.

She wanted all this to have been a nightmare. *Please, God.*

And what you ain't gonna get, sweetie, a cruel little voice jabbed at her viciously.

The snow stopped outside, and the world glittered as if covered in rare white jewels, instead of frozen water. Emma hid in the cave's shadows and read books, pretending nothing was wrong. As the days sped by, she began to feel weaker.

Slowly, she lost her strength. But still she wouldn't go out and feed. Wouldn't hunt down and kill a human being, just to soak up the blood like a sponge with teeth.

Oh, she was afraid of dying, but she was even more afraid of living like that. As a blood-sucking killer.

Seven

Long before it began to snow, Matthew knew he was in for it. Something about the way the skies and the clouds looked. A feel in the air. It would be a full-fledged blizzard, no doubt about it.

He was out in the middle of the wilderness, at least two days' walk or more to a town. Even if he could find an inhabitable place with a decent house to take shelter in, he'd never make it there in time.

He'd been camping out in the new free-standing tent he'd procured from an abandoned sporting goods store, on one of his rare forays into a town. He hadn't stayed around the ghostly place very long . . . a nearby volcano had been erupting, and the empty town could have been a moonscape with over six inches of concretelike volcanic ash covering the roads, houses, lawns, and discarded cars, like a bleak blanket of hard gray crust. The caustic air had been so full of ash and steam that it had been almost unbreathable.

And the weight of the ash on roofs had collapsed most of the houses and buildings that people had fled to. Matthew could still smell the decomposing bodies trapped in them.

Slogging through the sometimes ankle-deep muck, he'd gathered what he'd needed and had gotten out. Quickly.

He'd also purloined one of those new fiberfilled synthetic sleeping bags—that could retain up to ninety-five percent of its heating ability even when wet—a ground sheet, a lightweight Celestron 8X30 Binocular, a Buck Folding Hunter Swiss army knife, a rain and snow poncho, and—his pride and joy—a Foxfire crossbow with a scope, that could hit a nickel tossed up forty-five yards into the air. It wasn't that he'd set aside his Ithaca pump shotgun, but a gun made noise; a bow and arrow didn't. Sometimes noise was bad.

A thief, that's what he'd felt like, taking all those things. Yet they'd just been lying on those dusty shelves in that vacant store going to waste, he'd rationalized his innocent pilfering at the time.

So he'd been snug and warm so far, in his camouflaged tent with just one of those Pyromid eight-inch by eight-inch folding Freedom Grills, that reflected lost heat back on the food and into the air around it. But he didn't think the tent would be the ideal place for him when the blizzard hit. In normal times, yes, but these weren't normal times, and he wasn't sure how bad the storm would get.

So first thing that he had to see to, was locating a nice-sized hill, find the side where the wind wasn't blowing, tug his military shovel out of his backpack, screw in the longer handle, and commence to dig. An old Indian trick, a handmade cave.

It was early enough into the winter that the ground wasn't frozen, so it only took him a few hours. He made sure it was deep, so he could move around some in it, and build a fire bed. To allow the fire's smoke to escape, he carved out a small hole through the top. Then he made the walls more secure, by further bracing them with thick tree limbs he'd cut from nearby trees with his Buck Hunter knife.

It could snow all it wanted, but he'd be safe and cozy in his little burrow, sleeping on his fire bed, just like a bear hibernating for the winter.

The last thing he did was go hunting. He figured he'd catch some fish, and bag a small deer that he could make into a batch of venison jerky to prolong his food supply.

It was while he was out trampling through the silent woods searching for game, and maybe some more of those wild onions he'd come across the other day (good for flavoring), that he first caught sight of the people.

They were moving single file away from him. A group of scraggly-looking scavengers, whining among themselves and littering the woods profusely, as they stumbled through like sloppy children.

Grunting under his breath, Matthew slid noiselessly behind a thick tree and observed their passage. He'd been attacked too many times not to be cautious. And the truth was, even though he was feeling the pangs of loneliness more and more, he was mistrustful of everyone. Too many bad experiences.

He counted five men and two women, or what he thought were women. From the back some of them walked differently. Had to be women. They were all bundled into brand-new ski jackets, everything but their faces covered. Must have looted a sporting goods store, just like he'd done. Price tags still dangling on some of the clothing. Huge backpacks—way overloaded—weighed them down so, they moved awkwardly. Stupid, to travel with so much on them, especially in this sort of terrain. But the fleeting glimpse he got of their faces told the whole story . . . sly, dirty, with shifting eyes. They all carried weapons. Shiny high-powered guns with night scopes.

Hunters.

And Matthew thought he knew what they would

90

be hunting. People. Anyone weaker than they. Just the way they were skulking, reconnoitering their surroundings with their hard eyes lowered before them. Their evilness was a rank stench wafting on the air, a reek the Indian in him could smell. The hair on his body was prickling.

They were killers.

Matthew had seen enough of their kind in the last seven months to steer clear of them. They'd kill him quicker than a snake would kill a baby rabbit. He had no use for vermin like them. He waited until they were long gone, and then he purposely traveled in the opposite direction they'd been heading.

Discovering a small stream that wasn't frozen over, he used the old Indian method of catching fish . . . with his bare hands. Walking upstream, he startled the fish and watched closely where they hid, then he moved further upstream and, using a big stick, muddied the water as best he could. This would keep the fish from seeing or smelling his hands. Backtracking, he knelt down and probed under the bank with his fingers, until he felt a fish tail, and then very carefully moved his hands up under the belly, pulling it out by the gills to throw to the ground behind him. His father had always told him that the trick was never to try to grab the fish by the tail, they'd always slip out of your grasp. He caught two medium-sized ones and a runt. That was all. Too cold, he guessed. Lucky to have caught them.

A couple of scraggly wild onions cropped up under his feet, and he stuffed them into his pockets. Delicious cooked with fish.

He spent the rest of the afternoon tracking his deer, and bringing it down silently with the bow and arrow. He didn't want to alert those killers to his presence, if they were still in the vicinity.

Back at his improvised shelter before dark, he

cleaned the fish and started them cooking with the onions in his billy can on his Pyramid oven.

True night and the storm were coming, so he skinned and gutted the deer quickly. He prepared the jerky over a huge crackling fire, adding cardamom, marjoram, cayenne, black pepper, liquid smoke, water, and garlic powder, and when the meat concoction was ready, he deftly rolled it out, sliced it into long thin strips, and hung them out to dry over the open flames. Later he'd wrap the pieces of jerky in squares of aluminum foil. His people had been making this recipe of venison jerky for centuries minus the aluminum foil.

As he was carefully twisting the dried jerky into sections of the foil, the snow began. Time to pack it in, he thought.

He scooped the coals from the fire directly into his shelter, spread them out, and covered them first with a thick layer of dirt, and then a mattress of pine needles and leaves. A fire bed. It would keep him warm for over twenty-four hours, before he'd have to refill it with new live coals.

By the time the storm was in full force, he was warmly tucked away in his hole in the hill, sleeping peacefully. Dreaming.

The Indian with eyes like a wolf, and his people, again.

Long ago when the People were still great.

This time they were in full war paint, galloping across the land. Hunting party. The land before the white man came. Breathtaking. Mountains behind them and sun-dappled prairies all around. Going on forever, just like the tribes. Their lances and shields held strongly before them; their bows across their backs, their quivers filled with sharp arrows, and wolf fur flowing from their bronzed shoulders. Upon surefooted pintos with proud flaring eyes, draped with bright feathers. Prancing to their own music.

And the strangest thing . . . with the war party always ran the monstrous wolves. Huge, cunning-eyed creatures that galloped between the legs of the horses, or sometimes hung back on the horizon, watching. Always there. A mystery.

Off on the western horizon, the tepees shimmered where women waited patiently for the braves to return with fresh meat. Women of the People, with round sable eyes and silky hair streaming to their waists. Tiny children scurried about the camp like wild ponies, playing and smiling because they knew they were safe. Their warriors would protect them. The wolves that ran between their hide homes were their friends.

In this dream, the hunting party searched for the buffalo and deer that roamed the plains with the help of the wolves under a lowering sun.

It was the tall, fierce warrior—with a face like stone, his lupine eyes gleaming black and future-seeing—that first screamed the discovery of the herd as the wolves howled in the distance, and slapping his pony, prodded it into a ground-eating run over the earth as if it had wings. He brought down the first buffalo. Took the heart for himself and ate it raw.

Still squatting over the dead animal, the warrior turned and beckoned to Matthew.

Come. Come.

He waited.

Matthew tried to answer his summons, he tried, like he always did. The Indian didn't seem to be able to hear him.

He finally nodded his head sadly, jumped back on his pony, leaving the final butchering for the women of the tribe, who would come later, and galloped off.

The other braves followed as the wolves stayed behind to feast on the remains, their activities cloaked in a rising mist.

Such an unnatural partnership . . .

Matthew, grief-stricken at their going, stirred in his sleep, and heard the baying of the ghostly wolves as the familiar dream receded.

He awoke and contemplated the dark, remembering, as he always did, the dream.

It wasn't the first time he'd dreamed about the Indian. And it wouldn't be the last. Was the warrior with the wolf eyes *him?* His spirit, his protector? The dreams had begun soon after Sara had died, growing more persistent and vivid each time. Matthew was a modern Indian, didn't believe in all the hocus-pocus of his superstitious ancestors . . . and yet, the dreams were so *vivid*. So haunting.

It was true, Matthew yearned for people of his own. Friends, a mate, and children. Nibbling on a piece of jerky, he admitted it: he was lonely. But were the dreams true visions, or was his subconscious inventing a family for him? He wasn't sure. Only that he looked forward to them; couldn't wait to go back there.

Huddled on his fire bed, wrapped in his fur coat, he cleared out a small circle and made a tiny fire. For the company and light, as well as the extra warmth.

In the last few months he'd thought a lot about his childhood on the reservation, and all the people he'd known and loved. His dark eyes clouded as he remembered the legends about the end of the world. He stared into the fire morosely, his long black hair loose around his sharp face, falling to his shoulders, and gleaming in the firelight. It was all coming true.

Outside he could hear the storm raging, and he wondered how much longer he could go on alone in this hostile world, before he went insane. Oh, he could *survive* out in the wilderness forever. He'd proved that already. At first, that and his angry grief had been enough . . . but no longer.

He had to find a safe place . . . a place where he belonged. Wherever that was.

When he finally fell back into sleep, he dreamed again of the wolf-eyed Indian, this time in his teepee making love to his woman, and Matthew's rugged face softened into a sad smile. The woman didn't looked anything like Maggie, but Matthew was so strongly drawn to her, that he awoke later in a sexually aroused state that was painfully uncomfortable.

No, he told himself glumly as he tried to get back to sleep, he couldn't live the rest of his life like this. He might as well be dead.

Eight

Emma had been drifting in and out for a long time. She opened her eyes and gathered she was still alive. She had no idea how much time had elapsed, or if the blizzard had stopped, or, at first, why she was even there.

She only knew that there was someone or something in the cave with her, and for a second her heart was flooded with joy, knowing she wasn't alone any longer. Until she saw what it was.

A wolf glared at her from the mouth of the cave, with incendiary eyes like tiny flames that danced in the gloom. It was poised, so perfectly still for so long that Emma questioned if it were there at all. Then it seemed to see her. Its face tilted, and the hair rose up on the back of its neck.

It growled low in its shaggy throat, and advanced a few halting steps into the cavern.

And Emma's slack face mirrored disbelief.

Byron had come back! He had never died at all. In her delirium she believed that.

"Byron?" Emma's voice so feeble, it emerged a squeak. She tried to sit up, but couldn't.

No, Byron's gone, she agonized. He who made me like this. Byron the vampire. Emma experienced a small flutter of the earlier hatred, but it faded, she couldn't hold on to it. Too weak. Too lonely.

It padded closer. She could hear the animal panting

as if it had just run a long way, as its enigmatic eyes flicked away from her. It was swaying and shivering, its coat all tangled and snow-matted, its ribs poking out from its thin sides, its tail dragging. Unsure whether to stay or leave. So spent it could hardly walk.

Poor creature. Wet fur smell permeated the cave. Reminded her of Midnight, her long-dead cat. Emma smiled faintly, remembering her pet and how he would purr when she snuggled him, how he'd give her little kisses on the nose, and then out of the blue nip her. *Kiss, kiss . . . no bite . . . no bite!* Emma crooned to the phantom cat in her mind.

The wolf jerked at the sound of her voice, but didn't run away. It watched her with strangely intelligent eyes; cocked its head and whined; lifted an ice-encrusted paw above the ground, as if it hurt.

For some reason Emma wasn't afraid of the wolf. She sensed somehow that it wouldn't—couldn't—harm her. It only desired shelter from the storm. She tried to stay awake, just to see what the creature would do, but she slipped away again.

She dreamt of Danny and the kids, of Midnight, and their home. She hadn't been able to do that for a long time.

Danny and Emma were watching television in the living room, snuggled on the couch, kids tucked in for the night; a freshly delivered pizza—with everything, the way she liked it— half-eaten on the coffee table before them. Watching a movie they'd rented at the video store. An old one they'd enjoyed many times before. One of the Star Wars *movies:* The Return of the Jedi. *Emma had loved those. All those astonishing special effects and those fantastic aliens. The wickedness of Darth Vader and the villainous Emperor; the innocence and spunk of Hans Solo, Luke Skywalker, and Princess Leia, and the wisecracking androids. Luke Skywalker was just informing the Princess that they were brother and sister, and Emma was scarfing down another piece of delicious pizza she'd just reheated in the microwave.*

Midnight leaped up on the back of the couch, and was licking her neck . . .

She was so happy.

The dream began to dissolve. Emma knew she was waking.

Something wet and furry brushed past her face a few times, and she murmured softly to it. Talked nonsense to it in her sleep, as if it were her beloved and lost cat. She tried to pull it into her arms. *Midnight, you naughty creature, you.* It sidled away.

Don't go, she begged it. *Stay.*

She fell back asleep and *the movie was ending . . . she and Danny were making out on the couch like teenagers. He got up, took her hand, and led her into their bedroom to their comfortable water bed where they made sweet love, and ended up asleep in each other's arms.*

Emma sighed in her sleep, her stomach cramping. How could she still be so hungry . . . after all that luscious pizza?

There was a warm, velvety liquid in her mouth, and she was greedily slurping it up, letting it run down her parched throat. She moaned as the nourishment brought her back from the murky depths of her dream world. She didn't want to wake up . . . she didn't want . . . But *why,* some deeper inner instinct, some last shred left of her great desire for survival, asked. Why not? Her hands found the small furry mound and gripped it tightly as she sucked. It didn't struggle. It was dead. Freshly dead. Tastes so good. So warm and salty. She couldn't get enough, and drank . . . and drank . . .

Blood.

Emma's eyes fluttered open and achieved only a soft focus, her heart began to pump just a little faster, gaining strength with every drop. Slight nausea. Not too bad.

She realized that she wanted desperately to live. She did! Everything she'd been through, and why? For

98

what? There must be a reason that she of all people had been allowed to survive this long. Had to be.

She fed, then drifted back to sleep. A real sleep this time.

The blood stayed down.

It went on like that, Emma finding the new kills in her hands over and over. She fed and grew stronger.

After a while she awoke fully. Her eyes sharp in the dark cave, her senses all singing loud and clear. She smelled fur. Animal smell.

Across from her, curled up like an overgrown puppy, slept the same wolf that had intruded into her fevered state. For a moment the old human fear burned bright, and then she remembered. She was no longer human, no longer puny and helplessly frail. She was different now. She studied the animal, and as if it could sense her awareness, it leisurely opened its somnolent eyes and returned her look.

There was something between its paws. Stretching first, its head went down and its jaws clamped into the small mound, then it came gracefully to its feet, and trotted noiselessly toward her.

Now, Emma marveled, she knew where the food had been coming from! The wolf had been caring for her, like a mother would a sick child.

It was only inches away from her amazed face, when it plopped the dead rabbit into her lap. Emma held her breath. Didn't want to scare it away. Up close its eyes were dark, feral pools. Extraordinarily intelligent. Its face and body beautiful in its savageness; its smell, one of the wild.

"I can't drink its blood," she said to the animal, wondering if it understood. By the way it looked at her, she believed it did. "It won't stay —" She'd *been* drinking animal blood, and she hadn't thrown it up. She didn't have to kill *humans* to survive! Emma felt a great sense of relief.

Never taking her eyes off the wolf, Emma accepted

the rabbit, and without a second thought sank her teeth—which had grown razor sharp—hungrily into its tiny throat, and drank.

The wolf seemed to approve, and sauntered away to settle down just feet away from her, its gleaming eyes viewing her from the blacker shadows. It didn't seem afraid of her in the least, either. Rather, it accepted her. Emma smiled, finishing her meal. For some reason the wolf was befriending her. Protecting her until she was well again. The creature wanted her to live.

Emma wasn't exactly sure how she knew this, but she did. As if the wolf's thoughts and hers were strangely attuned to the same wavelength. Perhaps, in her time of need, she'd even unconsciously sent for it. Some minuscule part of her that had wanted to go on living had.

Emma was feeling better and pulled herself to a sitting position, ran her unsteady fingers through her dirty entangled hair, and gazed at the wolf.

Come here, she ordered gently in her mind. *Come.* She patted the ground beside her.

The wolf languidly rose to its feet and ambled over to where she had indicated; its eyes locked with hers; the animal dropped down softly.

Emma grinned widely. *That's it, buddy.*

She slowly offered the wolf the rest of the rabbit, and the animal, after only a moment's hesitation, took it into its massive jaws.

Go ahead, eat it. You caught it, you deserve it.

The wolf backed off on its haunches a little, and then began to voraciously tear the remains apart. Emma figured it had eaten the others the same way, because, unlike the first time she had seen the beast, it was now fat and its coat glossy, its eyes not tormented with the earlier hunger.

Carefully Emma drew herself up from the bed of furs, and after the initial dizziness spiraled away, she put one foot in front of the other, her hands braced

100

against the walls of the cave for further support, and wobbled through the hanging draperies toward the mouth of the cave.

The blizzard had ended, probably days ago, and the world was a white and gray mizzling mist. Nothing different there. She squinted her sensitive eyes, shading them with her hand, to look out. The volcano had stopped spewing forth its guts, though. Still couldn't tell where the sky and the snow began, or what time of day it was. The wind was screaming.

She leaned back against the cave wall, her weak body quivering.

Why *was* she still alive? She really didn't understand it at all. But she'd made some important decisions. There must be a reason, and maybe someday she would know what it was—or maybe she would never know. Either way, she would have to learn how to survive as what she was.

But I will kill no humans. Ever, she swore fervently. *Only animals.* She didn't know what that would mean to her, if it would hurt her in the long run, and she didn't really care. Leave it up to fate.

She would live that way, or perish.

She heard the wolf coming from behind her, and stepped aside so it could leave the cave. She watched it nimbly make the long climb downwards and then lope away. With its silver coat it merged right into the gray whiteness and seemingly vanished.

Off to hunt again.

Emma knew it would be back. And for a little while, she wouldn't be alone.

Nine

The snowstorm raged unbridled for days. Tucked inside his shelter, warm and well-fed, Matthew lost count. He spent his time thinking about the past, keeping the fire he'd built inside kindled, so there was always a supply of live coals for his fire bed, and reading the William Johnstone paperback novels he'd had stashed away for a rainy—or snowy—day. It kept him from going completely stir-crazy, even though the story lines were a little too much like what he was living.

When a lull came in the storm one morning, Matthew knew it was time to restock his food supply, and get some needed exercise. He had a feeling the respite wouldn't last long. The storm wasn't over.

He'd fashioned himself some snowshoes, with heavy, waxed string and whittled wooden frames, and put them on. Shouldering his Ithaca pump shotgun, he eagerly headed out into the white wilderness. Pleased as punch to be able to get out, if only for a short while.

Just the thought of fresh meat made his mouth water. A rabbit or a couple of squirrels. Jerky was fine for a while, but not everyday, day in, day out.

He must have made quite a picture, with his long hair whipping free, smoky sunglasses, fur coat, and leggings, his shotgun slung from his shoulder. Chortling at the thought, he trekked across the snow searching for game, careful of where he put his feet. The snow in some places was six-feet deep and not only were there rips and gullies to avoid, hidden under it, there was also quicksand.

It was cold out. Darn cold. Well below zero, he'd wager. The trees were glazed in at least an inch of ice, and everywhere he looked there was a transparent glistening. It didn't take him long to be glad he'd had the sense to acquire the glasses, either. Cloudy or not, the powdery stuff still had a glare to it that could eventually blind a man.

Matthew ended up foraging farther away from his shelter than he'd planned. Game couldn't be found, but since he understood this could be his only chance to find fresh food before the next onslaught of bad weather, he had to take full advantage of it. So he trudged on.

The large rabbit came out of nowhere, moving fast. Matthew unslung the Ithaca, his fingers brushing lightly against the checkered pattern on the wooden stock, raised the butt against his shoulder quickly, loaded a shell into the chamber, aimed, and fired, all in a blur. The rabbit fell in its tracks as the shot echoed and ricocheted around him.

Roasted rabbit. Real tasty. Matthew's mouth salivated as he snowshoed his way toward his kill. He wrapped twine around the rabbit's back paws, and tied it to the loop on the side of his coat.

He wanted to catch one more before he called it a day.

Hours later, growing weary, his eyes cocked nervously at the threatening skies, and another rabbit hanging from his waist, he started hiking back toward his cave.

The dark and the temperature came down like a curtain. Hours back he'd raised the fur hood over his head and covered his face with the wool mask. He didn't need a case of hypothermia to take home with him. Fatigue and wetness were the two main variables that could lower the body temperature to a dangerous level and bring on body chill. And he was sure tired, and sweaty under his clothes from his exertion. He was doing fine so far, he was still shivering. As long as the body had the energy to shiver, it still had the energy to create its own heat.

Later, he imagined it was that last shot that called their attention to him. It couldn't have been anything else. He'd been stupid, let his guard down. Walked right into the trap.

Suddenly he was surrounded by some of the same rabble he'd seen traipsing through the woods days earlier. He recognized them by the tagged ski coats and the dirty, sneering faces.

"Been out hunting, half-breed?" one of them drawled, shifting his scoped high-power rifle from one arm to another. A guy with milk-white skin and hair, a hard square jaw, and a strange glint in blue eyes so pale, they were almost albinistic.

"I have," Matthew said flatly. Their eyes locked, and Matthew saw the man's madness. He'd seen it before. Too much in the last year. The inner hatred glinted back at him like a beast.

His two cronies stood back, their eyes glued to the rabbits at Matthew's side. Not killers, Matthew thought, but followers. Lemmings.

"Done better than us." The man shifted his eyes to include his friends.

"Yeah, sure would taste good for supper . . . those rabbits. Nice fat ones," one of the other men, short, with a mustache and a sharp nose commented. Unlike the others, he had a flimsy coat on, ripped in about ten different places. His eyes took in Matthew's fur coat greedily. "Indian, that there coat of yours looks real warm. Fox?"

"Yes."

They were going to kill him, he absorbed the truth of it in that second. That's why they were there. Oh, they'd say it was for the rabbits and the coat, but that would be a lie. It was their sport, their reason for still existing. Matthew had met a few other men like that before in his life, but the laws of society, or lack of opportunity, or his own protective savvy, had kept him from being one of their victims.

The world was different now. No laws. No police, lawyers, judges, or juries. Survival of the fittest was the name of the game. Survival of the fastest.

He'd been careless.

"Game's scarce," Matthew stalled, trying to give himself the time to form a plan of action. "What with the storm. Another one coming." He made a big show of squinting up at the sky, but still keeping the three in his sight.

The one with the ragged jacket whispered something into pale eyes' ear; he nodded.

"You don't say?" Pale eyes pursed his lips in a thin slash. Matthew noticed the man's finger tightening on his gun's trigger, and his stomach lurched.

This is it.

Matthew moved faster than any of them, got in the first two shots. Pale eyes lay screeching in the snow, holding his bleeding stomach, and the one who had coveted Matthew's coat lay silent, eyes staring into space, a huge hole dead center in his forehead.

Matthew ran, the snow and the snowshoes making him slow, clumsy. He thought he'd gotten away, when another man stepped out from behind a tree somewhere to his right and shot him.

He went down just like the first rabbit he'd bagged that day.

Before the pain and the blackness claimed him, someone was already tearing the coat from his bleeding body, stealing his shotgun; they cursed him as they kicked him over and over in the head and ribs.

Then nothing. Nothing.

The wolf had come back all right. Bringing Emma its fresh kills. Day after day. Rabbits, or squirrels, or sometimes just rats or mice.

Emma learned to close her eyes and partake of whatever was offered, her hunger had become so rapacious. As if by beginning to drink the blood, she had released all the floodgates and no longer could plug them again.

They were only small creatures, she defended her appetite, *God put them on earth for us to eat.* What difference did it make if all she used was the blood? Was it so awful, all in all, was it?

Sometimes it seemed the carnivore could read her mind, hear and understand her voice. If it was gone and she called it in her mind, it always came.

Emma talked to it for hours through the long nights, named it Friend, and tried to get close to it — as close as it would allow her.

In time, it would even lie beside her, let her pet and cuddle it. As long as she didn't overdo it.

She couldn't comprehend why it was aiding her. Couldn't understand its attraction to her. But the wolf had saved her, she knew that, and she was thankful. Since she had found out she could live on animal blood, her life suddenly seemed worth living again.

In time Emma ventured out, well enough to walk, hunt for herself. She couldn't let the wolf feed her forever. He must have a pack somewhere that missed him. A mate somewhere who waited for him. Emma just seemed to know that.

Daytime. Or she believed it was day. The blizzard had ended, and the foggy grayness was so close to night, she wasn't sure. The atmosphere as well as the weather must really be fucked up, she mused, climbing easily down the cliff to stand upon the solid sheet of iced snow before her.

She couldn't believe it. She could actually walk upon it. Either it was so hard-crusted that she could tread upon it thus, or her condition accounted for it.

Emma still avoided putting into actual words what she was . . . that would shatter her fantasy. Her security. Deep inside she knew she should be dead, but she wasn't, knew she was something unnatural . . . but guilt and an intense sense of survival wouldn't allow her to acknowledge either yet.

The wolf accompanied her on the first of her hunts. Always close by her side. Before long Emma could run down the quarry and track almost as skillfully as the wolf; could throw her knife at anything, even in solid darkness, and usually hit it; could hunt for hours in the frigid climate before she became weary. If she was scratched or stumbled, the bruises would heal within hours.

She and Friend became great buddies.

They frolicked and hunted the nights away, and slept through most of the days. Emma always felt there was something he was trying to tell her, but couldn't get across.

Then one night, when they had finished their hunting and were heading back to the cave, the wolf wouldn't leave the edge of the thicket and make the final climb up the cliff with her.

After staring at her for a long time from the shadows, and whimpering low in its throat, it simply evaporated into the woods. All her calling wouldn't bring him back to her side. Heavy-hearted, she let him go.

It was time, she supposed. The wolf had to go back to its own kind. Back to its world.

Like any fledgling, she was being pushed out of the nest, and whether she would fly or fall was now up to her.

Thank you, Friend, she sent the thought lovingly out into the emptiness after the wolf. *Goodbye.* Come back anytime.

She'd miss him terribly; she'd grown quite fond of the shaggy thing.

And the loneliness clamped down upon her with sharp teeth. Again.

The following days were a learning experience for Emma. She had little trouble in finding and catching her prey. But without Friend, it wasn't the same. She began to wonder what she should do next.

She couldn't stay in the cave forever.

She should be moving on. To what and where, she had no idea.

Something was calling to her . . . somewhere. Who? And why? Like a siren song just beyond her understanding.

All she knew was that she had this urge to keep moving, to go east. She believed it had something to do with her sister, Margaret, seeing if she was still alive. Though, heaven only knew how she'd hide what she was from her sister. They'd been so close years ago. Thought alike. Could almost read each other's minds.

Margaret was her older sister. Three years older. Short dark hair, petite, with almond-shaped eyes the color of sapphires. Looked nothing like Emma. Acted nothing like Emma. She was a school teacher. English Lit. Ken, her husband, was a long-distance truck driver. The last letter Emma had received from her sister had been over nine months ago. Margaret and Ken had still been working part-time, but not enough to pay the bills, so they'd begun taking in boarders. That was hard to imagine. Her sister taking in people, cleaning their rooms, and feeding them, like a bed and breakfast. That hadn't been Margaret at all. But then, Emma reflected, everyone had had to change that last year. Times had been tough.

How would Emma hide her condition from her?

But how could she stay here? Looking around at the cave one night, she knew she couldn't. There was no longer any reason to hide. She wasn't fully aware yet of what she was actually capable of doing, but it was time she found out. She'd been given a new life; she should make good use of it.

Find her sister. *Or find others like me.* It was a scary idea.

She began to pack up what meager belongings she had, and make plans.

In just a few days.

Though why she felt she had to wait was another puzzle. Weather didn't affect her, and the overcast was so heavy, even during the day, there was no danger for her. She was probably more sensitive to bright light, than what was out there.

Then she understood . . . a couple more days. For Friend. In case he came back.

Useless. When she knew he wasn't coming back, and yet . . . she still waited. Three more days.

The night before she had decided to leave, she went out hunting.

She had expected to find game, a small mammal or two to quench her thirst . . . but what she found in the snow, covered with wet dirty leaves, half-frozen, coatless, and nearly dead—was a man.

A man with long dark hair and tan skin. Handsome. Big.

A human man. Emma's body went rigid. She hadn't fed yet, and forced herself not to think about that.

She wondered what had happened to him; how long he had been out there. What was he doing there. Was he sick? The plague? Or had he just wandered out here in the middle of the blizzard and given up?

The night looked to be bone-chilling; the man was covered in ice and unprotected. A frozen lump curled up under the leaves and snow. And it was beginning to snow again, the wind whirling around her, tearing at her clothes and hair. The world felt alien, glowing like the insides of one of those snowy Christmas scenes, the kind you could shake up.

Then she saw the blood trickling into the snow at the man's side.

He'd been shot.

Emma knelt down next to him, started to reach out to touch him, but brought her hand back like she'd been burned. She stared at the blood — ebony against the white snow — at his throat, and licked her lips. Her hunger was a fire consuming her. The scent of his blood was making her dizzy. It would be so simple, so easy to just . . .

No! She stood up and stumbled back blindly. *She would never take a human life. Never.* If she did, then she'd be just what she abhorred. A ghoul. She should just leave him there. He was in more danger with her than he was from the cold, the wilderness, from other men. He was none of her business.

Thinking like one of them already, huh? A human life meant nothing? she reprimanded herself, remembering something Byron had once said to her. *I've never done this before. Saved a human.*

The man in the snow shivered. She heard him groan, his hands clutched at the snow, and suddenly his eyes flew open. She could see them watching her, full of pain and shock in the darkness.

Help me, his gaze begged. His fingers reached for her.

He'd be dead by morning unless she helped him.

Whatever that was still human in her, ached for him. Yearned to help him, and not be alone again.

110

Unforgivable . . . that she was actually afraid to aid a fellow human being. Afraid she'd drain him of his life's blood like some demon from hell.

"There were . . . four of them," he whispered so low that only her acute hearing allowed her to catch it. "Four . . . not three! Didn't stand . . . a . . . chance . ." Then he seemed to lapse into unconsciousness again.

And like a whirlpool, she was sucked back into the memory of when Byron had rescued her. When those awful beasts had beaten and tried to rape her.

Someone had helped her.

Emma still perceived herself as more human than not.

And she knew what she had to do.

He was as light as a feather as she scooped him up from the ground and carried him back to her cave. Just as Byron had once done for her.

She built a fire for him and set out the candles. Her foremost worry was that the bullet—or bullets—were still in him. She'd never performed surgery on anyone before. Would never have dreamed of it . . . in the old world. The old Emma hadn't even been able to stomach the sight of blood, much less think of living on it.

But then, that Emma didn't exist anymore. She'd been through far too much.

One must do what one must do.

She undressed the man and found the two bloodied holes. Here the survival magazines and the medical books Larry had had in the old shelter proved again that they'd been worth their weight in gold.

Now, if she could recollect how it was done.

She boiled water over the fire, wishing she still had Larry's emergency first aid kit, or at the least forceps or tweezers and antiseptic. She had nothing like that. She'd just have to do what she could, the best she could, and hope it would be sufficient.

Using her fingers, she was amazed to discover how effortless it was for her to probe for the tiny hunks of metal, and maneuver them out of the flesh. They hadn't hit any vital organs as far as she could determine. The hardest part was smelling the fresh blood . . . not because it made her sick, as it would have in the old days, but because she craved it. Wanted to kiss her lips to the gaping gore-rimmed holes, and suck the man's life fluid from his veins.

It took every ounce of her willpower not to.

When she was done, she cleaned his wounds and him up, covered him warmly. Proud of herself that she had probably saved him; excited that maybe now she'd have someone to care for, someone to keep her company.

The only problem she could see was hiding what she was from him.

The man talked in his sleep. About a woman named Maggie and someone called Sara. Emma could tell he had really loved them. What had happened to them? The man dreamed, a soft smile lighting up his face.

In the firelight, her face turned serious. He'd hate her if he discovered what she was. Be repulsed. At the least, he'd run from her—at the most, try to destroy her. He wouldn't understand . . .

And the thought of his animosity affected her more than she would have imagined. So, she was still human after all?

And he was a fine-looking man, she mused, studying his face from where she sat, cross-legged next to the fire. Had his hair grown that long since the disaster, or was that the way he always wore it? Beautiful hair. He looked part Indian, though it was difficult to tell, she had never been good at placing people's nationalities. One thing for sure, he was healthy, or had been before he was shot. An outdoorsman. A survivor. His upper chest and arms sinewy and well muscled.

112

There was a fifty-fifty chance he'd make it.

When she was sure he was sleeping, and there was nothing else she could do for him, she left the cave and went back out into the snowy night.

She still had to take care of her own needs, and bring back fresh meat for the man. He'd need food if he made it.

He'd need a miracle.

Ten

"How did you find me?" Matthew asked, his voice still slurred with the fuzziness of pain and the fever that had just released its death grip on him. "In all that snow . . . in the dark?" He'd done nothing but ask questions since he'd come to.

Then he slept for three more days and nights. Recuperating. In the last two he'd slowly become aware of his surroundings, of Emma; gaining strength with every hour and every meal she fixed him.

"I was out hunting . . . and I stumbled upon you, you might say."

Out hunting, he thought, in this weather? He couldn't believe his luck. He couldn't believe she had taken the chance and somehow lugged him back to her cave. "Did you see the ones who attacked me?"

"No. You were the only one around."

Their friends must have come and taken them away.

"I think you'd been there for a long time."

"Unbelievable . . . that you even found me," he muttered.

Emma said nothing, squatting over the fire, roasting the flesh of another rabbit for him. The smoking meat had no effect on her. It didn't repel her or entice her. She turned it again. Almost done.

When the silence became unbearable, he tried

again. "You've lived in this cave awhile, then, huh?"
It had been so long since he'd had anyone to talk to.
He watched her as she moved around the fire. Noticed the knife sheath at her waist. He wondered if she was good with it.

"A few weeks," she answered. Her back still toward the man.

"It's nice. Cozy." His voice was weak, but eager.

"It wasn't mine," she said over her shoulder. "I kind of inherited it, you might say, from the last occupant. He didn't need it any longer." Then she shut up again.

"That's some knife you got there. Can I see it?"

After a moment she rose from her crouch and walked over, pulled the knife from the rugged black sheath, and handed it to him.

Matthew held the hilt and studied the blade. A nine-inch clip point. The handle a Kraton Pachmayr type. He whistled under his breath. "It's a Cold Steel Trailmaster Bowie . . . beautiful knife."

Matthew looked up at her face. She was so lovely. That hair, those eyes . . . like black diamonds. Somehow she was familiar to him. He smiled at her. "Are you any good with it?"

He thought he caught a twinkle in her gaze. Just a tiny one. Gone as swiftly as it had come.

"Pretty good."

I bet, Matthew speculated to himself. The way she moves, like a panther.

"Who taught you?"

She tossed him a strange look. "No one. I taught myself. I was alone. I've been alone since the St. Louis earthquake. I've taught myself how to survive."

Matthew knew better than to try to pry anything else out of her. He recognized that set to her jaw. So far he knew very little about her, and she seemed to like it that way.

115

She went back to the fire, away from him.

"Emma?" he finally demanded gently as the silence ticked away, unable to keep his frustration with her uncommunicativeness in any longer.

"Yes?"

"Are you scared of me—or something?"

Emma's back stiffened. She'd been expecting this for a long time. They'd introduced themselves, and Matthew had told her quite a bit about himself over the last day. Emma was content to listen. To stay physically away from him. She'd been afraid he'd take it wrong. He was a very perceptive man, her inner voice warned her. Too perceptive.

"No . . . I'm not scared of you," her tone sounded weary, but cautious.

"I mean," his hurt voice touched her from the other side of the fire, "exactly *why* did you save my life? I can see that you aren't ecstatic with me being here."

Emma sighed inwardly. She hated lying. This was going to be harder than she'd ever dreamed. "Because it needed saving. You would have died if I hadn't brought you here. You were already half-frozen." She tried to put just enough indignation in her words to throw him off.

But he was too smart not to see through her ruse. "Yes, you're correct, I would have died, if not for you. Yet since I've come to, you've acted as if I had the plague or something."

Emma couldn't help but flash an ironic smile when he said that, though it really wasn't funny.

"I sense this . . . barrier between us," he went on, uncomfortably. Introspection wasn't something he was good at. Talking a lot, either. But he had to clear this little problem of theirs up right away, or he knew he'd never win her over.

"Is something wrong?"

"No," Emma mumbled between clenched teeth.

Matthew was about to give up. If that's the way she wanted it, so be it. Then, looking at her in the firelight softened him. With her face hard, but so beautiful it took his breath away, and that long silver white hair of hers, so unusual, those eyes as black as space, and her tall, shapely figure, he couldn't do anything but soften. She reminded him of a wild animal. Untamed, strong, and primitive.

Maybe something awful had happened to her somewhere along the way. Something that had made her like this.

"All right, Emma . . . I didn't mean to push. I just want you to understand, I won't hurt you. I owe you my life. I'm damn grateful. And if you want me to, when I get well enough, I'll leave. If my being here is so distasteful to you." The disappointment sneaking in again.

Emma sighed, stood up, and walked over to stand above him. She had a plate of steaming meat in her hands. For the first time, she truly met his look full on.

He was lying on his side, his one arm supporting his lean frame. His wounds were still puffy but healing, and his face finally had a healthy color to it. He stared at her sometimes in just the same way Friend had. Penetrating, dark eyes that seemed to read her innermost thoughts. Wolfish. It unnerved her.

She surprised even herself when she murmured, "You don't have to leave. It's just that it's been so long since I've had human companionship. Decent companionship." She grinned hesitantly, handing him the plate. He made her somehow uneasy. Half of her—the woman in her, the human—wanted to please him, and the other half, well, it wanted to drain every last drop of his blood and toss away the husk.

"I know. There aren't many people left, but so far

the ones I've met — except you — have been scum."

Emma didn't deny it.

"I feel like I'm in heaven. Not only are you friendly, but you're . . . beautiful."

Emma was still enough of a woman to appreciate the compliment. "I guess I'm just rusty, Matthew." It was the first time she'd spoken his name, and it sent shivers down his spine. Her voice was so damn sexy. "I'm sorry. I've seen too much, I guess." She shrugged her shoulders.

"Don't be sorry, Emma. Nothing to be sorry about."

She went on with what she had been saying. "Maybe I'm a little apprehensive. But I've had some . . . unpleasant . . . experiences, too."

His eyes reflected instant sympathy. Ah, so something terrible had happened to her, then. And befriending her, gaining her trust, was going to take time.

"You can tell me about it, I'm a good listener."

Her attention shifted away from him. "Someday, maybe. Not now," a hushed entreaty.

"Okay." Take it slow. "I just want us to be friends, Emma. Can we be at least that?" For now.

Emma nodded. "Of course."

Matthew observed her as she waited for him to eat. She was a strange one, he had to admit. Real strange. She was so stunning to look at, that when he had first come to, and seen her hovering above him with that pale hair that glimmered in the darkness like spun silver, and that white perfect face, he'd been nearly speechless. Surely he was dreaming. Died and went to heaven. Every man's wildest fantasy, to be nursed back from death's door by an angel.

She aroused feelings in him that he had never known before, not even with Maggie. At first it had mystified him, that he had become so *attached* to her

118

so quickly—her smile, her husky voice, her very presence. As if he'd known her somewhere before.

He kept telling himself that he'd been lonely for so long, his life so desolate, that it only stood to reason that he'd be smitten with any half-acceptable woman who came along . . . especially someone as different as her. She utterly intrigued him. But it was more than that. Looking at her now, he knew it was more.

But certain *unusual* things about her had gotten under his skin. Bothered him. He'd never seen her eat anything. Sometimes he'd wake in the middle of the night, and she was nowhere to be seen. Where did she go? Mysteries. She never showed any emotion, never seemed—

"You're staring at me again," she spoke calmly with an amused smile, and then pushed the plate in his hands at him. "Eat."

"Sorry." He snapped his attention back to the present. He brought a piece of the warm meat to his lips and bit in. Around bites, he said, "Emma, aren't you cold in just that skimpy top and pants?"

"No. I feel fine."

"I have—had—" He winced at the memory of losing it for more than one reason, "the warmest fur coat. Those bastards took it, along with my shotgun. Gonna miss them both. But I can make another coat. I can make one for you, too."

For the first time he saw what he believed was anger flush her pretty face. Her eyes seemed to boil. "Not wolf fur!"

Her reaction surprised him. "No. It doesn't have to be wolf, mine wasn't wolf. It can be rabbit or fox. Fox is good." He rubbed the side of his scratchy face. Needed a shave soon. "As soon as I get better, I'll go out and hunt. I'll make you one," he said, proud to be able to do something for her. "But *not* wolf."

Emma knew better than to tell him she didn't need

119

a coat. She needed nothing. But if it would make him happy, she could wear it for him. No skin off her nose, so to speak.

"Besides," he added. "I wouldn't kill a wolf . . . especially now."

"Why not?"

"The wolf is one of my protectors . . . from the spirit world."

"Protectors?" Her somber eyes studied him thoughtfully, as if seeing him for the first time.

"In my dreams there have been wolves," his voice devout. "We Indians believe that an animal or a being can contact us from the spirit world, and then can act as our personal guardian—watching over us, protecting us in our life." He didn't tell her about the warrior with the eyes of a wolf. She'd probably laugh at him. White people didn't always understand the spirit world.

"Anyway I haven't seen any wolves around here, have you?"

"Yes," she responded matter-of-factly. "Timber wolves, I think."

That wasn't what he wanted to hear. Timber wolves could get nearly six feet long and a hundred pounds. As much as he revered the wolf, he sure didn't want to run across one someday out in the snow . . . especially a hungry one.

"So you really are Indian, then?"

"Half. My father was Cherokee. I was raised on the reservation." He smiled bitterly. "But after I met and married Maggie, I left it. Never went back."

"You didn't like the reservation?"

His face was stormy, barely hiding his hostility. "Would you like to be put in a pen? Treated like an animal? The best parts of your land taken away by thieves?"

"No, I imagine not."

Matthew said nothing more on the touchy subject. But she could sense him brooding about all of it in the corner.

She walked back to rekindle the dying fire. Better keep that going. She didn't want him asking anymore questions than he had already. Kneeling over the tiny flames, she stoked it with a stick and added more wood.

The coat reminded him. "What's it like outside these days?"

Emma's brows went up. "We had another horrendous snowstorm the night I brought you here. Lasted two days. Worse than the first one. Out there," she gestured toward the mouth of the cave that he couldn't see, "it's solid ice and snow. Looks like the Antarctic." She did a shiver to make it look good.

"Nice in here, though. Caves stay a constant fifty-six degrees in all weather," Matthew told her.

She cocked an eyebrow at him. He sounded like someone she used to know.

Done fooling with the fire and with nothing else to do to keep her hands busy, and no way to avoid it any longer, she went to sit cross-legged across from Matthew as he lay on the fur bed. When she'd dragged him in, she'd divided the furs, making two piles out of them. On opposite sides of the cave room.

Emma had just settled herself, when an earth tremor pulsed through the cave. It dislodged rocks; she could hear them sliding down the cave walls. Her face in the firelight was tense.

"Whew," Matthew hissed when the movement had subsided. "That was a bad one."

"Third one this week," Emma calculated, her voice brittle.

She turned frightened eyes on Matthew.

"I've thought about what's been happening to our

121

world. The earthquakes. The plague." She suddenly needed to talk about it, get it off her chest. "I mean, I've had enough time to think about it.

"Why is this all happening now? Why?" she whispered, eyes troubled.

"I believe," and he was smiling cynically, "the Great Spirit has had enough of man's greed and evilness, and has decided to end it all."

"You really believe that?" she asked, astonished.

"I . . . don't really know, Emma," he confessed nervously, as if by speaking the words aloud he'd actually cause it to be.

"You've got to understand, I'm half-Indian, and I was raised in the old ways. So part of me believes in the spirits of the earth. That if we anger them, they'll punish us.

"But, on the other hand, I've seen more of the world than just the reservation, been introduced to other beliefs, ideas, and religions. So I'm what you might call a modern Indian. I doubt everything." His eyes danced mischievously. So she didn't know whether he was being totally serious or not.

"Well, if the world isn't ending, how long will the quakes continue? How long will the weather be like this? Crazy, destructive." Her fingers massaged her wrists, her eyes unreadable as she stared into the cave's shadows beyond the firelight.

"I don't know. For a while, I think." Her hair looked so soft. He wanted to reach out and touch it. What was the matter with him anyway? "There's so much junk up there." His eyes rolled upwards, indicating the sky above the cave. "It's screwing the normal weather patterns up real bad."

He grew thoughtful. Leaned his head back. So tired again. He wasn't the same man he'd been last week, that was for sure. His wounds had leeched the strength from him.

"Emma, when it clears up outside, and I'm feeling up to it, I need to go back to *my* cave." He'd told her all about his hole in the hill. "And get the supplies I left there. Food, weapons, extra clothes. Everything I have in the world." Pictures of Sara and Maggie, he thought sadly. Tender mementos. Clean clothes. What he had on was becoming rank.

And he was glad he'd left the Foxfire there that morning.

The ends of his lips drew down. "If those bastards who jumped me haven't found the shelter yet."

Emma patted her legs lightly, and brought herself gracefully to a standing position, gazing down upon him. He needed sleep. She could tell that. Almost unconsciously, she thought: *Sleep . . . sleep.*

"Not likely they've discovered it. Not in the weather we've had the last couple of days. All your stuff is probably still there, untouched. We'll go as soon as you're able."

"All right," he grumbled, his eyes growing heavy and lowering. A moment later he was sleeping.

Emma nodded, watching him for a while, making sure he was truly asleep.

Then she quietly left the cave, relieved to get away from Matthew and his questioning eyes, the blood smell. She was hungry. And the night was calling her.

It was a good week later before Matthew was well enough to travel. A pile of dead foxes had mysteriously turned up one morning outside the cave. He'd looked at Emma suspiciously when she'd discovered them, even though she swore she hadn't the slightest idea where they'd come from.

He'd skinned and scraped the pelts, cutting slits into the main pieces, and using smaller strips of hide to lace the sections together, to make them both simple coats.

But the timely appearance of the foxes wasn't the only mystery that nagged him. He'd been wondering how they always seemed to have fresh meat and drinking water, since the weather had kept Emma from going out. But then, how did she ever go out, with no coat, leggings, mittens, or boots? Unless she had them hidden somewhere.

Yet she had found him out in the snow that night. The night of the blizzard. So she was lying to him. But why?

He strongly suspected, as insane an idea as it seemed, that she slipped out at night while he was asleep, but he could never prove it. Since the attack he'd slept like the dead at night. That baffled him, too. He'd always been such a light sleeper, especially since the earthquake. The survivalist in him. Now, he thought mockingly, a whole gang of ruffians could come crashing in and kill them both in their furs and he wouldn't wake up.

Dwelling on the inconsistencies only made him crazier.

The longer he spent with Emma, the more confused he became. She was so . . . different. An enigma he couldn't fathom. There were times he could have sworn she wasn't even human. But that was so ridiculous a notion, that Matthew would feel guilty for even letting it cross his mind.

It was just the world now. Their queer situation. That was all. Everything was bizarre. Not just people. Everything. But she sure did have some peculiar habits, no doubt about that. And she still kept him at arm's length. In every way.

Some days he couldn't get two words out of her. Sometimes he actually believed she hated him, though she was always civil to him, and kind—

124

in an aloof sort of way.

Sometimes he believed she was just a figment of his fevered imagination; that she and the cave were only in his mind. That he was still out there in that snow, dying, and hallucinating to beat the band.

So he stopped driving himself nuts, and just took one day at a time. He knew he should be thanking all the spirits that he was even alive, not asking for more.

The time passed.

"I'm ready," he said cheerfully one morning. Dressed in his dirty, stinking clothes and anxious to get out. He still wasn't his old self, he was a little wobbly in the knees yet. But he had told himself that once he got out in the fresh air, he'd be fine. After all, his wounds were mending better than he had hoped for. There wasn't even any pain anymore. Emma had done a damn good doctoring job on him, as he had told her many times. And just as many times she had sluffed it off, as if it had been nothing.

"You sure you're up to this?" Emma was poised a few feet away from him, her arms folded over her chest. She had on the fur jacket he had made for her. She looked beautiful in it, with her silver hair and dramatic eyes. Her face shone.

"I'm up to it. I have to get out," he almost growled, as he covered his hands with the fur mittens he had made.

"I know." She gave him that funny lopsided smile of hers for the first time in days. "You're feeling like that caged animal again?"

He stared at her, his mouth open. He'd been thinking those exact words. He closed his mouth, turned, and walked through the hanging rug over the inner entrance, down the winding tunnel toward the mouth of the cave.

Emma followed meekly behind.

125

Outside he tramped through the snow and stood looking over the edge of the precipice. Like every day since the last earthquake, it was a dismal, leaden day. The low-hanging clouds hung like a shroud over the sunless land. It was more like evening. Gray, brushed snow blanketed the world below them. Smoke coiled into the sky in the distance. Matthew immediately began to shiver inside his coat, his breath a fine, frozen mist coming out of his mouth.

His eyes widened the longer he looked down. What a climb. Then it hit him. There was no other way up to the cave but that one way—up the face of the cliff.

He blurted it out before he could stop it: "How in the hell did you ever get me up here that first night, Emma?"

"I threw you up."

He swung around and looked at her. She actually had another smile on her face.

So she wasn't going to tell him. Matthew's eyes hardened. When would she start telling him the truth about herself?

What *was* the truth?

"We'd better get going," she reminded him. "You're in no condition to be out too long."

"You're right."

At least, he thought, this side of the cliff had little ice and snow on it.

"Since you know the way, you lead down. I'll follow." He had no doubt in his mind that she could handle the climb quite expertly. Why he thought that, he didn't know. He just did.

He almost lost his balance three times, almost fell twice. Once she saved him. Her strength, as she held his arm so he wouldn't plunge down against the rocks, staggered him. But he said nothing.

At the bottom, she let him rest. He was huffing and puffing. Sweating and dizzy. Emma wasn't even breathing hard. Remarkable woman.

"I told you it was too soon."

"Which way?" he demanded to know.

She pointed toward the west, her hair blowing against her face in the wind. A gleam of real worry lingered in her eyes, but Matthew didn't catch it.

He pulled himself up and started walking, his back stiff and proud. Damn if a woman was going to make him look like a child!

Emma kept pace with him silently, as they stumbled through the snow into the forest.

Matthew wished he still had his snowshoes. He'd have to make them some. But the snow had an icy crust on it, so it wasn't as bad as it could have been.

The forest was lovely. All white and serene. But deadly. He'd never understand how he'd avoided frostbite the night he'd been attacked and left to die out in the woods. Some spirit must have been watching over him, to have sent him Emma.

He led, and she lagged in his footsteps.

"Some places might be hiding fissures, sunken holes, or even quicksand," he advised Emma. "I've seen a lot of that since the earthquakes. So be careful."

"One wrong step and I'll disappear forever, huh?" she bantered back, but her voice was strained.

"You could say that." He related the story of his truck the day of the earthquake.

"Okay. I'll be careful." *If he only knew how I roam these woods at night, unafraid of anything. If he knew the powers I possess.*

At night. Emma didn't want to admit what she was learning about herself. Daylight, even daylight as diluted as this perpetual gloaming, physically weakened her. She tried not to let Matthew see it. Keeping her eyes down, she kept to the shadows as much as she could.

127

They plodded through the trees and the coldness, to where Emma had found him that night. Everything was wrapped in new snow. Matthew wouldn't have recognized the spot. Her instincts, it seemed, were sharper than his.

But from that point on, he knew where he was. It didn't take long for him to locate his hand-fashioned cave. He was jubilant. Everything was as he'd left it.

"Emma," he called out to her from inside. "It's all still here! My tent, my weapons . . . dried food, herbs, and . . . everything!"

She wouldn't follow him in, though there was room enough for two; saying she'd best remain outside, to keep a lookout in case someone came along. As he rummaged around in the shelter collecting his things, she told him the story of Larry's bomb shelter and what had befallen her. How they'd come along and stolen everything she had. She left out the rest, not wanting to explain how she'd been rescued from rape.

He poked his head out of his hole. "How did you get away?"

"Pure luck. I waited until they were otherwise occupied," she murmured vaguely, "and somehow slipped away. They didn't come after me. It was dark."

She neglected to tell him the rest of the story. And he didn't push her to. He was just happy that she was talking about anything.

She helped him pack up his belongings, so they could take them back to the cave. Matthew marked that she was moving sluggishly, resting whenever she could. Not the Emma he'd come to know.

"Are you all right?" he asked her a few times, concerned, and she would always say, *Yes, I'm fine. Nothing's wrong.* But her actions belied her words.

He cleared out his stuff as rapidly as he could, and

they loaded themselves down and headed back.

Emma flushed out a thin rabbit as they traipsed back through the snow, and as it skidded wildly away, Matthew used the bow to bring it down. Emma was impressed.

"You *are* a true Indian."

For the first time Matthew laughed.

As he retrieved the tiny body, he stood up and caught a glimmer off in the distance, and started walking toward it. That was when he made the grisly discovery.

A campsite. Or what had been a campsite. The glimmering had been faint sunlight glancing off a pair of eyeglasses. Smashed eyeglasses lying in the snow.

Emma came up behind him.

"Maybe you won't want to see this," he warned her. Too late.

Her eyes took it all in, yet she remained mute.

The tents had buckled in on their inhabitants under the weight of the snow. A shoe sticking out here, a mittened hand there.

A circle of small, glittering, frost-covered lumps huddled before the dead fire. Their faces blue and snow-dusted, soulless eyes now just glazed over ice. Quick frozen people. One of their ski jackets still dangling price tags. Their bodies wedged so deep in the snow, only their shoulders and faces, in some cases, left in view.

"They're all dead," Matthew stated bluntly, shuffling around the silent camp. He counted at least six bodies. So one of the two he'd shot hadn't made it.

"Stupid city folk. Didn't they know enough to take better shelter during a blizzard?" He had no pity for them. They'd left him to die in the very same manner. "Serves them right."

Emma caught the heartlessness in his voice, as her

fevered eyes stared hungrily at the corpses.

"They're the ones who wounded you and left you for dead, aren't they?"

"Yeah." He kicked his foot out at the man who'd jumped and then shot him. He'd never forget that ugly face. Now it was dog meat.

His sneer was full of scorn. "Kind of a weird justice in all this, I'd say." His eyes hooded as he looked up at Emma, leaning back in the gloom of a tall oak. "They left me to freeze into a popsicle and, instead, it's happened to them."

Matthew felt the tremor right about the time Emma stepped out of the murkiness, her expression shifting quickly to alarm. She put her hand out instinctively toward the tree, to support herself as the earth began to jump.

"Earthquake, Matthew," she panted, and he was amazed to see her running toward him. "It's going to be a big one." Unwelcome memories of the St. Louis earthquake still haunted her. As indestructible as she was, she still feared nature's fury.

She was shivering in his arms when the full force of it hit them. Her eyes were wild.

"This way!" he yelled, grabbing his packs, shoving a bundle at her. He knew they couldn't afford to lose any of the stuff. They needed it. Then Matthew started running, dragging her behind him.

Emma glanced over her shoulder, and with numb eyes watched the whole campsite, including the frozen ghoulish figures in the snow, being sucked into the earth within seconds. The tents, everything. Gone. The tree she had just moments ago been propped against, gone. Then the ragged tear in the earth closed up, the edges grinding together like angry teeth.

They ran through the clinging snow, dodging flying limbs and falling trees, toward an open space ahead of them. She remembered vividly how Larry had died and ran faster, even though her legs were shaking and her head swimming. If only it were night.

"We've got to get out of the woods," Matthew hollered back at her, as they sprinted across a widening split in the ground. Emma barely made it. If it hadn't have been for Matthew and his firm grip, she would have slid over the edge. She saw no bottom.

The rumbling grew louder, not weaker, as they ran. It was going to get worse, she thought frantically, not better. Whole sections of woods and ground behind them caved in and started sliding to different levels, gnawing against themselves.

Matthew fell, his packs spilling everywhere, one slithering away into a yawning crack and out of sight forever. Emma helped him get up and regather the rest hurriedly.

They continued stumbling through the snow, Matthew breathing hard, his eyes veiled, his face determined. Earlier he'd tied his hair back into a ponytail, but now it was loose and disheveled around his face. It made him look even more like the Indian he was. Emma thought: this is a strong man. A special man.

The earth rocked. They made the open space.

As swiftly as it had begun, it was over. Emma and Matthew toppled to the earth with their supplies, and just lay there together catching their breath — and their wits.

"We were damn lucky that time, Emma," he gasped, wiping the sweat from his brow before it froze.

"Yes, we were," she sighed back, examining the face that was so close to hers. The strength of it. The way his dark eyes studied her.

"Might not be so lucky next time." He was thinking that if they were smart, they'd get the hell out of the area altogether. Too damn many quakes lately.

She smiled faintly back at him. "They seem to be getting worse, don't they?"

"Yeah." His face had slackened, the color draining off until it was as white as the snow.

She got up, brushed herself off. "We'd better get you back to the cave," she said, holding out a hand to him. "It's getting darker." Which it was. "And you look half-sick again." Which he was.

He acknowledged her concern with a curt nod; let her tug him up. They collected their belongings and started trudging back toward home. Matthew dreamt of the cave's warm fire, fur bed, and hot food.

The rabbit hung at his waist. He couldn't wait to see it roasting over the flames. He still had some of those wild onions and herbs, in his retrieved packs. Rabbit stew sounded good. A rest and a good meal was all he needed, he told himself, to get his strength back. All he needed.

With Emma's help (she seemed to have mysteriously recovered from her earlier lethargy), Matthew made it back to the cave.

But when they got back to the bottom of the cliff, they stared up at the cave entrance in the encroaching darkness in shock.

What once had been an entrance into their cave, was now solid rock. The earthquake had swallowed it.

"Great," Emma slumped to the rocky ground. The snow wasn't that deep there. The cliff protected it from the deepest drifts. "Now what the hell do we do?" she swore. She was getting tired of losing her homes.

Matthew grinned for the first time that day. "Simple. We use what we have here." He motioned at their packs. "Could be worse," he said resignedly, seeing Emma's face. She didn't know what he had in the packs yet. "We should just be grateful Grandmother Earth gave us the time to get it all out. Though I don't recall what I had stashed in that small pack we lost.

"I hope it wasn't the tent."

Emma's eyes turned away, she didn't want him to see the hopelessness in them. Losing the cave meant more than just losing her shelter, her sanctuary from the day and the world. Losing the cave just reminded her again of how precarious their existence from day to day was. How the world, and she, had changed forever in the last year. How hanging-on-a-frayed-thread their very lives were, especially Matthew's, who was still human. Matthew. Anything could hurt or maim him. Kill him. For some reason, she didn't like to think about that.

But she looked at the packs, squaring her shoulders, knowing Matthew was right. It could be worse. "Yes, at least we still have what we have."

"Well," Matthew said, exhaustion heavily apparent in his movements as he started digging into the packs. "No use crying over spilt milk. And we're both okay. That means something, too." He looked up one last time to where the cave had been.

"Let's set up camp for the night. Right here."

"Right here?" She was puzzled.

"At the base of this cliff. Good as place as any. Better. Not much snow." His eyes scanned where they were. "Some protection from the wind . . . and it's almost dark.

"We can't be choosy." He had found the pack with the tent in it.

"Here, help me. I'll show you how to set up a free-standing tent."

He caught the dejection in Emma's face.

"Ah, Emma, it'll be cozy, you'll see. Come on."

"All right," she said. He was right. No use crying

over spilt milk. What was done was done. Go on. Like she had so many times over the last seven months. Keep going on.

She was so tired of it all, though. So tired.

Yet she jumped in, and together they set up camp as the night fell. She had to admit that the tent wasn't all that bad. But she grieved for the safety of her lost cave.

Hours later, after their rabbit dinner (which she pretended to eat, but slyly tucked away to bury later under the snow), as Matthew slept, she listened restlessly to the mournful sounds of wolves howling out in the distance somewhere. The eerie cries on the wintry night air made Emma think of Friend.

She wondered where he was, and why he hadn't come back.

She also thought about those frozen bodies at the campsite. Damn. What a pity they'd been devoured by the earth. She could almost imagine herself warming them up to thaw, sinking her teeth into their scrawny necks, tasting their blood on her lips. She could almost . . .

Horrified at what she'd been contemplating, she sat bolt upright in the corner of the tent. Crawling out of the sleeping bag Matthew had forced her to take, while he slept in his coat, she was acutely aware of his steady breathing as he slept, could smell his blood coursing enticingly through his veins . . . too damn close. She had to get out.

Not worried about the noise she made (Matthew wouldn't wake up, she'd seen to that), she escaped the tent.

To hunt.

I should strike out on my own. I should leave Matthew before I hurt him. I should. She fought with herself about it all the time she was gone. As she stalked her prey and drank its blood, she debated it.

But she knew she wouldn't leave him.

Couldn't abandon him now. He needed her, she kept telling herself. *Who are you fooling?*

You need him. He's given you a reason to go on living. Taking care of him has been the sweetest emotion you've experienced in a long time. Someone to care for, to talk to, to laugh with. Someone to keep the darkness at bay.

Everytime she thought of walking away, the sharp thorns of loneliness pricked at her again; the apathy, the despair she'd had to bear since her husband and children had been taken away from her. Then Byron. Then Friend.

She couldn't go back to being alone again. Just couldn't.

That's the excuse she gave herself in the end. To stay with Matthew. She didn't even dwell on the fact that there might be another reason. That she might be growing fond of him. That she had begun to care for him as a person, as a man.

You're falling in love with one of them! her inner voice accused her, contemptuously.

One of them. Then she'd hate herself for thinking that way.

I'm still human, she cried aloud in the darkness to the night. *Human!*

She stayed away from the tent, though, until the gray of dawn seeped back into the blackness, and she made sure her hunger was satiated fully before she did.

Matthew had come to mean far too much for her to ever harm him. Far too much.

Eleven

The earth shook itself again in the early hours of the morning, waking Matthew.

Emma wasn't in the tent. But her coat was.

When she snuck back in a little later, Matthew feigned sleep. She'd saved his life, but he had no rights on her. He'd come to the decision that what she did at night was her business.

As long as she came back. With or without a coat. If she hadn't frozen before now, it was unlikely she would. She'd survived, and that was more than he could say for ninety-five percent of the country.

Matthew, still strung out from their escapade of the previous day, spent most of the next day in the tent, resting in his Ensolite sleeping bag, hunched over the Pyramid stove, feeding it the wood Emma gleaned from the nearby woods. They ate from his store of venison jerky, and the pemmican he'd made from part of the dried meat that he'd had stashed away with the supplies in his packs.

When he offered her a bowl of it, Emma just stared at the pemmican.

"What's this?"

"Pemmican, an Indian dish of concentrated dried meat and crushed berries. Go ahead, it's good," he encouraged her to try it, as he chewed his portion. "I even warmed it up on the stove for you."

Matthew conveniently looked away. Out of the corner of his eye, he saw her mush the food around on the plate with her fingers to make it appear like she'd eaten some, when she hadn't.

What *was* she eating? It had to be something. No one could live without food of some kind.

Again, he believed it was none of his business. Let her eat what she wanted. Do what she wanted. Stronger minds would have broken under the strain she'd lived with the last year.

"Emma, what did you do before?" he asked, licking the residue of the meal from his fingers. "Before the earthquake?"

Inside the tent it was dim and toasty. Matthew could hear the wind slapping against the side of the sturdy tent.

It was the first time they'd discussed their previous lives.

"I was an artist." Emma wiped her fingers off on a rag that Matthew handed her to use. "In an advertising company in St. Louis. A graphic designer." Behind her eyes she was seeing the old office, the cubicles, each with their own Macintosh. Saw herself as she'd been back then, talking and laughing with her co-workers. Going out to lunch . . . in a real restaurant. A working woman dressed in a classy navy suit and white lace blouse. Matching jewelry and heels. Her hair done up in curls. So civilized. She'd had a car, a home, and a family, too. Had that Emma ever really existed? The vision depressed her, because she knew she never would exist again. Ever.

"An artist? I should have guessed." He wasn't surprised. There was just something about her that made him think of a creative person. Maybe her eccentricities, her independent mannerisms. Her moodiness.

"You miss it?"

"I miss it," she said, turning her face away so he wouldn't see the naked yearning in it. It was all coming back. She'd locked it away for so long, and now here it was again to taunt her. Not just the people she'd lost, the world, but herself.

Matt understood. He listened as she wove out the myriad stories about the company she'd worked for. Her friends there, their talents and quirks. The silly feud with her art director. The sort of work she once did. Ads, brochures, and publications. The pride she'd always feel when a difficult, tricky project had reached completion — and it would come back from the printers perfect.

She confided a little about Danny and her kids. Her lost family.

"In those first months in Larry's bomb shelter, I believed they were all with me. I'd talk to them like they were real.

"Do you think that was . . . crazy?"

"No," Matthew responded gently. "I know what you went through. I still talk to Maggie and Sara sometimes. I dream of them."

And Matthew told her about how he lost his wife and child. The guilt he'd carried all this time, because he hadn't been there to save them that last day. He'd never realized how cleansing, how therapeutic just talking about it could be. How good to get it off his burdened shoulders.

Some hard core inside Emma seemed to melt as they compared tragedies. As they talked about themselves. She was no longer thinking of Matt as a stranger. No longer considering him as just another human . . . or as another meal.

Hours later, talked out, Matthew inquired, "What do we do now?"

"Let you rest. Those wounds still aren't completely healed, Matthew. Yesterday was too much for you. You'll get sick again if you don't take it slower."

"After that . . . any plans?" Matthew's eyes took in Emma's flushed skin, her jet black eyes glistening like tiny beacons. The silver in her long hair glimmered. She looked healthy, even if she wasn't eating much.

"I don't . . . know."

Matt detected her hesitation. "What is it?"

She gazed over at him. "Before I found you—" *And before those savages cornered me, beat me, and Byron did what he did to me.* "I was on my way to Maine."

"Maine!" Matthew exclaimed. Would the woman never stop surprising him?

"I have a sister, Margaret, and a brother-in-law, Ken, who live up in Bar Harbor. I wanted to see if they were still alive."

He was quiet for a moment, and then said softly, "That's what we'll do then, Emma. We'll keep moving . . . across the states until we get to Maine."

"You're kidding? You'd actually go with me? That far?"

"I have nothing to hold me here. I was wandering aimlessly before you found me that night.

"And to be truthful, I think we should leave this whole area anyway."

"The earthquakes?" she said.

"There's another big one coming. All the signs point to it. Maybe it'd be better if we were faraway when it did."

Emma was smiling. Searching for her sister gave another purpose to her life. It made her feel more human. Something she desperately needed. She didn't think Matthew comprehended what he'd done for her. Yet, in a way, he might. The thought of being on the move again invigorated him; but it would make Emma happy, and that's the main reason he would do it.

"Thanks, Matthew," she murmured.

"Well, then, we'll pack up and start moving this morning."

"No . . . in a few more days. You haven't recovered fully, and I don't want you keeling over on me on the road."

"Let's compromise, Emma. I'll take today to rest up, and then we start out at first light tomorrow morning. We'll travel short days at first. Take it nice and easy in the beginning."

She bestowed on him a pensive look.

He waved her doubts away. "The exercise will be good for me. I've never been so inactive in my life. I'm raring to go."

"All right. Tomorrow morning we leave," Emma conceded.

"You got it. Tomorrow we leave."

And Matthew lay back, grinning, until the earth beneath them began to rumble and growl again, then his grin quickly ebbed away.

Matthew had been right. The daily exercise of traveling revived his strength. Gradually Matt got better; his injuries healed.

At first, they only traveled four or five hours a day, pitching camp early, but not so much for him, as for Emma.

As he'd perceived the day they'd gone back to his shelter, Emma never seemed quite herself during the heart of the day. And in deference to her, as the days progressed, he gradually adjusted their traveling time to later and later, into what he once would have called evening. Though who could tell anymore with the constant fog? Well, some people just weren't day people, he told himself. Besides, the temperature was so changeable, that other than the absence of light, the evening was no worse to travel in than the day.

It warmed up and the snow began to melt. Matthew shook his head in bewilderment over the fickle weather. They didn't need the heavy fur coats, so Matt made them lighter coats out of deer hide.

As they journeyed, Matthew caught fresh game with his crossbow, and Emma marveled at times how accurate he was with the thing. She liked to watch him hunt, his lean body graceful as he ran, his hair wild around his sharp-featured face, the way his brown eyes lazily took in everything without seeming to. His skills in the woods were remarkable.

Emma had never met a man like him before. His survival expertise made Larry look like an amateur, and they almost rivaled her own newly acquired skills.

"You must have been Robin Hood in another life," she teased him one afternoon, after he'd brought down a wild turkey with one shot.

"I'm Indian. I've used a bow since I was knee-high. I should be an expert at it.

"But you . . . how did *you* ever learn to use that knife like that? You remind me of one of those carnival people . . . the ones that have assistants tied up on round spinning platforms and then they throw the knives at them. The ones that never miss. Or Jim Bowie." They were standing out in the snow, packs on their backs. The sun was a pale ghost ball on the far horizon behind the misty clouds. "You're that good, Emma. Never seen anybody as good as you, woman."

Emma had just brought down a rabbit for supper with her knife from an incredible distance.

Matthew's eyes had been full of admiration and awe, his lips curved in a secret smile. "Here we are, Robin Hood and Jim Bowie on our way to Maine," he laughed.

"I'd go anywhere now, Emma, with you watching my back. I'd have nothing to fear from ambush, I'll tell you that."

His praise had really touched her.

As time passed, Emma and Matt came to accept each other, respect each others privacy. Matthew no longer cared that Emma disappeared most nights. No longer cared about her odd behavior.

He knew he was falling in love with her, even though she continued to keep him at a distance.

He taught her how to use the bow, set up camp, build a fire the old way with flint and steel, how to locate and dig up the starchy *yampa* root—which was not only good for them, but delicious—how to find and cook with the forest herbs, how to bake fish in billy cans in an earth oven (when the ground wasn't too hard). To make wild mint tea and ash cakes and concoct a campfire cobbler with bread dough and wild currants. Not that she ate much of any of it, but it was fun to share the cooking with her. She caught on quickly. A smart woman.

And Emma taught Matthew about loving again. Caring for someone again. Happiness.

It wasn't just her beauty, her stamina, that overwhelmed him as the days added up, but her intelligence and sensitivity. Her heart. Her eccentricities meant less and less to him as the weeks went by.

They moved across the land, staying to the woods and backroads; avoided what was left of the towns and cities. Fearing they'd be like St. Louis. Chaos, sickness, or total destruction. Matthew knew, though, that it was only a matter of time before they'd have to enter a town somewhere along the way. To restock their supplies.

The time came as they passed into Indiana, and Terre Haute was spread out below them like a tranquil patchwork quilt in the late afternoon. Earthquakes and mudslides had demolished most of the city, but there were still stores and houses standing along the perimeters that looked safe enough. Some of them would have what they were looking for.

"Need to pick up a new shotgun," he informed Emma. The bow and knife were fine in the woods, but he'd feel better with a gun on his shoulder these days. "And you need your own sleeping bag. I'm getting tired of sleeping in my coat." Since the doomed campsite, they hadn't seen anymore people, but he believed it was only a matter of time before they would. Not everyone in the country could be dead. They were hiding somewhere. He wanted to be prepared.

"We could both use some different clothes." She grimaced, looking at his ragged jeans, frayed shirt. Emma's clothes hadn't fared any better. They were a mess. "And some combs, razors . . ." She grew thoughtful. "Toothpaste and toothbrushes. Other things." No matter what she had become, she still needed to care for herself. They'd lost a lot in the cave, and Matthew's grooming supplies had been in the pack that had gone into the pit that day.

She hadn't had a comb for her hair, or shampoo, for weeks. They'd been washing their body, teeth, and hair in melted snow water whenever they could. No soap. Using their fingers as combs. They both looked like electrified scarecrows.

"Maybe there'll be news," Emma offered, hopefully. "Of what's been happening in the world. Of Maine." She was relieved that she still cared.

"It'd be great if we could find a car or a truck . . . hot-wire it. I'm getting pretty sick of hoofing it."

"And a car or a truck would get us to Maine faster?" Matthew interjected what she'd really been thinking. He knew she was worried about her sister.

"Yes."

"I'd say a jeep or a truck with four-wheel drive. If we can find one still functional."

"Sounds good to me."

Matthew was studying the suddenly turbulent skies, as the wind eddied around them. The storms seemed to come up so swiftly these days, without warning. "I think we're in for some more bad weather. Anytime. I've never seen a sky look like that before." He was scratching the side of his stubbly face, peering up at the darkening air. It had been almost warm the last two days. It was time for the weather to go screwy on them again, Matthew reasoned.

"Just what we need." Emma glowered up at the racing black clouds in a neon crimson sky, and then back down into the empty city. "It looks pretty safe down there to me. I don't see anything or anyone moving." Like a lot of cities, it was covered in a light coating of ash, soot, and dirty snow that hadn't melted yet. A sleeping city with a gray blanket.

"It looks like a wasteland," Matthew announced, shivering. He kept waiting for someone to walk out of one of the houses and stroll across the street. Waiting for a face to appear at a filmy window. Or a dog or cat to bounce across a still yard. None did. "But that doesn't mean it isn't dangerous."

"I agree," Emma said. "So we go in nice and easy." They started down the hill toward the outskirts of the town, guarding their backs, weapons ready.

It was literally a scene from a science fiction movie. The streets alien-looking, deserted. Eerily silent.

Up close the city was a wreck. Paper littered the streets, and everything was covered in a film of grime, the remaining snow melting, untracked, and undirtied, from slushy piles into trickling streams of water slicking the roads. They walked the streets, trodding through six inches of gooey mush, and leaving a clear signal that they'd been there.

"Did *all* the people leave here, too?" Matthew uttered under his breath as they explored, looking for a store, pushing deeper into the town. "Can't believe *every single one* is *dead.*"

Emma had a fleeting image of all the homeless that had flocked to St. Louis in those last months before the earthquake. That hadn't occurred here. No one had migrated here, or if they had, they had all left. Why?

That smell. Emma covered her nose and mouth. She knew where the people were. "They're still here," she said through her fingers, trying to keep from retching.

The plague kills us also, Emma, slower perhaps . . . but it

makes us sick, and then kills us. Of those four men who at-
tacked you, three had it. I could tell by their . . . smell. Was
this the stench Byron had been referring to?

"I can smell them."

Matthew sniffed the air. "Your sense of smell is
more acute than mine. I don't smell anything."

"Wait, you will."

The light was receding from the streets, and unnatural sounds sighed all around them like phantoms.

They strolled into a grocery store. Its shelves were
picked clean like bones in the sun. Not one can, not
one box of cereal left. The dusty floors between aisles
were strewn with discarded, smashed packaging.

"Looks like a cyclone whipped through here," Matthew whispered, as they worked their way through the
store. "I was hoping that there'd be something for us to
salvage. Anything useful or edible. I can see that there
isn't. Not even a crumb." He dragged his boot through
a pile of rubbish, scattering it in a wider swath of debris. "I was hoping for a stray Hershey bar or something." He loved chocolate.

All the other stores they found were just the same.

Matt and Emma began going through the houses.
Most of them were ransacked and barren, but they
were lucky and in a few of them found some things
they could use. Stuff tucked or hidden away by the
previous owners and missed by the earlier scavengers.
Clothes, underwear. Some canned goods, matches,
and the bathroom toiletries they needed.

One of them always stood watch outside or through
a window, as the other one searched. They weren't taking any chances.

"It sure is strange," Emma remarked once, after
they'd left what had been a restaurant of some kind.
"Even after all this time . . . I still can't get used to
walking into one of these places and just taking what
we want. I still expect someone to come strolling in
and accuse us of stealing. Calling the law on us."

145

"Yeah. You know, I miss just walking into a store, having real food at your fingertips," Matthew piped up behind her, as they turned a corner in the abandoned street. They were still seeking a gun and a vehicle, and had decided to keep looking until they found something they could drive. So far all the trucks and cars they'd come across had been either stripped for parts, or wrecked. Junk. It'd been a disappointment.

"I miss . . ." Emma continued the bittersweet game they had begun to play, to ease the pain of loss. "The ringing of telephones. Noisy cars. People laughing. I miss newspapers. Danny and I loved Sunday mornings, reading them over coffee and danish, sharing the comics with the kids." Emma's face wistful. "God, what I wouldn't do now to be able to watch an old "Star Trek" episode, a comedy—"

"Me? I'd kill for a fresh orange, or an apple. One of those danishes you were talking about. Cherry cheese." He licked his lips.

And I'd kill for a pint of warm blood right now, Emma thought acidly. The night before, on her hunt for food in the woods, she'd found nothing except dead animals. Lots of them. She wasn't sure what they'd died of, either. She prayed it wasn't the plague. If the only other food source she had started to die out from sickness, she didn't know what she'd do. She brushed the worrisome thoughts away, and continued, "You know what else I miss, Matthew?"

"What?"

"Coming home after a hard day's work. Getting dressed up and going out to a movie or a concert. Music. I miss all of it."

"Yeah, me, too," Matthew commiserated with her.

He halted in his tracks, grabbing Emma by the elbow. "Shhhh," he alerted her in a soft voice. "I hear something. Listen."

Emma did. Shook her head. Then she heard it, too. Crunching sounds . . . footfalls, as if someone were

146

following them. The ash and soot on the streets gave them away. They stopped.

"I'll go on ahead, Emma, and circle back around. You wait here."

Before she could stop him, he was gone into the shadows beyond the next building. She knew he shouldn't have done that. Her heart thumping so loud she could hardly hear her own footsteps, Emma unclipped the sheath at her waist under her coat, and very quietly slid the blade out. She fell back against the wood of the building's outer wall, out of sight.

Noise up ahead of her now. Heavy breathing, cursing. That sickly sweet odor again of sickness. Plague carriers. The walking, stalking variety. Death bringers.

Some instinct jump-started her into moving toward where Matthew had gone. She had this feeling that he was in terrible danger.

She was right.

She began to run, faster than any human, her eyes scanning the open and closed-in spaces. The knife blade was gripped in her strong fingers, ready to fly from her hand.

Up ahead she spied Matthew, stealthily crossing the street, his bow still slung harmlessly across his shoulder. Unaware that his enemy, a dark creeping form, was only two feet away from him, closing in rapidly . . . some sort of club raised, poised to strike at his head.

Emma was too faraway to help . . . the club was falling! She screamed the same second she sent the knife spinning viciously. Impossible distance. For a human. Not for her.

The knife whistled like a bullet through the air, and buried itself in the enemy's head before the club hit Matthew. It dropped from the man's hands and clattered away along the street.

Matthew yelled as his assailant careened into him.

He shoved the body away, and it toppled to the ground.

Emma was at his side before the yell ended.

Matthew was gaping down at the writing body in shock. "Where the hell did *he* come from? Are there more?"

"I don't know," Emma answered, breathing hard. "But don't touch him. He has the plague."

"A little late for that." Matthew disgustedly rubbed his hands against his coat. As if that would help.

The man went quiet and motionless. Dead.

Matthew looked up into her frantic eyes. "What a throw . . . Jim." And she could see him grin. "Thanks for saving my life. Again."

"We'd better keep moving. He might have friends." Emma bent over and very carefully pulled out her knife, wiping it as clean as she could on the man's clothes. She resheathed it and stood up.

Matthew took her hand, and they headed back the way they had come.

Emma was the first to realize that they still weren't alone.

Her body went rigid, and she grabbed Matthew's arm, bringing her fingers up to her lips to let him know to stay quiet. "There's someone else following us," she told him in a hushed tone. "Lots of someones."

He nodded his understanding, squeezed her hand, and they began to run, careful not to create any more noise than absolutely necessary.

They flattened up against an old brick building in a narrow alley to rest and catch their breath. The packs weighed heavy on their backs. Emma's eyes glowed like embers in the lightless alley.

Angry shouts behind them. They'd discovered the body. More footsteps.

There was a large building, perhaps a church, to their right, the large double doors thrown wide open. An escape route.

"Come on, through here," Matthew urged, as he pushed Emma through the doors into the dim building.

It was a church. Emma recognized the pews and the elaborate altar immediately. A Catholic church. And the smell of plague death was overpowering from the moment they stepped inside.

There were shadowy figures filling every pew, murky outlines of people kneeling at the main altar, still forms lying in the aisles. People. But as Matthew and Emma's eyes accepted the lightlessness, Emma was the first to see that they were all crawling with fat pale worms, covered in flies. The corpses glistened black with the repulsive insects. As chilly as it had been, the bodies must have been there quite awhile for that many parasites to exist. Other things skittered across the pews—rats, mice—disturbed from their meals.

There were a couple of thin-ribbed dogs fighting over a human arm at the other end of the room.

Matthew just stared, wide-eyed, and gulped. The color drained from his face.

"Oh, God, more plague," she hissed coldly, in the same moment Matthew ran back out the door to puke all over the steps.

She backed out the door to follow Matthew.

"Now we know where most of the townspeople went," he said wretchedly, still bent over. Shaking, he finally straightened up. "The rest are chasing us."

"I figured that out myself," Emma retorted.

"Now I remember why I stayed out of towns the last eight months." He closed his eyes, weaving on his feet. When he reopened them, he said, "Forget the sleeping bag, the truck, all of it. We'll get it somewhere else. Let's get the hell out of here." Matthew surrendered, his face sweaty as he wiped off his mouth.

Emma didn't even have time to answer before he was dragging her through the streets again, toward open land.

They didn't make it.

Someone tackled Matthew, and with a scream of rage Emma saw him brought down, with squirming bodies piling on top of him. She heard the thud, then his cry of pain as his body crumpled to the ground.

Someone huge and smelly caught her around the waist and lifted her from her feet, before she could get to Matthew to help him.

"Got her!" a sinister voice yelped in triumph. "Damn, pretty one, too!"

Emma got a glimpse of a bearded face, a flash of decayed teeth, the stench of his foul breath, as she fought with the man who had captured her.

It all happened so swiftly—the violent attack and her instinctual retaliation—Emma didn't have time to ponder the ultimate ramifications. She was fighting for her and Matthew's lives.

She just reacted. And the man was no match for her. She picked him up by the throat and threw him. The body slammed against a nearby wall. She heard the bones break, and she grinned wickedly, reveling in her superhuman strength as she turned to deal with the ones who were beating Matthew.

She flew into them like an avenging demon, and one by one snapped their necks. Not even giving them time to cry out before their bodies flew to the bloody street. All except one man.

He escaped, whimpering like a baby in terror, scampering away from her on his hands and knees. She ran after him, lifted him up to see his ratlike face, and before she could stop herself, in the heat of the killing blood lust, she sunk her fangs deep into his unprotected throat as he thrashed and fought against her.

She took his blood with unleashed relish, until the struggling ceased. The warm liquid coursed down her throat and filled her with a rapture unlike any she'd ever known.

Then, in dawning horror, she released the corpse, and it fell to the wet street, as she stumbled blindly backwards.

What had she done? My God . . . after she'd sworn never to taste human blood. Sworn it!

And then her numbed mind filled with Byron's death. The disbelieving look on his face after he'd changed from the wolf and back into human form . . . to die.

Plague. The man might have had the plague, like all the others back in that church — and she'd be as doomed as Byron.

No. Her fingers touched her throat. But it was too late now.

Matthew!

She spun around and ran back to him. He was sitting, his bloody head propped in his hands, moaning, in the middle of the road. He gawked up at her in confusion. "I'm okay," he professed right away.

"You?" His trembling hands found hers, and pulled her into his arms.

"I'm okay."

"What . . . happened? They knocked me out." His voice in the dark came out wobbly with pain and incredulous. "How did we get away, Emma? Where did they all go? What happened?"

Saved. Thank God he was so confused that he couldn't remember what had actually transpired. It should be easy to make him believe he hadn't seen half of what he saw. *Easy.*

This time.

"They just started dropping like flies . . . I think they were sick to begin with," she lied boldly. "Plague."

He fell for it, because he had to. Needed desperately to.

"Emma, let's get out of here," he rasped, his voice urgent. His daughter had died of the plague, and he recalled her agony vividly. Even after all this time. He

151

didn't care what had really happened. As long as they were free. Another close call. Too close. He wondered when their luck would run out.

"Might not be so lucky next time." He stared around them with slitted eyes. His brain cleared a little more. "There're bound to be others lurking about."

As if to underline that statement, off in the distance somewhere, they heard a series of bone-chilling shrieks.

She helped him up, relieved beyond measure that he was all right. Emma snatched up their packs, handling them and Matthew easily enough.

They stepped over the dead bodies as they left, scurrying for the woods, as night clamped down firmly around them. A light drizzle pelted them, turning into a heavy rain as they passed by the empty houses and stores. Black windows mocked them.

They left the city behind them, as the rain pounded down from the night skies; a freezing wind tore at their retreating backs.

No one followed them this time.

But they didn't slow down until they were far from the city. And safe again. For a while.

Twelve

"Matthew, look . . . a house." Emma spotted the tiny building nestled in the heavy woods through the rain. They'd started their retreat with her helping Matthew, who'd been dazed; now he was the one supporting her.

Something was wrong, she couldn't run any longer, could barely walk. The world spun. She was nauseated. And she wasn't used to feeling that bad anymore.

Oh, she knew what it was . . . she was being *punished* for what she'd done back there in the city. In her wretchedness, she believed that. She'd gotten the plague from that man's blood . . . and now it was her turn to suffer and die, as she'd seen so many other pitiful souls die. Like Byron had died.

Her fault.

They were out in the middle of nowhere, soaking wet and exhausted. They weren't sure if anyone was trailing them, but they weren't sure they weren't. In the state Emma found herself, she was as vulnerable as Matthew.

He followed where her eyes were directed, squinting through the downpour and the night. They moved closer, until Matthew could see the house's outline.

"It's been damaged in one of the earthquakes," he reported. "See, the south end of the house and the car-

153

port all gave way . . . looks like there's a vehicle under it."

"I don't care." She leaned up against him. She hadn't felt this bad since those savages had attacked her. "Even if only part of it is still standing. I'm sick. I want to stay in a house. Not a shelter, a cave, or a tent, but a real house with a roof and windows. Beds. Please?"

"We're far enough from that city. We're safe."

Matthew held her close, hoping she was right. Her body was hot with fever. She didn't always respond, but kept going in and out of consciousness. Here he'd thought she'd done all the damage back there . . . but maybe she was right, the knock on the head had given him hallucinations. Made him see things that hadn't really been there.

He *thought* he'd seen her charge into those men, and heave them into the air as if they'd been *weightless*. He *thought* he'd seen her ripping one of their throats out, hunkering over the body like a rapacious bird of prey, blood dripping from her mouth. Crazy.

Of course, she'd vehemently denied it when he'd told her.

"That's impossible now, isn't it? I'm just a woman after all. And you had your hands full, so how could you have seen much of anything? What you probably saw was me kicking and hitting them. Fighting for my life, as you were doing."

"Probably," Matthew had grumbled. But the bizarre images kept replaying themselves over and over. The men's screams. The blood. What had really gone down?

He wished he could remember.

"And it was almost dark."

"Yes."

"You were hurt."

"Yes."

They'd gotten a couple of good hard licks in at him. There was a nasty cut on his left cheek, and an expanding bump on his forehead the size of a peach pit. He was still dizzy, but nothing like he'd been earlier. Water dribbled down his battered face, as he studied her in the murkiness. Now it was Emma who was acting hurt, and he was worried.

She was a dead weight in his arms, her eyes half-closed. He couldn't just lay her down in the mud, in the rain, and leave her.

He lifted her into his arms and carried her the rest of the way, suspicious of every noise, every imagined movement anywhere around him. There were no lights shining from the black windows. No smoke coming from the chimney. He stood in front of the house and made a decision. Emma needed rest. She needed a secure, dry place. She wanted a house. This could be it. Just because most places were unsafe, didn't mean that this one would be. Maybe they'd be lucky for once.

"I don't think there's anyone here." His gaze explored the house and the yard. There was a stack of precut wood piled along the whole front of the porch. Dry wood. "But just in case, you wait here, and I'll go in first and check it out."

"No," Emma's voice strained. "Where you go, I go." She hadn't realized until she'd seen him fighting for his life back in those streets, how much she'd come to depend on him being there. She needed Matthew. Nothing must happen to him.

"All right."

He placed her on the porch, and climbed up behind her to rest a moment or two. It was a relief to be out of the rain. When they got to the front door, he simply reached out and twisted the doorknob. It opened.

Inside it was pitch-black, dry, cold. The electricity was off, like in every house in the world. Matthew settled a groggy Emma on the floor, and rummaged quickly around in one of his packs until he came up with a book of matches; he lit one, his hands cupped around the baby flame. The room was in pretty fair condition, as far as he could tell. It seemed to contain only the usual clutter one expected in an empty house. Dusty, stale-smelling. Some loose debris toward the other side of what had to be the living room. And there was a fireplace.

It would do nicely.

He pulled a candle out of his bag and lit it, wedging it between two old books he found lying on a nearby table.

He turned to Emma and said, "We'll stay . . . until you feel better. Clean it up a little, and it'll be real comfy." But she hadn't heard him. She'd slipped away again.

He settled her down on the large couch, covering her with the folded blanket that had been on one end of it, and lit another candle. With the small light he searched the rest of the place.

The kitchen, living room, and one other bedroom were livable. The south end of the house — the rest of the bedrooms, what must have been a large den, and the attached carport garage — weren't. From a window he studied the vehicle under the wreckage. An old truck of some kind. He laughed softly, holding his aching ribs. As hard as they'd looked for one in that city, here, out of the blue, one was given to them. Life never ceased to amaze him. Tomorrow, when it was lighter, he'd have to dig it out and check it over. Most of the roads and highways were clogged or destroyed; many were almost impassable in some locations, but if they had a truck, it would be a whole hell of a lot easier getting to Maine.

He walked out the back door and saw the fresh graves. Four of them. Now they knew where the people had gone. Or most of them. Matthew had a theory. Maybe the owner had buried his family, just like he'd done, and then left, unable to stand living in the same house any longer.

Anyway, it was empty now. It was theirs . . . for a while. Emma would want to move on as soon as she could, but right now they both needed rest. Badly.

Matthew went back to check on Emma. She seemed to be sleeping, though uneasily; he didn't disturb her other than to add another blanket that he'd found. He fetched some of the wood from the front porch and built a roaring fire in the living room fireplace. He dragged a mildewy mattress out from one of the bedrooms, and positioned it before the fire.

In the kitchen he struck it rich and found a few large cans of food: soup, spaghetti, and tamales. A miracle looters hadn't found the house. Too remote, he guessed, hidden by the woods. Using his knife he opened the spaghetti, slid it into a pan he discovered in a cabinet, heated it over the fire, and scoffed it down hungrily. He'd never eaten anything so good.

Even the aroma of food didn't wake Emma. But she never ate much anyway.

Then, exhausted and his body aching in a hundred places from the beating, Matthew checked Emma one last time, and then lay down before the fire on his mattress. He watched the fire for a while. Watched Emma's sweaty face. She wasn't sleeping very well.

It was strange being back in a house after all those months, he mused, as his tired eyes traveled over the ceiling in the faint light from the fire. It was a nice house. Someone had loved it a lot once, fixed it up real pretty. He listened to the rain outside, and before he knew it had drifted into a deep sleep.

He didn't hear Emma moaning later on in the night; he didn't hear her crawl from the sofa, and stumble out of the house into the rainy night.

Some primitive instinct she had no control over drove her from the house and out into the woods. She'd shed her human clothes, leaving them back at

157

the house, so she wouldn't tatter them any worse than they were. It was cold and it was raining, but she felt none of these things. She only felt the pain that racked her body, and the burning in her blood . . . the mysterious urgency to be out in the wild alone.

A naked woman running through the forest in the dead of night.

She swept her blurry eyes across the cloudy, starless skies through the rain, and they were incendiary orbs of red. The pain hit her again, and she whimpered in her throat. She ran through the wet foliage like a madwoman, her shaking hands shoving her off from the trees that she would have otherwise crashed into.

Forcing herself farther and farther from the house and Matthew. As if whatever was happening to her might hurt him, and she was afraid of that. She could lose control . . . she *could* hurt him.

What's wrong with me? she screamed inwardly. *What is it? Am I dying . . . after all I've been through. Is it to end this way?*

Do I have the plague . . . ?

Have I given it to Matthew?

She fell to the ground, writhing in agony, frothing at the mouth like a mad dog, screaming out loud as her body began to transform. Her muscles tore. Bones snapped. Torture.

Something was happening . . .

She knew she was changing, but she couldn't stop it.

First her skin grew soft downy hair, and then the hair thickened, grew longer . . . down her arms, her torso, her belly, thighs, and her legs. Her hands touched her face, as the bones began to crack and agonizingly reform. Her screams turned into gurgling snorts. She was growing a muzzle, her head and her ears elongating and sprouting fur. A tail. Paws instead of hands. She grinned and felt the razor-sharp carnassials bared, curling at her lips. *Unbelievable.*

A wolf, her mind sang in awe, *you've become a wolf!*

Like Byron. Not sick, not dying with the plague, as you'd feared. A wolf.

Had it been the human blood, or was it just time?

Another one of the details Byron had neglected to relate to her, and in the end hadn't been given the time to.

On all four legs, Emma tossed up her head to the invisible moon, and her scream changed into a long, piercing howl of astonishment.

Part of her cringed at what her metamorphosis meant: She could no longer pretend vampires didn't exist; no longer pretend she wasn't one. The last of her fantasy wisped away like her old life.

She was.

But the pain had evaporated, she wasn't dying, and she was filled with such an unexpected ecstasy, she danced on all four paws. Splashing and rolling in the wet leaves and mud like a child. Or a happy puppy.

The night, adventure, life, beckoned her.

Faraway something else called. So faint, so sublime, she wasn't really sure she'd even heard it. Another wolf. Mournful, seeking . . .

Friend? So far, *fara*way, though.

Her ears perked up. Pulled by the call. Pulled by the human in the house behind her. She almost, but couldn't quite, leave him.

Instead, Emma galloped through the trees in the misting dark, reveling in her speed, her canine nightsight. The rain, the cold didn't touch her. The horrible sickness, the pain, was gone. She peered out at the changed world with glittering wolf eyes. She'd never felt like this. So alive. So free. Powerful.

Low to the ground, swift and deadly, she chased the small animals that were her prey, bounding joyously through the woods, shoving the decisions she knew she'd have to make sooner or later away . . . at least for the time being. Forcing herself to drink their thin blood (never would she partake of human blood again,

159

she promised herself. Never.), Emma filled her stomach until the hunger was assuaged.

She was different. This way. Her intelligence, her desires, her very thoughts. Wolf. Time meant nothing. Human dreams and heartaches meant nothing.

The night passed in a blink of an eye. All running and hunting. Singing with the night.

She made sure she was back sleeping on the couch at the house long before dawn, though she no longer needed the sleep she once had, as a human creature. And when Matthew awoke, she was sitting on the couch, smiling at him.

"How long you been up, Emma?" He rubbed his sleep-swollen eyes, sitting up in front of the dead fire. Scratching himself.

"Awhile. I've already searched the back rooms." She pointed at the floor at the end of the couch. "I found you a sleeping bag in a closet. A bit old, used, but I guess it'll do."

Matthew glanced at the pile of stuff. The sleeping bag did look worn, but it was a thick one. "It'll do just perfect. Thanks." A kid with a present couldn't have looked more pleased.

"You're better?" he declared, half-awake, but relieved. He was still trying to clear his head of the dream he'd had. It had frightened and unnerved him. He'd been in the Indian settlement again . . . but none of the braves, women, or children had been there. A ghost village. Everything just as if they'd strolled away for a moment, and hadn't come back yet. He'd stood among the empty tepees in a strange land of a huge, glowing moon, and had waited. They'd never returned. And all the time, on the night air, he'd listened to the musical lamenting of faraway wolves with a growing sense of foreboding. Then he had awoken. The dream still puzzled and worried him. What had it meant?

Emma was saying, "Yes, I'm better. A good night's

sleep does wonders." She had a hard time lying to him. But her romp in the woods was better than a night's sleep. She felt great. "Getting so sick must have been a reaction of some kind, to what happened to us in town yesterday." Her body quivered even as he watched.

"Could have been." He eyed her speculatively. She looked a hell of a lot better than he felt. "I'm glad you're all right, Emma. I was getting worried there." His eyes took in her tousled hair, her shining eyes, as she leaned back against the couch, watching him.

"How are *you* feeling, by the way? You're the one who got all the abuse in that fight, if I recall."

"I'm fine." Rolling his eyes, he crossed his legs, repositioning the blanket around him. The fire was only dying embers. "I was up last night; found real food. Canned stuff." He beamed. "And I checked myself out. Nothing broken. Just bruised. You healed me real good that last time, Emma. I'm better than ever.

"But I sure could use a bath." Sniffing at himself, he pretended the smell knocked him out, and toppled over from the waist to lie on the floor.

"Well, now we have real soap and shampoo — and a bathtub!" Emma reminded him. "We can both have baths." She rubbed her hands in glee. Then pushed her dirty hair away from her face.

"But no water," Matthew stated. "Unless you want to run out in the rain with a bar of soap?"

"Oh," Emma tucked her legs up under her on the couch languidly. "But we don't have to do that . . . we can get water from the creek out back, lug it in those two buckets out by the back door, and heat it up over the fire. There you are — a hot bath."

"There's a creek out back? How do you know that?"

"I looked out the kitchen window."

"Oh."

"I can't wait," Emma cooed, and stretched like a big cat. "That bath is going to feel *so* good."

"Yeah, I second that. I guess I'd better get us

161

another fire going then."

He shivered, getting up from the mattress, the blanket still clutched around him. "Brrr. God, it's cold. Got to get some wood. Be right back."

When the fire was blazing again, Matthew huddled before it a few minutes, then turned to Emma. "You hungry? I found some basics last night in the kitchen along with the canned goods. Flour. Sugar." Whoever had lived here had been well provisioned. As if they'd expected the end of civilization. "I could probably rustle us up some hotcakes, using water instead of milk, though. What do you say?"

She shook her head. "I think I'll skip breakfast. My stomach's still not itself. But help yourself."

Matthew made the pancakes hoping the smell would tantalize Emma into eating, but as usual it didn't.

Don't know about that girl. Doesn't eat enough to keep a bird alive. Is she trying to starve herself to death? he asked himself for about the hundredth time. But she looked too damn healthy to be doing that. It didn't make any sense.

In fact, this morning she looked beautiful.

Emma got off the couch and strolled to one of the windows. "It's still raining outside." She frowned. "If it keeps up like this, we'll have to build us a boat." She wasn't being funny, either. She meant it.

Matthew, perched on the floor before the fire, nodded, finishing up his pancakes. He'd listened to the rain pattering on the roof, he was aware it was still coming down. "I'm going to try to uncover that truck under the carport, soon as I get done here. See if it could be of any use to us. If we had a truck, it would be a heck of a lot easier getting to Maine."

Emma kept smiling at him. *He's going all the way to Maine for me. Such a good man,* she mused. Though she'd tried not to get attached to him, she was losing the battle.

Oh, last night had truly been a marvel to her, and

162

she still didn't know how to handle all the complicated emotions her changing over had created deep inside her. She wanted to run free forever, shake off the shackles of human form, and never return. It wasn't her world anymore. It had brought her only misery and loss.

But it was Matthew who had brought her back to the house. Matthew. And she didn't know why.

"Are we going to be able to travel, even in a truck? The roads are a disaster."

"Won't be easy, but I think we can get through. Might have to detour a lot, but with a truck, it could be done. Better than walking."

"Amen," she agreed. "I wasn't looking forward to getting soaked again, to tell you the truth."

"Or trudging through the snow that's going to come again," Matthew informed her. He was cleaning off the dish he'd used with a little water and a rag, and was putting it back into one of their packs.

"Oh." Her anxious face turned toward him, her back at the window. "You think we're going to have more snow?"

"Absolutely. We haven't seen anything yet. The winter's only half-finished—or just beginning. I think we've been lucky this last week or so. Enjoy it while you can." He spread his hands, gesturing to the steady rain outside.

"Yeah, some luck. Either blizzards or forty days and nights."

Matthew laughed and stood up. He put on his coat with his rain poncho over it. "Well, Emma, I'm going to dig out that truck. You get back on that couch and get some more rest. You still look awful pale to me."

Emma walked over to where he was standing and met his eyes. The closeness of him made her want to lean in against him, nuzzle his warm neck. He reached out for her, and before she knew what was happening, she was in his arms and he was kissing her softly. She

163

pulled away and looked at him.

For one moment she was distracted by the veins pulsing the blood through his neck, fighting the urge to sink her teeth into one of them and . . .

Then she saw the love smoldering in his brown eyes, and when he kissed her again more insistently, she'd won her fight.

She could never hurt Matthew.

Their kisses slowly grew in passion, and it was inevitable that they ended up on the couch in each other's arms, their clothes disappearing.

When they finally came together, Emma experienced something she'd never thought she'd feel again. Love. It was in every move they made, every touch, and every murmur between them.

He ran his gentle hands down her naked body, and told her how lovely she was. How he'd known from the moment he'd opened his weary eyes, that first morning in the cave, that he would love her. That they had been meant to find each other, to be together. The spirits had arranged it. That he would fight for her, die for her. Never leave her.

Emma was terrified that after what had been done to her, she wouldn't be able to love him like a normal woman, but her fears were soon put to rest. It was all so natural. So right.

And when he finally entered her, and she arched up to meet him, she knew her fate was forever linked to his.

"I love you, Emma," he moaned as he climaxed. The rain pelted the roof. The fire crackled behind them. "I love you."

But Emma couldn't say the words back to him. She couldn't condemn him that way to stay with her, when he didn't know what she truly was. A vampire. He would surely run from her if he knew. She was a lie. And the lie sealed her mouth to the words he so desperately wanted to hear from her; and that she could only say silently in her heart.

I love you, too, Matthew.

But he didn't demand it of her, wouldn't rush her. Instead, he cradled her lovingly in his arms afterwards and slept. She watched his handsome face for a long time before she joined him.

When they awoke, he got up and dressed again.

"I'd better get to work," he said. There was a new light in his eyes, a spring in his step that hadn't been there before. He reached out and brushed the wild hair from her face.

"Emma, I—"

"No," she objected, tilting her head up to smile at him. "Don't say anything else. For now, let's just be happy we have each other. Take a day at a time. Please? I'm so confused," came her whisper.

His face seemed to fall, but he nodded back. *All right.* He understood, and his face tried hard to form into the old smile. *I'm a patient man,* he told himself. *I can wait. Wait for you to love me. We have all the time in the world.*

Now she was getting up, getting dressed.

"What are you doing?"

"What do you think I'm doing?" She cocked her head at him, struggling into her shirt, her pants, her shoes already on. "I'm getting dressed, so I can help you. We're in this together, remember?"

"But you've been so sick," he responded protectively. His face hardened. "No way."

"Matthew," she sighed, fully dressed by then, even her coat. "I'm feeling fine, really. And I'm going to help you dig out that damn truck, whether you like it or not. I'm stronger than I look." She winked at him playfully. "So shut up and get moving." She shoved him toward the door.

His face showed respectful amusement. "Anybody ever tell you that you're quite a woman, Emma? Stubborn as hell, but quite a woman."

165

"Yeah, everybody. All my life. I never listened to them, either. Get going."

And they went out into the rain and the overcast day, to try to salvage a truck.

Thirteen

They'd been on the road for two weeks. It had rained a great deal of the time. Most of Ohio and Pennsylvania had been under water. New York hadn't been much better.

Vermont had been a wasteland.

"I was up here once on vacation with Maggie, before we had Sara. Most beautiful country you'd ever want to see. The forests and rolling hills were breathtaking. We'd just pull the car over on the top of the slopes, and stare out over the valleys. Now look at it. Burnt to a crisp, or under dirty water. The quaint little villages all ghost towns."

Emma said nothing. She'd been in Vermont before, too. She remembered. Talking about the devastation didn't change anything.

The truck was laboring to the zenith of a long rolling hill, and Emma saw them first.

"Look, Matthew . . . there's people down there!"

Matthew threw the clutch on the old Chevy, applied the brakes, and spun the wheels to a gravel-splattering stop. He looked. Through the obstacle course of trees dwindling down to tiny dots at the bottom of the hill, five or six people were climbing downward. Two adults. The rest smaller . . . kids. The bigger shapes seemed to be aiding the smaller

167

ones. "I see them." But his voice wasn't as excited as Emma's. "Looks like a family. They're unarmed, I can tell that." Their clothes, even at that distance, were just rags, and the people in them scarecrow-thin.

Emma had already jumped out of the truck and was poised at the edge of the projection overhanging the misty panorama. She wasn't sure how she knew, she just did: that they were harmless. On the run. She waved her hands at them, yelled at them, trying to get their attention, with Matthew, frowning, still sitting behind her in the truck.

She got it. One of them stopped and looked up, pointing. He said something to the others, and the next thing Emma knew, they were all skedaddling away into the woods, like swimmers leaving the water when a shark's been spotted.

Emma propped her hands on her hips above her knife belt, legs stiffly spread. Matthew got out of the truck, and coming up behind her, slid his arms around her waist. Since they had become lovers, they touched all the time. Couldn't get enough of each other.

"Sorry, Emma. I could have told you they'd run like frightened deer, when you started making a ruckus. They're scared. Of everybody. Do you blame them?" he whispered into her soft hair.

"No," Emma sighed, her shoulders slumping. She didn't know what she'd been thinking. Of course, like her and Matthew, they'd be leery of anyone they came across.

"But they're the first people we've seen since that plague city . . . I just thought maybe . . ." She shut up. Maybe what? That they could help and comfort them? Protect them? Sit around over a campfire and talk about what was new? Swap horrors and stories of loss? Why should she care anyway, when she

168

wasn't one of them any longer? Yet her eyes still swept the trees below, searching for them. Children. There had been children. Emma experienced a sudden jerk at her heart. She missed Peter and Jenny so much.

"It's all right, sweetheart," Matthew cajoled. "At least we know we're not all alone in the world." Something he and Emma had begun to seriously wonder about. "Maybe one day, we'll come across more people. Friendlier people."

"Yeah, sure," Emma said without much enthusiasm.

He laid a kiss on top of her head and led her back to the truck, so they could move on.

They drove a long way before the conversation began again.

They had been bouncing across some rough territory. Sometimes they'd have to backtrack or detour. Earthquake damage seemed to be even worse the higher up they went, and more than once Matthew feared they had made a mistake; that New England would be even less inhabitable than the Midwest. The earthquakes had quieted the last couple of days, though. He was glad of that.

He noted the alarming amount of water surrounding them. "Been a hell of a lot of flooding in these parts," he said, after they'd had to drive through another shallow lake. Any deeper and they weren't going to get through.

"You think we should turn around? Find another way?"

"No," Matthew said offhandedly. What good would it do? It was the same everywhere.

Emma kept talking, aware that he was becoming more worried with every mile, hoping to ease his mind.

Through the side window he continued to regard

the water racing along in the ditch beside them. More every mile. At first it had been a trickle, then a stream, now it was two lakes turbulently roiling by them.

"What's wrong?"

"I don't like the way the water's rising around us. With all the rain we've had, flash floods are very possible." He glanced at her, biting his lip. "You ever been in a flash flood?"

"No. And I don't believe I would want to be in one, either." Unlike the vampires of myth, Emma had found that water didn't affect her one way or another. She just wasn't a good swimmer, and she'd been wet so much in the last months, there was no love lost between her and the stuff.

Matthew was still studying the cascading water and the threatening clouds, hovering lower than usual over the moving truck.

"I'm so sick of this forever twilight. I miss the sun," he commented.

Emma wouldn't admit it, but she did, too—even though direct sunlight would probably make her deathly ill. But what you could never have, you wanted all the more.

In the last few hours, the rain had slackened to a meek drizzle, but now it began to fall in earnest. A waterfall drumming on the truck's old roof. Emma was glad they weren't out in it.

"We've just passed through into New Hampshire," Matthew announced. "We're almost there, Emma."

She could hardly believe it. The truck had made such a difference. They'd covered in two weeks what might have taken them months on foot, even though they'd had to backtrack a hundred times because of destroyed or blocked roads. Flooding.

Would have made the same mileage in a couple of days before the earthquakes and plagues, Emma thought. Those days seemed like centuries ago.

But the old blue Chevy truck had proven to be a hardy beast, and always got them through. Emma had been surprised at how much Matthew knew about trucks. When they'd first dug it out, Emma had labeled it a lost cause. It wouldn't turn over, much less run. The tires were half-rotted, the battery bad, and the gas tank was nearly empty.

Matthew somehow got it running, and the first couple of stops they made, once they'd left the house behind, was to forage for a battery, tires, and gas, out of abandoned trucks and cars along the way.

The truck wasn't much to look at, but it got them where they wanted to go.

They'd stayed another three days in the house in the woods, planning their future (Matthew more so than she), and making love over and over. Emma had almost not wanted to leave. She'd been happier than she'd been in a long time.

And as Matthew slept each night, she'd escaped to the watery woods and fields, returning to wolf form to hunt what she needed to exist. Emma returned to wolf form because she could no longer stop herself from doing it. The wolf was part of her now. She had to release it to be free, at least at night.

If Matthew was aware of her nightly escapades, he never let on or said anything. But he was an observant man.

"I could have sworn I saw a wolf at the window this morning, right before dawn," he told her once, his voice awed, baffled. "You must have been outside taking care of nature's business." The house's bathroom was unusable, and they'd just been going out back. "You came in right afterwards, I believe.

"Scared the hell out of me. To see this huge furry face peering in at me, as if it were actually looking at me." He'd massaged the side of his face, thoughtfully. "Then, just like that, it was gone. You see anything?"

He'd just finished up the truck, gotten it going for the first time, and they'd been making some supper. Emma had hesitated at his initial words, and then she'd innocently gazed back at him from where she'd been rekindling the fire in the fireplace. She'd cleaned up the main living areas of the house, swept and mopped, rearranged furniture. It was cozy. "No, I didn't see any wolf lurking outside the house or anything. You sure you really saw a wolf? Could have been a wild dog, you know?"

"Nah, it was a wolf. The biggest one I've ever seen. Man-size. It was dark silver with lighter white circling the eyes. Probably a timber wolf, just like the one you once alluded to. Remember?"

"No," she'd fibbed, going back to the fire. "I don't." She'd felt his eyes on her. She should have changed long before she reached the house, but she hadn't been able to resist a glimpse of Matthew while she was still in wolf form. In her wolf eyes, he had the most distinct aura . . . pulsating neon blue and white. She'd been trying to figure out what it meant since the first time she'd seen it. Did all humans have it, when she was in her other shape?

"Odd thing was, it had the most human eyes . . ." he'd stopped talking, and stared at the windows with the strangest look on his face. Not fear exactly, but apprehension. Outside it'd been dark. The rain had tapped on the glass, rippling down its smooth surface. A crack of thunder in the distance accented the quiet drizzling.

He'd sighed then. "Well, whether it was a wolf or a damn huge dog, you just be careful next time you go out, you hear, Emma?" And when his eyes locked with hers, she thought she might have seen just the tiniest bit of suspicion in them. Of course, that

172

could have been just her imagination.

"Don't want anything happening to you." His voice had been amused. He stole a sly look at the knife always at her waist, and she could almost hear his thoughts: *Not likely.*

"Don't worry, Matthew," she'd soothed him anyway, taking his arm and laying a kiss on his cheek, to get his mind off her alter ego. "Nothing's going to happen to me. You forget, I can take care of myself. Remember?"

Matthew had gathered her into his arms. "I remember," he'd said sullenly. Images—of her somehow getting him up to that lofty cave he'd first met her in; expertly throwing her deadly knife; of her fighting those men—crowded in on him, and he'd dropped the subject. He'd known it was true. She could take care of herself.

She was his equal in surviving, and maybe more.

He'd alluded to the wolf just one more time after that. When they'd been on the road a few days, he'd unexpectedly mentioned, with a nervous chuckle, that he thought the silver wolf was tracking them.

If it were raining at night, they'd try to find an inhabitable house and stay there; if not, they'd sleep in the truck cab. But it'd been one of those drier nights, and they'd been sleeping out in the tent next to the truck.

"Last night, I woke and had to go outside to relieve myself."

He looked sideways at her with canted eyes as they drove along in the rain. "You must have had the same idea. You weren't in the truck. Maybe your leaving was what had awakened me." He had shrugged as he turned the wheel to avoid a tree branch in the road. They'd just bumped over into the state of New York, staying far afield from New York City itself, because it had been bombed the year before. It would still be hot.

"Out in the mist, heading into the woods, I think I saw the wolf again."

"Oh?" she'd replied casually.

"Well, I couldn't be sure. But that silver fur, even in the dark, and its size . . ." He'd caught her grinning at him, and he'd shut up. "Probably just my imagination." He'd backed down again, but she felt sorry for her duplicity; she knew how he felt. Once *she* had thought she was being tailed by a huge wolf, too. And she had been just as stumped, apprehensive, and doubting her own sanity, as he was now.

Emma knew that from then on, she'd have to be more careful when she was in wolf shape. Matthew mustn't find out. Telling him about the wolf would mean she'd have to explain all the rest of it, and she could never do that. He'd never understand. He'd loathe her for what she really was. Recoil from her, stop loving her. Leave her.

She cared for him too much to chance that.

A vivid bolt of jagged lightning rippled across the gray sky, and a few seconds after that, a vibrating crash of thunder shattered the day.

Close, damn close, Matthew glumly calculated.

"My God, did you see that lightning?" Emma gasped, pointing to the opposite direction, where the last flickerings of another light was fading away in the sky.

Matthew squinted through the moving windshield wipers into the curtain of rain. "How could I miss it?" Sarcastically. "Not surprising. It's been unusually warm all day, and now it's getting colder. The two air masses are colliding. Big storm brewing." He stressed the word *big*, his countenance gloomy.

Another colossal pitchforked bolt crisscrossed from the ground and thrust into the layer of clouds above them. A spectacular but frightening show.

174

Emma's worried eyes mirrored the lightning spears until they dissipated back into the clouds, then she said softly, "Never seen anything like that before. It's awesome."

A roaring sizzled through the air around them like a monstrous freight train, and a few minutes later, on the horizon ahead of them, a whole wall of staggered lightning bolts erupted from the cloud and struck back at the earth.

"It's as if the sky and the earth are at war," she said just as softly. The earth rocked. Steam rose from where the lightning had just hit.

"We're having one hell of a lightning storm," Matt exclaimed, his eyes, too, reflecting the luminous fire of the lightning as he sat hunched over the steering wheel, trying to stay on the road. It was getting more difficult with every second. The flaring lights were so dazzling, they blinded a person.

Emma cringed as far back into the shadows of the truck's cab as she could get. The light made her skin tingle, burn. When she glanced down at her hands, there were tiny blisters forming where the skin was uncovered.

"Maybe we should pull over and take cover?" Emma had never seen anyone struck by lightning, but she'd read somewhere that hundreds of people were struck every year. It wasn't that rare. Many died.

"We're safer here than a lot of places," he assured her. "We're insulated—as long as you aren't touching metal."

Emma scooted away from the metal door.

"Worst place to be in a lightning storm is under or near anything tall. Like a tree. Or water."

Emma stared at the water flowing next to them. Was it her imagination, or had the level risen even higher in the last couple of minutes?

"If you're in a house, you stay away from electrical appliances, light switches, and telephones."

"Thanks, I'll remember that next time we're in a house."

He chuckled weakly. Emma could tell that he was really worried.

"They say right before lightning strikes you, your hair stands on end . . . of course, by that time, it's too late to do anything."

"Lovely. Thanks for the warning anyway, Matthew," she humphed.

"You know what causes lightning, don't you?"

"What?" she bit.

"The spirits of the sky fighting with the angry spirits of the earth."

"That's the Indian interpretation, I suppose?" She threw him a ghost of a smile.

"Yeah." He smiled back, his face veined with the shadows of the rain sprinting across the outside of the windshield.

"I suppose now you want the scientific explanation, too?"

"Of course. I always like to hear both sides."

"You want it simple?"

"Simple as you can. I was never good with science."

"I'm not as sure about that one. Something about the interaction of negative- and positive-charged particles, producing electrical fields in a cloud when the cloud passes over the earth, until the difference between these negative and positive charges are great enough that they overcome the electrical resistance of air and distance — and lightning results. Something like that."

"Not bad, Einstein."

Another bolt struck, not more than fifty yards away from them. It splintered a towering tree in a blinding white explosion, that sent hunks and rapier slivers of wood careening at them through the rain.

The windshield shattered, and the truck swerved off the road, crashing into a ditch filled with water. The truck promptly began to sink, water seeping rapidly into the cab.

Lightning crackled all around them in a strange dance.

"Shit!" Matthew swore, grabbing at all their packs; throwing some at Emma. "Get out of the truck. Now!" he ordered her.

She didn't question him, she shoved open the door and fell out of the truck, into the swirling flood of water that was quickly becoming a small river.

Emma was immediately sucked under, quickly bobbed back up sputtering and screaming for Matthew, who was being carried away by the water's swiftly flowing current.

The truck shifted behind her, and the front fender slammed against her on its journey downward, pulling her under again.

When she came up this time, she heard Matthew shouting at her: "Flash flood! Get out of the water! Get out of the water! It's dangerous . . . the lightning . . ."

As if to underscore what Matthew was yelling, a shaft of lightning hit a tree thrusting above the water between them, the lightning breaking up into thousands of tiny fireballs that skimmed around on the surface of the water, like cold grease on a hot skillet.

As Emma dove to escape them, she heard Matthew's piercing cry as he was yanked under. He probably wouldn't let go of those damn backpacks, she fumed.

She broke the surface, and abandoning her packs to sink without a second thought, she stroked strongly through the muddy, crackling water to where she'd last seen him go under. Emma didn't even realize she was frantically crying out his name over and over.

Her new strength aided her. She was no longer a weak swimmer.

Avoiding a rushing log, she just glimpsed the tip of his head, as he struggled before he went under again. Using every bit of her strength, she swam down deeper and deeper, until she encountered his shoulder, and desperately grabbing at him, dragged his body back to the top, and held him above the furious churning, until he'd spewed forth all the water trapped in his lungs.

"Emma . . . Emma," he cried, coughing and sputtering, clinging to her as the water continued to thud them against the floating debris.

Another log rammed against them and separated them; a split second later, a bolt of lightning hit Emma.

Her hair burst into flame and her body sank.

This time it was Matthew who plunged after Emma.

He found her, wrapped his arm firmly around her upper torso, and swam for the nearest shore he could see. When he thought he was too weary to swim another inch, he kept going, fighting the current, praying that Emma was still alive. She wasn't moving.

He almost didn't make it — and later he'd never know how he did — but he finally got them back up on land — then collapsed.

It was totally dark when he woke, lying next to her, his arms still wrapped around her thin waist. She opened red-rimmed eyes, moaning, and stared at him, then gave him a faint smile. She was a pitiful sight. All her hair had been singed off, and there

178

were terrible burns all over her scalp and face. Her eyes brimmed full of pain and tumult.

"Emma . . . Emma . . . you're still alive!" He gave a cheer, with his clenched fist hitting the air. His haggard, filthy face broke into a huge grin. He pulled her tighter into his arms and sobbed with relief.

"I thought you were dead."

"Not . . . dead . . ." she croaked in his arms, shivering. "Never die . . ."

He slid her down in his wet arms and looked at her strangely. His voice was a whisper when he told her, "I saw that bolt of lightning hit you dead-on." His eyes were confused. He shook his dripping head. "It's a miracle that you aren't dead. A miracle."

He tucked her back up against him and sat there in the mud, rocking her like a baby. "Emma, Emma," he crooned.

And Emma was amazed to see that there were real tears coursing down his cheeks through the grime.

"I'm all right," she murmured reproachfully. "Stop . . . making . . . fuss."

She closed her eyes, said weakly, "You lied to me."

"Lied?"

Her eyes opened, they were glittering. "Hair never . . . stood . . . on end." Her grin faded as her eyelids fluttered shut.

He somehow got to his knees and then to his feet, lifting her with him; he turned and tiredly started walking away from the edge of the water.

He knew he had to find them a safe place to spend the night, and get some food—they'd lost everything in the water. Get her, and him, out of their wet clothes. At that moment he didn't care about the truck or any of their lost stuff. Emma still could die.

The lightning storm was over, they'd escaped the flooding, but the temperature was plummeting. He could already see his breath puffing into ice particles before his mouth.

Holding her close to him for warmth, he forged forward, not knowing where they were heading, or what they'd find when they got there. Not caring.

He was just so happy that Emma was alive; he didn't give a damn how she'd managed it.

Fourteen

The night turned subfreezing, and as Matthew had predicted, the snow came.

They were on flat, featureless land, leaving the river behind them. No trees, not even scrubs.

He carried Emma for a long time. So long he wasn't sure his feet were still there below him, they were numb. He knew he had to get both of them dry immediately. Build a fire. But he couldn't find shelter, and the winds were so strong that to even attempt to build a fire out in the open would be futile. So he walked and walked through ice-glazed landscape and around shimmering pools of water. Night had fallen, another silent foe he had to fight, and he was weak from their earlier struggle in the water.

He was terrified that Emma was going to die, if he didn't get her warm, protected.

What he finally found was just a shell of weather-worn wood—what was left of a one-car garage—with slats missing and tiny broken windows, out in the middle of nowhere; a large battered swing-up door sealed one end of it. Empty. Dirty. But it was a buffer against the wind and snow, and he thanked all the benevolent spirits of the earth for giving it to them. If it had been attached to something larger, like a house, the house was no longer standing. The snow kept Matt from seeing them very well, but nearby there were metal skeletons of long-dead vehicles, pipes, and farm equipment, now all lightly coated with white powder.

He broke into the structure and laid Emma on a pile of moldy hay, covered with a filthy plastic tarp.

He could have made a fire the Indian way, twirling a stick until a spark was born. But always the survivalist, he'd hidden a supply of dried jerky, a pocketknife, and matches in a plastic bag in some of his pockets — along with other basic necessities. He would have done anything, though, for some dry, clean clothes for him and Emma, or a couple of fluffy blankets. Everything else had washed away in the flash flood. He'd tried to save some of the packs once he was in the water, but to rescue Emma, he'd had to let them go.

He sat forlornly looking around him at their meager shelter, and unbidden an image intruded and taunted him mercilessly: of his and Maggie's home back in Fenton . . . shiny appliances, a refrigerator full of frozen meat and vegetables that they'd merely popped into the microwave, and the bedroom with the large comfortable bed, stacked high with blankets and a thick comforter, the nineteen-inch television on the beautiful wooden dresser. Ah, the good old days, he yearned. Never again.

Thank goodness for the hay.

He gleaned slivers of wood and old trash from the shack's floor, and adding a pile of hay, built a blazing fire; he stuffed the cracks in the walls with paper and scraps of another tarp he found in a corner. Matthew spread hay in a pile on the ground close to the fire, and then he settled Emma in the middle of it. He stripped her of her wet clothes, and jury-rigged a frame over the flames to dry them on. His wet clothes were soon next to hers.

Gathering Emma into his arms, he crouched down

in front of the warming fire with her in the hay, and tugged the tarp tighter around them. He rubbed her body vigorously to get the circulation going again, studied her ravaged face in the light for the first time in hours, and experienced a mild shock.

The burns weren't as severe as he'd thought at first . . . no. He was staring at her, his eyes not believing what he was seeing. The burns were healing. Had already partially healed! Her hair was growing back . . . there was silver white fuzz all over her head. No longer was she unconscious, her breathing was regular and easy. She was sleeping.

Then another shock: she was mumbling in her fever . . .

"Why . . . save me, Byron? You killed all of them . . . all . . . how did you do that? Where is this place? Cave. Byron's cave. What's wrong with me, Byron . . . so sick. What have you done . . . to me!

"Vampire . . . ridiculous . . . no such thing," she raved on, her words becoming slurred and indecipherable for a while.

Then . . . *"Byron's dead. Plague kills them, too. He said so."* She laughed bitterly. Matthew watched her face, fascinated with what she was saying. If it were true, it would explain a lot of things.

"Scars gone . . . limp gone . . . so strong. Not human . . . anymore. Never die unless . . . Matthew must never know. Hate me. Need blood."

Then she cried in her sleep, as if her heart were breaking.

Matthew held her as his mind cartwheeled.

His good sense didn't want to accept what she was saying in her delirium, but there were facts he could no longer avoid. She should be dead. He'd seen that lightning *strike* her. Yet not only was she still alive, she was recovering at an astonishing rate. How could that be?

183

An old legend came to him. *Vampire.*

In Indian folklore there were creatures similar to vampires. They were evil spirits that took possession of people and made them do awful things. Matthew had never truly believed in such things . . . yet . . .

He cradled Emma in his arms, until her babbling ceased, and she went back to sleep.

Matt ate some of the dried jerky from his pockets and fought with himself on what he should do. He didn't want to accept all she'd said, but on the other hand, he couldn't completely discount it, either. Just too many coincidences that had suddenly fitted so neatly into place. *She wasn't human* . . .

In the end, still no closer to some peace of mind, he decided to do nothing.

He knew he loved and needed Emma. He could never stand to walk away from her. She was the love of his life that he had long ago given up on finding. The supreme irony of the whole situation was that life would be meaningless now, he realized, without her.

No matter what she was.

In her heart, Matthew believed, she was good. She'd saved his life twice, when she could have killed him. If that wasn't goodness, what was?

Still debating with himself, he eventually dozed off into a fitful sleep.

Hours later, or what he gauged to be hours, he awoke, and finding that their clothes were dry, got dressed, then did the same for Emma. Her burns were nearly gone, her hair was now a short cap on her head. She started to wake up, smiled at him sleepily, and returned to her slumber.

It was amazing. By morning she'd be as she had been before the lightning had struck her! And no matter how he tried to talk himself out of it, the whole damn thing made him uneasy after what he'd

184

heard from her own lips in the night. Not frightened, just uneasy.

Daytime realities quickly shoved away the nighttime fears. He fueled up the dying fire, worrying that if they were holed up long enough, they'd run out of things to burn. And eat. He could hear the wind howling and spitting outside, and meandered to one of the windows. Cold. White everywhere.

Where had they seen this before? He frowned. The air that hit him drove him back. So much for the fleeting kiss of balmy weather they'd had the last week. Would the weather ever be any kinder? Either the incensed sky spirits rained and flooded them, buried them in snow and ash, or attacked them with electricity. Why were the spirits of the earth so angry at them, that they would want to destroy the world? Matthew didn't know the answer to that one, either.

He hadn't dreamed of his spirit protector since they'd left the house, and then he'd not actually seen the Indians themselves. That worried him. Had his protector abandoned him? Was he angry at him . . . and why?

He glanced at Emma.

For the first time, Matthew speculated about their chances to make it. Maybe Emma might. *No, no, don't even think about all that!* It was absurd. Wasn't it?

Sighing tiredly, he went back to lie beside Emma in the hay, to try to get some more sleep. He had a feeling he was going to need it.

When he reopened his eyes, he reckoned it was morning by the way he felt. Not that a person could tell for sure these days. It was freezing; the fire had gone out. Leaving Emma curled up in the tarp, he searched the shack in the dim light. Nothing left to burn. Just long, thick boards that he wasn't sure he could break up. If only he had an axe. But there weren't any tools in the small enclosure.

185

He'd have to go outside and rustle up suitable fire-wood. Look around for game. They could use fresh meat.

Steeling himself to the inevitable, he slipped out the door and into the falling white stuff. He scavenged close to the shack, because the snow was already treacherously deep. He couldn't risk getting lost or hurt. Not with a sick Emma depending on him.

It wasn't easy finding wood that was hiding under the snow and ice. Mostly just scrub and sticker bushes. Matthew's bare hands and face turned raw-red in minutes. Coatless, hatless, and gloveless, he would soon be a victim of frostbite.

He wasn't sure how long he was away from the shed, but when he returned laden down with a meager armful of damp wood—all he could find—and no meat at all, Emma greeted him.

Emma, with her soft hair curling down around her ears, her face almost itself again, and her beautiful eyes tinged with guilt and fear. Of what?

"Matthew . . . I woke and you were gone," her voice meek. "I was afraid—"

"That I'd left?" He was shivering so from the cold, he could hardly get the words through his blue lips. Emma wasn't shivering. She didn't seem to be cold at all. He dumped the wood near the embers of the last fire, and knelt down so he could start a new one.

He looked up at her, gazing back at him with her innocent black eyes. She was so beautiful. Mesmerizing. That pale silver-white hair and those huge ebony eyes, that ivory skin.

Memories assaulted him. *Emma as he'd first seen her in that cave of hers. She hadn't had a coat on then, either, come to think of it. Emma rarely eating, or not eating at all. Mysteriously disappearing into the long nights, to do whatever*

186

it was that she did. Emma trudging alongside of him all those miles. Laughing and crying with him. Emma making love with him in that little house . . . her skin glowing soft and warm in the firelight. Throwing that deadly knife of hers and always hitting what she aimed for. Emma courageously battling those brutes back in the city, and what he'd thought he'd seen her do . . .

"I had to get us some firewood, that's all." He snatched up a piece of wood and knocked it against the side of the wall, shattering it, and venting his frustration and helplessness out on it. He used the inner drier splinters to start the fire, the larger ones to get it roaring.

He glanced up, and this time locked eyes with her.

"You're looking much better today," he said. *For someone who took over one hundred-and-twenty-five million volts yesterday,* he muttered to himself, and then hated himself for even thinking it.

The look of stunned misery in her eyes alerted him. *Could she read minds, too?* That was a sobering notion. And without being aware that he was doing it, he began to cloak his thoughts, closing his mind off to her. But he couldn't completely hide his doubts.

"I thought you were dead," he said, trying to smooth things over. Letting his feelings of worry for her overwhelm his thoughts.

"Lightning-strike victims sometime mimic real death, but it's only temporary death," she offered, squatting down next to him, sensing his ire, but not realizing it was directed at her.

Emma, are you going to tell me the truth now? Whatever it is? It just escaped his thoughts.

A confused look spread across her face.

Could she read his mind, or was she only picking things up intuitively?

Sadness filled her lovely eyes.

Guilt filled him.

When he couldn't bear her silence any longer, he captured her hand and pulled her down to sit next to him by the now flickering fire. His love for her overrode everything else.

"You've healed so quickly. You should see your face. It's almost a miracle." He reached out with gentle fingers and feathered them against her smooth cheek. The scars were all but gone.

"I guess I have great recuperative powers." She smiled radiantly.

Matt turned his face away from hers, biting his lip between strong white teeth. *Emma, don't you trust me? I hate being lied to. Stop it!* he ordered himself angrily. Learning to veil his thoughts was going to take some effort. Some time.

He turned back to her, and smiled, too. Then he wrapped his arms around her and kissed her.

This is Emma, he told himself. The woman who saved my life. In more ways than one. Who loves me. I can see it in her eyes. Loves me. And whom I love.

Emma.

Before he knew it, they were under the tarp making love, and it was better than it had ever been. And for a while, Matthew forgot all his doubts, all his fears. All he cared about was that she was with him, in his arms, alive and warm, and loving him back with more passion than any woman had ever loved him.

Matthew would have been startled by what Emma was thinking, if he could have read *her* mind. What truths she had at last and irrevocably come to: *It's true . . . I'm a vampire.*

No use running from it — or denying what is — any longer. I'm no fool.

I have great strength. Few things can hurt or kill me. I

188

can not only protect myself, but I can protect the man I love as well.

I can survive. A stronger more adaptable creature for this new pitiless world we now have. If I'd been as I was before, I'd never have lasted this long. Never have gotten to meet Matthew; fallen in love with him.

I'd not be here with him now.

I'd be dead.

And for the first time, Emma grinned inwardly. Grinned at what she was. No longer was she repulsed, or fearful of it.

But Matthew was another story. As close as he was to the truth of it (she could sense it), he wasn't ready yet. As she hadn't been ready a few weeks ago, or even yesterday.

She had to give him more time. Then she would tell him. Everything. Soon.

"Matthew?"

"Yes?"

"Let's not worry right now about why I'm still alive. Let's not worry about anything but surviving. About being together." Then in a husky voice, "Loving each other. Please?" Her fingers reached out to settle on his arm.

He gazed at her thoughtfully, as they lay spent, and satiated, in each other's arms.

She was right. Surviving was their top priority. Had been for nine months. Their love. Each other. That was all that mattered in this messed-up nightmarish world they now had to live in.

He nodded, knowing that in her own way she was trying to let him know that *she* knew what he suspected. Feared. She was trying to let him know that everything was all right. Would be all right. In time.

"Oh, Emma, I'm just so damn glad you didn't die back there. So damn glad." He clasped her near to

189

him, tightly, rocking her, his long black hair brushing her face softly.

"I love you. I trust you . . ." he whispered, then kissed her long and lingeringly. *Know you would never do me harm.* She could hear his heart thudding strongly in his chest.

And Emma knew from that point on, Matthew wouldn't worry about any of his suspicions again — until he was ready to accept what she had already accepted.

There were subtle changes between them after that. Changes they never discussed. Matthew stopped pushing food at her, and worrying over whether she was too cold or not. Instead she fretted over him. When she had fully recovered, a day later, she was the one that went out into the icy landscape and brought back wood for the fire, and fresh meat for him to eat. But she never told him that the game was very scarce. That she was seeing more dead animals every day. She had to hunt a long time to come up with what they'd both needed.

When the snow became sparse flakes wisping about and Matthew became restless, he fashioned them both snowshoes from thin tree limbs that Emma brought him, and they trekked back out into the wilderness heading towards Bar Harbor. Both of them felt the loss of the truck heavily, but they both agreed that the truck would have been useless to them in the snow.

"We're so close, Emma," he'd announced aloud. He knew she was frantically worried over her remaining family's welfare. *If they were still alive.* Matthew knew the chance of that was very slim. Yet he would never be the one to hurt Emma by pointing it out. So instead, he said, "We might as well keep moving. The snow could be here for months. So we either hole up here until spring or summer . . . or we get used to traveling in it."

"I say we keep moving." Emma was looking out the window. No one could have known that she'd been hit by lightning just a few days before. Her skin was flawless, her hair soft and silky around her face, though not as long as it had once been. But now there was hunger in her glittering eyes. She took great pains to hide that from Matthew, too. Perhaps further on there would be more animals.

"As you said last night, who's to say that the snow will ever leave? With the weather so unpredictable, tomorrow it could be eighty."

So they left the shack behind. It had served them well.

"If we spot any houses still standing, let's scrounge through them. Recoup some of the things we lost in the flood. We need sleeping bags. We need clothes. I need a weapon, if we can find one," Matthew planned ahead as they stalked over the first hill. But he was no longer as afraid of prowling gangs and scavengers as he had been before. Not with Emma next to him.

Until he could find a new weapon, he made do with a homemade bow he made the first day, out of a willow tree and small animal guts; the arrows were just straight pieces of a hardwood tree sharpened at the ends. It wasn't the best bow, but it made him feel a little better.

Sooner or later they'd come across a village or houses again, and they'd snoop around until they'd find everything they needed. Again.

Fifteen

The wolf peered out from the nocturnal gloom at the human family lumped around the campfire under the trees, its eyes gleaming red embers and its ears alert. It slunk closer toward the words they were uttering, and closer to the smell of warm blood.

It'd been hunting since full darkfall. Hours. It had only caught a few scrawny rabbits and a possum, which lay, bloodless now, under its paws; it still hungered. There'd been many animals, frozen and long dead—useless to the wolf—in the forest. Too many. Its breath froze on the heavy air.

It listened.

The woman rubbing her hands over the fire was saying, "If we don't find food soon . . . I don't know what we'll do. Elsie's so weak now, she can hardly walk." The woman was bundled in what looked like rags, from head to toe; only her pinched face, all tragic eyes and thin slash of a mouth, showed. "Wesley's feet are nothing but bloody cuts and bruises." She glanced behind her at the other three bundles huddled together on the ground. "So thin. They're all so thin." For a long moment or two, she just stared at them, then looked back toward the man who was still shivering before the fire.

"Maybe we never should have left that last place . . ." her voice sounded doubtful and weary, "no matter how bad it had become. At least the kids had food." She lowered her face into her covered hands, her shoulders quivered.

The wolf cocked its head. Faraway the siren song whispered enticingly on the dark breezes. Stronger every night. Then the human noises intruded again.

"Picking this place was smart, Susan," the man placated her. As if he hadn't heard anything else she had said. "You were right, the trees give us protection from the wind. Firewood, too."

The woman was weeping now, and the man finally got up and went to hold her. He was a man with massive shoulders, but a squat, compact body. A dark beard covered most of a gaunt face; a woolen cap held down unruly carrot-colored hair. His eyes were red-rimmed with sleeplessness and anxiety, but astute, and tinged with true compassion. He'd been a roofer before the world had gone crazy. Just a hard-working man who had loved his family. There were times he still couldn't believe the cruel tricks life had played on him. But he'd protected his family so far, he told himself tenaciously, and by God, he'd see them through this as well.

"It'll be all right, honey, you'll see."

"I'm hungry, Jack. I'm cold. Where are we going to go now? What are we going to do?"

"We'll find us an empty house somewhere and settle down. Just us, like it used to be. Safe. Tomorrow, I know I'll find us something to eat." It didn't seem to comfort her.

"We should have stayed." Her face was upturned, tear-streaked. A tiny woman with chocolate brown eyes and dull brown hair.

"No. We did the right thing. We had to get away from Gerald and his people. All those strict rules. The bullying. They were nuts. Worse than nuts.

They wanted our kids, for God's sake . . . to do heaven knows what with. And nobody takes my kids away from me. Religious man or not. Nobody."

"Then we should have answered those people we saw—"

"No," the man emphasized. "Don't trust nobody. That's how we got in that last mess with that nut Gerald."

Gerald Chandler, the wolf picked up the man's thoughts. *The settlement they'd just escaped from. A clever but paranoid man who had once been a nobody, but who had somehow changed as the population had dwindled.*

"If he and his cronies hadn't had all those guns to protect all that food," the man laughed sarcastically, licking his cracked lips, "we would have split long ago.

"We were stupid, not to see sooner that he was making us all meek sheep. Making us their slaves." He shook his head. "But when he started all that crap about being God's chosen, and how the new world had to be different . . . and made us do all that praying and fasting, that was the end. No way I was goin' to take anymore of that craziness . . ."

The wolf still heard the man's angry thoughts after his words had dwindled away. *And all those bizarre punishments for disobeying him . . . God, the rumor was that he was going to start herding the children to other locations. Couldn't tell Susan about that. School camps, he called them. Didn't believe that for one damn second.*

Suspected Gerald always hated the children. Called them liabilities and unneeded baggage. I know he was sending them away to have them killed. Had to get us out then.

Not my children, the man named Jack fumed silently. His jaw rigid. *There are so precious few children left anyway.*

Had to run then.

194

Now we're alone out in the wilderness, freezing, starving, and lost.

Jack wouldn't admit it to his wife, but he really wasn't as sure of their ultimate survival as he was pretending to be. The wolf knew that, too.

The man's eyes roamed the night beyond the fire, and caught the tiny pinpricks of animal eyes reflected by the campfire. Wild animals. But what kind? Wild dogs had become a reality and a damnation since the fall of civilization; they'd tear you to pieces as soon as look at you — and he'd seen them do it. It hadn't been a pretty sight. He shuddered.

They were almost as bad as wolves.

He had no weapons. Gerald had confiscated them all months ago, and Jack hadn't any luck in stealing any before they'd left the settlement.

Jack hurriedly whispered something to his wife and built the fire up. The glow touched the bright red of his children's hair.

Then he handed her, from a pile, one of two large sharpened sticks, the other he laid across his own lap.

Maybe we should have stayed, his worried mind mocked him. *No,* his eyes rested on his children's peaceful faces . . . *no.* They'd done the only thing they could have done . . . and tomorrow they'd find a safer place to stay. An abandoned house or something. They'd find food.

If they could only make it through the night.

The wolf watched as the man made the fire bigger. It could smell his fear. It looked at the family and then at the dead animals at its feet. Slowly it lowered itself to the ground and closed its eyes. Soon the man and woman would relax their vigil and sleep. It would wait.

When the fire was small again, and the man and woman both dozed, heads down, the wolf crept silently and cautiously into the human camp.

In its jaws hung the rabbit and the possum's carcass. Like a ghost it wafted near to the sleeping man and laid the dead animals at his feet. Backing away from them, it picked up three of the sharpened sticks in its mouth, one at a time, and quietly laid them into an arrow pattern, pointing toward the east — toward an empty gas station that they could use as a safe shelter for a while. Where they'd be warm and dry.

For a moment soft lupine eyes gazed at the sleeping children, and then, its shaggy head coming up, it turned and disappeared back into the night.

Back toward the gas station that she and Matthew had discovered, and were using for the night before they continued their journey in the morning. She knew that if she didn't get back soon, he'd awaken and worry. Along the way, she retrieved the other dead rabbit she'd left in the snow beyond the trees. Matthew would also be hungry when his sleep was over.

Sixteen

Matthew and Emma's days and nights soon fell into a pattern. It ceased snowing, but stayed bitterly cold. Blackened clouds hung low over the land like a thick, dirty blanket that Matthew found suffocating.

Game became scarce, and then dwindled to nothing. Matthew tried breaking the thickening ice on the ponds and streams when he could, and the few fish he did catch satisfied his hunger, but did nothing for Emma's.

They traveled during the twilight-day through the thick woods, and found some kind of shelter right before total night fell. When they were lucky, it was a house, cabin, or garage. Once they stayed in a rickety lean-to Matthew constructed out of loose wood and debris. Sometimes caves.

They scavenged through every house they came near, usually rubble, and painstakingly recouped the necessities they needed. Matthew dug out a rusty shotgun with ammunition that he cleaned up enough to use, a couple of knives, blue jeans, shirts, boots, and old coats for both of them. Emma donned the clothes, even the coat, and sheathed another knife on the other side of her waist. She was as lovely as ever in a man's oversized blue flannel shirt and ill-fitting blue jeans. Trying to be as human as she could be,

Matthew figured, but he said nothing. The damage she'd taken from the lightning strike was just a forgotten nightmare.

When they weren't lucky, they spent the night in a recess carved into a slight incline or hill, or out in the open under piles of dead leaves and forest debris, and covered with snow for their blanket. Emma didn't need the warmth or the rest as much as Matthew did. The knee-high snow and freezing temperatures that continued to plague them didn't affect her; she could see as well in total darkness as she could during the day. They rested each night for him, because he was the one who became tired and cold. He was the frail one. But she never belittled him for his frailties.

Matthew dreamed of the Indian with the wolf eyes once more. The Indians had returned to their village. The nearer the two of them got to Maine and their destination, the more he dreamed of the Indians. Like remeeting an old friend, Matthew was relieved. But the dreams had changed. Now Matthew was part of them, invited in by his warrior protector — and this time he was able to step inside.

Sometimes he rode with them on their wild hunts. It was so real, he felt the warm breathing flanks of the pony beneath him, the bow and arrow in his hands, and the warm air rippling back his long hair. Some nights he listened to their talk in the cozy teepees. It wasn't the language of his youth, so he couldn't understand what they were saying to him. But he felt the love; welcomed the comradery. He used sign language, and sometimes they answered, but usually just shrugged and smiled enigmatically back at him.

So Matthew laughed with them; ate meals with

them. Traditional Indian dishes he hadn't had since he was a child. It tasted so good, especially since he was always hungry. Strangely the warrior's woman had begun to look a great deal like Emma, except her hair was as black as Matthew's, and she wore it in long silky braids to her waist. She cooked the fresh meat Matthew and the other warriors brought her, and saw to many of his needs, yet never talked to him. Still, Matthew was happy among them.

He was one of them. He belonged as he had never belonged anywhere else. There was always love, plenty of food, and warmth . . . during the day the sun was like a large golden ball, crowning the sapphire blue skies. No earthquakes, molten lava, ash, or plague.

Nevertheless, Matthew always knew he was dreaming and would awake saddened . . . and hungrier than before. He wished fervently that he and Emma could just escape into the dreams and never come out. Back to the cold hell that was now earth. But that, too, was just a dream.

One night as he lay sleeping, the warrior appeared to him. Agitated. Gesturing wildly toward something Matthew couldn't see. Something over the far horizon. Something dangerous. To be feared. Matthew sensed these things, but the dream Indian dissolved into mist before he could actually show Matthew what he was so afraid of. On the air, in the remnants of the dream, wavered the cries of wolves. Some sort of premonition. A warning. But of what?

And at night as Matthew dreamed and slept, Emma would steal out of whatever shelter they were in, and become the wolf. Loping alone through the frosty nights, hunting for prey that increasingly wasn't there, and listening to the strange summons that had grown stronger each night as they neared Canada.

Wolves, she was sure it was wolves howling faraway on the midnight air . . . seeking her. For what reason, she hadn't a clue, but as the nights went by, she had the eerie premonition that they weren't normal wolves. Their cries touched something primitive inside her, and there were times when she was tempted to follow the distant night noises. But she always relented and returned to Matthew. His pull was always greater.

The devastation, as they crossed over into Maine and tediously worked their way up along the coast, was massive; more than in any other place they'd been. The desolation was heart-rending. How could there have been so much destruction? What had happened here?

There were no people, none at all, for a long time. Emma often remembered the red-haired family around the campfire, and she hoped they'd made it.

Matthew and she fretted about the absence of people, as they made their way across the barren land. Then one day they had what they believed was their answer. They came upon what was left of a fishing village; they'd been aware of its existence long before they crested the last hill overlooking it and the ocean.

A pungent stench permeated the air around them for miles. And it wasn't the smell of the sea. Emma had encountered that peculiar odor before. The fetidness was death.

Plague burnings.

As they gaped down at the burning town in the gray dusk, they watched in horror as cart after cart of screaming and sobbing people were drawn up to the edge of a tall scaffold silhouetted against the smoking sky, herded like cattle across it, and then cruelly tossed into the flames by men. Men bearing guns.

Some of the doomed wretches wouldn't go willingly into the fire, and they were shot, then their bodies pitched in. Some clung onto the outer planks, and gun butts were smashed against their hands until they let go and plummeted into the pyre.

Emma silently counted maybe thirty, coated, thin-lipped men corralling the prisoners to their deaths. Hats, tied down securely with heavy scarfs, covered their heads and eyes.

The scene was like something out of an old-fashioned apocalyptic movie.

She gazed down on the hellish melee, and her skin crawled. But her eyes were ice chips. She'd seen too much in the last year for it to have the old effect on her.

The victims' screeches of agony floated up to Matthew and Emma, and twisted in their guts like hot burning coals.

"Pitiful creatures," Matthew moaned aloud in a muffled voice, his hands clenched like claws around the stock of his shotgun. But his face was radiating a barely uncontrolled fury. "I've seen a lot of loathsome things in the last year, but this has got to be the vilest."

"But . . . Matthew, they're as good as dead, one way or another." She laid a warning hand on his trembling gun arm.

Emma tried to feel pity for the humans as they died so hideously, but all she could think about was all that sweet blood going to waste. Her mouth watered just thinking about it. She'd caught no animals to feast upon for over three days now, and she was more than hungry, she was ravenous. The game just wasn't in the woods any longer. The dead ones she discovered were everywhere. She licked her dry lips. She could smell the blood cooking below in the fire, and it was driving her slowly mad.

No, they were not for her. They had plague.

The shrieks crescendoed into a fevered pitch that made Matthew's hair stand on end, and violently broke the spell he'd been languishing under.

"Dear God in heaven, we must do something!" Matthew cried, his face a sickened grimace, as he brought his gun up and began to take aim.

Emma continued to look out over the grisly scene with flat eyes, and almost without thinking, she violently nudged the barrel of the gun downward.

"No! It would only call their attention to *us*, and we aren't staying," she hissed. *And if she remained here much longer, she'd lose what good sense she still possessed, and go charging into the midst of them and gorge herself on their polluted blood.*

Her instinct for survival was stronger than that.

"Emma!"

"NO!" She was stronger than him, and the barrel of the gun remained down.

Matthew had squeezed shut his eyes, trying desperately to block out the horrendous pandemonium below. But when he opened them again, it was to see a cart of what were no more than children hauled up and thrown into the flames, kicking and wailing in terror. That did it.

"I can't stand here and watch this . . . I've got to help them!"

Emma's fingers closed firmly around his shoulder, and—trying not to hurt him—brought him to his

202

knees. The meaning was clear.

With a gasp, Matthew went white, hid his face in his gloved hands, and crumpled onto the icy rocks.

"That humanity has come to this," he snarled hatefully through gritted teeth from the ground. "I can't take anymore!"

But Emma had already wheeled around and climbed back down the way they had come.

He followed her.

"Why are they doing that to those people?" He had grabbed her arm and jerked her to a halt. He was trembling with anger. "And why in hell did you stop me from helping them?"

"Plague. They all have the Red Plague," she sighed over her shoulder, still moving swiftly away from the bedlam. "I've seen this" — she waved her hand back the way they'd come in disgust — "before. Never on such a monstrous scale, though. The healthy people are so terrified of becoming infected, they immediately burn any person who exhibits any symptoms at all. The sad thing is, that some of those people don't even have the plague, I'd bet. But the rest are so paranoid, they kill them anyway."

"It's barbaric!" Matthew growled, wincing as the screams rose louder behind them. *When there's so few of us left anyway.* "Can't we do *anything* to stop them?"

Emma halted, spun around, and stared into his flashing eyes. "Matthew." She shook her head sadly. "You can't stop them. They're insane with fear. There's too many of them. And they have guns. They'd kill you." She wasn't afraid for herself, just for him.

"Besides, if we were to somehow stop them this time, when we were gone, they'd go right back to it. Unless we kill every last one of them. There's over thirty men, Matthew."

A stricken look washed over his face.

"They've gone over the edge. Didn't you see the way they all looked? Half-starved, filthy. The manic way the ones doing the killing are behaving?"

Emma saw the hope die in his eyes, and tears fill them instead. He simply nodded.

She encircled his hand with hers, and gently led him away from the stink and the billowing black smoke.

But it was a long time before they were out of range of the sound of human suffering, and Matthew knew he would hear those pathetic cries as he drifted off to sleep at night for weeks, maybe for the rest of his life, and he would cringe. Cursed.

They kept moving. Neither talked of what the other already suspected. That Margaret and Ken were probably as dead as the landscape they were traveling through.

The long arctic days collected into weeks. The earthquakes resumed, and Emma and Matthew found themselves often running to escape the splits that would open up in the ground like hungry vicious mouths. They had some very close calls. But, together, always managed to save each other.

The state of the world was only getting worse, and they both knew it.

As was the availability of food. Emma couldn't find game. The cunning of the wolf was no match for the brutality of nature. She'd run all night long, her tongue hanging out, her wolf eyes fiery orbs in the night, seeking the blood that was her life, the animal flesh that was Matthew's. And finding nothing. Three days without food stretched into six, then seven . . .

Emma had thought she'd stay with Matthew forever, but she'd never counted on not having animal blood to sustain her. Never realized what the hunger would do to her. It burned her stomach like acid, and then spread through her veins. She was on fire. In agony. She whimpered, at times, as they walked, but hid it as best she could from Matthew.

She didn't want to scare him.

The night whispers continued to beckon her from between the clacking ice branches on her night runs. Followed and taunted her. Entreaties on the winter night from somewhere up in Canada. Stronger and more insistent the more her ribs stuck out.

Emma wasn't sure what was happening to her, but she was still changing. What had once seemed monstrous to her—the drinking of human blood—didn't seem so any longer. She was so . . . *hungry*. All the time.

She grew lean, her eyes haunted and glittering with the hunger. Not human eyes at all any longer.

Matthew, too, grew emaciated, weaker. His handsome face became haggard. No longer could he catch fish. The water was too cold or frozen over; the fish wouldn't or couldn't come to the surface. The sea (they had been trekking alongside the coast toward their destination for days already) was barren, as well, as if all its occupants had fled to inhuman depths.

Seven nights seeped into eight.

They were both starving.

Emma began to find herself tormented, even salivating at the thought of sinking her fangs—just once . . . just a little—deep into Matthew's luscious throat. And the very idea of that repulsed her. Petrified her.

If she didn't find prey soon, she'd have to leave

Matthew — or she'd end up preying on him.

That she couldn't do. She'd promised herself. *But it had been a human promise* — and she no longer felt human.

Inevitably the day arrived that they came to the end of their long journey. Suddenly it seemed that all their suffering had been for *something*.

The Atlantic Ocean pounded against the rocks as far out as the eye could see. A dead gray color, just shades darker than the sky. Night was coming. Emma had been up to Maine once before with Danny to visit Margaret and Ken, years ago. Now it just seemed like an old movie she had watched, and not something she had done herself. But she recalled the small town of Trenton very well.

The town was on Route Three, and Route Three scooted right up to the Atlantic, and then became a thin bridge onto Mt. Desert Island.

Bar Harbor, where Margaret and Ken had lived, was on that island. So was Acadia National Park, and a quaint little restaurant in the middle of that park that sold those delicious popovers with strawberry jam. Five dollars for two. Emma and Danny had driven up to the top of Cadillac Mountain, and then on the way down had stuffed themselves on the pastries. Cadillac Mountain was the second highest spot in the Northern Hemisphere, she'd read on one of those road signs along the way. She'd forgotten what the highest was.

But when Emma and Matthew stood there on the outskirts of what had once been Trenton, and read the battered roadside sign that proclaimed they were coming into Trenton, and underneath it the words Mt. Desert Island, and then Bar Harbor with arrows pointing in the appropriate directions, there was nothing out there but a jagged ribbon of highway that disappeared into the water. Then just ocean . . . and a craggy spiked piece of rock that came sharply into focus and then blurred out, as Emma realized what she was actually looking at. The tip of Cadillac Mountain. Just the tip.

Mt. Desert Island was no longer there.

It was gone.

And so, then, was Bar Harbor. Margaret and Ken's house. Margaret and Ken.

The wind whipped around them, tugging at their coats and hair. Emma had known the Atlantic to be a bitterly frigid ocean, but it had never been so bitter as it was at that moment. Emma squinted out at the gelid and forbidding water that stretched on into eternity, her eyes reflecting the no-color of the frosted liquid. Her empty eyes searched for what wasn't there anymore. The people she had once loved. The last of her family. Her old life. All swept away like ashes on the wind.

"I'm sorry, Emma . . . I'm so sorry," Matthew told her then, seeing her desperation, reaching for her, genuinely hurting for her.

Emma slumped into Matthew's arms, buried her face against his chest. But only because he expected it of her. There were no heaving sobs and hysterics. She couldn't cry. Not even over Margaret.

Because Margaret and all the others had died long ago. Perished like the old world. It was only the fading dream she had to let go of . . . and that was easier than she would have imagined.

Now the last thin thread that tied her to humanity was Matthew. Only Matthew.

And Emma was afraid that wasn't enough to hold her. Not anymore. She looked at him, and all she could see, all she could smell, was his blood.

Night was falling, and from somewhere there rose a plaintive call of a wolf. Then another, and another.

Very close now.

They were coming to get her.

Or Matthew.

Emma pushed Matthew's arms away and stepped back. Their eyes held, and Emma's began to change. A lupine glint transformed them. She tossed her head, her mouth slightly open, her lips skinning back from sharpening teeth.

"No, Matthew, it's I who am sorry," her voice was so husky he could barely make out the words. An inhuman voice.

"As much as I love you, need you . . . I can't stay with you. Don't dare stay with you." She smiled, but it was a hopeless smile, and her fangs emerged. "I'd kill you if I did. There's just not enough food, Matthew. The kind of sustenance I need." She licked her lips wolfishly, and spread her hairy hands in a gesture of explanation. Her eyes were glowing brightly now, as she fell further back along the sharp rocks.

"But I can't hurt you. I love you," she spoke softly, her eyes tender. So sad. "And because of that, I must leave you now."

The yammering of the wolves was coming closer, and Emma's eyes shifted nervously away from Matthew toward the sound.

So close. If she didn't leave him soon, they'd find him. Kill him. And she wouldn't be able to stop it. She must go now. She began to remove her clothes, all of them, dropping them to the rocks, until she was naked in the freezing wind.

"Emma . . . *don't leave me!*" Matthew pleaded, the truth finally sinking in. He took a hesitant step toward her. She **was behaving** so strangely. Not like Emma at all. She was frightening him.

"I can't live without you!"

"You can't live *with* me, believe me when I tell you that."

"Emma —"

They were too close. Now.

It must be now.

"No! You mustn't follow me. You hear me? *They'd kill you . . . understand . . ."* and the humanness of her voice turned into a throaty growl.

Dumbfounded and immobilized, Matthew could only stare at Emma's human form, as it crouched down to the ground and remolded itself in a heart-beat into the large silver wolf he'd seen so many times before.

And then, with one last look of misery in its animal eyes, it whimpered at him, pawing the ground, then whirled in one furious motion and raced down the rocks and along the beach, away from him, and toward the howling sounds.

Matthew stood there until the wolf disappeared, and then, as if he'd been slapped out of a trance, he whispered Emma's name on a sob, his eyes filled with tears, and he scurried frantically after her.

He fell on the rocks, it was getting so dark, tore up his knee, but that didn't stop him. He dragged himself up and went on.

"Emma . . . Emma!" he screamed in panic. *Wait for me! You wouldn't hurt me. I know that. You love me!*

"Let me help you!" he screamed to the dead sky.

But the wolf was long gone, and soon, too, were the other mysterious animal sounds. The sounds swiftly dwindled away into silence.

Emma was going to fight or join the pack, whichever way they wanted it. Live or die. She didn't really care.

As long as she led them away from Matthew.

Seventeen

Miles away Emma headed off the wolves at the edge of the forest in the descending dark. There was a pack of them, their shadows slinking behind like phantom mascots. Forming a loose circle around her, the hulking, man-size beasts with incandescent crimson eyes and silver fur settled to their haunches. They studied her intently, slavering tongues hanging out.

They were fiercely majestic, beautiful. Deadly.

She wasn't convinced that they were true wolves. Something about the way they examined her — muzzles lifted, eyes sentient and shrewd — reminded her of Friend. But there was a human slyness to their actions, a vitriolic tension to the way they seemed to be silently communicating with each other. Up close they were undernourished, their coats bedraggled and their paws bloodied.

They'd been traveling far distances.

Emma's heart was racing. Were they of her kind; were they the ones who'd been calling her?

Byron had believed there were none left.

Was this where she belonged? With them?

She already missed Matthew. A dull ache she refused to acknowledge.

Yet some primal instinct warned her that the

211

wolves weren't friendly. She'd recognized their expressions: voracity.

Some of them were snarling low in their throats, the ruffs on the ridge of their backs standing straight up. Their teeth were bared.

One of the smaller wolves padded toward her, white streaks rippled through the silver of its thick fur, and its ears laid back flat at her in open defiance. It insolently pranced around her as the others looked on, and then, without warning, sank its fangs deep into her flank, ripping out a chunk of her fur and flesh.

Emma howled with pain as the animal swallowed the chunk and wheeled in for another. *Why were they attacking her? She'd done nothing to them.* Unless it was hunger.

She could have fought them, she had the power. But a finely honed intuition advised her not to: *They aren't normal wolves . . . and there are too many of them.*

When the slashing jaws came down again, Emma was no longer in the same spot. She was running, nimbly dancing away from the multitude of snapping teeth that were everywhere, with every ounce of speed her four legs could pump out for her, her blood flying out behind her like a bright red banner spotting the snow, tantalizing the rest of the pack into a kind of frenzy.

They took chase.

Through the icy, darkening forest, the wraithlike shapes pursued her. She purposely led them in the opposite direction of where she'd left Matthew. A human wouldn't have a chance against them.

She didn't have time to think, she fled, the miles clicking away under her fleet paws. If they brought her down, she would be their supper.

The pack howled and yapped behind her, and the

night swallowed her up. Emma had the distinct feeling that they were herding her . . . toward Canada. She'd hear a growl somewhere to her right and would veer left, only to hear a snarling to her left and she would move more toward the right.

Perhaps because she was stronger than they, or faster, or through dumb luck, she kept ahead of them . . . for a while.

Then she came to a wall of rocks, and the truth of what they'd done to her hit home. They'd trapped her.

The pack howled.

Emma pivoted and faced her attackers with head lowered and teeth showing. She was prepared to die, if that was the way it was to be, but she'd take a few of them along with her.

That's why when they bounded from the woods and penned her in again, she didn't wait for them to come at her, she went for them yowling in animal rage, her ears pointed up and her eyes smoldering with blood lust.

She hadn't fed in a long time, either.

Her fangs tore into two of the wolves' shoulders, and she bit a moving tail before they all moved away from her, falling to their haunches in the snow. From their circle, they glared at her like stone statues with glittering ruby eyes. Unmoving. Ominous.

Then abruptly all of them melted back into the forest. One moment there, the next gone, like smoke.

Emma was left dazed, ready to fight, with nothing but imaginary night demons to battle.

Then the calling began. Like singing. The wolves howled to each other mournfully across the night air, their voices merging into a chorus of unearthly, yet hauntingly beautiful, music.

She knew they could have killed her back there by

the rock wall; there was a reason they hadn't. Almost against her will, Emma was drawn to the ethereal sounds . . . and as they floated past her, she followed.

For miles.

She was loping across an open, snow-covered field when they fell back in around her. Silent ghosts. She ran with them, glorying in the freedom and the beauty of running with the pack. It didn't matter if they were like her or not. They had accepted her. She'd passed the test.

They ran all through the night, heading toward some preordained destination. North, Emma thought. They were somewhere in Canada probably. Emma just moved with them, in the center as if she were being escorted; thinking it peculiar that they weren't hunting for food. They didn't stop for anything. Her side where she'd been bitten had stopped bleeding, was already healing. It had never been meant to cripple her, just make her angry.

As true night passed into a murky predawn, and Emma began to feel the strain on her hungry body, they led her into a tiny cave in the side of a great mountain. It soon opened up into a series of larger caverns.

And Emma understood.

It reminded her of the cave Byron had brought her to; the one she'd in turn brought Matthew to after she'd found him wounded out in the snow; the cave that had been destroyed by an earthquake. A *living* cave.

As the last of the wolves skidded into the main chamber, the mystery was revealed.

In the undulating light of a central fire in the large stone pit, the wolves were metamorphosing into people in front of her eyes . . . coming up from their four legs into a crouch, and then rising up on two human legs.

Emma just huddled back on her haunches in a corner and watched in awe. She was a vampire and a wolf, but she had never seen herself change; she had only seen Byron change once, as he was dying, and had wondered if all vampires had the power to shape-change. It was mind-boggling to see a whole pack of giant wolves transformed in seconds into nude men and women.

Perfect humans.

They all had silver white hair and glittering black eyes like hers. But that was where the similarities ended, they were all quite different-looking other than that. Yet, all were very well built and good-looking, straight of limb and possessing a sinuous, graceful beauty that allowed no room for modesty. Their bodies were exquisite, and they knew it. Accepted it as if it were their due.

One of them, a tall, heavily muscled man with tattoos all over his arms in exotic patterns and vivid colors, placed his huge hands on his nude hips, and winked down at her, laughing.

"One of the prerequisites for becoming one of us has always been physical beauty. We don't make ugly vampires."

Another male, smaller and thinner than the man with the tattoos, but apparently just as arrogant, walked up to her. "Well, are you going to change or not?

"Isn't it time we see what our net hauled in?" He cocked his head toward the silent others behind him in the shadows. And they began to move in closer to her, staring at her. Most were men, already clothed, but there were women as well. Emma counted at least fifteen or twenty in all. Scrutinizing her. Waiting. Faces came into the light full of cautious curiosity, but cold eyes. Byron's eyes.

She accepted they meant her no harm. Not now.

"Don't be shy, darling," a slim, lovely woman with hair past her waist purred. "None of us are." Then she laughed throatily. "She'll learn, no doubt," she tossed off to a man standing behind her. "She's a clever one, she is." Emma caught just the slightest bit of envy.

Emma did feel embarrassed. There was enough human left in her to be embarrassed. Their ways weren't her ways. Yet. She'd been alone for a long time. Even accepting Matthew had had its problems. But Matthew had been aware of her shyness, and had taken every step slowly. He'd never pushed her for more at any one time than she could give. He'd understood.

But she was among her own kind. She'd have to be as they were, to be fully accepted. Had to forget her human timidity and embrace their ways.

She changed.

"Now I see why you were brought into the family. You're lovely." The huge man with the tattoos smiled approvingly at her.

Her hands lightly covered the half-healed wound on her left side, right above her waist.

"It'll be like new by tonight," he assured her. "Not like the gash you ripped in poor Ann's shoulder. Or Dean's tail, which you nearly bit off. You're very good, very quick, you know that? For one so young. A real scrapper. We admire spunk."

Young? In real time or vampire time?

"Is that why you didn't kill me?" Emma probed carefully, her eyes bravely meeting his. "Because I fought back like I did?" She dropped her arms to her side.

216

His bushy eyebrows lifted, and his mouth spread into a wolfish grin. "Smart, too." Then he tossed a handful of material, and a rope-belt, at her. "But then you'd need to be, to have made it this far. And even more so to face the horrendous future that's coming."

"Thank you," Emma murmured to the man, slipping the dress, a mid-calf-length shift of a shimmering dark midnight blue, over her head and belting it. It clung to her supple curves like a second skin. Emma hadn't worn anything so pretty in ages.

The others were all dressed as well. Simple clothes in a silky cloth that was usually of a dark hue. For her benefit perhaps?

"You're welcome," the man answered, then took her by the elbow and directed her around the circle. "We have much to discuss." His piercing, forceful eyes held hers. "But for now we'll take it slow. It's been a long, long night, and we're all exhausted. And hungry. But introductions are in order. My name's Stephen."

"Emma Bloodworth," she offered.

"Nice to meet you, Emma Bloodworth." A spark of humor at her name was evident. She recalled it had amused Byron, too.

He positioned her in front of a man, stocky, with a broad face and broad shoulders, in a soft leather outfit of pants and sleeveless shirt. He had a sharp nose, high cheekbones set in a narrow face, and a thick silver mustache tucked down around thin lips.

"This is Dean," Stephen said with a chuckle. "The one you bit in the tail?"

"I'm sorry."

Then to the man: "Does it still hurt?"

"Not very. Just my pride."

He swung his gaze to Emma. "No one's gotten me

217

like that in . . . a long time. But I'll hold no grudge against you." But Emma thought she caught a simmering animosity under the outward calmness. It was all around her. Tension. Why?

Unlike Matthew, and other humans, their minds were guarded and closed against her. They were like creatures from another planet, wrapped in their mysteries and secrets.

Emma shivered deep in her soul.

Another woman materialized in front of Emma, her face was beautiful, classic, her hair short and feathery. She was petite and wearing a belted tunic of black and some kind of leggings underneath. Intricate silver jewelry glittered at her throat, and silver and diamond rings sparkled on all her slender fingers. Emma wondered what became of the jewelry when she changed into wolf form. Did it drop off, or would there be a wolf out there running in the woods with rings and necklaces? Emma hadn't noticed it then, but then it had been very dark, and she'd been very busy.

The vampire fixed raging black eyes on Emma. There was sincere malice in that glance, and Emma warned herself to remember that.

"If Stephen would have let me, I would have killed you," she spat. She shoved her clothing away from her left shoulder, and Emma viewed the ugly teeth marks. "And I don't care what he says, I still might.

"The truth is, I don't like you. There's something . . . queer about you." Her eyelids slitted, she said, "And as much as the pack needs new blood—" she grinned jagged, razor-sharp teeth at Emma, "—for mating purposes, that is, I think you'll be nothing but trouble." Her delicate nose wrinkled up, as she cast Emma a spurnful and haughty glance. "You even smell human. Taste human."

Emma's hand unconsciously strayed to the wounds at her side. *So she's the one who bit me? Bitch.*

Then the female vampire, in a voice honeyed but dripping with hatred, added: "So watch your back, child.

"Because the next time, I'll be sure to finish what I started. Unlike Dean, I hold grudges forever." She turned and strode away hotly.

What a performance, Emma thought.

"That was Chelsea. Don't mind her, she's just irked because you bested her, and she's never before been bested by anyone. Not in this century, anyway. And she's probably jealous because you're such a looker," Stephen added astutely. "Up until now, she was the queen of the cave.

"But still, watch your back.

"Now." He grabbed her hand. "Come and meet the rest of us." She lagged behind him as they strolled around the cave to greet the others.

"This is Peter. Joyce. Edgar. John. Jill there poking at the fire. Robert there in the corner glowering at you. David's the one petting the wolf."

He must have seen the quizzical raising of her eyebrows. Or read her mind.

"Yes, Emma, a real wolf. We have a great affinity with them. And why not? We're their brothers. There are always wolves about. Sometimes we even take them on hunts with us. They take care of our leftovers, so to speak."

"I know about the wolves. It was a wolf back in Illinois that saved me, when I was too weak to hunt for myself." She related the story to him about Friend, and he seemed impressed. And she wondered if she'd passed yet another test.

"It was so human, I kept thinking he would change into a man at any time."

219

"Thought it was a werewolf, huh?" he asked her with a touch of whimsy.

"No . . . I'd seen one of you change from a wolf to a man long before I knew I could change." Then she thought of something.

"Do werewolves really exist?"

"No. There never were such things as werewolves."

"No?"

"No. It was always just us. Vampires. One branch of the family, I mean. Some vampires are shape-changers, but just one *gift* to each . . . some of us can change into wolves, bats, or panthers. Some can't change into anything, but then they have other special talents. They can read minds, predict the future . . . or move from place to place instantly," he snapped his fingers in the air like a showman. "Or become invisible. Most of us here can't do any of those things. We here can only change into wolves. No other talents."

Emma was listening attentively.

"The families don't usually group together." He gestured at the people in the cave. All going about their business, but watching them avidly. He scratched a large finger against the side of his massive jaw. "It would seem that the wolf shapechangers had the best natural defense against the plague. All the others I'm afraid have died out. That's why we're all the same here. I'm afraid there aren't any vampires who can change into anything else, or have special gifts, left these days—or, at least, I haven't run into them." He shrugged, as if that discovery didn't really bother him.

He went on with the presentations: "This is Clive. He likes to be left basically alone. He's from England, and is as eccentric as hell most of the time. Used to love the old horror flicks. Poor guy, he misses them now.

220

"Here's Brian. He's the fastest among us." Another face tilted curiously toward her and smiled.

"And Kathryn—over there with the shaved head." A thin woman with no hair and the most beautiful, piercing eyes Emma had ever beheld nodded shyly at her. Clothed in a white Roman tuniclike garb, she flicked Emma a nonchalant wave before she joined a man, and disappeared into the shadows with him, arm in arm.

"She likes to be shocking," Stephen chuckled in an intimate aside. "In every way, believe me."

Emma tried to meld the faces with the names, but she knew it would take awhile.

"There are three missing. Out hunting still; should be back any minute: William, James, and Graham. Graham is especially tall, a veritable giant. Can't miss him. We're sixteen in all. There were more of us once, but we've been ravished by plague, just like the Others."

"No last names?" Emma commented, curious, sitting down cross-legged on a pile of fur-covered foam of some kind, rather like a low couch. The cave was very comfortable, though strange, furnished the way it was. Rugs and furs on the floor, and heavy draperies on the walls . . . even pictures. Each person seemed to have a cubbyhole of their own sectioned off for private use, sometimes separated by a hanging tapestry or a curtain.

Stephen laughed. "We don't need them." He dropped down beside her. "That's a human invention. We've decided to drop them here. There are so few of us." Some of the vampires had gathered around, while others were off doing one thing or another. Sleeping, talking with each other, or cleaning. Just like normal people, Emma couldn't help but compare.

"Why do you live in caves," she asked, her eyes scanning the small low-to-the-ground, carved wooden chairs and the flickering candles on similar low tables, "when there are plenty of abandoned houses you could choose from?"

He looked horrified at the question. "Live in humans' houses? Never! They're our food. Surely, Emma, you wouldn't want to live in their places? It would be like living in barns."

Matthew and I have stayed in worse places.

That was the first concrete inkling Emma had as to how different she was from them.

"Besides, these caves are perfect for us." He spread his hands, encompassing everything around them. "Most importantly . . . they *hide* us from the Others. It's the way it's always been. We've learned to be *cautious.*"

Emma felt a tingle of foreboding at his words. These vampires feared and hated humans. The realization silenced her further on the subject. She'd have to guard her mind, watch her step. Her thoughts touched on Matthew gently. *Where are you now?* She prayed he was all right . . . out there all alone in the frozen wilderness, and hoped he had forgiven her for running out on him, and had found shelter and food somewhere.

The thought of food made her weak. How long had it been since she'd fed? Eight or nine days? Her head was dizzy, her body feeble. How long would it take her to die of starvation? She didn't know.

Emma fished for something to say, she'd let the silence go on too long. "You knew I was coming?"

"Not until we found you in the woods. You heard us . . . and you came. We were calling friends. We just never expected a *new* vampire. These days anyway."

222

When there's so little human blood to go around. She read his mind for the first time. Loud and clear.

Emma flinched at being called a vampire for the first time aloud, but quickly hid it from Stephen by yawning, and pretending to stretch.

Emma had never really understood in full how one made a vampire. Byron had never told her how he had made her. He hadn't had enough time. And she'd been too sick to care. He'd given her his blood, she remembered that. But was that all? Or was there something else he'd done? It was something she'd mulled over after she and Matthew had been together for a while, whenever she'd daydreamed about making him like her. Some fantasy. She wasn't even sure how it was done. She knew all the myths; who could tell which ones were true or false? She sighed silently.

But then that was before she'd known what kind of man Matthew was. He'd die before becoming something so . . . unnatural. Evil. Matthew had a strong religious streak through him. His Indian religion. *Much* deeper than hers had been.

Evil people were believed to be possessed of evil spirits, he'd told her once, and those spirits must be cast out or they would devour an Indian's soul. Which was the worst thing that could happen to an Indian, since most Indians lived their life in preparation for a good afterlife in the spirit world.

No, Matthew would die before ever allowing himself to become like her, or those she now sat among.

Thinking of her lover only made her feel worse. She leaned back against the cave wall, fighting to keep her eyes open. Her weariness not so much physical, as it was mental. Her unappeased hunger was gnawing viciously at her insides; her wound thudded with pain, though not as sharply as before. She shifted her body uncomfortably.

223

"We've been calling all of our kind for months," Stephen continued. "What's left of us. I'm afraid this is it, or near to it. Before this worldwide cataclysm," his voice low and distressed, "you never would have found so many of us together. We vampires have always been solitary creatures. Selfish. But now . . . it's different. We're dying off, just like the human race is. And those left are banding together for the survival of us all."

"I know. The plague," Emma commiserated, rousing herself back to the present. "Byron told me."

"Byron? Byron was the one who brought you into the fold?" He seemed genuinely astounded for some reason.

"Yes."

"Where is he now?"

Emma was taken aback. *I thought you knew everything?* "He's gone . . . plague."

For the first time, Emma thought she saw some sort of real emotion play across his perfect features. Shock. "Byron? It got Byron, too?"

Emma nodded.

"He was one of our finest, cleverest, and strongest. But a self-proclaimed hermit. He was over nine hundred years old, Emma. I don't know what amazes me more—that he made a *new* vampire or that he's gone. Byron *loathed* the Others."

Then he caught himself. Emma had once been one of them. But he didn't apologize, all he said was, "He must have believed you were something very special."

"No," Emma told the truth as she knew it. "I think he was just lonely. Terrified that he was the last of his kind. He said he hadn't seen another one like him for a very long time."

"That explains part of, then," Stephen's tone rueful. "But not all."

Stephen turned to someone behind him. Some sort of secret communication was going on which she was purposely being left out of. They didn't trust her. No surprise. She didn't trust them yet, either.

His attention roved back to her, but his eyes were now cloaked. "The way the world has become, Emma, savage and lonely, I can see why Byron would create a companion for himself." She met his eyes, but Emma couldn't read what was in them. They were cold, like the stars.

"I don't think it's going to change anytime soon. We that are left will probably end up starving . . . because mankind is dying as well.

"And when there are no humans left," he gestured eloquently around at the closed faces listening, "in the end, there'll be no vampires, either."

One of the other vampires interjected, "I still think we should gather up whatever healthy humans we can find, pen them up, and breed them. So we'll always have a blood supply."

Stephen gave him a dirty look.

"Robert, we've already discussed that option. It won't work. It's been tried before. Humans don't take kindly to captivity. They commit suicide, or die trying to escape."

Emma followed the conversation without a flicker of emotion, but inwardly she was seething. They talked of human beings as if they were less than animals.

"Well, maybe it's time to try it again," Robert whined.

"No, Stephen's right! That's not the solution," another one said indignantly, and launched into what he believed they should do.

Then another joined in, until the din was unbearable. They all had ideas, and they all thought theirs

225

was the best solution.

Stephen ignored the quarreling vampires, shook his head at them disgustedly, and threw his hands up in mock defeat. "You've picked a hell of a time to become one of us, Emma. Once we were invincible, now . . ." his voice ended in a sigh of futility. "Now we squabble among ourselves like spoiled children. Divided and lost."

I didn't pick anything, she thought. *It was picked for me. Against my will.* But she hid her anger. She had an idea that they wouldn't like her attitude. Best to play humble and ignorant.

"I guess I have more to learn."

"I'm afraid you do. Though, at times, I think all of us have a lot yet to learn." Cupping his chin in his hand, he rolled his eyes as the others debated what they should do with the humans. "If I can get them to be quiet long enough to try.

"And here we are supposedly friends. Most of us are very . . . old. Most have met at one time or another. Been enemies or lovers. You know we're capable of love." His eyes slid down the length of her body caressingly, a blatant sexual invitation that made Emma nervous, even though it was meant to be flattering. There were very few women in the pack . . . and she remembered, uneasily, Byron's appetites. All of them. Remembered how the vampire took what he wanted, never asked. She wondered if Stephen was the same. If all of them were the same. She had a feeling they were.

"I know," she said, refusing to meet his eyes. A subtle rebuff.

Matthew's memory plagued her again.

"How long *were* you with Byron before he contacted the plague?"

"Not long. Days," Emma responded, unsure of

226

what he was getting at. And he was getting at something.

He stared at her, suspicion creeping into his face, and the smile evaporated. She had to hand it to him, though, he recovered quickly.

"Days . . . then it's a miracle you've survived. Without instruction. Without guidance. With the plague and the way humans have begun to hunt us—"

"Humans hunting *us?*"

"Where have you been these last nine months, Emma?"

"It's a long story." She let out a breath she didn't know she'd been holding. "I'll tell you about it when I'm not so—" She almost said hungry, but caught herself in time. "Weary." There was no way she was going to show them any weakness. Any at all.

"Well, that will have to do. For now." Mistrust tinged his reply. "Yes, humans hunt us. Things have changed. In this world of horrors, humankind hasn't found the existence of vampires quite so difficult to swallow.

"And some of it's our fault. I'm afraid that without as many humans as before from which we can pick and choose, we've become . . . careless. The people, at least around here, not only believe in us, they openly attack us when they see us. A few of them even know how to destroy us."

Another of the pack had overheard Stephen's remark and jumped in. "Not that we're afraid of them. No vampire is afraid of a human." A sneer reformed thin lips. His hair was combed straight back from a high forehead, and he was wearing drab leather. No jewelry. He reminded her of Byron for some reason. Maybe the dreamy look in his smoky eyes. The somber clothing.

"His name's John," Stephen supplied the name to her under his breath, in case she had forgotten. She had.

"They can't stop us from taking what we want." John smirked cynically. "Their blood. Their lives. We do what we want. Always." There was cruel power in the way the vampire spoke so callously.

"But coming here I saw no one. No people. The villages are empty rubble," Emma pointed out. "What do you feed on?"

"There were people around here . . . once. No longer. The villages are empty because we've already sucked them all dry." John's face was impassive as he said it. "Killed every man, woman, and child we could find. That's why we're in such bad shape now. We have to look longer and harder, and farther away to find them now. Pity.

"It's such a bother having to work so hard to find our meals," John bemoaned. "Nothing like the old days." He sighed longingly, then turned to confer with someone else.

They weren't like her, Emma thought. Whatever they'd once been, they were predators now. Killers. No conscience. No regrets. How in the world was she going to fool them?

Emma *knew* without a doubt that whatever she did, they mustn't learn of her aversion to human blood.

They'd never allow her to stay if they found out. They'd destroy her, and she didn't need to read their minds to know that.

Suddenly Emma only wanted to get away from their prying, knowing eyes, but Stephen was still digging for information.

"How did you learn what you were capable of, or not capable of, if no one was there to instruct you?"

he wanted to know.

"Trial and error. At first I was so sick, I didn't care; I didn't know what to do." All of them were listening. All were watching. They knew this story well. "I didn't know what was happening to me." *I was terrified.* But she didn't think they'd understand that. "I drank animal blood in the beginning. The wolf brought me animals when I was too sick to—"

His eyes bored into hers, and she realized that the cave had fallen quiet. Too quiet. Some of the vampires were studying her with grimaces of disdain on their icy faces.

She'd already said too much, and regretted it. But she was weakened, too confused to think straight, or really care. Their faces were blurring in her vision, like faces in a fun house mirror.

Stephen stood up. His manner shifted like mercury in a bottle. He spoke to the vampires who were crowded around. Hulking vultures, that's what they reminded her of. "Emma, we're vampires, but even vampires can be wearied. You've come a great way, endured a lot, and you're weakened from the hunger. I've already been an unfeeling host.

"So, Emma, let me show you to a place you can rest. I think we all need it. Tonight we must begin our search for food again. Farther and farther. We'll all need strength. We'll continue our talk later."

He'd helped her to her feet and was leading her away from the others. He looked down at her in the dimness, and his eyes were like tiny coal beacons.

What was he thinking? And did she really want to know?

He led her to a tiny enclosure with a fur bed and nothing much else, in the back of the cave—and furthest away from the entrance. She crumpled down to her bed, feeling more like a prisoner than a guest.

"Thank you, Stephen."

But he'd already pulled a curtain across in front of her and was gone.

For what seemed like an eternity, Emma could hear the whispers in the cave, as she drifted into unconsciousness. Talking about her. Plotting, perhaps to kill her if she didn't measure up. How could she? When she didn't understand why she was the way she was.

These vampires have no heart, no soul. They'd been turned into stone over the centuries. Not Emma, though; that was her problem. She still had both.

So she was in a trap, a trap she couldn't get out of no matter what she did. They were too strong for her.

The cave of vampires seemed like some nightmare she had stumbled into. They were so . . . unreal. But then, her whole life for a long time, seemed just as illusory. Except for Matthew.

I hope Matthew's okay, was her last waking, but protected, thought. *I wish I were still with him. God, I miss him.*

She wasn't sure how long she was left alone, but at some time during the night, she sensed someone was hovering above her. Watching her.

Stephen.

When his weight came down on her and pinned her to the furs, and his feverish lips came down forcefully to stifle her cry, she knew it was him.

She had no chance to protest or plead — not that she would have. She already understood one thing about the pack. They took what they wanted. This could be just another test of her loyalty.

So she put up a slight struggle at first, just to make it look good, but in the end submitted. Stephen

230

could have overpowered her easily anyway.

Like Byron's, his lovemaking was a ferocious conquering, and had little to do with love, but rather with total possession. He wasn't intentionally brutal with her, but the results were the same.

Afterwards, she felt hollow and battered.

Nothing like the way it had been with Matthew. And Emma's heart wept silently, the only tears she could weep. She wept because she still felt human inside; still wanted to be loved like a woman, caressed and cherished like a woman. Not like vampires love. She didn't want to live like this. With them.

But what other choice did she have?

When he was done, telling her he'd leave her alone to rest, he disappeared the way he had come. As if it had never happened. Emma would always know it had, and she was sure it would be the same for all the coming nights until Stephen grew tired of her, or until one of the other male vampires decided to fight Stephen for the right.

With all her powers, she was just a pretty prize to be fought over. As helpless again as she had been back out in the world, before she'd become a vampire; she'd tasted freedom just long enough not to want to buckle back down to a woman's age-old slavery. All her life, from her father, husband, and art director on, she'd been held back, held down. She couldn't bear to become that helpless woman again. She'd rather die.

Matthew had never treated her like that. With him, always, she had been an equal, or more.

It took Emma a long time to calm down, to curb her insane wish to just get up and flee from the cave and the vampires, the kind of life they represented. Yet she knew that she wouldn't get too far. Their maniacal pride and their paranoia of her turning against them would send them after her in full force and fury.

It took her a longer time to fall into a half-sleep. The only kind of sleep she seemed to be able to steal since she'd become a vampire.

She woke to the sound of the pack leaving the cavern.

It must be night. But when she tried to move, she slid back down. Everything she'd been through had taken its toll. Not just physically. She had no desire any longer to do anything. Life wasn't worth living. This way.

Someone was standing over her. "The pack's leaving now, Emma. To run . . . to seek out a village where there are still humans left alive for us to feed upon." Stephen's voice, intimate because of their new relationship. "But tonight you stay and rest."

He bent down and set a large ceramic bowl on the fur close to her. Something sloshed around in it, foaming an ebony stain along the rim. In the dark she could see the ivory flash of his fangs.

His fingers stroked her cheek, then her thigh, down her leg. Emma recoiled from his touch. He didn't seem to notice.

"Sustenance, my sweet Emma. Drink. Get your strength back. You're very weak. We haven't much in reserve any longer, but I'll share my portion tonight with you.

"And soon, when you have your strength back, you'll hunt with us."

Then the shadow that was Stephen was gone.

Emma heard the pack's brooding cries weave away into the night. Hunting humans.

Had they really left her alone? Stephen must be

very sure of his hold on her—or he was sure of the pack's hold on her.

She leaned over and dipped her finger into the bowl and brought it to her lips.

Blood.

Human blood.

God, she wanted to drink every sweet drop of it! She was so hungry. She thought of Matthew. Of her old life, of her promises. Her mind clouded. What should she do? She knew that if once she succumbed to the drinking of human blood, she'd never go back.

No . . .

Emma gently picked up the bowl, rose to her knees, and then to her feet, quietly made her way from her bed and out into the main cavern, up to the burning fire, and dumped the contents into it. The flames licked up the blood greedily as Emma's mouth watered. She leaned against the pit, and a million images crowded into her exhausted mind.

The old world. The life she'd once had. Her friends and family. She must have cried out, the anguish was so heavy. She wanted it back so badly . . . but, she realized with a shiver of guilt, she wanted it back with Matthew.

She looked around, thinking the cave was empty, that no one had seen or heard her. The cavern was silent. The shadows flickered on the walls around her like a macabre and invisible audience. Judging her. Condemning her.

You don't belong here. You aren't one of them.

She explored the cave, peered into its corners.

"Ah, so you're awake after all?"

She jumped.

It was Stephen.

"You didn't go with them?" She was unsettled by his sudden appearance. Had he seen her empty the

233

bowl? Heard her cry out? Read her mind?

"No. Someone always stays . . . to protect our home." He looked around him. Then his gaze came back to Emma. For the first time, Emma caught just a glimmer of compassion. If she had to belong to one of them, he was a good choice. He was the best of the lot, she decided in that moment. The best, but still not like her; not like Matthew, her mind echoed.

"And I wanted to be here when you awoke. I just didn't think you would be up so soon. You're very weak. The hunger has been eating on you for quite a while, I'd say. You need to feed. Or you'll die, Emma, that I can promise you. A slow agonizing kind of death, unknown to our mortal counterparts. The hunger will eat you alive like a hellish cancer."

Unfortunately, Emma knew he was speaking the truth.

She sat down next to the crackling fire, her weakness finally asserting itself. "Thank you for the . . . blood. You shouldn't have gone without for me."

He just looked at her. "You're welcome . . . for what good it'll do," she thought she heard him mutter, but not unkindly. "You'll need much more.

"Looking around, were you?"

She forced her voice into an unfelt pleasantness. "I just wanted to stretch." Crossing her legs she watched the vampire settle his large bulk on the furs next to her.

"And curious, too? Like the rest of us. This must be all quite a jolt to you. Finding us. Not to mention what you've gone through since Byron turned you."

And even before that. Emma smiled faintly. Though it wouldn't have crossed Stephen's mind that she'd had it even harder when she was still human.

"I still remember what I went through . . ." Then he fell silent.

"Yes?" she urged. She really wanted to understand them, glean any goodness in them she could. After all she had learned, a tiny part of her still wanted to give them one last chance. Since she was there, and it didn't look like she was going anywhere else anytime soon.

He closed his eyes, pursed his lips. "Never mind. We aren't much for tender reminiscing. We must live in the present, or go insane, Emma." As if he was telling her something important.

She made no comment.

"You know some of the others want to get rid of you."

So it starts.

Emma's hair prickled across her arms. "They told you?"

"They didn't have to."

No, she guessed not.

"Emma, you're not like us. You know that. They know it. There's more to being one of us than just having the hunger and the powers." Stephen's strong-planed face turned away from her.

"And I sense—they all sense—that as of yet, you have no concept whatsoever of how great your powers really are. You burn brightly, Emma, like a candle among us. You could be one of the brightest . . . or you could be a formidable enemy."

"Why do they hate me?"

He let his gaze slide away from her, and confessed in a whisper, "You have something most of us lost long ago."

"What?"

"Love of life. A thirst for it. You still *care*. The youngest," he stressed, "the very youngest of us is over four hundred years old. We no longer remember what it was to be human, like you do. Vulnerable.

235

Happy, sad, or even in love. Oh, we have sex, but it is merely lust." Emma wondered if he was referring to what had passed between them just hours ago. It made her look at him differently.

"We have lost belief in everything, but our own petty needs. It's not a real life. We've seen and done things you will never be able to imagine . . .

"We're jaded. Or warped. Worse, some of us are just evil." He had picked up a twig that had burst from the fire, and he tossed it back in with a twirl of his hand. "We really don't want to go on living any longer, but haven't the courage to end it.

"You'll find that the longer you live, Emma, the more afraid of death you will become. But you'll run like hell from it — and, eventually, out of fear, from life itself. So . . . they envy you."

"They shouldn't."

"And the other reason they dislike you, is that to them, Emma, you're still more human than vampire. Your ways are still human. Your thinking."

"They're not going to let me stay, are they?"

"They haven't decided yet. But, on the other hand, we can't let you leave, either. You know too much. Seen too much. Catch twenty-two. We've had our share of traitors through the years, always with disastrous results. Betrayals. So Emma, you had better fit in. Become one of us."

He was forewarning her.

She nodded. "Thanks for the warning."

They sat in silence for awhile, until he murmured, "I can't believe Byron is gone.

"He was so strong. I remember the last time I saw him . . . in Athens . . . oh, it must have been around the turn of the century. Such a country gentleman in his sprawling villa on the hill, feeding on all those naive peasants." He was lightly rubbing his leg, growing maudlin. Reflective. Something he'd said that vampires never did.

"They worshiped him. Never suspected for a moment that he was the one killing all their children."

His words made her sick, but she leaned back and listened as he talked about Byron and the others, and the atrocities they had gotten away with through the centuries. Their war with man was an ancient, rancorous one.

Finally he came back to her. "So . . . tell me about your adventures. Tell me about the last nine months, Emma, and how you managed to survive."

Emma told him. How Byron rescued her, butchered all the brutes who had tried to beat and rape her, and how he had made her a vampire.

"You had the glow," he shook his head knowingly. "Not many humans have it. It's how we can determine—usually—if a human is susceptible to turning."

"The glow?" Emma questioned, hiding her excitement. She recalled Matthew's appearance, when she saw him in her wolf form.

"So that's what that bluish aura is that surrounds some humans when I'm a wolf?"

His eyebrows shot up. "So you do know about that little secret, do you?"

"Yes," Emma fibbed, wanting to make him think that, so she could pry more out of him.

"It's rare, too. Not many humans can be turned; that tells us they have a pretty good chance of it. Some chemical in their blood that allows it, we know now."

"Turning?" Emma pressed.

"Since you know most of it, you might as well know the rest. You can turn some humans into vampires by taking their blood every night for seven nights, and giving them back yours—if they have

237

that aura you were speaking of. But *only* if they have that aura. Otherwise, they always die. Humans are weak, you see. Those with the aura are not."

Now I know how to do it! Emma thought. The knowledge was like an unexpected gift. Though why it mattered to her, she didn't know. She'd never see Matthew again anyway.

She went back to her story: About what happened to her after Byron was taken by the plague. The wolf nursing her back to health. How she discovered what her powers were, and that she could change into a wolf herself. She asked him about that; why it had happened after she'd drunk human blood. He informed her that that had nothing to do with it.

"Everything comes in time, as you'll see. The longer you are a vampire, the more things will be revealed. Your strength will grow. Your powers."

Emma said nothing about the reason she'd traveled all the way up to Maine, and nothing about Matthew. And she tried not to think about him, either. Emma knew it was safest that way.

The earth rumbled uneasily beneath them. Matthew had believed the end of the world was coming. Maybe he was right, and all this soul-searching she was going through now would be useless in the end anyway. Let it come, she no longer cared.

Stephen's eyes glittered with the first fear she'd seen. "I've seen eight centuries, Emma. I've seen so much," he confided. "But this—" He spread his arms to encompass what had become of the world. The earthquakes. "I've never seen its like.

"My comrades believe it will pass. In time. That, like everything—wars, pestilence, famine, the dying of civilizations—we will outlive it and go on. Like always." The earth bucked again, and in the distance could be heard devastating explosions.

"But you don't?" She said it for him.

"I'm not sure. The planet has lived a long time, Emma. It's tired. And perhaps, like all things, it's time for it to die.

"Everything should be able to die . . ." he uttered in a melancholy voice. Emma had the impression that he was talking about himself.

And suddenly she wanted answers.

"What are vampires . . . what have I become, Stephen? Tell me. Where did you come from?"

"You? *We*. You act as if you aren't one of us, Emma, when you are, you know."

"All right, have it your way, where did *we* come from?"

He laughed cynically. "It's an interesting story, really. The stuff true legend is made of. We're aliens, if the truth be known. The first aliens."

"Aliens?" she smirked in the darkness. "Are you mocking me?"

"No." He studied her from behind mysterious eyes. "From an ancient civilization, galaxies away. Or so the legend goes.

"We landed here long before man emerged from his caves. But not by accident. It was planned. No one knows now if we were escaping something, or just looking for new territories to conquer, it was so long ago. A fresh source of food. We were always looking for food. And there was food for us here. Humans.

"We could even mate with them, make some of them, with the glow, like us, as I told you before. Though we can never have children, not among ourselves or with humans."

Stephen waved his hand lazily in the air. "Man was easy to prey on in the beginning. So clumsy, so slow-thinking. While we were swift and cunning. We had

239

the knowledge, science, and philosophy of our forefathers . . . unique *talents*. We dominated the savages effortlessly. Were worshiped as gods."

"What happened?" Emma asked.

"We both changed," he sighed tiredly. "Man grew sharper-witted, stronger, built a civilization of his own, and we *forgot* the ancients' technology . . . went backwards. We couldn't reproduce as humans could. That was part of it, too. Only once, maybe twice, in our long lifetimes, Emma, can we take a human and make him one of us. If we are lucky enough to find the right human." He stared into the stygian depths at the back of the cavern where the light couldn't reach, as if his peoples' history was hidden there somewhere.

"And here we are," he spread his arms widely, "back in the very caves man began in." He laughed wickedly then, as if it were all a joke. On them.

"I only know all this, because when I was a young vampire like you—seven hundred years ago—I met one who was old enough that he had known, in his youth, one of the very first ones. One of the last of those who landed in the great spaceship from Vasha. Vasha . . . that was the name of our original planet, Emma.

"Pretty name I've always thought," he mused aloud, but his deep voice stayed emotionless. "A place of purple seas and apricot skies, I was once told. Vasha. Ice glaciers and mountains. No grass anywhere. We lived in the mountains in glass and steel castles, and we fed on creatures much like humans, except they were imbecilic things with the personalities of cattle. Which is why we thought nothing of feeding on earthlings when we arrived . . . until they grew into these sly, intelligent beings that we now hunt. What a surprise to us. Imagine one of your cows picking up a gun or a stake and attacking *you* when you tried to butcher it for meat." Another caustic laugh.

"And we were *many* then. Now . . . we're the last of our kind. Here." His head had come up in defiance, his nostrils flared like an angry bull's. "Contrary to the human's idiotic myths about us, there are ways to kill us. This damned plague will finish us all off in the end, I know it. It reminds me of that old science fiction movie, *War of the Worlds*. Remember?" His face was hard, but his eyes were strangely disconsolate.

"When everything the human race could do to rid themselves of the alien invaders failed, and they were pitifully beaten and on their knees ready to give up . . . it was the earth itself, the very air itself, that saved them; it killed off their enemies." As if in agreement, the earth trembled beneath them one last time, and Stephen produced a sullen smile.

"Maybe there are more somewhere?"

He didn't answer her, just gazed into the fire. For the first time, she saw the centuries play across his face. He grew lost in the flames, as if she weren't even there.

A face so *alien* it made her cringe.

Emma took that moment to slip away. She rose unsteadily from the ground. "Stephen, I'm going back to my bed now." She wasn't as weary as she was anxious to be alone, so she could think.

He only grunted, lost in his own memories. Emma almost pitied him. Almost. She couldn't forget the cold rape of the night before.

She left him there in front of the fire, and made her way back to her corner in the cave. As she passed near the entrance, she thought of leaving. But where would she go?

If she tried to find Matthew, they'd track her down. They'd kill him and her. They'd have no

241

mercy.

They can't let you leave . . . you know about them. Where they are. What they are.

As if on cue, Stephen's steely voice admonished her. "Good night, Emma. I'll watch, so no one will disturb you."

More like, *so you won't escape.*

Emma trudged back to her furs and tried to rest. But she kept seeing Matthew's smiling face in her mind. She couldn't keep it out.

Glaring around at the dank cave, with one of them out there guarding her, her days with Matthew suddenly seemed like heaven.

And now she was in hell.

She was beginning to hate them.

The days swirled past Emma like a fog.

Stephen and some of the others kept bringing her fresh blood. She held out, as hungry as she was, and dumped it back into someone else's bowl, or into the fire.

When the others went out hunting (still not sure of her, they left her behind), Emma sometimes— rarely—was able to sneak out herself and feed on animal blood. It sustained her, but the small amounts left her weakened.

Stephen used her every night, and she gave in to him, but it sent her heart deeper and deeper into a blackness where she felt nothing. The other males leered at her whenever they caught her alone. If it wasn't for Stephen, they'd have had her as well.

It was getting harder and harder to hide her thoughts, her growing abhorrence of them, as they told their endless, gloating stories of cruelties to the humans who had crossed their paths through the

242

years.

No wonder men hunted them. Loathed them.

The animals she needed grew harder to find. Here, like back in Maine, Emma began to see the mysterious sickness that was killing so many of them again reappear. So many nights out in the beautiful woods, Emma would yearn to just keep on going . . . away from the cave and its vicious inhabitants. But she didn't dare. They'd find her wherever she went. Stephen had told her so.

The constant but so far futile search for humans to feed upon, had caused a rising tide of tension in the cave. The vampires were fighting among themselves. Emma knew it was only a matter of time before war would break out among them. There was just too much jealousy and selfishness, too much desperate fear of what was happening, for the pack to bear.

But between the feuds, the sulking, and the fights, Emma began to learn about the vampires. Their habits. Their hatreds. Their unbelievable and colorful pasts. Some of them avoided her, some openly detested and spurned her, some—to help them get their mind off their hunger—treated her like an amusing new toy. A few accepted her, mainly because of Stephen's patronage.

She tried to fit in.

At night after Stephen had finished with her, and left to do whatever it was he did the rest of the night, she'd lie there and listen to the other vampires making love—or what they called making love. They paired off. Fought over their women just like humans. They were lusty beings. Undead or not.

She wondered what would become of her. Growing weaker every day, more miserable. The vampires hungrier and shorter of temper.

The earth beneath them grinding and growling

more each day.

Emma didn't need to be able to predict the future to know that something terrible was about to happen. The whole world felt it.

She wasn't sure exactly how long she'd been with the vampires, when she rounded a dark corner deep in the caves one day, and heard a few of them discussing the human they'd captured out in the woods and killed the night before.

A lone man with long dark hair. Heading this way.

"He was a fighter, that one. Any other time I might have let him go free, just for his bravery. But these are lean times, and the scent of his blood was so . . . overpowering. I couldn't wait to tear open his throat and slurp . . ."

Emma's head reeled, and her vision clouded to black. Her tingling fingers touched the cave's cool walls to support her, or she would have fallen in a heap right there. She'd swiftly drawn back into the shadows of the cave passageway, when she had first heard the nature of their conversation.

". . . not enough for all of us . . . took three to hold him down . . . strong . . . left him in the snow for the wolves to finish . . ."

Their words tore into her heart like a knife, for she believed they were talking about Matthew.

She hadn't wanted to listen. Couldn't not listen. But they mustn't see her, or know she was eavesdropping. She was already a pariah in their midst. Even though she hadn't actually done anything to warrant their hostility, she hadn't done anything to win their trust, either.

She'd made excuses every night not to hunt with them, preferring to hide in the cave. There was no way she could get away with killing and drinking animal blood, if she were with the pack.

She'd wanted time to adjust. To decide what to do. Then she'd overheard them.

"He shot at us," the one named Edgar said dismissively, "but it did him no good."

They'd drank his blood until he'd died.

As they drifted away on their nightly hunt, Emma stood there frozen in the dark.

Could it be that Matthew was dead? Possible. He'd come after her, then. And why should she be surprised at that? He'd loved her.

And she'd loved him.

She wanted to tear after them and demand they tell her everything about the man. To be sure. But that would have been sheer folly. To show that much interest in a human, would give them just one more reason to ostracize her. Mistrust her.

She fled back to her private sanctuary to mourn in peace. To hide. With Matthew's death she felt a part of herself spin away forever. The part that could still see and feel beauty; the part that could still love. The hatred she wanted to feel for the ones who had killed him was tempered with the bitter truth: Now there was no going back. If she didn't fit in with her own kind, she would have nowhere else to go.

She'd be alone. Again.

This time forever.

Her wild eyes gazed into nothingness for a long time. Her mind felt numb, her heart as dead as her lover.

When someone finally entered her space, her eyes traveled up and met with cold assessment. It was Ann, the one whose shoulder she'd ripped up on that first night. The wound had healed days ago, just like Emma's had. Not a trace remained.

"I thought everyone was gone," Emma said in an empty voice. *Except the one Stephen always orders to stay here in the shadows and watch me.*

"They are. I'll catch up. Now that I'm well again. See," she showed Emma the unmarred creaminess of her right shoulder above the edge of her garb, "the shoulder is all healed now. It is as good as new." Her rich voice still had the heady warmth of Spain in it. Her hair, streaked gray through the silver, was neatly tied back into a bun at the nape of her neck. She was a beautiful woman, with wisdom in her eyes. It was hard to believe she was a cold-blooded killer.

That she was five hundred years old.

She'd told Emma that in the early fourteenth century, she'd been a Spanish noblewoman, sold off and wedded at the tender age of thirteen, to a sadistic brute of a count by her two greedy brothers. Her husband had beaten and tortured her for years for his own pleasure. Her brothers hadn't lifted a finger to aid her. When she gave birth to a beautiful daughter, her spiteful husband had the baby put to death, because it wasn't the male heir he'd wanted.

That's when she ran away to the woods, and when the vampire had found her. Later, reveling in the power she had, she returned to her home in the night and killed her husband, as well as her two brothers.

Ann smiled at her. Besides Stephen, she was the one who was most willing to accept her. She held no resentment toward Emma for defending herself that first night, and had let her know it right off.

"I deserved it. I would have done the same if I'd been in your place. And it was the best thing you could have done, otherwise we would have torn out your throat."

At least Ann was fair.

But Emma was in a sour mood. Maybe Ann had

246

been one of the ones who had fed on Matthew. She'd heard the voices, but hadn't been able to tell who they'd been. The cave's echoes had distorted them. "Is there something you want, Ann?"

Ann gracefully lowered herself to the furs. "Yes, there is. I've come to tell you of Chelsea's scheming. She wants to have you exiled or, better yet, killed."

"Why?"

Ann chuckled sarcastically. "Simple. She hates you. Until you came, she was Stephen's first choice. Now everyone knows *you* are.

"That's why you're still here," her voice conspiratorial. Her lovely face gleeful. "You are under Stephen's protection. For now. Chelsea claims you won't kill humans. Won't drink their blood. That you'd turn us all in to them the first chance you got because you're one of the very rare ones that never *turn* completely. You'll always be half-human."

Oh, so that's it, is it?

"She's going to insist you come with us on our raid tomorrow night."

"Tomorrow night?" Emma asked innocently. Stalling. She knew what Ann was getting at. She'd be a fool if she didn't know.

"Yes, a populated village has been found. A village of Others . . . just waiting for us. For once," Ann's eyes were glazed with hunger, her small frame taut with anticipation, as she licked her lips around gleaming fangs, "our empty bellies will be full."

She looked at Emma sharply. "And Chelsea will make sure that if you refuse to go . . . or if you do not join in the raid and the killing, she will destroy you without a moment's hesitation."

"Why are you telling me this?"

Ann stood. "Because I hate that conniving bitch Chelsea. She always seems to get her way. Even now

247

she is one of those who want to leave the safety of the caves. She thinks we should pair off — she and Stephen, of course — and divide, go out into the wilderness as in the old days. That would surely be the end of us. I believe, as Stephen does, that strength lies in numbers now. Times have changed. Chelsea hasn't.

"And . . . long ago she and I crossed paths. She hurt someone I loved dearly." The woman's eyes flashed with an old hatred. "I owe her, you might say."

Emma's broken heart didn't care about anything Ann had said, but her brain wouldn't let the warning go so easily.

You want to be alone again? Matthew's gone. They're all gone. The world you once loved is gone. Forever. What else have you but the pack now? What else?

You must fit in, Emma, Stephen had warned her. *Fit in or die.*

And the need to survive, as always, was stronger than her damaged heart.

She'd go with the pack tomorrow night, and she'd kill. She would. She must forget being human, forget the world she'd once known, the people she'd once loved. Forget Matthew. Forget her ridiculous promises. Promises made to be broken.

She was a vampire, and damn it, it was time she accepted it. All of it. What were humans to her?

The Others, she thought with feigned disgust. Her enemies. Her prey.

"Well, are you going to come with us tomorrow?" Ann wanted to know.

Emma came out of her angry brooding, and replied softly, "Yes. Tomorrow I'll come." It was time.

Ann seemed pleased as she left.

Emma sank down to her bed, her mind and heart at war. Her mind won.

"Damn you to hell, Matthew . . . for leaving me here alone. For not being stronger than them. For not making it here to rescue me. Damn you!" she hissed in a whisper, pounding her hands against her thighs, her heart-rending grief giving vent to silent rage.

She was not going to spend the rest of her life alone.

She was going to become one of them.

One of the vampires.

She was sick of starving, hurting . . .

She was so hungry!

Eighteen

Hands were shaking Emma awake. The world was uneasy. Another earthquake. Not so bad, this time.

"Come on, foundling, it's time to go. Time to feed," the voice was a woman's; the touch rough. Emma's eyes were adjusting. A woman with no hair, a scarf wrapped around her head gypsy fashion. Dressed all in red. Burning eyes. A cruel smile. Kathryn.

"The big hunt, Emma. We haven't fed on fresh blood in so many nights, I've lost count. Any of us. I can see you're starving . . . we're all starving. But tonight, at last, we break our fast, and we'll dine well. We've found a village . . . with lots of people in it. At least ten families. Maybe thirty or forty of the Others."

Families?

"More people there than we've seen in a long time. It'll be quite a night, Emma, great sport, and we can all gorge ourselves." My God, the creature was drooling. She pinched Emma hard. Emma wanted to slap her across the room for it, but held back her ire. This vampire, Chelsea's sycophant, already disliked her, no sense in making her a full enemy. Kathryn was pushing her on purpose, probably also on Chelsea's orders.

Gorge ourselves. Revulsion flooded Emma on one level, but her hunger leapt up like a vengeful albatross on the other. She no longer wanted to fight it. She wanted to give in to it. See what it would feel like.

To kill her own people. To be one of the pack.

Now that Matthew was gone forever, there was no other place for her in the world, but here, with them.

Yet, gazing up into Kathryn's sadistic eyes, Emma still experienced loathing. Why? She kept her doubts to herself. *I'm becoming very good at it,* she thought smugly.

Emma struggled to her knees in the dimness of candlelight, her brain feverishly trying to make connections. She'd been dreaming that she was still with Matthew in that little house in the woods. A lovely dream. But only a dream.

Don't think about Matthew! No, it's all right now. Matthew was dead. Dead. They can't hurt him now. They can't touch my memories, either. Her head spun, her senses blurred . . . where was she?

"You're with us," the woman jeered, and shoved at her again. "Come on, weakling, get up. This time you're not staying behind."

By Chelsea's instruction, no doubt. Kathryn couldn't think for herself usually.

"No one is. We need every set of fangs for the coming battle. The humans are barricaded in their stronghold; they have weapons."

"Weapons?" Emma mocked cynically. She was wide-awake now, shivering, but not from cold. Nerves. She knew this was coming, had prepared for it, or thought she had.

"Nothing we can't handle, of course."

Kathryn tapped her foot impatiently, anxious to be on the move, her arms folded across her chest. "You come—now—or we'll tear you to pieces." Emma could tell by the woman's voice that she would like that just fine.

"Come on! We're gathering the troops and leaving in minutes." A whoosh of air and the vampiress was no longer there.

Outside Emma's tiny room, she heard the commotion. The snarling and growling of animals. They were changing into wolf form, preparing for the raid.

Emma dragged herself from her lair, so weak from lack of nourishment that she could barely move. Her appetite felt like a raging, wild beast in her veins, demanding fulfillment. Demanding blood.

One part of her was fighting with another part: *What's wrong with you? You've made all the other transformations. You're with your own kind. It'll be easy to follow them . . . do what they do. So natural.*

You are what you are . . . and this, as you've learned, is a horrible new world. Survive. You must survive. You must kill what vampires kill. Drink what vampires drink.

And Stephen was correct, animal blood over an extended amount of time kept her just existing. Barely. She wasn't as strong as she had been in the beginning with Matthew. Soon she wouldn't be able to crawl from place to place, and then the pack would finish her off. Survival of the fittest.

She moaned, burying her face in her arms and leaned up against the granite wall.

She already saw so many dead humans' faces . . . all the people she'd known and cherished in that other life of hers. Matthew's. Danny's. Her children's. Larry's. The people she had worked with. All those dying faces through the Rover's windows as St. Louis consumed itself in ashes, flames, and water.

Someday would her mind be filled with all the faces of her victims as well?

Mustn't think like that.

Those people in that village they were going to tonight. They might just be cattle to these predators, but they were feeling, thinking, sentient creatures—human beings.

How could she kill them?

The pack was whimpering in the main cavern, anxious to be on the move. Hungry.

How could she not?

"Emma?" a husky voice commanded through the dark to urge her out. Stephen. "We're waiting." She had nowhere to go. Trapped.

Emma staggered through the passageway and faced the pack. Shimmering rubies in silver fur faces. Huge shaggy beasts from hell. Teeth and fangs gleaming white. Death on four paws.

Her judge and jury. Her guards. Her new family.

Emma changed faster than she ever had. Without thought. Second nature already. It felt good. She was stronger as a wolf, even now.

She watched the pack fly by her with wolf eyes, and engulf her, hauling her along like a fish on a hook.

Out of the cave and into the pitch-black winter's night, through the ice-crusted woods, paws clicking and slipping across the frozen snow, the pack ran, accompanied by three or four timber wolves. The mist was so thick, it was like swimming through cold pea soup. A light drifting snow curdled around them.

Emma had trouble keeping up. They were all more robust than she. Better fed. She kept bumping against furry heaving sides, stumbling. Sharp teeth nipped at her, moving her up and on. A dream . . . it's like a dream, she kept telling herself. Am I really going to become one of them tonight? Am I really going to become a monster?

The miles sang under her bloody paws. *If you don't feed, you weaken. You die.*

She didn't want to die.

Emma tortured herself about what she'd do when they got there.

They came to an ice-covered river, and the pack milled around on the bank for a few seconds, then the lead wolf—Stephen—gingerly padded out onto the glimmering surface, and the rest trailed behind like lemmings. Except Emma. She held back just a little . . . she heard something.

Something. Don't go on the ice. Don't . . .

Then Ann was beside her, teeth sharp in her flank. *Move.*

No. Emma dug into the ground, slashed back, missing, and howled.

The fringe of the pack turned to glare at her.

The ice had begun to split; short whiplike cracks ripped the stillness of the night, as the wolves in front of Emma slid back wildly toward shore. The bulk of the pack followed her.

Stephen, stranded in the middle of the small frozen river, began to growl low in his throat and found himself abruptly dunked, yowling to the night skies, into the choppy water, as the others scattered to avoid the same fate. He struggled at the edge of the hole, bobbing up and down in the icy black water, as the pack howled on the shore in panic. Unlike the others, Emma watched his struggle from the bank silently.

He painstakingly worked at it until he'd clawed his way out. When he made it back to firm ground, the other wolves licked the icy water from him. A tribute.

And on they raced, crossing the solid river further down where it was narrower and safer. This time they all made it.

Emma smelled the village long before they clambered the last hill and reconnoitered the shacks below them. A small country town that had somehow survived. As usual the clouds obstructed the stars and the moon, but wolf eyes could see the human figures huddling before the fires through the cracked windows. See the pens of farm animals, cows, sheep, some chickens.

Something nagged at her memory, though: Another scent underlaid all the rest. Where had she encountered that odor before — and what was it? Her hunger was too far out of control to allow her to place it, and later she would recall that.

Thirty lupine eyes contemplated the feast below, canine tongues lolling over sharp fangs. Fifteen animal minds furiously wrestled with the quandary of how to lure the humans from their shelters.

The settlement was a snug collection of crude wooden cabins. Smoke escaped from chimneys and bled into the black sky. Rambling corrals encircled all the cabins and various other tiny buildings. From the sounds emitting from them, they housed the domesticated livestock. Goats, sheep, chickens, and horses. Cattle clustered together along the sides of the houses to evade the chilling wind and drifting snow. It was a scene right out of another century. Even Emma's wolf senses told her that what she was looking at was humanity regressing.

The cabins looked flimsy enough to tear down with their teeth.

Stephen growled low in his throat and, tossing his head, led the rest of the pack back over the rise. He changed swiftly back into human form behind a copse of wind-swaying trees in the wintry night.

The others followed suit, including Emma, until they were all crouched on the ground around their leader. Naked. Waiting. As the wind wailed around them.

"I have it . . ." his voice was still husky from the change, half-growl. "The humans will die for their

255

animals. So to get them out of their homes, we threaten their animals. Simple."

Simple. They changed back.

The pack slunk up the hill, over it, and moved in.

They slithered under and over the slatted fences like crazed rats, and began to attack the bellowing cattle; some of them crashed the thin barn doors down and went for the sheep and horses in the rickety barns. The fracas would have woke the dead.

Emma went along with the flood — Chelsea right behind her, breathing down her neck — and found herself slinking along the side of one of the dwellings. She heard some familiar noises coming from within, and she stood on her hind legs and peeked into the small window. Through the curtains she could see a man yelling at a woman, grabbing his coat and his gun. Apparently he'd heard the commotion. There was a young boy sitting at the table, his face horror-filled; the table still set out for a meager supper. Such a sweet-looking child.

Emma jumped down from the window and ran for the nearest lean-to, where she could hear sheep bleating in terror. She never heard the splintering of the cabin's door or the startled cries of the man, woman, and child as Chelsea and two other of the wolves smashed through and sunk their teeth into them, dragging them down to feed upon.

In the barn the sheep were cowering. Lugging one of them out into the yard, she ripped its throat out; so ravenous she greedily sucked up its spraying, gurgling blood, and gulped it down without second thought. Then, realizing what she was doing, blood dripping from her jaws, she looked around guiltily. The others were too busy killing to have noticed what she had done. Chelsea was gone.

The animals were screaming, stampeding, trying to defend themselves — and the trap had tightened.

Stephen had been right.

The humans had come running out with their guns, pitchforks, and sticks to save their livestock, thinking they were only fighting wild dogs or wolves. They'd hastily thrown on coats over their night-clothes. Sent their dogs out. The dogs didn't last a heartbeat before they lay dead in the blood-spotted snow at their masters' feet.

By the time the humans saw what they were up against—wolves with superhuman strength and a hunger for human flesh and blood—they were already doomed.

The wolves leapt at unprotected throats, ripping them out in chunks; the ravenous creatures brought down women and men without a qualm. They howled in ecstasy as they drank the first fresh plentiful blood they'd had in days.

The human screams and agonized cries of confusion rattled Emma, halting her dead in the middle of the melee and keeping her from attacking, as her conscience battled with her hunger. All her previous intentions of being just a killing machine fled like cowards before a bloody charge.

It was Armageddon. It was a scene from hell. There were families here. *Families.* Children. Everywhere Emma looked, there was carnage. Pieces of bodies. Rivulets of blood sullied the snow her paws trod on. Her senses reeled, her legs swayed under her.

Why were they butchering them? Why were they eating their flesh and scattering the rest all over the place?

And she was torn. She wanted to feed . . . needed to feed—but *something* stopped her. She could feed on animals, but she couldn't bring herself to kill the humans.

A woman in a nightgown and coat battled two of the vampire-wolves with a pitchfork. The wolf that took the curved prongs into its flesh squealed its pain, but managed to squirm off the points, and still jump on the woman, bringing her down . . . and it fed as she shrieked. A man was shredded into pieces by two of the pack, who then ate his limbs and lapped the blood from the hard icy ground.

Emma saw the children eventually emptying from the houses to aid their dying parents. The children died just as the adults had before them.

Behind Emma one of the pack was dragging a small child, a tiny boy with red hair, kicking and crying, from a house. A trail of crimson blood on the snow. The wolf had crashed through a window to get him.

Emma froze, her head hanging. *Children with red hair. Like that family she'd left the food for that night out in the woods.*

She'd had children once. A boy and a girl.

He was crying in pain now, howls that electrified Emma's heart. She began to inch forward, unsure what to do, when a man bolted out of the door of a nearby house with a flashlight and a rifle, his face distorted in rage.

He had carrot-colored hair and a beard. It was the man . . . the family . . . from the camp. Somewhere in Emma's brain she knew it wasn't the *same* man or the *same* family—that had been faraway from here—just people who looked like them, but that didn't change her feelings. It was as if they were that family.

He emptied the gun into the wolf hunkering over his child, then, when that didn't stop it, he ran at it and slammed the butt of the gun against its head, over and over. Yelling at the top of his lungs above the screeching wind. A father fighting for his child.

A small girl ran from the house behind him, crying for her brother, followed by a woman trying to restrain her.

258

Emma couldn't let them die!

The wolf fell back just long enough for Emma to act.

She threw her body over the boy and growled menacingly up at her comrade. *This is mine . . . mine!*

The other wolf—Dean—grinned at her in brothership, and then pranced away leaving her with the prize. There was plenty of prey.

Emma stared at the man, the cowering woman now holding back the girl. He raised the rifle and fired at her. The bullets lodged in her flesh, but didn't bring her down. Bullets alone couldn't hurt her. The man finally stopped pulling the trigger and stared at her in disbelief and shock, cringing back against the woman and the other child. Trying to protect them with his body.

Emma slowly backed away from the still boy at her feet, waiting. She lowered and cocked her head at the boy, and tried to get her message across. Her eyes looked toward the distance. Go. *Go.* At first the man seemed confused. Then she backed away further. The man lurched in to scoop the frail body up, and along with the woman and other child, scurried off into the night.

Emma watched them go, her head lowered, her eyes luminescent, a subtle undercurrent of sadness permeating every move. Now she knew . . . she couldn't kill them. She'd tried, she really had. She just *couldn't.*

And there was Stephen, panting, and scowling down at her with knowing eyes, his jaws clamped firmly around an old woman's bloody wrist. The huge wolf had brought the woman to Emma; his paws held her down on the snow. An offering. *Eat.* The woman was beyond fright, almost comatose, her watery eyes glazed and peering up at Emma, begging for mercy. Stephen stood and watched.

259

Emma placed her paws on the woman's scrawny throat, and bringing out her fangs, made a great show of lowering her head to the warm flesh, pretending to gnaw at the tender throat, to suck. The woman passed out.

Satisfied, Stephen whined approval and bounded off to attend to his own needs.

When Emma was sure he was gone, she lifted her paws and left the woman lying there, unharmed, in the snow.

As the killing went on into the night, Emma dragged dead sheep behind a pile of wood, and fed until her hunger was appeased.

The others were too damn busy feasting to see that she'd fallen away; and later too busy to see her glide silently back among their ranks before they moved out.

Or so she thought.

After they'd had their fill, the pack took a different route, in case they were being followed, and skulked back to the cave through the night.

Most of them barely changed back into their human form before collapsing into deep, sated sleep.

Only Emma was restless. She couldn't get the haunting images of the people's gruesome deaths out of her mind. Their cries. The sounds of the savage killings. She hoped the family and the old woman had gotten away.

Except for those negligible acts of bravery, she had done nothing.

But what could she have done? Warned them? Turned on the pack and fought for the humans' lives? Run away? No, the others would have chased her and brought her down. A traitor.

No, there was nothing she could have done, other than what she had done, little as it was.

But I can't stay with these monsters, I can't, she admitted, her eyes staring at the curtain.

But where else can I go? Even if I find people, I could never live among them. Or could I?

She'd fooled Matthew, hadn't she?

If any people survived.

She thought of the vampires sleeping like the dead so near to her, and she shuddered. Then wondered for the hundredth time why she didn't feel a kinship to them, even partially. Why it disturbed her so much to become like them.

She touched the bloody bullet wounds that were healing. They didn't hurt any longer, her body had dissolved the chunks of metal. *Bullets can't hurt us.* She *had* helped some of them.

By tomorrow the holes would be gone.

Emma was still worrying about her problem when Stephen's terse voice broke through her reverie.

"Emma . . . I know you're awake. We must talk."

The last thing Emma wanted was to talk. With any of them. But Stephen's tone sanctioned no argument.

"Come in," she bid him. After what she'd witnessed that night, she'd have to be vigilant, not let him know how she'd come to loathe all of them. It wouldn't be easy.

Stephen came through the curtain with a candle. "Though we can see in the dark, a tiny glow of light still brings comfort." He settled down next to her, an inscrutable expression on his face.

He was finding it difficult to express his intentions.

"Yes? You came to talk . . . talk."

"I shouldn't be here." He shook his head. "I should follow our rules. Ancient rules."

Emma's face closed. Her heart began to thud. *And what were those rules?*

He put the candle down and looked into her wary eyes. "You're not like us, Emma . . . I sus-

261

pected it from the beginning, but now I'm sure."

"What are you talking about?" Emma breathed innocently.

"Oh, I'm sure you know what I'm talking about. You're clever. Oh, you're special, too, Emma. Strong. I even suspect you have talents besides the usual ones. But I've been a vampire for hundreds of years, and I can spot the ones that *won't* make it."

"And I'm one of those?"

"Yes. But not the way you think." His eyes gazed vacantly ahead of him. His face shadowed. "You have power, Emma. I can feel it in you. But you're a baby in our world. This world." He gestured outside the curtain. "You think you can hide your true intentions, keep things from us . . . well, you can't."

Emma was frazzled, sick at heart, and the last thing she wanted was to play games.

"Stephen, can we discuss this tomorrow? I'm so tired." And that she didn't have to pretend.

"It can't wait," he said through gritted teeth, belligerently. He leaned forward toward her. "I saw what you did tonight, Emma. Or didn't do. You let that old woman go."

"I'd already fed, I was full."

"Emma," he tsk-tsked and moved closer, running his hand along the rise of her breasts. Emma gently took his hand off of them. He moved them back and continued what he'd been doing.

"She was . . . tough."

He laughed skeptically.

Emma deflated. He'd seen what she'd done. How many others had? His hands continued to caress her. Under them Emma tried not to flinch. So it was to be blackmail then? Why wasn't she surprised.

"Emma . . . I saw you helping that family, too." He drew back and really looked at her. She was the most beautiful woman he'd ever seen. Emma looked

262

like them, but she was different somehow. And the stories she could weave.

One night after they'd made love, he'd asked her politely about her earlier life. He'd been bored, nostalgic. Wanted to be entertained. It had been a delightful surprise that when Emma had, under pressure, been forced to begin her nightly stories about her life before becoming a vampire, he'd soon fallen under their spell. Tales of her mundane home life with Danny and the kids. What it was like to work in advertising. Her life as it had been before the final earthquake. He liked her survival adventures as well, but he cared most for the simple stories of her home life. Called them quaint. Emma couldn't figure him out. At times, she had thought, he was almost human. Then had had a good chuckle over it.

"I don't remember my prevampiric life. Or much of it," he'd revealed to her. "So long ago, and such a minuscule time compared to what I've lived since. I'd forgotten what it was to live a normal life." He'd grown silent after that, and had been content to listen to her reminiscing.

He'd nicknamed her his Scheherazade, and had taunted her gently with the name ever since.

Emma had not been amused.

"You're just fortunate that one of the others didn't catch on to what you were doing," Stephen whispered snidely. "They would not have been kind." He should want to destroy her. The others would have, if they'd caught her doing what she'd done tonight. Especially Chelsea.

Emma wasn't like them, maybe never would be. But she intrigued him, amused him . . . and it'd been a hell of a long time since anyone had done that. He didn't want anything to happen to her. Yet.

So she was safe. For now.

"You're going to tell them?" Emma asked nervously.

"Should I?" He drew her to him and stroked her hair.

Emma's head went back and forth. *No.*

"Besides, my little Emma, I'm hoping that in time, you'll see what is best for you, as you have always done before, and you'll accept the life we offer. It's the only life around." His hands were everywhere. He was insatiable. They all were.

Emma remained mute. Relieved that her secret would stay a secret for a while longer. Could he be right? That eventually she'd accede to what they wanted her to be? That she'd kill as cold-bloodedly as they did? *No.* Never.

She shoved Stephen away from her. "Tonight," she wanted to know, her eyes sparking with controlled anger, "in the village . . . why did you have to tear the humans all to bits?"

"Simple, my dear. Do you recall what I'd said to you before, about us having become careless and giving ourselves away? How humans were hunting us?"

"Yes."

He shrugged. "If we just drained all the bodies of their blood, leaving puncture marks on all of them, and left them strewn about like so much discarded flotsam . . . what would the ones who discovered them — if anyone does — believe?"

Emma shivered. She understood all too well. "Vampires."

"Exactly! And they would continue to seek us out. So we muddied the waters a little, so to speak. If they find the settlement the way we left it, cattle and people alike torn apart into bloody hunks, what will they think?"

"Wild animals. Dogs or wolves."

"Clever woman," Stephen congratulated her.

"All right . . . why kill the women? Children? And kill *all* of them, every last one?" Emma could still see the bodies bleeding on the snow. It didn't turn her stomach as much as it would have once, but it still troubled her. Dead children.

"Would real wild animals discriminate?"

"No." He had her, and he knew it.

She wouldn't give up easily, though. "But, Stephen, you yourself told me that mankind is dying out. We both know that. You said that when the humans are gone, we'll be gone, too. So why kill *all* of them? Is that wise?"

This time he almost seemed at a loss, then recovered. "If any had been left alive, they might be smart enough to guess what we really are . . . and . . . and . . . I couldn't have stopped the pack anyway. Their hunger was too great, it'd been too long."

Emma was astounded he'd admit such a thing.

"I thought you were their leader?"

"No. I'm not their leader. Vampires don't bow to anyone. We are separate here. I just happen to be the one with the coolest head. They come to me for advice. They listen to me only when they want to, and I can't make them do anything they don't want to." He laughed cynically.

"Well, then you'd better tell them that things must change," Emma said stubbornly. "They'd better listen. If you kill every human you see, soon there'll be none left." Emma stared at him intently. "All I know is, that times are changing, Stephen . . . you're facing your Armageddon, and if the vampires don't change, find a different way of existing, we'll go the way of the dodo bird. Humans are becoming an extinct species; they have plague, and it kills us. We must change."

Stephen chuckled. "What a bizarre metaphor." She never failed to intrigue him. "But, my dear naive

265

vampiress, we have been around for centuries, and I have no doubt that we'll go on for centuries longer, and probably outlive humans. Wouldn't that be ironic?"

She sighed. He'd just proved her point, but didn't get it. He never would.

"Besides," he said. "Graham has located more prey for us. A whole town this time . . . and if we're careful, we can feed from there for weeks, maybe months."

Appalled, Emma had to fight to subdue her facial expressions as well as her thoughts. A whole town? That meant they'd be going on another raid the next night, and the night after that, and after that. She saw that doomed village in her mind again, heard the screams, saw the slaughter. She couldn't go through that again, much less over and over. She couldn't. Wouldn't!

"Emma, by the way, why *did* you let that family and that old woman go tonight?" Stephen was asking her.

"You drink the blood I give you, but you won't kill. Why?"

So he didn't know that she'd been dumping the human blood. Hadn't figured out yet that she snuck out to kill animals whenever she could, usually during the day when they were all in their sleep. She imagined after centuries of hiding from the sunlight, their habit was harder to break. While she could come and go almost as she pleased, because the clouds obscured its light from the earth.

She had to lie, she knew she did. The look in his eyes. "I'm having a hard time getting used to killing. You've been this way for centuries. Not me. For me it's been only months. And before that . . . I was one of them."

"So, what you're saying is what I've already deter-

266

mined, you just need a little more time, huh?" He seemed pleased that she saw it the same way he did.

"Yes." *If he'll swallow that, let him. I'm tired, sick of all of them. I just want to be left alone.*

Stephen narrowed his black eyes at her in the candlelight. Emma had the feeling that he could see right through her. He knew she was lying, but for his own selfish reasons, was playing along with her.

"Emma, just remember what I told you . . . you think you can exist on animal blood. You're wrong. Oh, it'll do in a pinch. But just for short periods. That's all.

"If you don't drink human blood, eventually you'll sicken." His tone was meant to frighten as he muttered, "It's hideous what happens to us when we deny what we are.

"And it's hideous what the pack will do to you if they ever catch you doing what you did tonight," he warned her.

She looked down. There was blood on his clothes. He reached out and took possession of her body again with his hands. His skin was cold to the touch. He began to slide her tunic off her shoulders, let it fall around her waist so she was half-naked.

"You've been alone far too long," his tone was a soft caress. He tugged her clothes off the rest of the way. Emma didn't protest. What good would it have done?

He didn't know about Matthew. He'd never know. Emma pushed thoughts of her dead lover back into the recesses of her mind, as her new lover lowered his head to her breast.

She played her part again. He took her body with an appetite equal to his blood hunger, and then left her when he was done. She was more than usually grateful when he did.

Outside Emma's sleeping quarters, Chelsea had already slipped away from her earlier hiding place. She'd heard everything that had transpired between Stephen and the hated usurper. So she'd been right all along? The foundling couldn't kill. She wasn't one of them, and she'd never be one of them. A half-changer. She'd always be part human, and therefore sympathetic to their enemies. Sooner or later, her kind always betrayed them. Would bring dissension and disaster down upon them.

She had to find a way to get rid of the bitch. That's all there was to it. Chelsea swiftly cut through a shorter passage to get to her sleeping place before Stephen got there. She smiled wickedly in the cave's belly.

Stephen still spent part of the sleeping time with her. She still had a hold on him that way. The new bitch was just a novelty that would soon wear off. Very soon, if Chelsea had anything to do with it. She made it back to her bed just before Stephen arrived, and she was there with open arms. Even for a vampire, he was endowed with the most insatiable sex drive she'd ever seen. When she was rutting with him, she almost felt alive again.

There was no way that wishy-washy bitch would ever take him away from her. She'd see to it. Tomorrow night.

Emma lay alone on the furs in her little world for a long time after he'd left, her mind exhausted but busy. Her stomach felt bloated from all the animal blood, her mind bloated with the images of the mutilated bodies back in the village. The looks on the peoples' faces as they died.

And they were going to do it all again the next night . . . only on a grander scale. A whole town.

No, not again. Never again!

She buried her face in her arms, disgust and guilt overwhelming her. She was in hell with devils — with enemies, she knew it.

The undeniable truth hit her. She had to get out of there. *Now.* It might be her only chance. With the vampires as full as ticks and in a dead sleep, maybe she could get far enough away so they'd never find her. Escape them before their vile evilness corrupted her heart and soul, or what was left of them. Before the next massacre.

How many more times could she deceive them?

The difference between her and them was that they reveled in killing people, seeing them suffer. They fed as much on the fear and pain they caused as the blood itself. Time did that. How much time did she have before she became like them? *They were evil.* This evil was engrained as deeply in them as the need for love, being good, was embedded in her.

She would never be like them, and they would never allow her to exist any other way.

It was better to die. Or to live alone for eternity rather than be forced to kill the way they killed. What was the use pretending that she could somehow, someday, fit in, when she knew she wouldn't.

She had to get away, before they realized that, too. Then the trap would spring shut, and they'd destroy her. She had no doubt that they knew ways to do it. Painful, lingering ways. It could happen tomorrow . . .

She had no choice but to leave. Now. It'd be her best shot.

Emma waited just until she was sure they were all in dead sleep, and then stealthily crept through the cave. No one had stayed up to watch her. God must be smiling down on her.

Soon she was back out in the cold night. Free again.

As the snow fell in heavy flakes around her, the lone silver wolf took off running. Back toward the United States. Back home. Emma decided to go back to Illinois. There was nothing up here for her but the vampires, and she wanted to put as many miles between her and them as she could. Light years would be best, she grinned in the night, happy to be away from Stephen, his lust, and all the others, but continents would have to do. She didn't think they'd follow her that far.

If she was to be alone the rest of her life, she might as well be alone in a place she'd once loved. Where she'd once had family, a husband, children . . . memories.

Maybe she could find a nice home out in the woods somewhere, near the places she had once known.

Maybe, she could even find Friend and his pack, and then she wouldn't be totally alone.

Her hopeful thoughts flew ahead of her racing body through the night, right behind the fear of pursuit. She ran faster.

Nineteen

The places where the bullets had rammed through her ached. But the pain was lessening with every mile. The holes were just faint outlines now.

Emma was leaving tracks, but there was no help for it. She needed to get as much distance between her and the other vampires as she could get, as hastily as she could. There was no way she could be sure they were or weren't following.

Now, if she could have changed into a bat, as Stephen alleged some vampires could do . . . she could fly. No such luck. So she plodded on four legs through the clinging whiteness through the night and the next day, as weary as she was. Sooty clouds hid the sun like all the other days, and Emma kept in shadow as much as possible, and kept moving. She must have come to the limit of her endurance, her strength, as a vampire, because she felt so awful she could have been human again.

Stephen had cautioned that animal blood was not enough. But, she told herself willfully, if being half-alive was the price she had to pay . . . damn, she'd gladly pay it . . . rather than be like them.

The frozen tundra stretched on for horizons. America didn't even look like herself anymore, Emma brooded, as she journeyed the plains and the forests. She saw no people anywhere. She ached to rest, to

271

burrow into a dry hole somewhere and hibernate.

You can rest once you're out of their reach. Once you are far-away from here and safe. From them.

She still found animals long dead from the mysterious sickness, but Emma was lucky and also found some alive and healthy. As Matthew would have said, a good spirit must be watching over her.

She retraveled the same route she had come on the way up, or as near to it as she could remember. It had been night, and she'd been terrified, running for Matthew's life with the pack nipping at her heels. But her senses were animal sharp, and she seemed to have a gift for direction since the change. Soon she came to the very place she'd left Matthew. Was it only weeks ago? It seemed longer. Another life.

He'd followed her. He'd loved her. He'd died for it.

For the first time, she could stand to think about their time together without heart-wrenching sorrow. Remember the adventures they'd had together, the love. Strangely, the memories comforted her through the long days and nights of her flight.

She stood on the very rocks where she'd fled Matthew, and noted that she could no longer see the tip of Cadillac Mountain out in the ocean. The water had taken more of the land. After watching the roiling sea for a short while, she moved on, retracking their earlier route. She wondered if Matthew had kept her clothes and her knives, where they were now. Most likely buried in snow next to the remains of his body. She had no clothes with her, of course, to change back into, so she just stayed in wolf form day and night. Though, she thought wryly, what difference would it make if she wandered around buck naked . . . there was no one to see her.

Awareness of the vengeful obsessiveness of the vampires, especially Chelsea, their possible attitude toward being outwitted, and the boredom that made them do self-destructive acts just for the thrill of them, pushed her past her limit.

She wouldn't be surprised if they were chasing her. That they might even travel to hell and back, just to have something exciting to do. Just to teach her they were as omnipotent as they had pretended to be.

She couldn't let them catch her.

Then her intuition was overloaded with the suspicion that something very bad was about to happen. Something horrendous. It'd been dogging her for weeks, and she'd had *that* feeling before. It was in the air; she was aware of it in the other creatures she encountered, or fed upon, as well. Fear. The earthquakes were a constant now. At least two or more a day.

She left the coast line behind, because the oceans were coming in on leviathan tidal waves and ravishing, eating the land, like a monster from the deep.

Emma had never seen anything like it. Within a day, half of Maine was submerged in water, and more every hour, she skittering right before it. The plague village where she and Matthew had seen the burnings was no longer there. The ocean had reclaimed it. Were any of those poor wretches still alive? She doubted it.

Pushed to a frenzied haste, by something she couldn't explain, she only let herself rest the few hours that were the heart of the day, and then was back on the run.

Pressing inland.

Another premonition was what ultimately tipped her off: she was being followed. One of those extra gifts of hers that Stephen had referred to? Like when she knew before all the others that the ice of the river was going to crack under Stephen the night of the

273

raid. She felt the same way. By nightfall, as the world went black, she knew it unequivocally.

The pack was somewhere behind her. She could smell them.

She sped through the night, not even stopping to feed or rest, and then doubled back as a feeble imitation of dawn was breaking.

She was going to take a chance. During the day, when the vampires were at their weakest, maybe even resting somewhere, she'd find where they were . . . and then sneak past them and go another way. Carefully camouflaging her trail if she could. Or she'd hide somewhere. Even if she couldn't succeed in throwing them off her scent, perhaps she could confuse them long enough to get a better start.

She knew she was close to them, and then the human screams in the distance began. A human in extreme danger. Wolf snarls almost drowning him out.

Emma sped through the close-standing trees misted in the end of night. Sped toward the sound of the fray. Not knowing why she felt the urge to do so, just following her instincts. She broke through to the top of a low hill and there below her . . . one lone man surrounded by the pack. The wolves were attacking him. One against many. Something about the way he was standing alerted her. The ramrod-straight back. The gray, borrowed coat, tattered around the edges. Packs lying next to him in the snow. Old pump shotgun held so familiarly at his shoulder. Long dark hair . . .

It couldn't be.

The vampires were slithering in for the final kill.

He shot two of them, but since his bullets weren't silver, the wolves just picked themselves up from the crushed snow and kept coming. The man reloaded. They were circling him now, drawing the noose tighter, lower jaws down and open as their long canine

274

tongues flicked over fangs, lips drawn back in fierce grinning snarls, their eyes filled with blood lust and greed. Emma recognized them. Stephen . . . Ann . . . Chelsea . . . Peter . . . Dean, and perhaps Graham. Where were the rest of them?

Graham lunged at the man and sprawled him, bleeding, in the snow, gun still clutched in his hands. There were scratches down the right side of his cheek ending in a mutilated ear, blood everywhere, and his clothes were in tatters. The man groaned as he moved. They'd torn up his legs, trying to cripple him so he couldn't run. Rolling away from the snapping teeth, he laid low to the ground and tried to get a bead on Graham with his gun. *They'd been playing with him. Torturing him.*

But, damn, he was a fighter, and hadn't given up like most would have.

Then another wolf came at him from another direction. Stephen.

Emma felt a deep stab of admiration and pride, as the human let out a war cry of his own, and slammed the butt of his gun into an attacking wolf's head, sending the animal spinning to the ground.

It was that war cry that sent Emma's heart humming with joy, and answered her question.

The man *was* Matthew! He *wasn't* dead. Emma had been wrong. The man whose death she'd clandestinely overheard being discussed by some of the vampires hadn't been Matthew at all. It'd been someone else entirely. Matthew, her Matthew, was there in front of her eyes, fighting for his life with her enemies. They'd kill him as easily as they'd swat a pesty fly.

Not giving herself time for further thought, she acted. Emma raced wildly down the steep hillside toward the predatory yowls, the shouting, and the gunshots.

What the hell had he been doing out here anyway, she fretted to herself. Had he been tracking her and come across the pack? While *they'd* been coming after her? Yes, that had to be it. Somehow their paths had crossed. She frowned trying to figure it out. Then the answer came, so simple it almost slapped her in the face.

He'd been looking for her. He'd never given up.

He just happened to come across them first. Or he had been trailing *them* . . . hoping they would lead him to her, or hoping she was with them. *Oh, Matthew.* Emma's heart swelled with love. *You really did come for me. You really were strong enough. I just gave up on you too soon, left too soon.*

And what miracle had brought her to this very place at this exact moment, she didn't know and didn't care. She was here and she would save him, or they'd die together trying.

Stephen had picked himself back up, and with a bestial growl, had leaped at Matthew again, this time sinking his teeth into the arm that was steadying the gun. Matthew cried out and fought with the huge wolf, as two others squeezed in for the kill.

And Emma's cautious good sense peaked into a murderous rage she couldn't stop. She burst into the conflict with a blood-curdling howl and went for Stephen's shaggy throat first. He was the strongest, and if she could bring him down, the others might fall back.

The element of surprise is what gave her the edge, and sent the pack into disorder. The vampires hadn't been expecting reinforcements. Especially one of their own kind.

It was enough of a distraction to enable Matthew to get away. And he was shrewd enough to see his chance and take it. He couldn't hope to defeat all six vam-

276

pires, so a strategic retreat was his best option.

He hesitated just a brief second, looking back at her in the middle of the furious battle with agonized eyes — he knew who she was — but she slammed against him, shoving him on his way, and he obeyed her. He ran.

The last she saw of him, he was hobbling toward a line of rocks, leaving a sprinkle of fresh blood from his wounds on the white snow, and glancing back every once and a while at the deadly trap he'd left her in, as if he were still not sure he was doing the right thing by running.

He evaporated into the night, leaving Emma to pay the price. Which she did gladly. Her hellish anger at what they had done to Matthew, and her hatred of all they stood for and all they were, was her only defense against their greater strength. It was enough . . . for a while.

She fought valiantly. She kept them from chasing Matthew down, alternately attacking and falling back, so they'd have to follow her deeper into the woods. Even in her weakened state she turned out to be faster than any of them. Strong and ferocious as any two of them, she couldn't kill them, only maim or slow them. Just like they couldn't kill or catch her — one on one, anyway.

But though she got her revenge — biting off Chelsea's ear, ripping Peter's flank down to the bone and muscle, and doing as much damage as she could to the others as Matthew escaped — they finally outsmarted her. If they couldn't catch her as wolves, then they'd do it another way.

They cornered her in a steep ravine, herded her in, and then formed a tight gauntlet Emma couldn't evade. Changing back into their human shapes they subdued her, and stood over her in the dark, glaring down at her as if she were a slug. Their wrathful eyes glittered coldly.

"Change back," Stephen commanded her, his voice breathless. The gaping wounds she'd inflicted a condemnation. His face mutilated where she'd gotten to him. His eyes slits of fury.

She did. A body slashed and bitten into a mass of cuts and bleeding wounds, she huddled at their feet, half-dead.

"Finish me off . . ." she muttered in an indifferent voice, not meeting their eyes. They would know how to kill her, maybe not with fangs and claws, but in other ways. Knowing it was coming, she welcomed it in a way. No more guilt. No more loneliness. No more being torn between two worlds.

And she'd saved Matthew. She'd denied them their prey, and that gave her great satisfaction.

"No!" Chelsea, holding her ragged ear with a bloody hand, sneered down at her. Her glowing eyes cruel. "I want her to be given the traditional punishment for turning on, harming, one's own kind; for choosing an Other over one of us and allowing him to escape. *I want her to perish in the old way.*

"I want her to *suffer,*" she hissed.

Stephen looked from Chelsea to Emma, and Emma caught the indecision in his impassive gaze.

Emma's heart nearly stopped. She didn't know what Chelsea was talking about, but by the *way* they were talking about it, she knew it was bad.

"Chelsea, is that truly called for?" he sighed.

She turned on him. "What, are you going soft on us, Stephen? Are you siding with a half-changer? A traitor? Would you like to join her?" There was more than an idle threat in the vampire's inhuman voice. There was insanity.

"And especially now . . . you want to release her?

278

Now? When every enemy we can count is one too many?"

Emma realized that there was something else wrong. Something else had riled them to this murderous rage. Again Emma was aware of how few they were. Where were the others?

The rest of the vampires watched him from beneath heavy eyelids. Waiting. Most of them wearing injuries she had administered. They wanted their pound of flesh.

From someone.

Stephen grabbed her by the shoulder and yanked her to her feet. "All this," he growled into her battered face, "for a *human!* You fought us over *him?*" Disbelief mingled with his underlying disappointment.

I had plans for you. Us. You betrayed me, Emma, his thoughts burned into her mind. *You could have been one of us. A special one. It's gone too far. I can't save you. I dare not.*

She remained mute. Uncaring what he'd wanted or what he thought of her.

All for that Matthew . . . that human lover of yours. The one you'd believed was dead. Fool.

Emma's eyes flashed. *You knew about him all the time?*

Yes. I told you you couldn't hide anything from us. Bitter jealousy like bile. *You'd throw your existence away for him? A human?*

She threw her head up in defiance. "Yes. And I'd do it again. You were torturing him." Her hatred was palpable.

"Killing for food — to survive — is one thing, but you do it for sport." Her angry eyes traveled from one soulless face to another, condemning. "You're all monsters. I'd destroy you all if I could. I'll never join you. Never."

"You little *fool.*" He lifted and shook her violently,

279

then flung her back to the ground in disgust.

One of them, Dean she thought, gave her a laugh of pure contempt. "She is hopeless," he muttered, tossing his hands up, and turning away. "Chelsea was right."

Ann said, hurt, "Emma . . . we offered you our protection and acceptance, you ran away like a guilty thief in the night . . . and now this." There was genuine sadness in her eyes, but no pity. No pity at all.

"Yes," Emma exploded, vehemently. "Protection and acceptance—*on your terms*. No! I couldn't stand the way you butchered those poor people that night; couldn't stomach it. And there was to be more. A whole town! No, I'd not be party to it. So I ran away." She didn't say anything about Matthew, that she still loved him. Maybe the others hadn't picked up on it as fully as Stephen had. It might fuel them to go after him even now; knowing hurting him could hurt her far worse than any barbaric punishment ever could.

"I'm not like you," Emma said through clenched teeth. "I don't want to be like you."

"So we've learned," Stephen said with a strange finality. Then he took her by the chin and made her look into his eyes.

"I'm giving you one more chance, Emma. Join us . . . *now* . . . or pay the price."

She shook her head and turned away. Not caring anymore what they said or did. She should have died when her family died. It was past time.

She wasn't afraid to die.

"No! No mercy," Chelsea snarled. "After what she's done. *No mercy*. I don't want her in the pack. What's left of us anyway."

Stephen looked at her in the dark. "That's why I'm giving her the choice, Chelsea . . ."

He pivoted back to Emma, his hand still tight on her shoulder. "That village the other night had the plague . . . all of us but six have become infected with it; have perished or are wasting away with it even as we speak."

Ah, so that's what that stench had been. Plague. She should have remembered. *Just what you deserve,* Emma thought bitterly. A slow, smug grin slid across her lips. "Too bad."

"That's it," Chelsea said with her own gloating smile. "Get rid of her, Stephen. She's trouble. She knows too much about us."

And I'm too great a threat to just turn loose.

"Get rid of her, or I leave," Chelsea threatened.

The other vampires exchanged looks, some of agreement, some unsure. One of them said, "It's our law that she must be punished. Anyone who puts humans above their own kind."

Stephen said softly, "Then do it. But leave me out." He stalked away. He knew what came next and didn't want to witness it.

"Weak stomach, hey, Stephen?" Chelsea snickered. "Don't go too far, my love . . . we'll be ready to leave in a few moments."

Chelsea then told the others, "We have to take her back to the cave first. There's something there we'll need, and,"—here she rested pitiless eyes on her victim, and gestured at hers and the others' nakedness—"I couldn't bring it along, as you can see.

"Take her . . . you know what to do." She nodded at the others and moved in as they did.

They crowded around Emma, held her down, and took turns drinking her blood, until she nearly passed out. As she lay moaning on the ground, her fuzzy mind asked, *Is this it? Is this how they dispose of unwanted vampires?*

Wiping her mouth off, Chelsea bent over and whispered in Emma's ear, "No, my dear, that would be too easy. We're just preparing you for the journey back to the cave. Take some of the feistiness out of you. Act up and you'll get more of the same.

"Now change into your wolf and come along quietly."

Like a robot, Emma found herself following Chelsea's orders. The leeching had befuddled her mind, her will. She changed and watched, swaying and dazed, as the others changed. Then they began the long journey back to the cave, Stephen dogging in their wake, refusing to acknowledge her.

Emma remembered little of it. She loped along, head drooping, in their midst for what seemed like forever. Going where they wanted her to go. Thinking, feeling nothing. In a twilight world where dead people walked along beside her, telling her their secrets. No one she knew, though. Just spooks. Probably all those poor souls that the vampires had slaughtered in that village.

When Emma's mind finally began to uncloud, they had already been back to the cave. The other vampires were dressed, she wasn't, and she was now in human form, trudging behind the others through the snow toward some mysterious destination. Her first clear thought was: *Where are they taking me?*

"A special cemetery on the other side of the woods," Chelsea, who was nudging her along before her, answered the unspoken query. "That's where we're taking you."

Emma, still unsteady on her feet, stumbled. She was so weak. No one aided her. She was having a hard time recalling what she was doing with them. Hadn't she run away from them? Escaped them?

Why did she feel like this? Debilitated, and her memory out of focus. She'd felt like this once . . . back in the sixties, that time when

282

she'd tried marijuana. High as a kite. What a night. She'd never done that again.

Why were they taking her to a cemetery? Why . . . Another layer of confusion melted away, and Emma began to remember. Then wished she hadn't. Her head began to pound along with her heart.

She'd saved Matthew. Attacked the pack. She was going to her punishment. But the whole trip back to the caves, and to this very moment, was still a blank. But it was evening again, almost night. Where had the last days gone? She didn't know.

Shaking her head to clear out more of the cobwebs, she gazed around her. Stephen wasn't with them. That's right, he'd washed his hands of her. She didn't care, she detested him almost as much as the others.

The guard of vampires drove her on through the woods, up a steep hill and down. She tried to ask questions of them, her tongue too big for her mouth. They wouldn't talk to her, just prodded her along like a condemned prisoner heading for the gallows.

They arrived at an old snow-covered cemetery. An earthquake had demolished it at some time, leaving a lot of the graves gaping open, tombstones crumbled alongside. In the dwindling light, the snow gave it an eerie glow. Spidery trees lay like dark webs across the white ground where they had fallen.

One of the vampires stopped for a moment to tear off a part of a stout limb, about five feet in length, and brought it along.

They roughly pushed her over the graves, and up to a vast mausoleum with the name Lawton across its huge stone door.

As she looked up at the forbidding stone structure, Emma's head began to unfog quickly. A surge of strength washed over her, born of fear. *"No!"* she mouthed faintly, her voice still a shadow of its old self, as she began to fight. Strong hands were suddenly there to subdue her and move her along.

Into the cramped blackness of the crypt they dragged her, by then totally aware and kicking and biting like a crazed animal heading for the slaughter table. She didn't waste her breath or her energy talking or pleading for leniency, from them there'd be none. She spent it fighting, but she was too drained, and they were too powerful for her.

The crypt was full of the dead. Large dusty coffins were set into larger stone enclosures like snug-fitting boxes. They hauled her deep into the heart of the mausoleum to an inner chamber, and stood her before a casket.

Three of the vampires held her, as Chelsea dumped out on the ground a blanket-covered bundle she'd tucked into the thick leather bag she had pulled there along behind her, careful to keep it as faraway from her body as she could. Using the stick, she poked at the blanket until she'd uncovered a massive chain. She didn't touch it with her hands once, again using the stick to heft it into the air in front of her. She seemed afraid of it.

"I came prepared." She threw Emma a wicked smile. "This chain is pure silver, Emma. Do you know what that means?"

Emma's eyes opened wide, she knew what the silver chain meant. The old legend: Vampires couldn't stand to touch silver. But her mouth wouldn't move. Her eyes glued to the glittering chain, all she could think was: *They're going to bury me alive. Oh, dear God, no.*

It had always been one of Emma's secret terrors. Being buried alive like Boris Karloff in *The Mummy. Buried alive. Left alone in the dark to feel the air slowly drain away; to claw fingernails and fingertips into bloody stubs trying to escape the confines of the tiny wooden enclosure;*

284

screaming until your voice was hoarse and your throat raw, lips bloody with teeth marks.

But being a vampire gave the act even more unspeakable horror. She'd die excruciatingly slow . . . it would take a long, long time. Alone. Without hope. Forever.

Emma's eyes burned like two coals in the dark, full of hate and panic; her fangs came out as she hissed at her executioners, and tried to lunge free of their grasp. She couldn't.

The chain was silver, and it would hold her, trap her in the wooden box. For eternity.

Chelsea, chuckling with uncontained, malicious glee, pulled over an occupied coffin and opened it. A skeleton in rags holding a cross stared up at them with gaping holes for eyes. Chelsea didn't even bother to empty it, she jerked her head at the three who were restraining Emma, and a moment later they slammed her into the coffin right on top of the earthly remains of the original owner.

Then the hands fell away, and as Emma arched up trying to get out of the coffin, they dropped the chain over her, thrusting her back into the wooden box, like a bug under someone's descending shoe. The chains burnt her skin like heated irons. The smoke and stench of burnt flesh rose into the night air.

Chelsea leaned over and peered down at the captive with a cruel smile. "Let's see how brave you are now, bitch. I'll tell you this because you might not know it . . . it takes months, sometimes *years,* for a vampire to actually die this way." The vampiress ran her slender finger lovingly along the rim of the wooden coffin. The others were lurking back in the shadows, their faces all showing just the tiniest traces, perhaps, of genuine pity.

Don't do this, Emma implored silently. *Don't.*

285

"First your hunger will turn the blood left in your veins into acid that will burn as cruelly as the chains . . . then you'll be awake to watch your own flesh waste away, your hair fall out, and the bones poke through what's left of your parched skin."

No . . . don't leave me like this!

"The last to go will be your eyes . . . but you'll still be aware up until the last second before your body crumbles into dust. And only then will you finally be released to die.

"It could take years in this place." She let her eyes slowly scan Emma's stone prison. "Where your friends in the end will be the very worms that eat you from the inside out." She laughed sadistically, and gestured to the others that it was time to go.

"Goodbye, Emma . . . enjoy yourself."

Don't go . . . don't leave . . . don't . . . don't . . .

Fully awake now and finally finding her voice, Emma wailed unashamedly in panic and terror, as they shut the coffin lid over her, and plunged her into the blackest night she'd ever experienced.

Inside the coffin she felt herself lifted and dropped unceremoniously into the stone sarcophagus; heard the marble lid seal her in for eternity.

Silence. She knew they were gone.

She screamed . . . and screamed . . . and there was no one to hear her.

Twenty

Matthew staggered through the early morning woods, seeking shelter and a place to hide, near fainting from his wounds and loss of blood. Running as if devils themselves were breathing down his neck. As far as he knew, that's exactly what they were.

Those wolves . . .

He had this theory that they weren't real wolves, and after seeing Emma change into a wolf that day on the rocks, anything seemed possible.

Weeks ago, after Emma had run out on him, he'd followed her, her and that large wolf pack she seemed to be running with. Followed the tracks and signs for weeks, until he'd found their lair, a well-hidden cave. Looking for Emma. Worried for Emma.

While he tried to decide what to do that first night as he staked out their cave, the wolves had come barreling out like an angry tornado. He couldn't tell from a distance whether Emma was with them or not, but on a wild hunch, he tailed them, and was soon glad he had. They didn't go back to the cave. Though he couldn't keep up, their tracks were clear enough in the snow to trace even in the dark — with the help of a flashlight.

The next afternoon, their tracks ended at the mouth of another cave. Matthew had caught up with them. He figured they were on a journey to somewhere. A determined journey. According to their tracks, they hadn't veered off for anything, hunting or resting, but had moved in a straight line.

He'd hid himself behind a large rock and guarded the entrance of the cave the rest of the day, catching naps with one eye open until they came out that night. Some of them were acting strangely, stumbling and weaving as they ran off, some dragging behind the rest. They acted sick.

Early the next afternoon, he caught up with the pack again, hibernating in another cave. He watched the entrance, slept some, and again pursued them. They soon outdistanced him, and he again used the flashlight to follow their tracks in the snow through the night.

Where were they going? Why did they sleep only during the day? Didn't make sense to him. Wolves were not usually so nocturnal, especially in such glaciate weather. And most important, where was Emma?

Time and time again the word *werewolves* popped up in his mind.

Was Emma a werewolf? And the wolves? Matthew didn't know.

He tracked the pack for a long time, repeating the same pattern of watching them leave a different hiding place each night—usually a cave but sometimes nothing more than a thick canopy of leaves from overhead joining trees, brambles, and walls of shrubs—and then catching up with them sometime later the next day. He'd steal as much sleep as he could, but they traveled like wildfire, and keeping up wore him out. He ate on the run.

Each night, though, there were less wolves than the night before, until there were only about six or seven left of the original fifteen or sixteen. Once Matthew even checked the cave to see if some were staying behind . . . there was never anyone there.

He must have grown lax, or they had. Gotten too

close. That's when they must have caught on that they were being followed, and laid that trap for him.

The pack had emerged from the frosty mist in the fading dark and had encircled him. Up close, their eyes had glowed with unearthly fire, malevolence. Their movements seemed far too human as they had taunted him, attacked him, tearing little pieces out of him like he was some stuffed scarecrow hung out in a field for their sport. Always one step ahead of him. Emma's image as she'd turned into that silver wolf haunted him as he fended them off.

He'd shot at them, but their bullet-riddled bodies would rise up from the snow and keep on coming. He'd known. A gun or a knife wasn't going to save him.

Werewolves.

His people had had their werewolf legends as well as the white people, but Matthew had never expected to encounter any. He hadn't believed . . . until Emma had transformed right before his eyes, and now these *creatures*. Matthew racked his brain in the little bit of time he had. The Indian belief was that werewolves were evil spirits trapped in human form, and they were almost impossible to kill. You needed silver to kill a werewolf. A silver stake, blade, or bullet. Did wooden stakes work on werewolves? Or decapitation? He wasn't sure.

He only knew that he had no silver anyway, and was fated to die a horrible death—but he'd wreak some havoc with the monsters before they ate him for supper. He was losing and had just about resigned himself to dying, when that other wolf had launched itself into the fight, and allowed him to escape.

And here he was.

He squinted back over his shoulder, his eyes wide and glazed with pain. If he didn't stop somewhere and tie up his wounds, he'd have escaped for nothing; he'd bleed to death. Dead just the same.

Were they coming after him even now? He wasn't sure, and just the thought that they were spurred him on, stumbling and swearing under his breath.

Matthew even now couldn't make sense of what had happened back there, couldn't believe the power and uncanny intelligence of those animals — or whatever the hell they were. They'd been playing with him, and hadn't acted like any wolves he'd ever seen before. The word *werewolves* kept whispering in his ear.

He could have sworn that last wolf had attacked the others on purpose. Why? Matthew experienced the same uneasiness he'd felt when the wolf had come tearing into the skirmish.

To save him?

Something about that wolf had been familiar. It had been trying to help him.

Emma.

That lone wolf had been Emma. He'd suddenly comprehended that. She'd come from somewhere and saved his skin again. He leaned his head back, trying to catch his breath, and not pass out.

Matthew couldn't go another step, the truth and his profusely bleeding wounds pulled him up short. He slumped down against a base of a tree, and laid his gun across his lap. There was more light, so he checked his wounds. His legs were covered in blood, but he didn't think anything was broken. Just deep slashes. He'd seen worse. They'd heal. Using his knife, he slashed a couple of cloth strips from the inside of his coat and used them as tourniquets. It helped some.

He snatched another tense glance behind him, watching the shadows swirling into threatening shapes. He thought he saw wolves slinking at him from everywhere, his adrenaline working overtime.

He was shivering with cold, the gloves on his hands had been tattered in the fight, as were his clothes. His

290

face and ears were numb, but, at least, not bleeding any longer. He clamped his hands under his armpits to warm them. His legs were numb, the blood freezing into a crust. There was ice around his lips. He'd dropped his packs of supplies somewhere back there, when the wolves had first closed in. Gone now. Food. Blankets. Tent and sleeping bags. Emma's clothes and her knives. He was damn lucky to still have his gun.

But guns can't hurt werewolves.

Matthew's thoughts went back to Emma. She'd fought her own kind to save him. Because she loved him. She hadn't abandoned him back there in Maine . . . she hadn't run away . . . she'd led those wolves— those fiends—away from him. Protecting him. He remembered that evening and the sounds of the wolf pack. Thinking back, for the first time Matthew saw all the pieces, and they neatly snapped into place.

And he'd left her to fight them . . . alone.

I should be helping her. She doesn't stand a chance against all six of them. Yet he'd tried to fight them, and what good had it done? If Emma hadn't come along, he'd be dead right now.

Matthew hung his head, fighting nausea, and tightened the grip on his gun. He was in no condition to help anyone. He wasn't sure he could even walk, now that he'd quit moving.

Though I should be getting used to being beaten up and mauled by now, he mused.

You should go back.

Too late . . .

Then pursue them. Or go back to their cave. Maybe they'll take Emma there. Maybe she isn't dead.

The beauty of Emma's face lingered behind his burning eyes. The way her hair softly fell around her face as they made love, the way her eyes sparkled. The way she looked out in the woods throwing those damn knives of hers like some circus performer. The fierceness of her face as they fought off those thugs in that plague city. Emma's lovely body shifting into a great silver wolf . . . like those others. Matthew's head throbbed, and he put a shaking hand up to soothe it.

But she wasn't like those demons. They'd smelled of evil. Were evil. Not Emma. Emma had been kind to him, loved him. Emma had saved his life over and over, not tried to maim or kill him. Emma was *good*. He was sure of it.

He squared his jaw in preparation for the fresh pain, then using the tree trunk as a crutch, he stood up on his trembling legs and started back the way he'd just come. This time moving as quietly as he could. Once he'd gotten close to the place where he'd been ambushed, he slunk down behind the bushes and the brambles until he came to the exact spot. Trying not to grunt with pain at every move.

This is insane, he chided himself. Whatever those things had been, they were malignant and dangerous. But he couldn't forsake Emma, if there was any chance to help or save her.

There was no one there. No dead wolves, or parts of wolves. Just his own blood spotting the thrashed snow. But his packs were still hidden behind the trees, where he'd dropped them before the attack. At least he had his supplies. Food.

Retrieving his packs, he worked his way through the woods and located the end of their trail, where they'd converged on something. Emma? There was a little blood, but again no body.

Maybe she wasn't dead. Maybe they'd taken her back. *Or else they'd merely eaten every hank of flesh, bone, and hair.*

He studied the direction of the paw prints in the snow. He had a strong suspicion, though, of where they were probably heading. *If they'd been chasing after Emma all along, and they had her now . . .*

Back to their cave.

He stared into the distance and tried not to think about the days, the miles and miles he'd have to travel to get back there. He shouldn't do it right away. He should rest, get his strength back. Tend to his injuries.

Instead, he hiked his worn packs higher up on his back, and began the long journey back, nibbling on a piece of dried meat from his supplies on the way. His legs were killing him, and he couldn't do anything past a fast hobble, but it would get him there sooner or later. If he didn't die of blood loss and exposure first.

The thought of Emma as prisoner of those beasts spurred him on.

In the days to come, as he slogged through the snow, resting very little each day, and in pain, he thought about Emma and the wolf pack.

It not only unsettled him that the wolves were not what they seemed, and had almost killed him, but that they had come into his life at all. Now. That Emma could change into a wolf. Ever since that had happened, he'd been uneasy. All those dreams he'd been having about the Indian and his village . . . dreams of wolves.

Wolves a lot like the ones he'd been mauled by. Wolves like Emma could change into.

That one dream where the village was empty at night . . . where had the Indians gone? Matthew was afraid to speculate. But the dreams where the wolves hunted with the braves, and were part of the Indian village, those obsessed him, too. Had they been omens of what had come, of what was to come? He hadn't dreamed of the wolf-eyed Indian since Emma had done her changing trick.

In his worst moments, he could almost believe that

293

the wolves had escaped out of the dreams. Were in his world now. Except the wolves in his dreams hadn't been like those monsters. And he hadn't seen any Indians on war ponies yet.

At least he got a chuckle out of the whole idea. Which didn't last, because the hopelessness of his quest closed in as he shuffled along the cooling trail in the cold and wet. He had a long way to go, and not much time.

Matthew limped faster.

He'd been traveling almost nonstop for days, when he came to the village. For a long, stunned time, he could just stand and look at it, his face vacant.

Nestled in a valley, it sprawled out before him, ghostly with the shacklike cabins silent, and hunks of glittering ice-coated trash littering the dirty snow all around. There was no smoke coming from any of the chimneys. No movement at all. He listened and thought he heard . . . chickens somewhere.

Puzzled, he moved up to the splintered fence, tossed his packs to the other side, and stiffly climbed over it. His legs were not healing correctly, probably because he was pushing himself so hard. They hurt like hell still, and when he had taken the time to check his wounds, they were festering and swollen. He knew that was bad.

His feet crunched as he walked, his head down as his eyes took in all the garbage lying on the ground. Slowly it sunk in that the chunks weren't trash at all . . . but eviscerated human bodies, and pieces and gobbets of bloodied, raw, frozen body parts. Everywhere.

Matthew's stomach lurched, and he had to turn quickly away, stare up at the sky and breathe in deeply, or he would have emptied his stomach of whatever was left in it right there on the ground.

People . . . these had once been whole, walking,

talking, alive people. Now they were only blobs of raw meat. Something had massacred all of them. And left *most* of them. What animal would do such a thing?

His narrowed eyes swept the areas around him; he began to patrol. He checked all the buildings, his gun cocked, and all the ground around the cabins. The carnage was everywhere. Animal as well as human.

There had been people and animals living here. Families. Children, for heaven's sake. All of them dead now, ripped to pieces by . . . what?

Matthew saw something fluttering, embedded in the sliver of a slat of the wooden fence. He strode up to it, laid his packs down again in the snow, took the worn glove off his right hand, while cradling his shotgun in the crook of his arm, and tugged the scrap off with bare fingers.

A hank of silver animal fur. Wolf fur like those creatures who had set upon him. Fur like Emma's. He slipped his glove back on his red hand.

Matthew stared around him, his face thunderous. There was silver fur everywhere, now that he noticed it. Feathering across the snow, frozen in the blood of the victims. Everywhere.

The wolf pack had been here. Days and days ago, though, by the look of it. Maybe weeks. The arctic weather had preserved the grisly scene like meat in a freezer. No way he could even bury the poor bastards. The ground wouldn't give them up without a fight, and Matthew just didn't have the energy, the heart, or the time to fight it.

Matthew leaned up against the fence, hid his red-rimmed eyes in his hands, and shook his head despondently. He wanted at that moment to just give in and give up so badly. He was tired. Sick. The world had somehow changed into hell. Plague and destruction on and on and on. Endless. Now werewolves. *Maybe we're all dead and there already, have been all this time, and just didn't know it.* He'd seen a hell of a lot the last year, but somehow this was what sapped the last of his soul away.

The temperature had dropped; night was coming in. Matthew was exhausted, cold, and starving. The cabins, even with the human debris around them, looked inviting. A few brief hours in a real house, in a real bed, with a real fire, and maybe real food, sounded like something he desperately needed. He couldn't go on, not another step without some sleep. Just a little.

His shoulders slumped in misery, he trudged to the nearest cabin and started to enter it. Out of the corner of his eye, he caught something lying in the snow to his right. He turned and went to it. A dead man, or what was left of him . . . but still clutched in his right hand was a hunting bow. Matthew pried it from the corpse's fingers. Hefted it up. A Golden Eagle "Cam" Hunter bow of multilaminated yew wood and hardrock maple with a textured, black handle riser and black hardware. Axle to axle length about forty-six inches. About four pounds in weight, designed for the advanced bow hunter. This particular bow was nicked and worn, well used. Well taken care of.

Matthew gathered the arrows from different places. Some were stuck in the earth, some in the side of the cabin. Apparently the man hadn't any luck in shooting his attackers.

Of course, regular arrows wouldn't harm werewolves or demons.

Now if the tips were dipped in real silver . . . Matthew frowned at his bizarre thoughts, and took his prize and himself into the small cabin.

It was empty, as he'd assumed it would be. Two tiny beds in the corner. Decaying food sat on the crude wooden table, as if the occupants had been having supper when the attack had occurred. He searched the sparse cabinets. There was food. Canned stuff and dry. In a homemade wooden box right outside the back door, he found eggs and milk, even slabs of bacon. He recalled the dead cows and the live chickens out in one of the barns.

There was a fireplace with an assortment of cooking pots and pans hanging above the mantel. Metal hooks had been inserted over the hearth for cooking. Firewood was stacked neatly next to the fireplace. Matthew quickly had a fire going, and he attached a large black skillet to the hanging wires, then fetched the eggs and bacon from the icebox outside the door and started them sizzling.

As he cleared off the table in preparation for his meal, the bacon and eggs smelled so good they made his mouth water. Couldn't remember the last time he'd had them. Oh, yes, at home, with Maggie and Sara. The memory made him smile. He collected a clean plate, a glass for the milk, a fork and a knife, and set the table. It was the most civilized he'd been in a year.

The food was delicious, and he ate like a starving man would. Ten eggs and many slabs of crisp bacon. Three glasses of the milk. Stale homemade bread he'd found wrapped in one of the other cabinets. He silently thanked the people who had lived there before, for his feast and the use of the cabin just when he'd needed it the most. But the cabin and what lay outside all around him made him sad, jumpy. He knew the wolves wouldn't be back, and yet he kept hearing things in the night. He never let his gun out of his sight.

After his meal, he was just about to lay down when the idea hit him again.

He gazed at the bow and arrows he'd discovered outside. *Silver-tipped* arrows might kill them, if they were what he suspected they were.

He methodically searched the rest of the cabin. A

woman had been living here, he could tell that by the way the place was prettied up. A woman might have silver jewelry, or silver service plates for special occasions.

Excited, he found what he wanted under one of the beds in a beautifully carved wooden chest, the kind that women stored their treasures in. This one had little jewelry, mostly gold, but there was a tissue-covered package with an exquisite silver plate in it, elaborately etched with fruit designs and borders. It looked very old, very expensive. Something handed down from her mother's mother, perhaps.

He silently thanked the dead woman for the gift, begged her to forgive him for taking it.

Matthew spent the next hour melting the plate down over the fire in a large kettle; dipping the tips of the arrow in the silver sauce. He did the same to one of Emma's knife blades and one of his. When he was done, he smiled with satisfaction at the nine arrows and two knives gleaming with silver.

Whether they were werewolves or not, and whether he believed in them or not, at least he'd be prepared when he met them again.

Using soap he found in the cabin, he heated water and spent a little time cleaning and checking his wounds, bandaging them. They were healing, slowly; he'd have to be careful or full infection would set in and he could die. He'd never rescue Emma then, if she were still alive. Then, weary beyond the point of exhaustion, he crawled into one of the beds and fell immediately into a deep sleep, reminding himself: Just a few hours, no more.

He couldn't delay any longer than that, or going after Emma would be futile.

Matthew dreamed of the warrior and his people for the first time since Emma had run away from him. He was so glad to see them, he could have cried.

298

But it was a strange dream . . . all the villagers were silently gathered around their teepees in the dark, like ghosts. The Indian with the wolf eyes walked up to Matthew, and threw his arms around him. He smiled at him and Matthew grinned back.

"We haven't been gone, we've been here all the time. We'll always be here . . . Whitefeather." Then his face went solemn.

"Go after her. Your Emma. Go after her and get her back. Hurry. You haven't much time."

Matthew wanted to talk more, but they were fading, swirling back into their world. "Wait!" he screamed. They didn't.

"Use the silver arrows," the Indian only whispered, backing away from him. "And do not be afraid of the wolves. You're right . . . they're evil. You must destroy them if you can. I—we—will be with you," he promised.

"You have done well, my son."

The warrior waved at him, and in the murkiness of the dream, Matthew gasped in astonishment as all of the Indians of the village metamorphosed into huge black wolves with gleaming eyes and white shining fangs . . . and soundlessly bounded off into the night. Baying at the huge orange moon.

Leaving Matthew alone in the empty village glaring after them in openmouthed shock.

When Matthew awoke, he recalled the dream vividly.

What the hell had it meant?

But as he packed hurriedly to leave, taking as much of the food (even killing some of the remaining chickens, and cooking them to take along) as he could carry, he thought he knew what the dream meant. He was just afraid to accept it.

* * *

He opened the cabin door and was ready to forge back out into the cold day, when he spied them.

People. Striding across the open space toward the cabin. A woman and three men.

If it hadn't been for the state of the world and the fact that Matthew hadn't seen any live people for so long, he would never have been caught so unprepared. He stood gawking a moment too long, and they spotted him, too. Started immediately toward him.

Friends or enemies?

He had his shotgun down from his shoulder and pointing in their direction a second later, and when they were within shouting distance, he yelled, "I don't want no trouble . . . Do you? I'm just passing through."

"No!" the resounding shout came back. Their hands went up in the timeless gesture of surrender and friendship. Something about the way their eyes met his straight on, the way none of them raised a weapon— when they all had rifles slung at their sides—let him relax.

Then the tallest one asked an odd thing: "Are the wolves gone?" There was fear in his voice.

"Yes," Matthew responded.

"They haven't been back?"

"No."

It was all he wanted to know. Coming closer, Matthew could see the relief on all their tired faces.

Matthew lowered the gun and smiled.

One by one, his smile was reflected back at him. One of them waved. By then the four of them were almost in front of him. He'd been correct, three men and a scrawny woman. Matthew couldn't help but stare at them. It'd been so long since he'd seen any people this close . . . that weren't either attacking him, or dying. Besides Emma.

"I needed a place to sleep," Matthew explained in a

rush. "Saw these cabins. Only shelter near here. Been on the road a long time. I was tired, hungry.

"I didn't think there was anyone left."

The woman remarked in a dull voice, "I don't hold it against you, friend. Times are tough. Food and places to sleep are hard to find. People do what they have to do." Her dead eyes had been fixed on the bodies around them as she spoke, as if she understood that he'd have had to be real desperate to stay in such a place. She was running one gloved hand over another in a continuous rubbing motion. Her eyes haunted. "It was our house. Once. I hope you got good use of it, mister."

"I did. But I'm sorry, ma'am, I found some food in that wooden box out back — eggs, meat, milk — and I ate some of it."

She smiled absentmindedly. "No matter. You were welcome to it."

The woman acted peculiar, like she wasn't in her right mind. Or like she was in shock. Under the circumstances, Matthew glanced at the frozen body parts strewn everywhere, perhaps that was normal.

The three men were all eying him, measuring him. One man was big like a St. Bernard, with a full beard and tarnished copper shoulder-length hair, compassionate eyes, and as tall as Matthew himself, while the other two were darker-skinned and clean-shaven. All bundled up like Eskimos. They seemed like nice people.

The men took turns putting out their hands, but Matthew just stared at them until one of them actually grabbed his hand and shook it.

"My name's Edward Cummings," the big guy offered. "This is Sally, my wife." He touched the woman's thin shoulder. She was so small and he was so huge, they made an odd pair.

301

"George Sadler."

"Mark Aggers."

"Sorry, I've forgotten my manners," Matthew muttered embarrassed. "It's just been too damn long . . . I'm Matthew Whitefeather."

"It's alright, friend," the big man said in a husky voice. "Like my wife said, times aren't exactly normal. But we're friends, don't mean you any harm. You're Indian?"

"Yes. Half-Cherokee. On my father's side." For the first time in a long while, his father's loving, well-wrinkled face was resurrected along with a brief vision of them hunting out in the woods together, his father patiently showing him how to hold the bow. How to track.

"A half-breed, huh?" But the man smiled in such a friendly manner, that Matthew knew he didn't mean it as a slur, like some did. There was a time Matthew would have become incensed at such a comment, no matter what the intention. That old anger now seemed trivial.

"Are you alone, Indian?"

Matthew could only nod. He still couldn't believe he was standing there talking to real people.

The woman was sneaking looks around him at the cabin. She had a pretty but somber face, melancholy eyes. Her skin the color of ivory, her eyes were green like new grass, her hair a brilliant red where it had escaped from her coat's hood. She reached out a small gloved hand and squeezed the giant's arm, as if she needed his support.

"So this was your cabin?" Matthew asked them.

"It was," he said, but his voice lacked emotion. "Until a pack of wolves came out of nowhere and forced us out."

The whole time they'd been conversing, they'd been steadily moving toward the cabin door. Now the

302

woman slowly walked past Matthew, who'd stepped away from the doorway, and into the cabin. There were tears in her eyes. The woman was older than he'd at first thought. Maybe forty. Or maybe she was younger, and the last year or two had just prematurely aged her.

"Memories," the man called Edward said to Matthew in a low voice, shaking his head. His eyes were sad, too. "Last time we were here, both our children were still alive.

"Losing our home, friends, and then our children, has been hard on me — but devastating on my wife."

Matthew thought of Sara, of Maggie.

"I'm sorry."

All of them were following behind the woman. She was openly weeping now, her shoulders heaving. Her husband went to her and put his massive arms around her, let her cry against his chest, then maneuvered her toward one of the beds so she could lay down.

Matthew didn't know what to say, what to do. He remembered losing Maggie and Sara, remembered the pain, and ached for her. He cleared his throat, saying, "I'll build the fire back up. You all look like you need the warmth. It's the least I can do for loan of the cabin the last hours." And that reminded him of the fancy silver plate he'd melted down. Guilt flushed his face. He'd never been a thief before in his life, not until lately, anyway.

The other two men plunked down on the wobbly chairs congregated around the table, their faces etched with weariness and cold. They were both short men with dark hair and eyes. Looked like they could be brothers. Wiggling out of their heavy clothes, they hung their wet coats over the chair backs. The cabin had retained some of its heat from the earlier fire.

Matthew stashed his packs and his weapons into a corner, grateful he had wrapped the silver-tipped arrows in an old shirt, and went to tend to the new fire. When it was a blazing inferno, he claimed one of the last two chairs, still studying the people. Their being there was like a gift. Like it was Christmas. These were good, decent folk, Matthew could tell just by the way they regarded him. Friendly and open. It'd been a long time since anyone had looked at him like that. It felt good.

The one called Mark slouched over in his chair at the table, and hailed the man comforting his wife. "Edward?"

"Yep?"

"Matthew here mentioned food."

Edward had gotten his wife out of her wet coat, cap, and gloves, and was gently taking her boots off. She was still crying on the edge of the bed, but silently, the tears trickling down her careworn face. The soundless tears, her stricken face, were worse than the sobbing, Matthew thought. He'd seen that empty look before.

"Yes, if our Indian friend here left us anything—"

"I did," Matthew threw in with an amiable laugh.

"There was eggs, some bacon, I think, maybe some milk, all out in that wooden box by the back door. There's even a stash of emergency coffee that Sally was saving for a special occasion. I can't think of a better time than now to dig it out."

"You're kidding? Real coffee?" the man, a small wiry guy with wire-rimmed eyeglasses, sounded as if he were going to cry. "It's been months since I've had coffee." He took his glasses off and set them gently down on the table. Glasses were more precious nowadays than gold.

"Well, wait a sec, and I'll dig it out for us," Edward told him. When his wife was tucked in, Edward ambled tiredly over to the cabinets, rustled his fingers around the top of one of them, and came to the table clutching a small, brown paper bag.

He showed it to his friends and Matthew with a flourish. "I'll just get us some water out back from the well and fill the old coffee pot, put it on to perk over the fire." He did that, and then after the coffee was brewing, shucked his coat, hat, and gloves, and also sat down at the table. "Heat feels good. Real good. Thanks for the fire, Matthew."

"You're welcome."

"I'll rustle us all up some food here in a minute," Edward promised, propping his head in the palm of his hand, elbow on the table. His eyelids drooped. "After I rest a bit. I can't stand up another second."

The other men exchanged knowing glances.

"Matthew." He met the Indian's eyes and cocked his head toward the woman in the bed. "I apologize for my wife. She's exhausted—to the bone. All of us are." He grinned tiredly.

"We've been on the road for days. No rest. Mark and George wanted to get here and get back. We're worried about the people back there, especially after what happened here."

"Then why did you come back?" Matthew questioned.

"We're here to try to bury our friends. Get some things. Recover any food we can find for the other settlement. They took us in when we came to them scared, frozen, and hungry. They need the food." He spread his hands, sighing. "To be truthful they need . . . everything.

"I tried to keep Sally from coming." The man's face looked ancient as he glanced over at his wife, sleeping peacefully now. "Her brother, Samuel, and his family lived here, too. Their bodies are out there somewhere." His eyes drifted to the window. "Sally has it in her head that they won't rest—therefore she won't rest—until she's given them all a decent burial.

305

"My wife's a good Christian woman."

"I understand," Matthew confessed. "I lost my wife and daughter, too, after the St. Louis earthquake last April. Burying them gave my heart some relief."

Edward gazed at him differently, "I'm sorry." Simple words handed back to him.

"Don't be." Matthew's eyes went to the sleeping woman, her face puffy above the thin blankets. "We've all lost. We're still losing. It can make you damn tired. I'm so tired I could sleep for months, and it still wouldn't help. Still would wake up to this world," Matthew snorted.

"Yep." A tiny word that said it all.

The aroma of brewing coffee wafted around them. Heavenly. It was warm with the fire. All of them sitting at the table, so normal. So cozy. Someone sleeping across the room. Real people. Matthew felt tranced. Unreal. It was hard to believe that bloody corpses landscaped the snow outside the cabin.

"What happened here, Edward?"

Horror flickered across the man's face. "You noticed the mutilated bodies outside, did ya?"

"Couldn't help but," Matthew answered gravely. "Wolves, you said, did this?"

The other two men waited to hear the story again. Now that they'd seen the damage, it was more believable. More horrible.

"Yes, we were attacked by these . . . wolves. If you want to call them that. I don't know what the hell they were." His voice dropped to a whisper, as if he didn't want to wake his wife. "A whole pack of the fiends. Big as men. Never seen such huge wolves. They came here one night about two weeks ago, slaughtered our livestock, lured us outside, and then did *that*." He gestured at the outside, and hung his head, his shoulders trembling slightly. "We were ten families. Thirty-one

306

people. I don't know how they managed to butcher all of us. But they did.

"We didn't stand a chance. They tore us to pieces. Even though we had weapons." He seemed suddenly confused. "Matthew, I'd never been a superstitious man, but I could have sworn . . ." his voice came to a dead end. He shook his head, rubbed his eyes. Shrugging it off. Then he said, "Never mind. I imagine the horror of what happened that night, and since, has pushed me a little over the edge."

Matthew deduced that the man, like him, suspected that the wolves weren't normal wolves. But then, unlike him, he hadn't seen Emma transform. Whatever Edward doubted, Matthew no longer could.

Matthew wondered what Edward would say if he knew that stuffed in the corner was a bundle of silver-tipped arrows and knives, and that Matthew believed that what he was chasing were werewolves.

"Anyway," Edward went on with angry eyes, "they killed everyone but me, my wife, and our two kids, Angie and Steven." The man clenched his hands on the table before him, as Mark got up softly and fixed them all steaming cups of coffee with cream in cups he was directed to in the lower cabinet. Even without sugar it tasted delicious.

"Never seen such animals," Edward groaned, sipping his coffee. "They were so damn *strong*." He paused, again obviously rattled over something he wasn't talking about.

"How did you get away?" Matthew wanted to know.

"Strangest thing . . . one of the wolves had my boy and was dragging him across the yard out there. I was right behind the bastard, trying to get my boy back.

"Then this other wolf showed up out of nowhere, chased off the one that had my boy . . . and . . . damn. You won't believe this, I still don't believe it."

307

Matthew waited. Mark was cooking food for all of them, having gotten tired of waiting for Edward to do it. The same meal Matthew had had a few hours ago. They offered him another plate, but he turned it down. He'd stuffed himself earlier, and he could tell these people were starving; the people back at the other settlement probably were, too. He couldn't take anymore of their precious food.

The woman must have been really beat, even the smell of frying bacon didn't rouse her. They'd save her something, Mark told him.

He felt even worse about the silver plate, but he couldn't bring himself to tell Edward what he'd done. Also, then he'd have to explain why he melted it down; he didn't want to do that. Didn't want to scare them anymore than they were.

"It let my boy *go*," Edward was saying. "Let all four of us go. It just stood there watching us with these glowing eyes, as we ran off into the night. Damnest thing I ever saw." He sighed, shaking his head. Gulped down another large swallow of coffee, caressing the cup. The fire crackled noisily behind him. Mark was turning the bacon, humming some elusive melody to himself as he worked. George's eyes followed every move Mark made with the food with hungry eyes.

"Somehow we got to the next settlement." Edward nodded toward George sitting next to him. "Last Hope, it's called. Appropriate name," he chuckled. "About ten miles away."

Then his voice became gloomy. "We escaped. But our children died anyway . . . plague."

Matthew jerked at the word, his face drained. "Plague? You have plague?" a hoarse murmur. His hands let go of the cup, and his body automatically moved farther back in the chair away from the table.

Edward shook his head, reaching out to touch Matthew's tense hand. "The settlement here had it. Angie and Steven died of it right before we arrived at Last Hope. We buried them out in the woods. For some reason, we lived, while our poor children died. It's alright, Matthew . . . my wife and I are not infected. The time span has long ago passed for us to be contagious. Last Hope is clean of it, too."

Matthew accepted that. The plague always killed children. Sometimes adults, like him and Emma, were spared. It happened.

"And you're safe, you can't get it from the frozen bodies outside, I'm fairly sure. Maybe when they thaw . . . but not now."

Matthew was relieved, realized he'd been holding his breath, and let it go. Mark had finished frying the meal, laid the plates on the table in front of everyone.

Matthew watched Mark and George scoff down the food. They sucked it up like vacuum cleaners. Licked their plates.

"Well, I told you why we're here," Edward said, between bites of eggs and bacon. "Now it's your turn, Matthew."

Matthew decided to tell the truth. Or some of it, anyway.

"Like I told you before, I'm passing through." His eyes were hard chips as he met theirs. "I've been tracking those wolves of yours. They attacked me a ways back. Took something very important to me. I'm going to hunt them down. Find what's left of them — and kill them."

He sipped his coffee, relishing the flavor of it.

"What's *left* of them?" Edward had caught that. "There was more'n a dozen or so of the hellish creatures two weeks ago."

"Yea, well, as of a few days ago, there's only about a half-dozen of them left."

Edward was surprised, but pleased. "You killed them?"

"No. They just disappeared."

Edward's face was incredulous. "Disappeared?"

"I've been tracking them on and off for nearly two weeks myself. The pack's been mysteriously dwindling. I don't know why. When I first started following them, there were fifteen or sixteen, now there seems to be only about a half-dozen left." As if mentioning the wolves reminded Matthew of his quest, he stood up. His face was hard.

"And I've already stayed here way too long. I was leaving when we met. It's time I got back on their trail, or I'll never catch them."

Edward seemed sorry to hear it. But seeing the look in the Indian's eyes, he understood. They both had their job to do. Matthew to destroy the wolves, and they to bury their dead, collect what they needed, and get back to the hungry people at Last Hope.

"I hate to see you go, Indian, but if you find those mothers . . . give 'em hell for me and mine, would ya?"

Matthew nodded.

"Matthew," George asked. "You've been out there?" His hand waved at the invisible horizon. He meant beyond the settlement.

"A friend and I came all the way from St. Louis."

George's mouth dropped open. "That far, huh?" His deep brown eyes were excited.

"That far . . . and I've been up to Canada and back, tracking the wolves."

"Any people left?" His voice sounded soft, hopeful. Matthew figured he must have family somewhere. He thought of Emma and her sister.

"I'm sorry, George, not many, not many at all. You people are the first sane and well ones I've seen in almost a year."

George's face fell, but he thanked him for the information anyway.

Then Mark cut in. "Some of us back at Last Hope believe that this is the end of the world . . . that the earthquakes will continue until the whole planet tears itself apart." His fingers were steepled in front of his mouth, his voice was almost religious. But Matthew saw the terror in the man's glittering eyes. He recalled what he'd told Emma, and saw again in his memory all the leveled cities, missing cities, and destruction; all the land along the coast was now under water. The tidal waves. Dying animals. The vicious weather. And the earthquakes had gotten worse.

"What do you think, friend?"

"I don't really know, friend," the Indian finally answered carefully. "I don't know."

Matthew collected his gear, slipped into his tattered coat and torn gloves.

"Wait a minute," Mark said, looking at Matthew's hands. Pulling his coat from the chair onto his lap, he tugged something from the pocket. "Got an extra pair of warm gloves." He shoved them at Matthew. "For you. Yours are just rags. Go ahead, put 'em on."

Matthew thanked him, almost speechless at the man's generosity. They had so little themselves. He peeled off his old gloves and put the others on.

"And when you're done killing those monsters, Matthew," Edward said, "you're welcome at Last Hope anytime. About ten miles this side of the creek. A straight line west from here. There'll be a place there for you, if you want it."

Mark nodded, adding, "There's about twenty people there. Women, children even. A few of the women are unclaimed. We can always use another good man."

George had stood up, too. Was shaking Matthew's hand goodbye, a warm smile on his face.

311

"Come anytime."

The offer was sincere, and it affected Matthew more than he could say. He had a place to go when this was all over. A place where he could belong. A home. If he wanted it. If he never found Emma.

Mark and George shook his hand again, too.

"You're welcome to take some of the food. We'll share," Edward offered kindly.

Matthew shook his head. "I've plenty. I'm afraid I also killed two of your chickens. I think there are a few left out back, though."

Edward scratched his neck. "Eat 'em in good health. And good luck tracking those wolves. We would have gone after them ourselves." He shrugged. "But if we couldn't kill them that night we were ambushed, with the weapons we had, when we were fighting for our wives and children — our very existence — then there was no way we could hope to kill them if and when we *did* find them. We decided none of us wanted to be martyrs. We have people we're responsible for.

"Just what you told us — that there are only about six of the demons left — has been miracle enough for us. We can't thank you enough. Hope your weapons are better than ours."

"They are," Matthew replied flatly.

He grinned at Matthew then. "Hope you catch 'em."

"Me, too," Matthew said. He glanced at the woman in the bed. "And I hope your wife is feeling better."

"She will, when this is done, and we're back at Last Hope. There's an orphaned baby girl there she's already sort of adopted. Needs her.

"We'll start a new life there. She'll be fine. She's a strong woman. Got her husband and her faith to comfort her."

"Say goodbye to her for me."

"I will."

They walked him to the door and watched him leave.

Matthew tried not to look at the butchered bodies he walked among. The gory images were already burned so deep into his psyche, that he'd see them, along with all the other atrocities he'd witnessed the last year, until the day he died. For the first time he was thankful for the frost in the air, the cold. There was no stench.

As he was entering the woods, he turned to wave one last time. They were still all standing there waving back, when he walked over the hill and out of their sight.

Good people, he told himself. He'd hated leaving them, he suddenly realized. He'd really wanted to go back to Last Hope with them.

His feet crunched in the snow as he turned his face into the wind, covering his mouth as a fit of coughing hit him. Must be coming down with something. He didn't feel too well. He kept walking. Already freezing. Lonely.

Wondering why he was doing it.

Because Emma's face wouldn't leave him alone, that's why. She was still alive somewhere—he could feel it—and she needed him. Needed him badly.

He had to find her. Kill those werewolves, or whatever the hell they were. His heart wouldn't let him rest until he did both.

Twenty-one

Matthew arrived at the wolf's cave a day later, right before dawn. If the pack followed the same pattern as the nights he'd chased them, they could return anytime—if they weren't already in the cave. He took the chance and entered it, his bow in front of him notched with a silver-tipped arrow, the rest of the arrows hanging at his waist. He believed his dreams, and his protector had implied that Emma was still alive to save, though there wasn't much time. Matthew couldn't afford to waste any.

They weren't there. Or, at least, he didn't think they were there. The cave was quiet. Felt empty.

He'd be there, hiding, when they returned. He'd kill them all, as soon as he found out what they'd done to Emma. The obvious flaws in his plan were, of course, how would he get the information out of them, and could he kill them before they killed him.

He wasn't sure they were like Emma—able to transform into human beings. He'd never seen them do it. And if they weren't like her, how would he be able to communicate with them? He didn't know. He'd cross that bridge when he came to it.

Matthew had an answer to one of his questions as soon as he entered their cave. By the looks of it, the cave was inhabited by human animals. Lit by a huge central fire that someone had been tending to quite recently, there were places to sit, bedrooms of a fashion, and personal belongings everywhere. He cautiously searched the place and discovered clothes and . . . books. All the classics. Fiction. Love poetry. Books Maggie had had in their old house. Werewolves read? Loved? Had dreams and fears. Thinking of them like that was disquieting, so he stopped, replacing that picture with the one of the slaughtered village.

So they were werewolves. Like Emma. Part of the time anyway.

By the furnishings he could tell that a large group of them had lived there. He remembered the pack as he'd first seen it, fifteen or more strong . . . now only six or less. The tracks the last two days had thinned, dwindled. He'd thought at first that some of them might have split off in another direction, or were doubling back to get him, but he bore in mind the puzzle of the empty caves along the way, when he was tailing them the last time. Something had been happening to them, and he mulled over the idea that the plague from the village had affected them, just as if they had been human. Why not? They were part-human.

Matthew stood by the low, dancing flames of the fire and studied the cave thoughtfully. It was a strange place. So silent, so empty — yet not. Ghostly echoes elusively frolicked and twittered around him, scampering to the farthest dark corners. The odor of wet fur and bat droppings permeated the air along with the dampness. The metallic odor of blood.

He couldn't forget for a moment how bloodthirsty the fiends were, how many people they'd probably killed. Perhaps the cave was full of their victims' specters. The thought made him afraid to look too closely at the darkness huddled in the corners.

"Stop scaring yourself, Matthew," he sighed, turning away from the safety of the light and exploring the adjoining tunnels quickly, to see if there were any other exits, painfully aware that the wolves could return at any moment. No. He couldn't find any if there were.

One way in, he decided unhappily, and one way out.

He concealed himself deep in the back of the main cavern in the shadows, his packs hidden away under some other things, his gun lying close by him; his bow, silver-tipped arrows, and his knives were cradled in his lap. He settled down to wait for them to come back, cross-legged, his head hanging.

He was tired. Tired of chasing, of being chased, of being cold and frightened. Of being alone. His strength was almost gone. And his heart feared for Emma. It'd been days since his run-in with the wolves, weeks since he'd last been with her. He missed her.

The wounds from that last encounter with the wolves still hurt, though they'd begun to heal, and even the people he'd met at that cabin the day before hadn't noticed or commented on his bloodied, torn-up pants. Maybe because he'd wrapped both legs in old rags right before they'd arrived, and they'd thought it had been done for warmth. Then again, nowadays, most of the people you met were scarred or injured in some way. A common occurrence in the new world. He gently touched his mangled ear. He'd forgotten all about that, too, and they'd never asked about that. Well, he'd told them he'd had a run-in with the wolves. Maybe they'd put two and two together. Or maybe they'd noticed, but had been too polite to mention that he was carved up like a day-old Thanksgiving turkey.

Matthew fought the sleep his body craved. He had to stay awake, alert. The wolves could return at any moment, and if he was caught unprepared, he'd be dead. To stay awake he thought about Emma and their time together, thought about the Indians in his dreams, and what that last dream had tried to tell him. He daydreamed about finding and saving Emma and taking her back to Last Hope, about them starting a new life with those people. He ignored the fact that she was what she was, and that they'd never welcome her there because of it. He was daydreaming, after all.

Outside, the day was dawning. The new kind of day, foggy. Matthew's stomach growled, and never taking his eyes off the distant entrance to the cave, he ate the last of the cooked chicken he'd taken from his packs, and washed it down with water from his canteen.

They'd be coming soon.

He had no idea how many. No idea if his silver-tipped arrows would do the trick. No idea if he could defeat them.

Matthew's whole body tensed. Something was coming.

A growl rose in the stale air, and a large furry shape was silhouetted in the murky entrance. Then another.

Matthew crouched back further into the shadows, holding his bow tightly against his ribs, holding his breath, waiting.

If they were werewolves, they might be easier to fight in their human form. He hoped if he waited long enough, undetected, that they would transform. Then he'd get them to tell him what they'd done to Emma—before he killed them.

The wolves lumbered into the cave. Matthew recognized the larger brute from the earlier attack. The one he'd shot up. There were no signs now of any wounds. It came slowly into the light of the fire and paused, its muzzle raised as if to smell the air, its eyes glittering like red diamonds.

The other one came dragging in behind it. The second wolf barely made it into the cave before it floundered to the ground, panting and groveling in pain. It whimpered some secret message, because the bigger wolf slowly turned and padded back to it, nudged it.

Then its massive head came up again, its form rigid, as its eyes tediously scanned the rest of the cave. Eyes like spotlights.

He knows I'm here, Matthew realized with a jolt, his fingers tightening on the bow. He very stealthily unsnapped the strap over the knife at his waist, heart pounding, sweat beginning to trickle down the side of his mauled face.

He waited as the agonizing minutes crawled by, yet the wolf never came for him, never even acted as if it knew he was there. Instead its attention was on its comrade writhing on the cave floor.

Mesmerized, Matthew watched as the reclining wolf evolved into a naked, beautiful woman with short hair and perfectly formed limbs. Delirious, she rolled on the cave floor, her knees drawn up to her chest, her animal sounds slowly turning into human.

The other wolf began to change . . . soon it was a large man kneeling over the sick woman. Naked as she was. The firelight shone off white skin and intricate tattoos. Long silver hair like Emma's.

A werewolf with tattoos?

"Chelsea . . ." the man crooned. "Don't fight it. Just give in." His manner was full of grief as he took the woman gently into his arms and rocked her. They weren't used to pain any longer, and the suffering had broken her.

The woman cried in tiny sobs. "Hurts so. Never hurt so. Stephen . . . don't want to die . . . don't want to . . ." Her mouth froze and she slumped in his arms, her neck falling backwards and her hair spilling away from her lovely face. She lay still in his arms, silent.

Matthew was stunned at the display of compassion. These were the creatures that had murdered all those people back at the village, the same creatures who had attacked him?

Suddenly the man threw back his head and . . . *howled.* Howled like a demented thing from hell. The mournful sound echoed and ricocheted around the huge cavern like a released, angry entity with a life of its own. Over and over.

Startled, agitated bats fell from the ceilings and circled the man's head in masses of black, that hid both werewolves from Matthew's gaze like a blanket, until the howls ceased and the bats swooped back to their perch in the depths of the cave.

Matthew crawled closer. He couldn't believe his eyes as the woman's shape in the man's arms began to flicker and fade, like a special effect in some horror movie. Her skin began to fizzle and smoke, and then dissolved into thin air until there was nothing left in the man's arms. He dropped them to his side and lowered his head in open grief, his body quivering.

Did werewolves weep?

Matthew had moved even closer, out of the shadows, intrigued by what he'd seen. *Now he knew what had happened to all those other wolves. When they expired, their physical bodies simply ceased to exist.*

Was it plague . . . or something else?

The werewolf slowly raised his head. His eyes riveted on Matthew's face.

Matthew was out in plain sight, with his bow. The werewolf had seen him.

Faster than Matthew could take in, the man began to change. His face grew thinner, a muzzle thrusted itself through the skin, fur dominoed across his nakedness into a thick silver pelt, as his body bent and he went down on all fours, his hands and feet becoming huge paws with sharp claws. A tail rose from between his hind legs, and his ears formed tall and pointed, while his wolfish muzzle had opened wide and now revealed rows of teeth and fangs. It howled like it had

319

when the woman had died, but the sound was one of fierce fury and animalistic savagery.

He'd forgotten how huge the damn thing was.

Matthew fell back on his butt from shock.

The giant wolf snarled, snapping at him with razor-sharp teeth that gleamed in the faint light, and then without hesitation, launched itself at Matthew across the space between them like a bullet.

Matthew couldn't react fast enough and was bowled over, but managed to push the creature off of him, rolled away, and sprang to his feet. His bow with the notched arrow had flown out of his hands and was lying a distance away from him. He scrambled for it. But the wolf was quicker and slammed it out of his hands again, and knocked Matthew back down.

Later he would admit that perhaps the werewolf could have killed him then and there, but for some reason didn't. It stood growling at him a few feet away, frothing at the mouth like a mad dog, its lips curled back to show the wicked fangs, bunching up its powerful muscles for yet another attack, giving Matthew time to retrieve his bow and renotch the silver-tipped arrow.

After the second attack Matthew might have questioned the wolf's strange behavior. Not at all like the predator it had been the last time he'd faced it and its friends. Its coordination and eyesight were perceptibly off. It kept charging him, but Matthew had only to step aside at the last moment, and the wolf would miss him and slam against the cave walls; it would drag itself up sluggishly and try again. Moving slower each time.

But Matthew's fear had overridden his usual powers of observation. He kept seeing the bloodied body parts buried in the ice and snow back at the village, he kept remembering their last ferocious attack on him.

Matthew aimed and let the arrow fly.

It struck the werewolf in the side. The creature screamed like a person, but kept coming at him. The look in its eyes sent icy slivers of panic deep into Matthew's heart. It hated him. It was going to kill him. The arrow still sticking grotesquely out of its side, it advanced on him, head lowered, jaws wide.

Maybe the legends were wrong. Silver didn't kill them.

Gasping, his hands shaking, Matthew pulled another arrow from his waist, where he'd had them hanging from a rope-belt, notched it, yanked it back, and let it go.

This time it caught the beast in the chest, plunging deep.

The wolf rocked to a standstill, weaving on its feet like a drunken porcupine. Its howls now whimpers of pain. It was only a few feet away from Matthew. It could have had him as he rushed to place in another arrow. But it didn't. It just *looked* at him with its narrowed eyes . . . flat and dead. No longer menacing.

What was it waiting for?

Finally, panting, it collapsed at Matthew's feet and began to return to its human shape. Naked. Retching. One arrow sticking out of his left side, and one right where his heart would be.

The werewolf's body stopped jerking. His voice became soft; Matthew had to kneel down beside him to understand the words. Not too close because of the plague. Even then, the stench of the dying creature gagged him.

"Don't be afraid," the man groaned. "Killing you wouldn't have done any good. Fresh blood won't reverse the . . . damage. Wasn't trying to hurt you.

"Lost Chelsea . . . so angry . . . at world . . . at humans and their damned plague." He spat out blood. Crimson liquid stained the floor around him, spreading pools of it. "I . . . want . . . to die. *No one left*. I'm

321

sick like the rest of them. Won't live long now. But plague horrible way to die. So much *pain*. Thank you."

So werewolves were susceptible to plague, as well.

"So all the rest of your pack is dead—from plague?"

"Yes." The man closed his eyes a moment. Opened them. A film of milky white covered them. "All dead. I'm the last one left."

His skin was mottled, like plague victims in the first stages of the disease. Weakly, he raised a hand to wipe the blood trickling from his open mouth. Then he was convulsing. Couldn't stop the blood coming from his mouth, sprouting from his nostrils and ears. His glittering eyes locked strongly with Matthew's for the first time, and his expression changed from one of pain and confusion to one of sullen misery.

"You . . . You were the one Emma saved. The one she loved." There was no animosity in his tone any longer, just resignation. A wisp of envy.

"Yes. Where is she?" Matthew demanded between clenched teeth. "Have you killed her, too?" He'd been prepared to hate this creature . . . he'd come to kill him. Kill all of them. Yet now, watching him die, he could feel nothing but pity for it, the earlier hatred seeping out like released pus from an infected wound.

"We thought our enemies were you Others." The creature writhing on the cave floor laughed bitterly, ignoring Matthew's question about Emma.

"We were *so* wrong," he went on, coughing up more blood, and grinning ghoulishly at Matthew, as it dripped down his chin.

"After all these long centuries . . . this is how we end. This is how we die." His laughter a death rattle in his throat.

"Where's Emma!" Matthew's hands itched to throttle the beast's throat, get the truth out of him, but he was afraid to touch the contaminated man. He shouldn't even be this close. The plague was so contagious.

"She was *right*," the werewolf whispered, still not answering him. "Smartest of us all. Wouldn't drink human blood . . . insisted on it . . . just animal. As if she knew this would happen . . ." His breathing, his voice had become very labored.

Matthew's anger was growing. The thing was dying, and what Matthew needed desperately to know would die with him. He needed answers. What difference that it was suffering, dying? Matthew steeled himself with the thought of all the people it and its kind had tortured, mutilated, and killed all the time it was on earth. Steeled himself with images of the destruction they'd left in their path. How old were these creatures?

"Centuries old, human," the man chuckled gloatingly. "And Matthew . . . we're not werewolves. We're vampires." And Matthew realized it had read his mind. He pulled back from it, loathing it and everything it stood for. *Vampires!*

"Where's Emma!" a hiss now.

The vampire's eyes opened wide. Age-old hatred mingled suddenly with the pain, then it swiftly ebbed away.

"She's not dead, you know." The creature laughed softly. "Worse than dead . . . but not. Poor Emma." Its eyes were misting, its body rigid on the cave floor. "Yet. I can still feel her struggling in her agony. She's *strong*."

Still alive?

Matthew inched a little closer again, hope rising. Was it possible? Emma was still alive somewhere?

"Emma's not dead?"

"Shouldn't help an Other. Enemy. But what the hell . . ." With its last gasp it mouthed, "Her punishment for helping you, human was to be buried alive."

Oh, dear gods . . . Emma.

Before Matthew could ask where, the vampire's eyes drifted shut, and it curled up into a fetal position. Unmoving.

"Where. *Where!*" Matthew screamed at it. His hands hovering inches above its face. Don't touch it. Don't.

Nothing. Silence. Then the bloody mouth moved and whispered, so low that Matthew had to put his ear almost right against it to understand.

"Graveyard over hill . . . four . . . trees. Lawton tomb."

Ash gray smoke rose from the body. The flesh melted like wax in the sun, revealing muscles, then bones . . . slowly its form began to dematerialize.

Matthew stared as the remnants dissolved into the air. To nothingness.

He fell to the ground, his mind gasping with the horror of what he'd just learned. The cave echoed with ghost sounds. Footsteps wandering down dark tunnels. Laughter and weeping deep in the ground.

Buried alive. Emma! What she must have been going through. How she must be suffering. He sat there for a time, shaking from what he'd just gone through. Facing and killing the . . . vampire. Hearing what had happened to Emma.

Vampires. They had been vampires. Didn't vampires exist on human blood? He tried to recall what Emma had eaten. That's right, she never seemed to eat. Yet there were those nightly sojourns of hers. Had she been out drinking blood . . . animal blood as the vampire had said?

So he had been right. She wasn't like those others. She wasn't evil as they had been.

The earth jolted, knocking him off his knees to the ground.

Earthquake. A bad one. The world heaved and groaned as Matthew scuttled toward the cave's entrance on all fours. Another shaking, harder this time, landed him on his butt again. Cracks split down the walls of the cave and brought rocks tumbling from the ceiling.

He suspected he had minutes to get out before the whole place gave way.

He made it, but barely. As he crawled out into the snow, the cave buckled in on itself behind him.

Then the earth settled down once again.

The vampires' lair was gone forever. Sealed like a tomb. Just like Emma's other cave back in Missouri. He made a mental note not to stay in caves anymore. Too dangerous these days.

"Damn . . . my supplies were in there," he moaned, remembering the packs stuffed under the rocks. "And my gun . . ." All he'd gotten away with was his bow and arrows. "Should be used to that, too," he mumbled gloomily.

Contemplating the now solid wall of rocks with a stoic stance, he slung his bow over his shoulder. Time was running out for Emma, if it hadn't already. He had to go.

Rapidly inspecting the terrain around him, he located a hill toward the west with four stark trees atop of it, two of them swaying in the rising wind, and two of them on the ground felled by the earthquake. He started hiking in that direction, praying it was the right hill, and that the graveyard would be right below it.

If the vampire had been telling the truth . . . Emma was buried in a tomb marked Lawton. Had been for the last seven or eight days.

Matthew's face was stone as he trudged through the frozen woods. He squinted up at the cloud-thick sky. Looked like more snow. At least the earth had quieted. He didn't want to dwell on what that graveyard might now look like after the earthquake. What condition the tomb was in. If it was still there at all.

He just began to run.

Twenty-two

At first Emma struggled violently, beating and clawing at the coffin's inner lid with her fists and fingers, but the silver chain and her lack of blood debilitated her strength to the point where she was weaker than a human.

She couldn't get out.

She'd never been so terrified, so alone, in her whole life. It was a million times worse than when she'd been in Larry's shelter, in agony over her burns. This time, the chain scalded her like hot iron, and she could barely move . . . trapped in a tiny box. The burning wouldn't stop; there would be no healing as long as the chain was there wrapped around her. And she wouldn't die from lack of air. It wouldn't be that easy. She'd prayed for that release in the early hours of her imprisonment, then grasped, her heart rising up in her tight throat to choke her, the fact that she *couldn't* suffocate. Not like mortals suffocate.

How long did it take a vampire to die this way?

Days, weeks, months? Surely not years? Lying fully conscious, painfully aware of every second's passing. *Hell. This is hell.*

When she dwelt on it, her mind went into a sort of paralyzing shock, and she couldn't make a sound or move for hours or she would burst into fits of screaming again, tearing at the sides of the coffin with bloodied fingertips. Crying would have been a mercy, but though she sobbed aloud, they were dry, impotent gaspings, not human crying.

Vampires couldn't weep, either.

After what seemed like an eternity of unrestrained and unstoppable hysterics, she forced herself into a false calmness. She'd never find a way to escape, if she didn't control herself. Had to think. Had to get out.

Emma . . . think! There must be a way.

But she could find no way to extricate herself, try as she could. No way, she tried them all. Few as they were. The silver chain—she couldn't touch, couldn't move, though she tried and had burned strips into the skin of her fingers, like steaks on a barred grill. The stench of her searing flesh gagged her. The coffin lid—she couldn't budge, no matter how she squirmed or pushed, because the chain kept her nailed to the coffin's bed. It was unmovable.

Hours went by, days, she couldn't tell. Only that somewhere along the way, she began to dream as she lay awake. Hallucinate.

Danny. . . .oh, Danny, it's so good to see you again, she whispered. He was squeezed right in next to her. His beloved face close to hers.

Well, Emma, you sure have gotten yourself into a real fix this time, he joked, but his expression was grave. *Woman, you sure can't take care of yourself, can you?*

I didn't do too badly at first, she responded with the last of her shredded pride, just relieved he was there. *Got myself through all those months alone. Learned how to survive out in the new world. Learned how to be a vampire—on my own—without drinking human blood. Met Matthew. Saved Matthew. I was even happy for a while, Danny.* The memories of those days with Matthew

made her forlorn. *I even got away from those monsters.
Didn't buckle down to them.*

*I gave Matthew his freedom, another chance to go on liv-
ing. I did good, didn't I, Danny?*

Yes, you did good, Emma. Danny winked at her in
the darkness.

But this . . . She shifted her sad eyes around her
tiny prison, shuddering a sigh. *I can't get out. I've tried.*

*I know, honey. I'm so sorry, there's nothing I can do. I'm
just a ghost, you know. Not substantial enough to do you
much good. Wish I could. I still feel there's something else
left for you to do out there, Emma* . . . His blue eyes were
shining sapphires floating next to hers. Emma felt his
hand brush her cheek. Like a feather. God, she'd
loved him once. And the children.

For a moment her mind flashed a muted picture
for her of her kids laughing and playing with the
family cat, then it merged into a picture of that red-
haired family huddled around the campfire, that
night in the freezing woods. Emma was glad now
she'd helped them. In fact, she wasn't sorry for anything she'd done. Even defying the vampire pack.
Saving Matthew. She didn't mind dying. As a mortal, she'd accepted the idea. She'd been on borrowed
time for months anyway. It was the way she was
dying that upset her.

I think this is the end of the line for me, Danny. Maybe,
she had the urge to laugh, *I'll join you and the kids, and
all the others, pretty soon.*

You still got a fighting chance to get out of this, babe, he
said.

*Oh, Danny, this time I'm really going to die. I just don't
know how long it will take* . . .

Will you stay with me? She reached out her trembling fingers towards the apparition. *Until the very end?
Please.* She looked into his ghostly blue eyes. He nod-

led, caringly. He knew what she was going through. He'd always known her innermost fears, known her horror of being trapped somewhere in the earth, in a landslide, or in a wrecked car, her life eking away. He knew she was nearly insane with fear.

I'm scared, Danny.

Taking her maimed hand tenderly in his, he kissed it. *Don't worry, babe, I'll be here for you. You won't be alone. And if you don't make it out, the kids and I are waiting for you.*

Then he dissolved back into her consciousness, and she didn't see him again for a while. She was too busy trying to find some way out, her mind scurrying around in its maze, like a LSD'd mouse.

Sometime later, Emma thought about Matthew. Was he looking for her, even now? If he'd made it, if the vampires hadn't gotten him. Well, he wasn't visiting her in the coffin like Danny did, so maybe he was still alive. She thought of how it had been with Matthew in that cabin. She could see him now, collecting wood and building the fire, fiddling with that old truck, and hunting with her out in the snow. See him sighting over that bow of his, the soft light from the misty day kissing his rugged face. See him rising above her as they made love. They'd been happy.

She laughed miserably to herself. *Even if he's looking for me, he'll never find me here. Never. He doesn't even know what I am. What those wolves were who attacked him. I should have told him! Foolish Emma. I'm doomed.*

They said that when you were truly dying, your life danced by in front of you. Emma was dancing. Watching her life like it was an old movie reel.

She was a child again. Eating candy buttons off the strips of white paper, and sucking out the soda from the tiny wax bottles from the corner store. Her ninth birthday she had a party and received a

Brownie camera, cashews, a box of pastels, and a big white drawing tablet. Her sister and brothers grinning at her over the birthday cake and banana ice cream. Later drawing pictures. Anything she could see, she could draw. She amazed all the grownups with her little trick. Impressed the Sisters at her Catholic school by reproducing the holy card pictures as she sat in the back of the class at her desk. They let her draw them all day. She won the weekly class art contest the very first week, her picture was hung on the board with the golden star. So proud.

Then she was a teenager. Going to the street dances, wearing bell-bottoms, and black eyeliner that went up at the corners. Dangling golden earrings that jingled. Flower child of the sixties. Drawing her classmates' portraits for spending money. She was sixteen when she met Danny Bloodworth. He was beautiful with his long blond hair, eyes that smiled. Tight pants. They danced at the Teen Towns to "Brown-eyed Girl" and "Tamberine Man." Went steady.

Grew up together. Went to college together.

Emma's smiling up at him through her lace wedding veil, walking down the aisle. Dancing with her handsome father and brothers at the reception. Happy, happy.

She's holding a tiny Peter in her arms, he's crying, squinting up at her with that old baby face of his. She's being pulled behind a running Peter, another baby, Jenny, clutched at her shoulder.

Her mother laughing with her one day at the kitchen table. Danny's gotten that job at the restaurant. Emma's working at an ad agency. Busy, so busy.

Emma dreamed of working at her Macintosh, finishing an important job for a prestigious client. Proud of her accomplishment. Then, she, Larry, and the others going out to a birthday lunch for somebody or other. It made her smile. Pizza at Calico's downtown. Salads so big, topped with cheese shaped like fat little ropes, and their famous house dressing. She couldn't eat it all. Took it home in a doggie bag for supper. Those had been great days. Great times.

Emma dreamed of being home again with Danny and the kids in their lovely two-story house. They were just finishing up a fried chicken dinner at the kitchen table on a spring afternoon, years before any of the world troubles started. The kids were outside playing on the tire swings Danny had hung for them, under the big oak tree out back in the late afternoon. There was *real* sunlight. And the sounds of their children yelling and teasing each other wafted through the kitchen windows. The ceiling fan gently created a cool breeze above their heads, as they lingered at the table after supper talking about the things that had seemed so important at the time. Getting a new, bigger television. Danny's promotion at the restaurant. Emma's disagreements with the new art director. Whether the kids should have those expensive brand tennis shoes that cost so much, or the cheaper ones. Should she buy that classy blue suit she'd seen in Famous's window downtown. How about dinner and a movie out on Saturday night. Get a babysitter.

She got up from the table, their cat, Midnight, brushing against her legs, always in the way, and prepared them both dessert: homemade shortcake and fresh strawberries with whipped cream. The kids came running in for their share.

God, those were the days.

Emma wanted so badly to stay there, happy, safe.

Because then the maelstrom began . . . the earthquakes in the west . . . the hordes of displaced, frightened people coming, always coming . . . the

bombing of New York . . . the economic collapse
. . . the end of life as they'd all known it.

Emma was in the ad agency reliving again that
fateful Saturday morning. Larry, too. Lying in her
coffin in another world months later, Emma wanted
to scream at that placid-faced woman that had once
been her, gazing out the window at the homeless below: *Run! Run back home to your family. Save them! Soon
it'll be too late!* But the woman didn't hear her, and the
earthquake came anyway.

The rest of her life whirled through her mind in an
ever-increasing downward spiral. Faster. Faster. She
and Larry escaping through the crumbling, shrieking
city . . . Larry dying in her arms . . . the fire . . .
her agony from her heartache and her burns all those
lonely months in the shelter . . . coming out . . . going back home through the barrenness . . . crossing
the dangerous Poplar Bridge . . . weeping in the ruins of her home that rainy night . . . being followed
. . . those bestial hoodlums that had beaten her and
almost raped her . . . dying . . . Byron . . . then the
changes . . . finding and saving Matthew . . . their
journeys . . . being attacked in that town . . . the
wolf . . . the abominable plague burnings . . .
searching for her sister . . . leaving Matthew to save
his life that day on the cold rocks . . . the vampires
and their cave . . . defying the vampires that morning for Matthew's precious life . . . the look of gloating and pure hatred on Chelsea's wicked face as they
put—

No! Abruptly the visions ended with a whoosh,
and she was back in the coffin, back in the ground.

No! NO! *NO!* She opened her eyes to the inki-
ness of her eternal prison, the hopelessness of
her situation, rocking her head back and forth
in misery.

What did I ever do to deserve this? Oh, God . . . what?

And time crawled by. Danny visited more and more often, as her strength dwindled away, and her hunger grew into a ravenous monster that ate her up from the inside like a raging cancer. She whimpered with the torture of it. Eventually the misery became her whole existence, and blocked out the memories and the dreams. She rocked back and forth in the box. She bit her wrists and sucked out her own blood, until her arms were nothing but raw bites. The hunger grew anyway. She didn't have enough blood to keep recycling. And it didn't free her from the coffin.

Danny wrapped his arms around her as she moaned and thrashed about, until she passed out.

She'd almost slipped into a place where nothing could touch her any longer, when the coffin began to vibrate like a huge tuning fork. Her eyes flew open and she screamed, hoarse grunts because her voice had long ago been used up. She tried to brace herself as the coffin bumped and knocked itself around, like a wild horse trying to unseat its rider.

Someone was digging her up! Matthew had found her somehow, she thought unbelievably the first few seconds, laughing insanely at the pure relief, joy of it. Pounding at the sides of her coffin with her bloodied hands.

He was saving her! Thank God! Thank God!

But her hope vanished like smoke when she felt the coffin—herself in it—falling . . . submerging deeper into the bowels of the earth, like a submarine into the depths of the sea. Dirt and rocks cascaded down upon the coffin's lid. She could see dust floating around her in the blackness.

She'd never get out now.

The earth had opened up like a hungry mouth and

swallowed her further into its maw. Swallowed he
alive.

So this was to be the way she perished, after all she'd bee
through . . . this was the way she would die—and sh
slipped away into unconsciousness again with the hic
eousness of it.

Twenty-three

"Vampires . . . damn, they were vampires! They looked like werewolves to me. Acted like werewolves to me . . ." Matthew was talking to himself as he fought his way up the hill and through the thorny bushes, using the bow to clear his way. The undead. And Indians hated the dead enough anyway, dreaded death. Some Indians even believed that when a person died, all that was left was the evil in that person, and that it took ghostly form, made trouble, and could make a live person sick. A *chindi*. Some tribes, after a person died, would get rid of the corpse as quickly as they could, and then never speak that person's name again, for fear that the person's *chindi* would hear and come for them.

Matthew had never truly believed all that. Otherwise, the last year, with all the dead bodies around, would have driven him insane. Evil *chindi* everywhere. But still . . . he had the Indian's aversion to the dead, and vampires were the *un*dead. That didn't make him very happy. Of course, werewolves weren't so great, either.

"Vampires. How was I supposed to know *that?*" He kept mumbling to himself to fend off the nagging doubts he was beginning to have. He'd seen what those creatures had done to the people in that village. What they were capable of. Would Emma eventually become like them? Had she run away from him solely to save him from the pack, or to save him from herself as well?

He wondered if he was insane after all. Werewolves. Vampires. But he was a strong man, and he knew what he'd seen. Just like he knew the wounds on his face and hands were real.

"Emma, if you've become like them," the hushed timbre of his voice was full of despair, "I'll have to kill you." Suddenly the bow in his hands felt like it weighed a hundred pounds. As heavy as his heart.

How would he know?

No, his thoughts fighting a fierce battle, *that vampire back in the cave told me that Emma wasn't like them.* That's why she's where she is now. Punishment. She wouldn't kill. She wouldn't drink human blood. They made her an outcast.

She fought for him, saved his life, at the cost of her own. She had to be different. He wished fervently that he could talk to his spirit guide about it, but he had a hunch that since that last dream, he'd never see him or the dream tribe again. They'd served their purpose. Whatever that had been.

Matthew shivered—not just from his dilemma—and coughed into his gloved hands. The cough had gotten worse just the last day. It hurt to breathe. He'd covered his face with a strip of cloth with three holes cut in it for his eyes and mouth, but he could still feel the ice forming on his chapped face. Though he was practically running, he was still so cold he couldn't stop his teeth from chattering. He'd been cold most of the last seven months, but the chill of the wind as he crested the hill was incomparable. Canada wasn't fit for human habitation any longer, as far as he was concerned. Neither was Maine or the whole East Coast. It was all going underwater.

When he found Emma, they'd move back south, back toward the Midwest again. When he found her. If he found her.

His heart sank as he broke through the trees and snow drifts and scrutinized the valley below him. The graveyard was there alright. Sprawling out below him like a ghost town. He hated graveyards, like sacred Indian burial grounds. *Chindi* everywhere. The earthquake had ripped a huge gaping crevice, a canyon oozing red lava, smoke, and heat, right through the middle of it, dividing it in half. Some of the graves and mausoleums had toppled into it. The chasm was at least a mile wide and miles long, gashing across the land like an ugly colossal scar. There was no way he'd get across, if the tomb he was looking for was on the other side of it.

Just what he'd needed, another obstacle.

Lawton was what the dying vampire had said. So Matthew would check all the tombs on his side of the chasm first.

He was freezing and he was hungry, his wounds still ached, but he knew that if he didn't find Emma soon, it wouldn't make any difference. He couldn't bear to think about what she must have gone through the last seven days and nights, couldn't stand to accept that she might already have died in agony. Alone. How long could a vampire go without . . . sustenance? He didn't know.

Matthew spent the next hour searching through the graveyard for the tomb marked Lawton. He couldn't find it. It must be on the other side of the abyss.

The crack in the earth went on as far as he could see. He knew he had to get across it. The rest of the graveyard awaited him. Emma awaited him. Somewhere. But he wasn't going to cross it here.

"Damn," he swore, and started hiking along the edge. "Emma, hold on. I'm coming! Hold on!" He'd have to keep going until he found a place where he could get over.

He walked for a long time, weary and coughing. He'd picked up a cold a few days back, and with his low resistance and his wounds, he was becoming really sick. It had come on so quickly, most likely from exerting himself too much. Now he was sweating under his clothes. Fever. He had to stop a few times and rest. He had a spasm of coughing that pulled something in his side, and when he got up and continued his trek along the pit, he was limping, it hurt so. Hell of a time to get sick, he fretted.

Finally he came to a place where the chasm had narrowed to a crossable place. Only about twelve to fifteen feet wide.

What he wouldn't have given for a coil of sturdy rope, but he had none, so he had to make do with what was at hand. Tree limbs.

It took another hour or so to find and chop off a section of thick branch with his knife. He'd have to use it as a crude bridge, and pray he didn't fall off, or that the limb didn't break under his weight. Shouldn't be too risky, he thought sarcastically, as he anchored the limb on the other side under a ledge of dirt and then on his side with rocks. He'd lost a lot of weight in the last few weeks tracking after Emma. He probably resembled a scarecrow.

Nothing to what Emma must look like now.

Removing his gloves and stuffing them in his pockets (he couldn't cross with them on, no grip), he lowered himself onto the branch, swung down, and hand over hand, he laboriously made his way across the gaping fissure, trying not to let the trembling in his hands or the heat from churning, boiling lava far below unnerve him. It was so hot, he was sweating from the moment he started across. His hands became slippery with it, and he didn't think toward the end that he'd make it. But he did. Then he collapsed on the ground on the other side, hacking his head off, his body shaking uncontrollably with fever. He must have drifted off for a while, because the next thing he knew he was waking up, his body stiff, his lungs burning, and it was considerably darker than when he'd crossed the breach.

He dragged himself to his feet and started the long hike back to the graveyard. Thought he'd never get there. When he breathed, his chest rattled like a junker car.

He tediously scoured the rest of the graveyard searching for the tomb, pushing himself. His head was spinning, his chest hurt so badly he could hardly take a breath without pain. But he found the tomb, or what was left of it. Stone slabs, one with the Lawton family name chiseled into it.

Teetering on the edge of the crevice.

Some of the stones had slipped into the hole, some had crashed onto a shelf about fifteen feet down, along with other debris lodged up against gigantic tree roots.

First Matthew checked all around the demolished tomb. Would they have buried her in the ground, or in a sarcophagus? No fresh graves that he could tell. But no coffins, either. Above the pit.

Peering over the edge, Matthew could make out coffins that had broken free of their stone sarcophaguses and were perched precariously on the ledge. The bubbling lava was a furnace about thirty feet down. Hot, like hell. Fumes eddied around his head, making him even dizzier. Damn, he'd have to find some way down there and open each one. If the ledge held. If he didn't topple into it.

Groaning with trepidation, he took his bow off his shoulder and laid it on the ground by the edge, found another tree branch, dropped it down the side of the pit until it lodged in solid ground, then cautiously climbed down to the ledge. Astounded, but relieved, when he'd made it.

He scuttled carefully on hands and knees from one coffin to another, prying them open with his knife and a hunk of wood he'd broken off the limb he'd come down on.

The first few were full of powdery bones or half-decomposed flesh. No Emma.

Shit, he muttered, looking down into the hazy fog of the chasm, there's two more down there on another ledge. Except that ledge was a great deal smaller, and more hazardous. Clenching his teeth, and grunting through them, he continued the descent and nearly lost his grip when one of the coffins slid off and went over the edge. He found footing and grabbed a stray branch limb just in time, swiveling away from the thing's path.

Praying under his breath, he watched as the coffin bounced against the wall of the abyss, splitting open, and spilling out its contents. Bones and tattered rags. The rest of it plunged further down and burst into flames, as the pieces hit the churning molten lava, disappearing beneath the fiery quicksand.

He glared at the last remaining coffin as he excruciatingly inched his way over to it. Always the last one, wasn't it? When you were looking for something, it was always at the bottom of the stack, the end of the line, the last one of all the others you'd looked at.

"Emma?" his voice reached out softly. "Emma, are you in there?"

He heard a very faint moan. Wasn't sure it wasn't just his imagination, so he bent his head down close. Yes . . . something was in there. Something alive.

He'd *found* her.

His dirty face split into a huge grin under the face cloth, but it quickly faded when he remembered the decision he had to make yet concerning her. When he looked into her eyes again for the first time . . . he'd know.

He still had the silver-tipped knife on his belt.

"Emma, I'm going to get you out, just be patient. Whatever you do, don't move. We're on a narrow ledge over a hole in the earth caused by an earthquake.

"But I'll get you out, I promise." Tears of relief were trickling down his face, as he pried stubbornly at the coffin lid. It popped off with a cracking sound.

As it opened and he met the glittering feverish eyes in her skeletal face, took in the heavy chain that bound her, and her bloodied hands, part of the shelf beneath them began to disintegrate.

Without a thought for his own safety, he snatched at the chain and yanked it off her, then grabbed at her reaching arms, tugging her free of the box, just as the coffin went plunging into the pit.

Her body dangled over thin air for a moment, then Matthew heaved her up into his arms. She was nothing but emaciated skin and bones, weighing less than a bag of prickly feathers.

The rest of their niche was crumbling under his feet, so he didn't waste time, but scrambled back up the way he had come, bringing Emma with him.

Back on top he slumped to the ground against a headstone, Emma wrapped in his arms, and cried as she clung to him like a weak kitten. He was horrified when he finally eased her away and gazed into her ravished face. She looked barely alive. There was blood all over her hands, cuts and slashes, ugly burns peeking through her torn clothes. The gleam in her eyes bordering on the edge of insanity. She didn't even look like his Emma.

She smiled a ghastly smile, so at odds with the haunted look on her face. "You came . . . you really came," her voice a raspy croak.

"Are you real?"

"Yes, I'm real."

She still couldn't believe Matthew was there and not just one of her hallucinations. He took off the cloth mask, and she had to touch his face, his lips, press up against his chest.

He began coughing. Deep, vibrating. Covered his mouth, trying to muffle them.

"You sick?" she mumbled.

"Never mind," he brushed her inquiry away. "It's you I'm worried about."

The sweet scent of his warm blood, as it pulsed in the veins under his skin, was driving her crazy.

"Not good." He didn't know if she was talking about his cough or about her condition.

Emma met his eyes, and the hunger inside her flared up fiercer than she'd ever felt it. In a trance, she found herself at his neck before she knew what she was doing, her arms tightening around him like a vise. Even as weak as she was, she was still stronger than him.

"Emma!" his voice came as if from faraway, warningly, and stopped her.

She pulled away and stared into his frantic eyes. She looked down. In his hand he held a knife. One of her knives that she'd left at his feet that day on the cold rocks, when she'd abandoned him to lead the pack away.

Startled at what she had almost done, she pushed violently away from him.

But not before she'd read his thoughts strong and clear. His fear of what she was, what he now knew her to be, a vampire.

What he was about to do to her.

Emma's eyes clouded with sadness. He knew what she was. What the pack had been. Reading his mind, she also knew that he'd seen the remains of that village. The slaughter. Knew that he would kill her if he had to. The knife was silver-tipped.

"No, Matthew," she finally spoke, her voice feeble. "I won't harm you. Even though I'm dying." She hung her head. She couldn't look at him. The hunger was almost too strong to fight.

"I'm not like them." She answered his silent question. "I'll never be like them. I'll perish first. And I'd never hurt you that way . . . I love you," a whisper.

His hand holding the knife hesitated, uncertain.

She was quiet for a moment, then said. "Use your knife then. End it for me. I have nothing to live for, if you no longer love me."

He put the knife slowly back in its sheath, as if he'd made an important decision.

"But I do love you, Emma," he said softly, cradling her again in his arms. She struggled at first, and then gave in. Let him rock her. "And I have my answer." There was finality in his words.

"Where are they?" She meant the vampire pack.

"Don't worry," Matt soothed her. "They're all dead."

"Dead?" Emma couldn't accept it.

"Plague," Matthew explained.

There was irony in her raw laughter. She was the only one who hadn't drunk the humans' blood. And now, after all that had happened, she was the one still here — and they weren't.

343

"How did you find me?" *Talk, keep talking. Fight the hunger.*

"I remembered where their cave was and cornered them there. There were only two left. One died before my eyes, and the other one attacked me. I shot him with an arrow dipped in silver, but he told me where you were before he . . . died."

Emma was amazed. "Told you where I was? Why?"

"I don't know. I think because he admired you. Big guy. With tattoos."

"Stephen. I—" she murmured, nodding, losing her voice. She closed her eyes; she couldn't talk anymore. Didn't want to talk anymore. She wanted Matthew to use his knife and end it. At least it would be swift. Merciful compared to the way she would have died if he hadn't found her.

"Matthew . . . put . . . me . . . out . . . of . . . my . . . misery," she begged. The world was spinning. She wasn't sure of where she was any longer. She felt strange.

"I can't, Emma. I won't let you leave me, now that I've found you," he said forcefully. "I'll never let you leave me again.

"Like the wolves, we'll be together forever."

Emma smiled dreamily. Her eyelids fluttered open, but her eyes wouldn't focus. She gathered all the last of her strength to keep talking.

"Can't. Dying, Matthew." She smiled faintly and her fangs gleamed in the dim graveyard. Her whole body shuddered. She truly was dying. "Only waited until you found me.

"At least I die out here, free, with you." She touched his cheek with a bony hand. "Love you . . ." She went away from him again. And he knew she didn't have much time left. But he'd made his choice.

Matthew had finally penetrated the mystery of his

Indian dreams. He knew what the wolf warrior had been trying to tell him. *He* was that warrior; his people were the wolves. Matthew was supposed to become one of them. With Emma.

Matthew shook her gently. "Emma, listen to me. This is important."

Her eyes opened just a little.

"I've thought about it. I know what I want." There was a passionate determination in his tone that roused her.

"Make me like you."

She laughed softly. "Never."

"No, I mean it, Emma . . . make me like you. It's what I want," he pleaded with her. "I understand now why you were so afraid all that time to get close to me, really close to me . . . you were afraid you wouldn't be able to keep from drinking my blood. Hurting me. But the strange thing is, now I don't care. I feel it's the only way." He scanned the graveyard with wary eyes, looking for *chindi,* and then came back to her guarded face. His request had her attention. She tried real hard to listen.

"I think the world's ending. I believe we only have a short time. I want to spend what I have left with you. Really with you."

He could tell she wasn't convinced. Yet. But hope was emerging deep in her apathetic eyes.

"I'm sick of hurting, sick of being hurt. Of being tired. Of being cold." He shivered even as he said it. "I'm not indestructible. I'm a weak human.

"And you're strong, Emma. As vampires, we'd have a better chance of surviving longer. You know that. Cold and heat doesn't affect you. If you can exist on animal blood, so can I. If you can be different than those other vampires, so can I. We don't have to be human-killers.

"It's our best chance, our only chance maybe, to survive as long as we can, don't you see?"

She studied him thoughtfully, her eyes glowing. A spark of optimism ignited for the first time in a long time. Maybe what she had become wasn't so bad. She wasn't evil.

"Don't you want to go back to Last Hope? Be with those good people, start a new life with them?" she asked guiltily.

She had read his mind. He stared out over the tombs and devastation that was now their world. Night had fallen. There was a tangy frostiness hanging in the air. His breath created a crystalline mist. It was snowing again. Getting colder, if that was possible. He coughed, his body shuddering with the effort. He was so tired. So cold. Those poor people in that village were doomed. They all were.

His eyes came back to fasten on her gaunt face. "No, Emma, I love you. I want to be with you. I want us to be together. This is the only way." She could feel his anguish as he held her. It hadn't been an easy decision for him. To give up his humanity.

But he's right, she thought, amazed at how rational it all seemed, when he put it like that. If the world was going to end anyway, why not see it come together, with the best of odds they could achieve?

As vampires. A new kind of vampire.

"And I love *you,* Matthew," she said tenderly, as she brought his lips down to hers, then gently nuzzled his neck. Just knowing that he would be with her forever had given her strength, the will to go on. She'd never be alone again.

"Yes," she murmured against his warm skin. "I'll do as you ask. Yes." Her hunger flared up like fire.

"Now, Emma . . . before it's too late." *Before I change my mind.*

346

Emma then whispered, "It will take seven days. And you'll become very, very ill, Matthew. You could die." She remembered his aura. "But I believe you have a very good chance of making it.

"And if you make it . . . you'll be like me. In every way."

Matthew thought about that for a moment, and then nodded his head somberly. "I'll make it. I'm never going to leave you again," he said firmly. "Do it."

She let out a tremulous sigh, and then sank her fangs into his neck before she could change her mind; quivering like a new lover, she hungrily drank the blood she so desperately needed to keep on living.

And when she was done, and her skin was glowing with newfound health, and the power was flowing back into her body, she bit into her own arm above the vein, and put it to his lips.

Without hesitation, he drank.

And so it was done.

Epilogue

The huge silver wolf hunkered down behind the brambles and howled, to let her partner know where she was. She'd spotted the deer in a nearby field, some with young, which would slow them down when they made their move. They'd take the small buck, leave the does and the fawns alone. Now all they had to do was run the buck down . . . and then feast. It had been a long time between meals. Game was scarce, and the wolf knew it wouldn't get any better as time went on.

But hunting in tandem with her mate, a great black wolf with crimson eyes, had greatly increased their harvest. He was clever, strong, and agile. Fast. They worked well together. Where one had starved, two could find game. Yet this was the first prey they'd located in a week, and they were ravenous.

Spring had arrived late, but it had arrived, for they'd feared that the world would stay in perpetual winter. They couldn't tell if it was any warmer, because cold didn't affect them anyway. The snow had melted, but the game hadn't returned.

They'd even thought of moving on, though the silver wolf didn't want to. She was still hopeful that Friend was alive, and that sooner or later they'd meet up with him on one of their nightly hunts. They'd been searching for him for weeks, since they'd ar-

ved back in Illinois. Illinois was home. She was
appy to be back in the places she'd known and loved
ll her life. Places where she had memories to glean.
he'd discovered that as time went by, even the worst
f the recollections could no longer hurt her. It was
he good memories she treasured. Even then, the old
world was dimming more every day in her mind.
Her old life. It was the same for Matthew, too. He'd
old her so.

They rarely saw humans. And they stayed away
rom the ones they did come across. Which wasn't
very often.

All that existed for them was this new savage world
f earthquakes, emptiness, hunting for the blood that
was their food—and each other.

As long as they had each other, it was enough.

Out of the blackness a black wolf, with dark silver
treaks rippling through his coat, emerged and slid in
next to the silver one under the foliage. Matthew had
made the complete transition from human to vampire easily. Emma couldn't recall how long ago now,
ime meant nothing to them. Unlike Emma, Mat-
hew had only become mildly ill. He seemed to like
being a vampire. As long as Emma was by his side.

By their minds they silently communicated. *Prey's
over there . . . see . . . to your right. Just behind those trees,
nestled down for the night. Four of them. There's a buck for
us.*

The black wolf woofed low in his throat. *I see them.
Let's go. Hungry.*

Together they panicked the small herd into running, cut the buck adeptly away from the rest of
them, and brought it down. They fed. One buck
wasn't enough for them. But they wouldn't kill the
does or the young. That would be like killing the
goose that laid the golden eggs. They had to think of

349

tomorrow and the next day. Let the does have mo[re]
fawns, let the young grow, and someday there wou[ld]
be a large deer with much more blood to feed them
The wolves were never completely sated, but wha[t]
they did consume kept them alive. They would ju[st]
continue to hunt until they found more game. If the[y]
didn't find more that night, they'd be a little hungr[y]
They were used to it.

When the night was over, they cantered back [to]
their home, a neat small cabin they'd claimed [as]
theirs on the Mississippi's bank. Metamorphosed in[to]
two humans again, they curled up together to slee[p]
the main part of the day away. Later when the[y]
awoke, they'd make love, talk, and plan the night[']
hunt.

Sometimes they'd go up on the bluffs and watc[h]
the strange fires and explosions in the distanc[e]
Towns and cities were still burning as humanit[y]
fought its last battles for survival, as the earthquak[e]
and plague ravished what was left, which wasn[']
much these days.

It was enough to stay alive themselves. What wit[h]
the ground always shaking, or spewing forth molte[n]
lava from somewhere deep in its bowels. Or floodin[g]
The air was still a thick fog, the sun a pale ball b[e]
hind the thick clouds somewhere.

Matthew said that the earth was splitting itse[lf]
apart, that it was only a matter of time now. A sho[rt]
time. There were few places they could hunt tha[t]
didn't have fiery craters, or slits gorged deep into th[e]
earth. Forest fires chased them from one huntin[g]
ground to another, destroying the animals tha[t]
couldn't run as fast as they. Even in the spring, mo[st]
of the land was blackened, parched, and dead
Everywhere. The streams and rivers were drying u[p]
even as they melted, and were soaked into the grou[nd]

350

g cracks of the world, as if the core of the earth
as a giant sponge. Matthew had told her of what
e'd seen months before along the coast. Emma won-
ered what was happening to the oceans now.

So far their cabin had been spared, was still safe,
nd on solid ground. They had a home. Found prey
omehow. Had each other. They were content. For a
hile.

But their time was coming to an end.

The spring was cruelly short, there was no summer
t all, and then winter closed in again with a white
elvet fist, freezing and killing whatever was left.
Man and beast alike. Their game gradually disap-
eared. They starved like all the rest of God's crea-
ures. There weren't even any cities any longer to
cavenge in, because there weren't any humans left.
They were gone. Their cities were gone.

One evening late in the winter that would never
nd, the two wolves emerged from the cabin, some
nstinct telling them to keep moving, their eyes glit-
ering with unassuaged hunger, ribs sticking out from
kinny bodies. Their gait lurched as they staggered
hrough snow against the gale-like wind. They moved
ide by side, up over the hill, as the earth shook vio-
ently. Over and over.

The silver wolf fell to her knees, and the black one
rabbed the scruff of her neck in his powerful jaws
nd pulled her back to her feet. He kept her moving
vith sharp nips on her rump, away from the spread-
ng destruction.

Topping the last rise they paused only a moment,
o look back with cold eyes as their home collapsed
nto a pile of rubble, and then slid out of sight into
he yawning pit.

Another rent in the earth started to snake toward
hem. Trees fell all around like matchsticks, as if an

351

angry giant was slamming them down. The bla
wolf urgently prodded her on, pushing her to ru
This way. This way.

Where are we going, Matthew?

I don't know. Somewhere . . .

And without another glance backwards, the tw
wolves turned almost as one and galloped off into t
trembling woods, until they were just tiny bla
specks in the white.